A Broken Mirror

Mercè Rodoreda

Mirall trencat
Translated and with an
introduction by
Josep Miquel Sobrer

University of Nebraska Press
Lincoln
Institut d' Estudis Catalans
Barcelona

Publication of this book was assisted by a grant from
the Program for Cultural Cooperation between Spain's
Ministry of Culture and United States Universities.
Mirall trencat © 1991 Institut d'Estudis Catalans,
Barcelona. Translation © 2006 by the Board of Regents
of the University of Nebraska. All rights reserved.
Manufactured in the United States of America. ⊗

Typeset in Adobe Minion designed by Robert Slimbach.
Typeset by Kim Essman. Book designed by Richard
Eckersley. Printed and bound by Edwards Brothers, Inc.

Library of Congress Cataloging-in-Publication Data
Rodoreda, Mercè, 1908–
[Mirall trencat. English]
A broken mirror = Mirall trencat / Mercè Rodoreda ;
translated and with an introduction by Josep Miquel
Sobrer. p. cm. – (European women writers series)
ISBN-13: 978-0-8032-3963-0 (cloth : alkaline paper)
ISBN-10: 0-8032-3963-7 (cloth : alkaline paper)
ISBN-13: 978-0-8032-9007-5 (paperback : alkaline paper)
ISBN-10: 0-8032-9007-1 (paperback : alkaline paper)
1. Sobrer, Josep Miquel. II. Title. III. Title: Mirall
trencat. IV. Series.
PC3941.R57M513 2006   849'9352–dc22   2005021030

Contents

Acknowledgments

My translation was begun years ago with help from poet Lisa Ress but was soon interrupted and abandoned for a long period. I returned to it during the academic year 2001–2, which I spent in Madrid, Spain. In Madrid I received the friendly encouragement of Señora Mari-Carmen (Mamen) Castaño, who urged me to finish the translation before ending my year's work at the Universidad Complutense; Amy Olson was always ready to help with a word or turn of phrase at critical times when I was trying to render a Catalan sentence.

Back in Bloomington, Professor Breon Mitchell, in his gentle, understated way, encouraged me to revise the translation and pursue publication. Professors Brad Epps, of Harvard, and Joan Ramon Resina, of Cornell, were kind enough to review a sample of my manuscript and offer helpful, and needed, suggestions. Professor Epps furthermore steered my introductory notes toward a more readable form.

The almost-final version was read with great care by another poet, Robin Vogelzang, who aptly guided my version to greater clarity and more acceptable English.

To all, my deepest thanks.

J. M. S.

Introduction

A Broken Mirror is the book on which Mercè Rodoreda worked the longest, which is not surprising given the novel's ambitious scope. The plot spans three generations; it presents in detail scores of characters of different ages and social classes; it reflects momentous historical events – most notably the Spanish war of 1936–39. More important, perhaps, the narrative technique of the novel parts with the first-person narratives of Rodoreda's preceding and ensuing works of fiction. And, as the related events develop, so does the narrative technique itself and even the prose of the narration. Beginning with a fairly standard story (the first chapter could be read independently as a realistic short story), the novel progresses toward more daring ways of storytelling, some of which blur the line between novel and poetry. In this sense *A Broken Mirror* can be seen as the watershed in Rodoreda's career, moving from the stark realism that characterizes her earlier production to the experimental poetic prose that characterizes her later one.

The critic Josefina González has pointed out the autobiographical elements in the novel. Foreseeing such claims, Rodoreda wrote a revealing, meandering foreword to the first edition of the novel. In it she declares: "All my characters have something of me, but none of my characters is me. Besides, my historical time interests me only relatively. I have lived it too much . . . A novel is also a magical act. It reflects what the author has inside without quite knowing she carries such ballast" (16).

Rodoreda also muses on the image of the broken mirror. Yet the title-inspiring scene was apparently a fairly late find. Rodoreda informs us that coming upon her title is what allowed her to complete the work, after several lengthy interruptions. She explains how different chapters were written at different times and not in the order she finally chose for her story. The first chapter that she wrote, for example, ended up as chapter 19 of part 2 (Rodoreda 15); the one she wrote next is now the seventeenth of part 1 (17). The novel as a whole, however, did not fully come into being until Rodoreda found the image that gives it its title – in the episode when a character drops, picks up, and stares at a handheld looking glass. This character, the servant Armanda, sees in its many pieces – some still within the frame, others fallen to the floor –

the bits of family life that constitute the novel. The novel offers thus a series of broken pieces – short chapters – held together by the overall narrative frame.

Rodoreda's life story can be said to have been shattered just as her fictional mirror. The only child of a lower-middle-class couple, Rodoreda was born in Barcelona in 1908. On the very day that she turned twenty she married Joan Gurguí – but only after receiving ecclesiastical dispensation: Joan Gurguí was, after all, her mother's younger brother (Casals). One year later the couple had their only child, a son. In 1930 Rodoreda began to write and publish fiction. In 1935 she took a job with the Ministry of Information (Comissariat de Propaganda) of the Generalitat, the autonomous government of Catalonia. In 1936 the Spanish Civil War broke out. In January 1939 Franco's troops were closing in on Barcelona.

Like many intellectuals on the Republican side of the conflict, Rodoreda left Barcelona early that year. At first, in her exile, she found a place in Roissy-en-Brie, a small town near Paris. Her husband and son did not join her, thus putting an end, de facto, to the marriage; the couple was never reunited, and after 1939 they saw each other only rarely. In Roissy, Rodoreda lived in a villa with a number of other exiled Catalan writers, including Joan Prat, who signed his writings as Armand Obiols. Rodoreda and Prat, according to all biographical accounts, fell in love and began a long-lasting relationship. They were to live together for a number of years but never married. (Prat could not get a divorce from his estranged wife any more than Rodoreda could from her husband in Spain).

In 1940 the Germans occupied northern France, forcing the Left-leaning Catalan refugees to flee from the Gestapo (who would have extradited them to Franco's Spain to face jail or even execution). They traveled south along with thousands of other displaced people. The fairly comfortable experience at Roissy had also been shattered. In their flight the couple Rodoreda/Prat dodged bombings and lived hand to mouth, until the war ended and they could settle down – first in Limoges then, successively, in Bordeaux, Paris (1946), and Geneva (1954). During this period, which lasted until 1979, Rodoreda continued to write in Catalan and, from 1957 on, to publish in Barcelona from her Swiss exile. Four years after moving back to Catalonia, on 13 April 1983, Mercè Rodoreda died.

A mirror that is broken at once distorts and enhances reality. By re-flecting a vision from several angles, a broken mirror reminds us of the inherent fragility of a unified viewpoint. The title of the novel, given the structure of the narrative, makes perfect sense. Furthermore, besides its reference to theories of the novel, the image of a mirror is fraught with symbolic and even magical signification. A mirror is a reflection, a mere illusion; a mirror is a symbol of vanity, a portrait in constant change. A broken mirror is thought of in many cultures as an omen of bad luck, and *A Broken Mirror* is essentially the story of the tragic disintegration of a family. The author reflects:

The first titles I thought I'd give the novel felt flat. A novel is a mirror. What is a mirror? Water is a mirror. Narcissus knew this. The moon knows this, and so does the willow. The whole sea is a mirror. The sky knows this. The eyes are the mirrors of the soul. And of the world. There is the ancient Egyptians' mirror of truth that reflected all passions, both high and low. There are magic mirrors. Diabolic mirrors. Deforming mirrors. There are little mirrors with which a hunter lures the lark. There is our everyday mirror that makes us strange to ourselves. (Rodoreda 22)

The mirror is also the emblem that realist novelists in the nineteenth century chose in order to explain their ambition to paint a lifelike picture of a segment of society. Rodoreda prefaced her notes to the novel with an epigraph – "Un roman: c'est un miroir qu'on promène le long du chemin" – which she took from Stendhal, who attributes it to Saint-Réal, an attribution Rodoreda does not question (Arnau 28). The illusion of fidelity is broken into the fifty-two chapters, grouped in three sections, that constitute *A Broken Mirror*. Each chapter could stand as a terse short story, with its own title.

A Broken Mirror is the only one of Rodoreda's novels that is not told in the first person. Reflecting on how she stumbled on her technique, Rodoreda wrote: "An author is not God. She cannot know what happens inside her creatures . . . I cannot tell the reader my character has lost all hope; I must make him feel she has . . . In other words: A novel's character may know what she sees and what's happening to her, but not the author" (16–17).

Essentially, Rodoreda echoes the recommendation of "show, don't tell" that is so prevalent in creative writing workshops. In *A Broken Mirror* each chapter is anchored in some character's point of view, often a character who is incidental to the development of the action. The technique, which Carme Arnau has related to cinematic narratives and to the free indirect style of such writers as Gustave Flaubert and Virginia Woolf, gives the novel its intensity (40).

In its overall plot lines *A Broken Mirror* is a family saga. Its main character, Teresa Goday, is presented in the opening chapter as what is indecorously called a gold digger. Reading on, the reader learns more and more about Teresa. Responding to a felicitous request of her editor, right before its original publication, Rodoreda added a chapter to the completed novel: chapter 2 of part 3, "Youth." Here a dying Teresa remembers her first love: an affair with a married man who left her pregnant with a boy, Jesús Masdéu, who believed that he was only Teresa's godchild. By way of the flashback our knowledge of Teresa comes full circle, and we realize the dimensions of the character. In her article "The Woman in the Garden" Maryellen Bieder points out "the reversal of male and female roles, with men the unadaptable victims and women the adaptable survivors" in Rodoreda's fiction (363). The theme of women's dominance and men's subservience or inadequacy is indeed a major one. But, underlying it, Rodoreda makes us aware that in a patriarchal world women's power has its limits. No one can hold onto the order of the material world anymore than one can hold onto life.

The description of Teresa's old age is as compelling as it is horrifying. In a scene in chapter 3 of part 3 Teresa rues the ravages of time when the young doctor who tends to her paralysis pats her on the face; she feels the psychological pain of no longer having smooth skin, which had been her weapon for seduction. Teresa sees herself die. Death is one of the themes that run through the novel. The narrative gives us examples of incest, fetishism, murder, suicide – and, less dramatically, but not less poignantly, adultery, sexual frustration, physical handicaps, class conflict, adoption. Women writers after Rodoreda, beginning with Montserrat Roig, later explored topics such as abortion, rape, and also homosexuality that would have been taboo to the Franco era bourgeoisie. Rodoreda herself continued the social exploration of the realist and naturalist periods. A sense of the harshness and utter unfairness of life is latent in this novel, as indeed it might be an essential trait of the modern literary tradition. Along with its bloodstained themes, however,

A Broken Mirror also offers scenes of joy and luxury, of love and hope, of laughter and delight – and of confusion, boredom, obsession.

Teresa is the founder of a matriarchal dynasty but one that seems doomed. The novel is as much about the devastating passage of time as about anything else. In *A Companion to Catalan Literature* Arthur Terry concludes that *A Broken Mirror* "is one of Rodoreda's most pessimistic novels" (114). Functioning as a central symbol, the villa that Teresa's second husband remodels for the family comes, like the family itself, to decay and is ominously destroyed by the wrecking ball at the end of the novel.

But the villa, and the mirror, are only two of the symbols interwoven in the seemingly realistic tapestry of the novel. Others are the garden, water, flowers (especially violets), and a laurel tree. These symbols blend with the changing lives of the characters.

A Broken Mirror is the saga of an upper-class family, but it finds many memorable characters among the working class. Several characters, including Teresa, find love across class barriers – loves that prove to be destructive even as the characters, most notably among them Eladi Farriols, attempt to keep desire under control. This theme ties in with another: the quest for a home. In an essay on *Mirall trencat* Gonzalo Navajas has pointed out the allegorical dimensions of such a quest. Just as Rodoreda, because of the forces of history, could never return to the independent Catalonia of her republican aspirations, so does the family mansion harbor disappointment and foster tragedy, destruction, or exile.

A Broken Mirror is a novel of and about Barcelona. Not perhaps today's sociologically complex and ethnically diverse Barcelona but the native city that could not but be idealized by a native writer who had been unable to visit it for so long. The chronology of the novel is a bit loose. The action begins in the prosperous 1870s and ends, shattered, with the advent of the Franco dictatorship. Rodoreda's is a monolingual Catalan-speaking Barcelona, a *Heimat* (a term Navajas has applied to this novel) more ideal than real. Yet the story at once carries, and moves, the reader. Its themes are the usual fare of fiction: love, power, hatred, betrayal, disappointment, and death – natural or inflicted. The main characters are female, and the men drift around them or avoid them. *A Broken Mirror* is a novel of relationships, a novel whose characters writhe under the passage of time, a novel of maturity.

If *A Broken Mirror* is sad and pessimistic, it is also shot through with beauty. Each one of its chapters sparkles with a rare lyricism; each moment is a beam of light floating on the wake of decay; each small narrative appears as cutting as a piece of a broken mirror. Each disappointment in the story is infused with an energy that can leave no reader feeling indifferent. Because it is broken into many pieces, the allure of the mirror is multiplied.

Life as a dance of contraries, yes. But also life as something fragile, eminently breakable. The novel's title congeals in chapter 5 of part 3. When Armanda, the faithful servant who has known all three generations of the family, slips and falls down the stairs, she breaks a mirror.

The mirror had broken. Most pieces remained in the frame, but a few had fallen out. She picked them up and tried to put them back in the spaces she thought they would fit. Did the pieces of the mirror, having lost their level, reflect things as they were? Suddenly, in each piece of the mirror she saw years of her life spent in that house. Fascinated, crouching on the floor, she could not make sense of it. Everything passed, stopped, disappeared. Her world took shape in it, with all its colors, with all its strength. The house, the park, the rooms, the people: young ones, older ones, corpses, the flames of candles, children. The outfits, the décolletages with emerging heads, laughing or sad, starched collars, ties with perfect knots, freshly polished shoes walking on rugs or on the gravel in the garden. An orgy of time past, far, far away. How far away everything was . . .

A set of lives, and a way of life, has passed. Like Humpty Dumpty, something has fallen and cannot be pieced together again.

REFERENCES

Arnau, Carme. *Una lectura de* Mirall trencat *de Mercè Rodoreda*. Barcelona: Proa, 2000.

Bieder, Maryellen. "The Woman in the Garden: The Problem of Identity in the Novels of Mercè Rodoreda." In *Actes del segon colloqui d'estudis catalans a Nord-Amèrica. Yale 1979*. Ed. Manuel Duran et al. Barcelona: PAM, 1982.

Casals i Couturier, Montserrat. *Mercè Rodoreda; contra la vida, la literatura: biografia*. Barcelona: Edicions 62, 1991.

González, Josefina. "*Mirall trencat*: Un umbral autobiográfico en la obra de Mercè Rodoreda." *Revista de Estudios Hispánicos* 30.1 (1996): 103–119.

Navajas, Gonzalo. "Normative Order and the Catalan *Heimat* in Mercè Rodoreda's *Mirall trencat*." In *The Garden across the Border: Mercè Rodoreda's Fiction*. Ed. Kathleen McNerney and Nancy Vosburg. Selinsgrove PA: Susquehanna University Press, 1994.

Rodoreda, Mercè. "Pròleg." *Mirall trencat*. Barcelona: Club Editor, 1974.

Terry, Arthur. *A Companion to Catalan Literature*. London: Tamesis, 2003.

Part One

I honour you, Eliza, for keeping secret some things.
Laurence Sterne

Vicenç helped Senyor Nicolau Rovira into the carriage. "Yes, Sir, as you wish." Then he helped Senyora Teresa. They always did it that way: first he, then she, because it took two of them to help Senyor Nicolau out again. It was a difficult maneuver, and he needed a lot of attention. They went along Carrer Fontanella and made a right turn at Portal de l'Angel. The horses picked up a trot, and the black-and-red, newly varnished wheels moved smoothly up Passeig de Gràcia. Senyor Nicolau told everyone how Vicenç was a great help and how without him he would sell his berlin because he wouldn't trust any other coachman. And, since Senyor Nicolau was generous, Vicenç was doing very well for himself. It was a brisk day; now and then, between two clouds, a faint ray of sun appeared briefly. Everyone – that is, their servants and some of their friends – knew that Senyor Nicolau wanted to give Senyora Teresa a present. When, to celebrate their six months as a couple, he had given her a beautiful black lacquer Japanese armoire with nacre and gold inlay, it had left her unenthusiastic, and he had been disappointed. "I see; I didn't guess right, and it's cost me a fortune, but, since I like it, I'll keep it and give you something that will please you better." Vicenç stopped the horses in front of the Begú jewelry shop, climbed down from his seat, and, setting his top hat on it, saw that Senyora Teresa had opened the door and jumped out like a doe. The two of them extricated Senyor Nicolau from the carriage – "from my closet," as he used to say. Motionless in the middle of the sidewalk, because after getting out of the carriage he could only straighten up with difficulty, he glanced sideways two or three times without moving his head, as if he didn't know what to do. At last he took hold of his wife's arm, and, very slowly, the two of them entered the jeweler's.

As they wished to see Senyor Begú in person, one of the clerks took them to the office. Senyor Begú was a handsome man with rosy skin, short-cropped hair, and thick eyebrows. "What happy occasion brings you here?" he exclaimed, rising as they came in. He had not seen them for some time, and he noted that Senyor Nicolau Rovira had grown much older: he must have been unable to resist the emotions of matrimony.

Senyor Rovira went straight to the business at hand. "We would like you to show us a piece, a real piece of jewelry."

He had seated himself in a straight-backed armchair that helped his posture and was thinking he ought to get one or two like it for himself. Teresa was looking at the jeweler's fingernails: impeccable, manicured, shiny. She glanced at him on the sly: he must have been over fifty, but he looked as though he'd just turned forty – tall, elegant in his dark pin-striped suit, and wearing a gray pearl on his tie. He was holding a pencil by both ends and looked at the Roviras with a smile.

"What type of jewelry would you like?"

Senyor Nicolau looked at Teresa, and Teresa said that perhaps a brooch . . . She had earrings, she had the ring, she didn't like bracelets. Senyor Begú pulled a cord and asked to be brought the brooch boxes, all of them. His eyes had darted toward Teresa; now he fixed his gaze on Senyor Rovira alone. He knew their story: Senyor Rovira, in his old age, had married a girl of low origins; who knew what those seemingly innocent eyes and that great beauty might hide? "These marriages work sometimes," he thought, "but it's better not to chance it." He didn't know what to say. Senyor Nicolau had coughed a couple of times as if about to die; the poor man must be suffering from bronchitis. "Too much tobacco and too much liquor." When he saw his assistant come in, the jeweler felt a weight had been lifted from his shoulders. The first box he opened was filled with simple pins, and Senyor Nicolau, barely glancing at them, told him he could put the box away. He wanted an expensive piece of jewelry. With a satisfied smile, Senyor Begú opened the other boxes and looked intently at Senyor Nicolau and his wife. Teresa, who had been motionless the whole time, bent forward suddenly and picked up a circle of rubies interlaced with two circles of diamonds. It was a pretty brooch, but her husband plucked it from her fingers with a sneer and dropped it on the desk. Then Senyor Begú went to his strongbox and produced a black velvet case.

"It's the best piece in the house," he said, tracing with one finger a bouquet of flowers made with diamonds and as big as the palm of his hand. Teresa gasped and shook her head as if what she saw before her was a dream from which she was trying to wake. Senyor Nicolau had removed the brooch from the case and was hefting it in his hand.

"Don't you think it's too much?" Teresa sighed, flushed with happiness. Her husband did not answer; instead, in a somewhat rusty voice, he asked the jeweler to pin the brooch on the lapel of his wife's dress. Then, while Teresa looked at herself in a display case mirror, Senyor Nicolau very calmly began to count out a stack of bills, which he set neatly on the desk. Senyor Begú saw them to the door. "How much money the man must have made on the stock exchange!" Before shaking his hand, Senyor Nicolau asked Begú where he had bought the straight-backed armchair. "On Carrer de la Palla, at an antique dealer's." Senyor Nicolau thanked him, and Begú wished them many happy returns. As she climbed into the carriage, Teresa was thinking that the brooch was going to be her salvation.

One morning, two or three weeks later, Teresa left home rather early. For the last couple of days her husband had been afflicted with a bad cold. She was going to see her dressmaker, she told him, but wouldn't take the carriage because she felt like walking and breathing fresh air. She'd been closed in with germs and eucalyptus vapors for two days now. Would it be all right if she wore the brooch? She wanted to stun her dressmaker. That pin, as Senyor Begú had said, would testify to the worth of any man. "People who see me won't think, what a fine lady! But, rather, what a fine gentleman!" From his bed he forced a laugh. Teresa was a pearl. He had first seen her as she walked by with a girlfriend while he was on the terrace of the Liceu. Her mother ran a fish stall at the Boqueria market. Teresa had explained that to him right away on that day when she had been out alone and he followed her for a while and then asked if he could walk with her. After that they saw each other a few times. That winter Teresa's mother died. She hadn't been buried a month when Senyor Nicolau asked Teresa to marry him: all he could offer her was his fortune; he knew very well that he was old and that no girl could fall in love with him. Teresa said she'd think about it. She had a big problem: an eleven-month-old son, a slip-up the size of a house. The father's name was Miquel Masdéu; he was married and earned his living, among other things, turning streetlights on and off, but he was a knockout. As soon as Senyor Nicolau asked her to marry him, Teresa hid her son at an aunt's, and after a few days she said yes. "And to hell with the fish stall!" It seemed all that had happened a long time ago, when in reality it was quite recent.

The day was sweet and the sunshine enchanting. Teresa walked as if she had wings on her feet. After a while she slipped into a doorway, unpinned her brooch, and put it in her purse. She felt nervous. She crossed Plaça Catalunya slowly. If her nerves didn't calm down, she wouldn't be able to do what she intended. And she had no choice but to do it. Her husband, who could spend a fortune on making her look good, doled money out to her with an eyedropper: he was bound to notice how quickly she spent it. But what worried her most was that Aunt Adela was growing old, she could die any day, and then what? Passeig de Gràcia was nearly empty. One of the windows of the jewelry store displayed a three-stranded pearl necklace, the pearls grayish, like the one on Senyor Begú's tie. Teresa pushed the door open and went in.

The store was dimly lit; perhaps it was too early. The young man with the boxes, who remembered her, smiled. "You're in luck, Senyora Rovira; Senyor Begú has just arrived."

Senyor Begú, who must have seen her through the curtains, came out at once. "What an honor, Senyora Rovira; will you please . . . ?"

Teresa looked at him with a mixture of curiosity and discomfort and followed him into his office. A lamp on his desk with a green shade left her in shadow. Better that way; she felt protected. She began by taking the diamond bouquet from her purse and laying it by the lamp. He will think that one of the diamonds has fallen out and that I am here to complain. Since Teresa said nothing, Senyor Begú asked her if something was wrong.

"Is the clasp not working properly?"

"No. I came here for you to buy this from me."

Senyor Begú got up, approached one of the display cases, turned around, and sat down again. It was a delicate situation; he didn't know how to begin.

"I would like to ask you something, but I do not dare . . . I don't have the slightest wish to offend you." He got up again, ran his hand through his hair, and finally made up his mind. "Does your husband know?"

Teresa answered quickly, "No."

And, looking at him with honeyed eyes, she added, "My husband does not know, nor should he ever know." What she wanted was for Senyor Begú to buy her brooch back from her, for less than it had cost, of course. Senyor Begú rubbed his cheek and kept eying her as if he hadn't quite understood. Teresa told him she needed money.

"You and I will make a deal: you must promise me that you'll neither show nor sell this brooch until, say, two or three months from now and, before selling it, if you do, that you will have someone copy the design." Senyor Begú smiled, his eyes full of cunning, and Teresa went on: "Would you agree to two-thirds of what my husband paid? I cannot promise you, but it's very likely that we will be buying it again." Senyor Begú stopped smiling and picked up a checkbook. Teresa, with a gesture of her hand, stopped him. "No, no checks."

Senyor Begú looked at her complicitly. "If I had gone to the bank yesterday as I intended, I would have been forced to ask you to come back." He opened his strongbox and took out a stack of bills. "Will you count them?"

"I don't have to, whatever you say." Then Senyor Begú, who had softly brushed her fingertips in giving her the bills, put the brooch in one of the drawers of his desk. Teresa got up, and he took her arm gently. "Shall we see each other again?"

Leaving the store, she answered in the most natural way, "It's almost certain."

Grasping her purse by its clasp, she went to the cab stand. When she arrived at Aunt Adela's, the neighbor sweeping the landing told her there was nobody home but that Senyora Adela would be back right away. If she would like to wait . . . Aunt Adela came after a moment, worn-out, carrying a shopping basket and the baby. They left him in his crib and sat down in the dining room. Teresa told her in a couple of words what she had to do: go see Miquel and give him the money. She took the wad of bills from her purse and divided it in two.

"Miquel will adopt the boy; we have talked about it – his wife agrees." The wife didn't know, of course, that the child was his. Miquel had told her a very sad and very complicated story, and, as they couldn't have children of their own, he had persuaded her. Teresa would give him the other half of the money after the boy had been baptized. "I will be his godmother so that when I'm an old lady he can come visit me and I can help him out: I don't want a son of mine lost in the world." Aunt Adela looked baffled, but to everything she said yes.

"This money will give Miquel and his wife some help." Naturally, Miquel had behaved badly; when she started going out with him he hadn't told her he was married, but she wasn't the rancorous sort and had been in love with him. Aunt Adela told her not to worry, she'd do everything in her power. "Do you want to see him sleeping?" The child slept like an angel. Teresa didn't quite like him because she thought he had a turned-up nose, like her own, but, while she liked her own, she found his ugly. She tucked him in. "I must leave, Auntie, I'm in a hurry." At the doorstep she gave her aunt some money – "This is for you" – and told her to rest assured, she'd never be in need.

She needed to find a pharmacy not too far from the dressmaker's because first she had to go for a fitting. There was one on the corner. As soon as she entered the fitting room, she told the girls to make it fast because she wasn't feeling well. Half an hour later, going down the stairway, she realized her hands were trembling. She stopped at the sidewalk. With a little luck everything will be all right, she thought, and then she slid to the ground, half-leaning against the wall. A few people crowded around right away, and a gentleman helped her to her feet. In the pharmacy they had her smell a vial; she said she'd had a dizzy spell: she hadn't been married long.

The pharmacist smiled and prepared a remedy. "Take half a spoonful with water every two hours."

The gentleman who had helped her up went in search of a cab.

"If you don't mind, I'll go with you."

"You'll be doing me a great favor." The doorkeeper saw them arrive together – this was what Teresa wanted – and helped her up the stairs. Felícia opened the door.

"If my husband asks about me, tell him I came in exhausted and that I am not feeling well." She went straight to bed. That night Felícia brought her a glass of milk and told her that the Senyor was still feeling wretched, but when he learned she had gone to bed he sent for the doctor. Teresa was alarmed but didn't need to invent too much; her pulse was fast and her temperature up.

The cries began quite late. Felícia was about to fall asleep when she heard the bell from her mistress's room. She threw on a robe, and, as soon as she opened the door, her mistress, who was standing before the dresser, disheveled and red-eyed, asked her whether she took the brooch from the lapel when she put her dress away. Felícia never lost her composure. "What brooch?" "What brooch do you think? The one with the diamonds." Felícia said she hadn't seen it. She had taken the dress, brushed it thoroughly, and, since the mud stains remained, she'd taken it to the cleaner's, but the Senyora could be sure there had been nothing on its lapel. Teresa covered her eyes with her handkerchief and burst into tears. First thing the next morning Felícia went out to ask if they had found a brooch on the lapel of Senyora Rovira's dress. The girl at the cleaner's said no, that before sending the dresses in for cleaning she went over them to make sure there was nothing on them. "They must have taken it from me when I fell," Teresa said in great desperation. "I wish I were dead." Felícia told Vicenç, Vicenç told the doorkeeper, the doorkeeper told the druggist, and the cook, when she went to ask Senyor Nicolau for her wages, explained that the Senyora had lost the diamond pin when she left the dressmaker's and had gone half-crazy out of sheer mortification. Senyor Nicolau, somewhat recovered from his cold, went to see Teresa and found her as pale as death because she hadn't closed an eye all night and, having said so many times that she felt ill, now really was ill and had convinced herself she'd lost her brooch. Sitting at the foot of the bed, Senyor Nicolau asked her why she hadn't confided in him and told him right away. Teresa, with almost no voice left, told him someone must have stolen it from her when she fainted and that he couldn't possibly imagine her vexation; she felt as if she'd been thrown into hell, not because of the jewel's value, which was great, but because it was a present from him, a proof of his regard. And she burst out weeping with her face to the pillow. Senyor Rovira took her hand and told her that he regretted it, of course, but he did not want to see her sad any longer; he'd find a remedy right away.

One morning, when she felt better and her cheeks had regained their color, because it was true that she had been suffering, they ordered the carriage. Senyor Rovira climbed in first, with Vicenç's help, as usual. Then Senyora Teresa got in. When Senyor Begú saw them he had to suppress his desire to laugh. Teresa explained to him the fiasco with the brooch, and Senyor Nicolau, interrupting her, asked if they had another one like it. "No, I do not have another one like it because it was a unique piece, but I kept a drawing, and, if you wish, I can have it made again. The hardest part will be finding diamonds as perfect as those at the heart of the flowers, but I will do the impossible, let me assure you." Two months later they returned to the jeweler's. Senyor Begú produced from his strongbox a violet case lined in white satin and placed it open on his desk. Senyor Rovira gave the satisfied jeweler a stack of bills, and Senyor Begú, pinning the brooch on the lapel of Senyora Rovira's dress and looking into her eyes, said, "No one would guess it isn't the same one."

That spring Teresa Goday de Rovira became godmother to a rather mature infant who had no mother, poor little thing; she'd died in the hospital in childbirth. Teresa explained to her husband that Miquel Masdéu was a worker whom she'd known from childhood, that he was the first cousin of the erring mother and, as the child had been left alone and Masdéu and his wife had no children, had decided to take him in. A big mess. "What nice folks," Senyor Rovira said, even though he hadn't felt up to accompanying Teresa to the baptism.

In a corner of the church office Miquel Masdéu, his eyes teary, shook Teresa's hand. "Thank you. Be happy, and may God repay you." And he stared, dazzled by the shine of candle flames on a gemstone bouquet that Teresa, married to a wealthy old man, wore pinned to the left side of her breast.

2. BARBARA

Salvador Valldaura closed his eyes as the violins unfolded the first notes of the allegro con brio. He was concentrating, surrounded by waves that carried him away and left him almost breathless. When after the three orchestral chords the piano repeated the beginning phrase, he opened his eyes. On the stage, in the first violins section, there was a young woman with a bit of lace hanging from under the hem of her skirt. That dangling piece of lace seemed so out of place that he lost his concentration for a moment. He closed his eyes again and tried to concentrate. The piano shaped the second theme, passed it on to the orchestra, and took it again with greater assurance. But it was hopeless. "They had to let a girl play in the orchestra!" How could he not have noticed her earlier? Before the concert began he had been busy reading the program, and then, when after a silence the orchestra attacked the opening notes, he had barely caught a glimpse of her arm and her bow among all the others. He felt annoyed because, with her untidiness, she was ruining the best part of his evening. All of a sudden, feeling his heart tighten, he looked at her more attentively: the young woman with the lace was the violinist he had seen five or six months ago playing in Salzburg, in a concert of conservatory students. Thin, blonde as gold, with very bright eyes, her hair done up but with two or three curls escaping down her neck. He had stared at her all evening, and later he thought of her often, somewhat foggily; she was so fragile that he thought life might end up damaging her. He had mentioned her to Joaquim Bergadà, his friend. A bad choice and bad timing: having just seduced the wife of the English commercial *agregé*, a woman with an amorous reputation, Quim had barely listened to him. "Is that so? Be careful; these girls tend to stick," and he had changed the topic. Valldaura resolved to never again mention her to anyone. She must have been Viennese; nowhere else in the world had he seen such fine young women or such graceful features. He had been sure he'd never see her again, and now he had her within reach. He heard, as a sigh, the last notes of the cadenza, and the music languished toward that almost unbearable finale. The kettledrums joined the piano. He closed his eyes once more, but it was useless: he saw her with her head bent and her eyebrows frowned, just as in Salzburg, and he thought the violins, the piano, and the flutes sounded farther and farther away.

Many years later, each time Salvador Valldaura was to hear Beethoven's Concerto no. 3, he would recall that night. He left the hall with the crowd and then strolled for a long while without knowing where he was going. It was cold, and the few people on the streets walked on quickly. He had the impression that things had changed and would never again be the same after that night. He did not see her for another two weeks. It was also a Sunday: she'd done her hair differently, parted in the middle and her curls gathered with a black ribbon. He could not see her eyes, but her forehead, extremely white, had a sweet shape. As soon as she stopped playing, she'd lower her head, absorbed and serene.

The next day Valldaura invited Quim to a restaurant and could not avoid mentioning the young woman from Salzburg.

Quim looked at him with a laugh. "You mean a girl who sometime plays in the Sunday concert series? Of course I know her! She is a relative of a friend. Her name is Barbara something-or-other. Some afternoons she goes to Dehmel's for tea, and she lives right behind the embassy. Flowerpots on her balcony and small glass panes in her windows . . . You can't ask for better! One of these days I'll introduce her to you."

When Joaquim Bergadà and Salvador Valldaura got to Dehmel's, Barbara and her cousin were already there. They sat in the back room at a table with a black marble top. The place was crowded. Barbara raised an arm as soon as she saw them: she was wearing an overcoat with a fur collar, and Valldaura thought that close up she was even prettier.

Quim made the introductions. An old waitress, dressed in light blue and wearing a big apron, served them. They were together for not even a half-hour. Barbara said almost nothing during that time. She listened attentively to her cousin, a red-cheeked middle-aged gentleman who talked music with Quim. Barbara appeared distracted, as if thinking of other things. Valldaura could barely speak to her, but taking advantage of a lull in the conversation he told her he liked Vienna a lot.

"Really? I like it too, but it must be because I was born here," she gushed with a smile.

He thought her French was perfect. She began to put on her gloves.

"Please, don't get up, but I must go."

They all stood. On the street Quim and his friend dropped back, and Valldaura asked Barbara if Sunday afternoon she would go for a stroll in the park with him. Barbara turned her head and looked at him with her gray eyes half-closed.

"Yes," she said in a thin voice.

He suspected she had accepted out of politeness. When he was alone he entered a flower shop and asked them to deliver a bouquet of violets to Barbara every day. The violet blooms were big, pale, more lilac than purple in color. But they had no scent, perhaps because they came from a cold climate.

The weather Sunday was splendid. Valldaura got up late and went to his hotel's barber for a trim. He took his time with lunch. As soon as he got out of his carriage in front of the house with the little balconies, he saw Barbara already coming down the stairs. She was dressed in gray and wore a velvet cape and a few violets pinned to her chest. After closing the cab door with Barbara seated at his side, Valldaura thought himself a lucky man. She, who had barely opened her mouth the day they had been introduced, was now chatting ceaselessly without looking at him. "A bit much," Valldaura thought. As they entered the Prater, she had already explained that she lived with her grandparents and that her mother, who was a beautiful woman, had let her hair grow so long that it reached her thighs.

"When I was five or six, she let me in the bathroom to see her bathe, but, as she'd begin to get dressed, she'd say, pointing to the door: 'Now, Barbara, you may leave.'" One day Barbara didn't see her mother anymore and for a long time, whenever alone, looked for her all over the place and called for her softly. She had fled with an old flame who lived in Italy. Barbara knew very little of her father: he traveled a lot, and she almost never saw him. But her grandfather . . . The day she told him she wanted to learn to play the violin he was elated. "He loves music." She fell silent. For a while all you could hear were the horse's hooves. Valldaura thought, "What must be the matter with her that she's telling me so much?" The avenue was almost deserted; the sunlight had weakened, and the air felt a little cold. Two officers in their light-blue uniforms appeared on horseback from a side pathway. The one closest to them held his kepi with one hand as he leaned to look in the carriage. The other one, who wore a monocle, said something, and they both laughed. Barbara followed them with her eyes for a little while.

"My grandfather was in the military, and I still remember sneaking up to pull the buttons off his uniform." She turned to face Valldaura, and, pointing at the violets on her chest, she said: "It's the first time someone sent me flowers." Valldaura felt the urge to grab her hand but thought that he better not startle her and spoke about Salzburg. Barbara smiled: "At times I feel discouraged and think I'll never be able to play the violin well." After a while Valldaura had the cab stop, and they walked toward the Lusthaus. She refused to go in. "I feel like walking; it's been so long since I was here last . . ." They were in the middle of the round opening, surrounded by forest, and they followed a dirt path with tall grasses to the sides, burned by the cold. With a flutter of wings two birds took off from a branch, screeching. Barbara started, and Valldaura took her arm.

"Don't be scared. It's just birds." She laughed. Valldaura had never seen a face change so much with laughter; she seemed a different woman, and her eyes betrayed a kind of maliciousness.

"My grandfather and I used to come here. Do you see that boulder down there? He always told me to climb it. Then we went down to the river. It's not far . . . But we used come in the summer when the trees were thick with leaves and the grass was soft." Delicious. At that moment Valldaura would have wanted to be God. "Let there be leaves on the trees and flowers in bloom," he thought with a smile. He wasn't going to leave the park without kissing her.

"Barbara," he muttered. She picked one of the violets from her chest and gave it to him, fixing her gaze on him. Valldaura brought the violet to his lips. Among the branches you could see the almost white sky; a bit of fog was coming from the river. Barbara picked up a pebble and threw it furiously.

"When I was little I thought I could kill fish with stones." They stood facing each other; Valldaura was looking into her eyes, the speckled iris, the darker pupil, the bluish white of the cornea. Without a word he took her face into his large hands and kissed her. They walked slowly back to the cab. Before dropping her off at her house, he asked if she'd like to have dinner with him the next day. Barbara said yes.

The maître opened the door and beckoned Valldaura into the private room. The ceiling was low, covered with the same material as the curtains. In the back, half-hidden behind a screen, under a big mirror, there was a sofa covered with cushions. Valldaura looked at the glass and saw two white fingerprints.

"Don't you have another room with a clean mirror?" The maître apologized profusely: impossible, every room was taken, but he'd have the mirror cleaned, it wouldn't take a second. "Quick, quick," he said when the maître returned with the waiter. Valldaura waited in the corridor. If Barbara should arrive right then . . . The maître and the waiter scurried away. Valldaura waited for quite a while. He strutted around checking every detail. He stopped in front of the table. It was round, it had two silver candlesticks, and the tablecloth fell all the way to the floor. The wine glasses were green with pink stems. Perfect. There was a knock on the door, and a waitress slowly began to light the candles. Before she had finished, Barbara arrived. Valldaura looked at her with some surprise. She was prettier than ever but was dressed entirely in black.

Barbara gulped the last glass of champagne. She had risen from the table and, wiping her forehead, was approaching the divan. After a few steps she came to a sudden stop, and turning around she shrieked, "Oh, please, this mirror!" Her eyes shone as in a fever. Valldaura asked her if she was feeling all right.

"I'm fine. It's nothing." But it took her a while to calm down. Later she explained to him that after her mother had left them she sometimes dreamed that a soft voice said to her, "Barbara!" And then she went into a mirror with a gilded frame just like that one and felt she was trapped inside. Valldaura did not know what to say. She looked around, grabbed her overcoat, and stepping onto the sofa covered the mirror with it.

"Done." She sat down and began to remove her hairpins. Valldaura, coming nearer, parted the hair off her face.

"What beautiful hair, how long and blonde." Barbara burst out in a laugh and put a finger to his cheek, pressing hard, as if to leave a mark.

"When a person dies, her hair continues to grow. Did you know that?" She unbuttoned her bodice and leaned back. She took his hand and brought it to one of her breasts.

Two days later Quim went to see him and showed him a newspaper: Barbara had committed suicide. She'd been found drowned in the canal.

He lived for a few months unwilling to believe that Barbara was dead. He thought he would see her again, some afternoon in the park, some evening in a café. He walked absently in the places where they had been together. One day, in the museum, he stopped before the Bronzino Holy Family, and his heart leaped: Mary was the spitting image of Barbara – the same arch of the eyebrows, the same oval face, her neck like a marble column, her parted hair, her head slightly bent. He went every day. He spent his afternoons sitting in his hotel room, near the balcony, staring blankly at the windows of the house across the street. His doctor told him that if he wanted to come out of the well where he had fallen he would have to seek some distraction. In the embassy people gossiped about him. Quim Bergadà had told them the story of Barbara, and they were all afraid he might do something crazy. The new post in Paris helped him a little, but winter saw him down again. After Christmas, on a visit to Barcelona, Rafael Bergadà, Quim's brother, introduced him to the widow of the financier Nicolau Rovira, a pretty and most charming woman called Teresa Goday.

3. SALVADOR VALLDAURA AND TERESA GODAY

Those velvety eyes and that contagious laughter seduced him. He was always to remember Teresa's entrance into the room, in her hazel moiré dress, a pink rose on her breast and a marten overcoat hanging down to her feet, and shivering, complaining about the weather. They barely exchanged two words, but when they parted she shook hands with him, laughing as if she'd known him all her life. He saw her again the day after Twelfth Night, also at Quim's brother's house. Rafael told him he'd invited the two of them for dinner because both of them were a bit lost: she'd been a widow for a little over a year, and he had no relatives in Barcelona. When coffee was served and the men were left alone, Valldaura asked, to what branch of the Godays did Teresa belong?

"I don't quite know," Rafael answered him evasively, "but since she's the widow of Nicolau Rovira she has many friends, and all doors are open to her."

Teresa and Eulàlia, Rafael's wife, had become intimate friends and once in a while would go window shopping together. One week after that dinner Valldaura, walking by himself along the Passeig de Gràcia, saw them get out of a carriage on the corner of Carrer Casp. Teresa wore a hat with bird-of-paradise feathers.

"What nice feathers," Valldaura said, stepping to her side.

"Are you sure you are not making fun of me?" Teresa looked splendid, and men turned their heads to look at her. He was about to take her arm but had second thoughts: one couldn't do that sort of thing in Barcelona. They walked together for a while, and before he left the women he said he wouldn't be seeing them for a while as he'd received a letter from Paris and had to leave before the end of the week.

One afternoon two days later Valldaura went to Can Culleretes. He had the habit of going to that café for a dish of whipped cream on the eve of his departure, once he was all packed. It was his way of saying good-bye to Barcelona. Lost in thought, he heard Teresa's voice: "May I sit at your table?"

The waiter came at once. "The usual, Senyora Rovira?"

Teresa laughed. "Yes, Joan, whipped cream and an *ensaimada*."

Setting her gloves and purse on a chair next to hers, she told Valldaura, who had not yet recovered from his surprise, "You see, we like the same things." They talked about the weather, of the Bergadàs, of Joaquim, whom Teresa had never met. Then they sat for a while, not knowing what else to say.

Teresa sighed. "How nice it must be to travel . . ."

He replied that he was beginning to feel tired of globetrotting on his own and that he'd always been afraid of marrying a foreigner. "It might work out, but I've never felt like trying." All of a sudden he remembered Barbara and blushed. Teresa took her teaspoon and toyed with her whipped cream; looking at him, her eyes filled with false innocence, she thought: I'll bet you've slept around plenty! They barely said another word. When they rose, Valldaura said good-bye reluctantly. He was smitten.

The next day, before he left the hotel with his suitcases, he ordered flowers to be sent to Teresa daily. "Violets, while they are in season." It would be as if the Vienna idyll had taken hold again. More realistically, however, he left a boxful of his cards. On each one of them he had written, "Devotedly."

When Felícia entered her bedroom with the first bouquet of violets, Teresa had just awakened. Without seeing the card, she guessed they were from Valldaura. For the past two days she had thought about him often. She could not say she disliked him: good-looking, blond hair, elegant.

"What would you do in my place, Felícia; would you marry again?"

The maid looked at her with happy eyes. "I should think so, Senyora."

Felícia left, and Teresa felt the sort of uneasiness she felt whenever she thought of the time she'd been married to Nicolau Rovira. For the first several months she'd missed him. She owed everything to him: he had tempered her; he had taken her out of poverty. Shortly before he died like a little chick, he'd said to her, "Now you can go anywhere you want." If on any given day she looked at herself in the mirror with the diamond brooch on her breast, she felt a wave of shame on her cheeks. She was getting used to living alone. But time was passing, and Nicolau had left a part of his wealth to his sister, a widow with two children. Teresa's endowment was not unlimited, and she was a spendthrift; she was beginning to fall into debt. She thought she might sell one of the houses but wasn't very happy about the idea. She might play the stock exchange – she had friends who would advise her – but Nicolau had once told her, "If you're not very good at it, you might find yourself a pauper in the blink of an eye." Valldaura was a pleasant man . . . but the day she met him she had caught him with a look she found disquieting. And she was bothered by that Vienna story – everyone knew about it – it had prostrated him. She didn't like the fact that he lived abroad. They said he was extremely wealthy. But, if you thought about it, first an old husband and then one with a foggy past . . . She closed her eyes again. Why was she wasting her time with these thoughts? No one had proposed to her yet. She set the violets on the night table and tucked herself in.

Every year at Carnival the Bergadàs gave a ball that had become famous in Barcelona. As soon as Teresa received an invitation, she paid them a visit. "I can't do it, Eulàlia. I stopped wearing mourning before a year had passed because you know I can't stand black, but going to a party is something else."

Eulàlia placed a hand on her knee. "What does a year more or less matter? Listen: don't wallow in your grief. We've only invited friends . . . Are you afraid people will find fault with you?"

Eulàlia didn't give up until she talked her into it. Before leaving, Teresa told her friend that Valldaura was sending her violets every day.

Eulàlia got up and kissed her. "I hear wedding bells."

Teresa burst out laughing. "Not so fast."

Eulàlia, who had sat down again and remained very serious, picked up her arms suddenly and clapped her hands: "I've got it! I'll have him come. Upon my word, you two will dance. Wear your best."

The next morning, quite early, Teresa stepped into Terenci Farriols's shop to buy material for her dress.

Terenci Farriols was a tall and thin man, extremely polite, "Senyora Rovira, you may not believe it, but I was just thinking about you."

Teresa sat down and laughed: "I don't believe you for a moment. Show me lace, will you please? And satin for a domino."

Farriols looked at her with surprise. "We have some exquisite lace, of a quality that you may never have seen." The attendant spread a few pieces of lace on the counter, and Teresa, after looking and looking, bought the most expensive one. The satins were extraordinary. Teresa hesitated before she decided on the color but, thinking of the violets, chose purple.

"You have chosen the prettiest color, Senyora Rovira; it will suit you beautifully," Terenci Farriols told her as he accompanied her to the door.

The day of the ball Teresa arrived at the Bergadàs's a little late. The first person to greet her was Salvador Valldaura.

"What a surprise . . . I thought you were in Paris."

She looked ravishing – her wasp's waist, the mask in her hand, gloves past her elbows, and naked shoulders; the white lace made her skin look darker. She had pinned a violet corsage by her heart and another one in her hair. She wore no jewelry. Valldaura thought: What a woman, once she turns forty!

Pointing at her corsage of violets, Teresa said, "Do you recognize these?"

He asked her if she liked violets. Teresa lied: "They're my favorite." The orchestra, which had finished a dance when Teresa came in, began a mazurka, and Valldaura offered her his arm. When they walked past Rafael and Eulàlia, who were dancing together, Eulàlia winked at Teresa, and Teresa turned her head away, pretending she hadn't seen her. Valldaura made her promise him all her dances.

Her cheeks burning, she fanned herself with one hand. "Do you think it's a good idea to dance only with me?" She spoke as she crossed out all the pages in her dance program. Her corsage fell to the floor, and Valldaura bent down to pick it up; before returning it to her, he smelled it.

"Fragrant . . . like all of them."

Teresa removed her mask to put the flowers on again, and, as she pinned them on her breast, Valldaura observed her long and curly eyelashes, her thick chestnut hair like a silk cap. They approached the buffet to eat sweets and drink champagne and, glasses in hand, went to sit in a corner. Behind them, on a golden column, stood a vase with white lilac branches.

"Flowers follow me," Teresa said as she straightened the tail of her dress. The tip of one foot appeared at the edge of her skirt. She realized Valldaura was looking at it, and she pulled it back. "Do you know what I like about champagne? The bubbles." They gave their empty glasses to a servant who had approached them with a tray and took freshly filled ones.

"Why don't you come to Paris?"

Teresa pretended she hadn't heard him, and Valldaura, who was about to repeat his question, felt suddenly shy and finished his champagne in silence. He looked handsome: his well-cut tails, his immaculate shirt front, and his blond beard slightly disheveled. As soon as the musicians began the Lancers Dance, Teresa, with her eyes sparkling behind her mask, picked up her train, took Valldaura's arm, and moved to the middle of the room. Now and then they changed partners, and whenever they came together they looked at each other and laughed. If I could, Valldaura thought, I would take her to the end of the world. The applause was deafening. Teresa, panting, her head thrown back, was telling herself that she'd never known a night like this one. She was hot. She took off her gloves slowly – they seemed endless – and wiped her face with her hand.

"What I'm doing must not be quite proper."

Valldaura shook his head, laughing.

"Just a moment," she said, "I'll be right back." She went to look for Eulàlia. "Please, let me borrow a fan; I can't take it anymore." Eulàlia gave her the one she had. "Keep it; it will serve as a token." Its ribs were mother-of-pearl, and there was an apple painted on the fabric; a silk tassel hung from the handle.

The musicians played the dance again. When it was over, Teresa said: "Whew! Shall we have more champagne?" She brought a glass to her lips and drank it in one swallow. "I shouldn't be drinking so much. It's gone to my head. You too?" She was fanning herself briskly; the apple was green, very pale, with a touch of pink and two large leaves to the sides of its chocolate-colored stem.

"I can drink a whole bottle and not feel it. Other things, though, go to my head right away."

Half-closing her eyes, flirtatiously, Teresa asked him, "What things?"

"Beauty, for example."

The party lasted into dawn. Before it ended, Teresa said she was tired and wanted to leave. The lilacs in the vase were beginning to wilt, but the splendor of the lights, of the dresses, of the silk in the gold-framed medallions, was ever lively.

"Do you want to leave so soon?" Valldaura asked her, as if he were never to see her again. To Teresa the air outside seemed like ice. They were standing by the gate. Valldaura didn't take his eyes from her. "How fast the night has gone!"

She gave him a long look and stroked his lapel with her fan. In the gray clarity of the new day, her hair a little undone, among her violet folds, Teresa looked less like a woman than like a dream. Valldaura helped her into the carriage and, his hand on the door handle, whispered: "I must leave tomorrow. May I write to you?"

Teresa's apartment looked very nice. She had gotten rid of her husband's furniture and bought better pieces under the guidance of an antiquarian. She had kept only the Japanese armoire, which, with the passage of time, she'd begun to really like. The walls in her living room were covered with straw-color damask, and, in a corner next to the sofa, she had installed a white porcelain nymph, as tall as she was, which gracefully held a round urn on one shoulder. Valldaura had returned to Barcelona a few times, and Teresa had him over for delicious teas. One afternoon he proposed to her. He spent a while holding his cup in his fingers, saying nothing, preoccupied. She remained thoughtful, with eyes lowered. She didn't answer yes or no. Simply: she had loved her husband dearly and still thought of him.

"What you just said is very flattering, but it's so sudden . . ."

Valldaura, who was looking at her intensely, leaned forward and took her hand. Why could they not help each other live? He left as he had come: without a definite answer. The next day he came again. He could not stand not knowing. Felícia showed him into the parlor.

"Senyor Valldaura is here to see you, Senyora; I asked him in."

Teresa, who was dressing to go out, took off her clothes in a hurry and, clad in her most sumptuous robe, entered the living room amid waves of perfume and the rustling of silk, asking Valldaura to forgive her for receiving him in such a manner but she had been resting and hadn't wanted him to wait. In a calm voice she inquired, "Are you all right?"

"Yesterday we left a problem unsolved," Valldaura replied, and, looking at her gravely, he added he had come there to get a kiss. "A kiss will mean that there is no problem."

Teresa brought a finger to her lips and then caressed Valldaura's cheek with it. "You have it." Then, giving him no time even to open his mouth, she asked, "May I leave you for a moment while I go and order tea?" Down the corridor, a hand to her neck, she took a few deep breaths.

That spring they were married in the church of Santa Maria del Mar. Valldaura decided they would spend the honeymoon on his estate in Vilafranca. "You'll see, what vineyards!" One evening, while they were strolling under the apple trees, Valldaura shook a branch and a shower of blossoms fell on them. Teresa spread her arms and hands and, examining a blossom that had fallen on her palm, said softly, "This flower, so small, is mine."

Valldaura embraced her. "It's all yours: these vineyards, this land, and I." He kissed her with his eyes closed so that nothing would distract him – such a long kiss that he almost suffocated her.

At the beginning of autumn, when they returned to Barcelona, Salvador Valldaura realized Teresa was sad. It must upset her, he thought, thinking she'll have to live in Paris. Without another thought he went to see Josep Fontanills, his financial advisor. Fontanills was a rather fat man, broad shouldered, short legs and arms; he had a reputation for integrity and for being a kind person.

As soon as he saw Valldaura, he broke out into excuses. "Why didn't you warn me? I'd have come to see you." He seated Valldaura in his best chair. Through the balcony doors they could see the hilltop hermitage of Sant Pere Màrtir. Valldaura had heard that, on clear evenings, Fontanills took time from his appointments to enjoy in perfect quiet the sun setting behind the hill.

Valldaura said: "I am taking my wife to Paris, but, as she is quite a Barcelona woman, I am afraid she might feel homesick. If she can't take living abroad, I'll give up my career. I would like you to find me a villa – and take your time – so I can begin refurbishing it to my taste."

"It just so happens," Fontanills replied, "that I have one for sale. It belongs to a miscreant heir, the Marquis of Castelljussà, who has squandered his parents' fortune. But it's in terrible shape."

That very day they went to see it, and Valldaura fell in love with the place. It lay in the upper part of Sant Gervasi, on a street that hadn't yet been paved, next to an open field, surrounded by a big garden, which, at the back, beyond an esplanade, became a woods. He would say nothing to Teresa until all was ready. Fontanills made an appointment with the owner, they soon agreed on the terms, and Valldaura took the closing papers to Amadeu Riera, the attorney of the fashionable set.

"Make sure there are no liens on the property and that everything is in order."

On the right-hand side of his desk attorney Riera kept a small vase with a rose. "As far as I know," Valldaura laughed, "you're the only attorney with flowers in his office."

They closed two weeks later. When the Marquis of Castelljussà left the office with a billfold full of cash, Amadeu Riera congratulated Valldaura,

"What are you going to do with a villa in a lot that's over three hundred thousand square feet?"

"Three hundred and fifty-six thousand," interjected Fontanills, who had not said a word the whole time. And he added: "If I had the money you have, Senyor Valldaura, I wouldn't have let that property slip away from me either."

A few days before leaving for Paris, Valldaura took Teresa to see the villa. Fontanills went along. As soon as they stepped out of the carriage, Teresa was so struck that she could only say, "My God, it looks like a castle!"

At the foot of the wrought-iron fence, a wide driveway, lined with chestnut trees, led to the house; at the end of the driveway, four stories high, with two towers and all the roofs tiled in green ceramic, covered by a creeper with leaves turning red, the house showed its outline against an autumn sky. It was windy, and the three steps that led to the main entrance were half-buried in leaves. To one side, next to the door, stood two large varnished pots, full of dirt, and a few flower pots with dead plants. Valldaura raised his walking stick and, pointing at the terrace held up by four pink marble columns to shelter the main door, said, "I'll have this enclosed in glass, and in wintertime it'll serve as a sun room."

Fontanills put the key in the hole and jiggled it. "Everything is rusted out, Senyor Valldaura; but we'll get it all fixed."

The vestibule was so large that it seemed like a ballroom, and, to the left, a staircase, with a wrought-iron banister, led in a single curving sweep to the second floor. They explored room after room; there were walls with hanging strips of wallpaper, and the dankness was oppressive. One reached the towers from the fourth floor through very narrow and high-stepped stairs; on the first landing there was a door that led out onto the roof. Fontanills opened it. "Do you want to look?"

Teresa shrieked, "Close it, it frightens me."

They climbed no farther. By the pots with the dead plants Valldaura asked his wife: "Do you like it?" Teresa said nothing and hugged him. Fontanills, not daring to look at them, thought: What else could one do? A woman like this is well worth a mass.

It was growing dark. They went around on the stone path that encircled the house. To the right, with its branches against the wall of the house, was a tree with narrow and shiny leaves.

"It's a laurel, isn't it?" Teresa asked.

"Yes, Senyora, and you will seldom see any others this tall."

Beyond the laurel there was a well and two stone benches under an arbor covered with dry wisteria. They crossed the esplanade, and Teresa, looking at the thickness of trees at the end of it, thought: It's beautiful, but scary. They were walking amid ferns and brambles. From the top of the trees they heard the cooing of turtledoves.

"This," Valldaura said, "has never been a woods; when they built the house it must have been a park."

"I think you're right," Fontanills answered, looking down at the ground so as not to trip, "it's an abandoned park."

They soon came to a pond surrounded by black ivy.

"This pond, Senyora Valldaura, never goes dry; at the center it is over five feet deep. At the end of the lot there are three ancient cedars. They are supposed to bring good luck. Would you like to see them?"

Suddenly, in the ivy, they heard the rustling of an animal scurrying away. Teresa moved closer to her husband. "Let's go." The wind, growing stronger, made the branches sway. They came out onto the esplanade, and Teresa saw it wasn't yet dark.

Fontanills extended an arm, pointing toward a little house near the edge of the woods. "It's the washhouse; it can also be used as a toolshed. There is a porch on the other side of it." He said he'd give them climbing roses to plant so they could cover its walls. "The old man who cares for my country house in Premià is always giving me cuttings from his rose trees; they grow flesh-colored roses as big as your fist."

Teresa did not like Paris at all; she found its houses too black and its sky too gray. The gentlemen with whom she had to deal, almost out of duty, were too ceremonious and the ladies too snobbish. Her French teacher was good only for making her feel ill at ease. She could not stand being by herself for even five minutes because she would begin to think about Barcelona, and, knowing herself so far away, she felt a kind of anxiety. But, if she went out for a stroll with the wife of one of her husband's associates, she suffered even more. When she became pregnant, it was worse. She spent whole afternoons thinking of the estate in Vilafranca.

"We'll have to go back to Barcelona," Valldaura told her one day, when he'd found her crying. And he added: "For good. I've never been all that crazy about my career, and, now that you are to have a child, even less so." He had become very jealous, and whenever he went anywhere with Teresa he felt cornered. Teresa was too attractive.

Overjoyed, she asked: "For good?"

"For good."

She was to have the baby in Barcelona, at home.

"If it's a girl," Valldaura said to her, "we'll call her Sofia, like my mother; if it's a boy, we'll call him Esteve because we met on the feast of Saint Stephen."

Teresa had a girl. Joaquim Bergadà, who was still living in Vienna, came to the christening: Valldaura had insisted that Joaquim be the godfather. Quim's sister-in-law Eulàlia was the godmother. The renovation had been completed, and the villa shone like a mirror. The gardeners had many more days of work in store, though, clearing paths, weeding, burning dead branches, and planting peonies and begonias in the beds they had dug on both sides of the chestnut tree promenade. One Sunday morning, when the movers had not yet delivered all of the furniture, the Valldauras moved to their villa with their servants and a wonderful wet nurse who wore lots of necklaces.

5. A STORM IN SPRING

After lunch Teresa sat by the great dining room window. She didn't feel like doing anything. If Valldaura had been at home, they would have gone out, as they did everyday, for a walk in the garden and to watch Climent water the plants. Climent was their new driver: an emaciated-looking man with black sideburns and eyes like coal. They had engaged him shortly after they got married because Vicenç, who for so many years had served Teresa's first husband and had been left unemployed in Barcelona when the Valldauras left for Paris, had decided to move back to Igualada, his hometown. Climent lived with his wife in the little apartment the Valldauras had fixed for them over the stables, an old porch in which Valldaura had arranged to keep the horses and the carriage; you could see it from the gate, far off, behind a privet fence, next to the wall on one side of the garden. Since the horses did not take too much of his time, Climent worked part-time in the flower beds to help the two gardeners who came a couple of times a week and were somewhat slow. Three days ago Valldaura had left with Fontanills to look over an estate near Montseny. Since he'd given up his career, he busied himself with his possessions.

Teresa saw the wet nurse go by with a small bundle. She must have changed the girl's diaper and must be carrying the dirty linen to the washhouse for Antònia to wash it. They had been very lucky with the nurse: her name was Evarista, and she was very pretty, with green eyes and skin so white that more than one lady would have envied her. And clean as a whistle, all starched and tidy, fresher than a rose. Perhaps too much: whenever she'd see Climent in the garden, she was all aflutter. Sofia had just turned six months old; she was thin, nervous, and had a tiny face. She wasn't growing all that well. "When I breast-feed her," the nurse would say, "instead of sucking, she plays." If for some reason Teresa tried to caress her, the girl turned around, clutched the nurse's neck, and started to cry. "Don't get any wrong ideas, Senyora; she does recognize you, but she is cranky in a bad way. I think her teeth are hurting her." Teresa heard people speaking outside. The nurse must be talking to Anselma, the cook, who had a shrill voice. It was quite a thing, given how fat Anselma was.

The heat was sultry, and Teresa, who was beginning to faint, felt a drop of perspiration fall down her cheek. She thought of the pearl she'd given her husband when they returned to Barcelona. It was a gray pearl, and she couldn't shake it off her mind. How many things had happened since that morning when she and poor Nicolau had gone to Senyor Begú's jewelry shop . . . She got up and went to the stairs. She couldn't remember whether he was wearing it before he left. She found it on the dressing table stuck onto a little cushion along with some other tie pins. He must have been afraid of losing it and had chosen another pin. She smiled, but she was feeling uneasy. It must have been the fault of those clouds that had begun to cover the sky during lunchtime. She opened the balcony and, without going out, looked at herself in the glass panes, in profile. She didn't show any belly. The midwife had been right. "Be patient. If you can stand these sheets for three or four days, your belly will be as flat as it was before." Doctor Falguera, who dropped in every afternoon to check on the girl, had laughed: "These women, they are always discovering something . . ." Teresa paid no attention; she spent a whole week in bed under the weight of three folded bedsheets and came out as flat as she'd been before any pregnancy. But something had changed. Her hair was a little darker; it was no longer the light chestnut it had been when she was twenty.

She looked around her room and went back downstairs. She couldn't sit down. In the vestibule she got distracted for a moment looking at the black mosaic pool; they'd had it built at the last minute: the water poured from a large stone basin, jutting out from the center, amid alabaster grapes and pears. It had been her idea, and she liked it better every day. Hidden among leaves, three water lilies were beginning to blossom: they were the first. She had ordered some red fish a couple of weeks ago, but they hadn't been delivered yet. She went into the kitchen and then outside. Antònia was scrubbing a large pot on the ground and rinsing it at the water spout by the kitchen door; Anselma made her clean the pot outdoors because she said that, being too heavy, it would scratch the sink marble and no one would be able to get rid of those scratches even with cleaning powder.

"I think we'll have some rain," Anselma said, without lifting her eyes from the girl.

"Let it rain already; otherwise, I will suffocate," Teresa complained.

Anselma licked one of her fingers and raised it over her head. "Not a bit of wind." Teresa laughed and crossed the esplanade slowly. She might find a cool spot under the trees. She could not understand how it could be so hot in May.

Anselma saw her move away. "If she had her nose stuck to the oven the way I have, then she'd have reason to complain about stifling heat."

At the foot of the trees Teresa turned around to look at the house. She still hadn't gotten used to living there. She had spent the whole winter going from one room to the next; she leaned out the balconies to look at the yard. When the room warmers were lit, she'd run through the house in the dark and spent long hours seated before the fire in her room with her eyes fixed on the embers. Now she was beginning to get used to it. She walked on among the trees. A ray of sun had just come out between two clouds, but it could barely get past the leaves. She heard noises from the branches: they must have been full of birds, but Teresa, who stopped to look up from time to time, could not see a single one. There were many in the laurel tree by the well. At certain moments the sparrows came in and out incessantly, cheeping like mad. She walked to the pheasants' cage. It was a very large and tall cage, the top in the shape of a pumpkin and crowned with a golden ball. Valldaura had it filled with peacocks, pheasants, and guinea hens. At dusk the peacocks let out spooky shrieks heard everywhere. The guinea hens were lying down, their beaks half-open, and when she went near them they all rose at once. A pheasant, perched on the dead tree that stood in the middle of the cage, looked at her with one eye. She opened the gate and stepped inside. "Little ones, little ones . . ." She came closer to the pheasant on the branch, which had not moved, and plucked a feather from its tail. The bird didn't stir: perhaps it was sick. The water in the drinking tank was very murky. She should tell Mundeta and reprimand her; she was the youngest of the maids and took care of the animals. "That such lovely birds have to drink dirty water . . ." The guinea hens were all bunched up in a corner – dark, with light spots on their feathers, their tiny heads. She felt like leaving the cage door ajar; those creatures would be happier if they could run free under the trees. As she left and closed the door behind her, she asked them, "Don't you think so?" A few steps beyond the cage the pond's water was green, almost black, full of tadpoles swimming up and down. Gathering up her robe, she walked to the wall at the end. Before she got there, she came to an opening with three cedars, very close together, very old. The cedars that brought good luck. The wall, quite high, was crowned with broken glass. She touched the wall. "You're mine." And she laughed. Where had she gotten this habit of touching things that were hers? She turned around and went by the cage on tiptoe. The pheasants slept on the branches, and the guinea hens, lying down, had closed their eyes. She heard above her the cooing of turtledoves. Neither she nor Valldaura had ever seen them. If she dared, she'd have many trees cut down; it was amazing that they could live so close to one another. And it was going to get worse every year because they were full of shoots. The lilacs that Valldaura had planted next to the cage and in some other spots were about to bloom. "If he'd had them planted in the sun, they would have bloomed long ago." Everything was very green, very dark . . . A large lizard ran by her feet like an arrow and disappeared behind a growth of grass.

Halfway through dinner, when Teresa asked Gertrudis to change the water in the pitcher because it was not cold enough and to bring her some pieces of ice, a flash of lightning lit the whole esplanade up to the line of trees. Gertrudis had remained at the foot of the door, very quiet, with a pitcher in her hand. The sound of thunder came right away, and the first drops, big and far apart, began to fall. Teresa pushed her dish away – she was no longer hungry – and grabbed the little basket with the nuts. She heard someone running up the stairs; Sofia must have wakened.

"She's been very nervous the whole afternoon and hasn't stopped spitting up milk; she's feeling the weather," the nurse told her when she brought the crying child into the dining room.

Another flash of lightning lit a whole patch of sky. The nurse had rested Sofia's little head on her shoulder, and Teresa, holding her breath, waited for the thunder. It was as if the sky was being rent. She got up all shaken, with the nutcracker in one hand, and Gertrudis, who'd come back from the kitchen, white as a sheet, said in a barely audible voice, "I've broken the pitcher, Senyora; if you knew how bad I feel . . ."

Teresa didn't even listen to her: "Go tell them right away to close all the shutters and make sure there's no balcony open." Without realizing what she was doing, she broke open a nut and left it on the table. "Do you know what, Nurse? We'll go to the drawing room; we'll be more protected there."

As they crossed the vestibule, they heard the wind drawn in underneath the door. Once in the drawing room, they sat on one corner of the sofa. The laurel was hitting the wall.

"It looks as if it wants to come in," the nurse said, while wiping the eyes of Sofia, who was wailing as if someone were killing her. Gertrudis opened the window and, bending down a little so as not to let the rain fall on her face, closed the shutter, which twice flew free from her hands. Sofia was still crying. The nurse, trying to calm her down, bared one breast; the child moved her head from side to side.

"Leave her alone, Nurse. Don't waste your time." Teresa was nervous and felt like checking to see if anything had happened. In the kitchen, seated in a corner, Antònia, who had left the dishes half-done, was crying. Teresa barely looked at her.

"Make strong coffee for everybody, Anselma," she told the cook, "and as soon as this one calms down tell her to bring the bottle of cognac and the glasses." Before leaving, she turned around: "And, if you're frightened, come, all of you."

From the foot of the stair she heard the slamming of a door and saw Filomena running down. "It's the one in the tower, but I've been too afraid to go that high."

Teresa took her by the arm. "Come with me."

They climbed to the third floor and lit a candle, but as soon as they got to the staircase a gust of wind left them in the dark. They had to grope their way down. In the drawing room the nurse was rocking Sofia, who was quieter but still sobbing now and then. "Poor little one," Teresa thought, looking at her, "even I feel spooked." And she felt like crying. Lightning had frightened her mother a lot, and, whenever she heard thunder, she covered her ears. "If she were alive," Teresa thought, "I would have her living like a queen."

Anselma and Antònia brought the coffee. The last ones to come in were Gertrudis and Mundeta, who had gone up to shut the turret door after Teresa and Filomena had come back; the latch had broken, and they had to secure the shutter with an ironing board. They were all very quiet, a little intimidated, unsure of what to say. Mundeta was explaining that in her town, when she was little, lightning had killed a man. Filomena sat on the floor because there weren't enough places on the couches and she'd been afraid to leave the room to get a chair. Gertrudis made the sign of the cross at each flash of lightning. "You've crossed yourself enough," Anselma told her, as she brought her cup to her lips and blew on the coffee before each sip. Teresa had gotten up and opened the window; in between the slats of the shutter she saw a river of water running through the yard. When she was about to close it again, she was stunned and felt as if the night were torn in half. "It hit next to the wall, by the laurel," Anselma said, coming close to her. Sofia, who had fallen asleep, woke up startled and started crying with her mouth open. "Senyora," the nurse said, "she's got her first tooth." Teresa lifted her child's lip with one finger: to one side of her upper gums a little white point showed.

At dawn the storm abated. They could only hear the noise of water running down the gutters. Filomena, stretched on the floor, had fallen asleep. "Don't wake her up," Teresa said, and with all the other girls they went out to see what damage had been done. The air felt cool, and the clouds were shredding away. Next to the well there was a big puddle of water. Only half of the laurel was left standing. Climent, with his cap to his ears and wearing a very old pair of shoes, was dragging the fallen piece of tree. When he heard Teresa and the girls, he raised his head. "I'm moving this so that it doesn't stand in the way; better the laurel than one of us, don't you think, Senyora Teresa?"

The following afternoon, when all was calm, Anselma told Senyora Teresa that her niece called Armanda was to take her First Communion.

"May I have leave to attend, Senyora?"

Teresa said yes.

6. JOAQUIM BERGADÀ IN BARCELONA

Seated at his desk, his back to the window, Valldaura opened the last letter and, before he had finished reading it, said to Teresa: "Quim says he will arrive next week and will spend a few days in Barcelona. I would like to invite him to stay with us."

Teresa, who had been served breakfast in the library as usual, took a sip of coffee and raised her head. "It would make more sense for him to stay at his brother's. But if you like . . ."

Quim arrived one Saturday afternoon. He had asked them not to pick him up and had wasted almost a half-hour driving around the neighborhood because the coachman could not find the villa. Valldaura thought he looked older. "You haven't changed a bit."

"Neither have you," Quim said, giving him a hug. Then he went to Teresa and kissed her hand: "Excuse me, Teresa, but you look even better than when I came for the girl's christening."

They heard running steps, and Sofia came in; she was now four. Quim sat her on his knees. "I wouldn't have recognized her."

Teresa thought: "Some idea! He hasn't seen her since she was in diapers."

A little scared, Sofia asked her: "Who is this gentleman?"

"I am your godfather," Quim said to her. And, caressing one of her eyebrows with a finger, added, "And what are you looking at, with these Japanese eyes?"

Teresa, displeased, took the girl by the hand and led her away. "Let's go, you're in the way." By the door she turned around: "I'll have your suitcases brought up." She was rather enervated by Quim's arrival.

He'd been assigned to Bogotá a little over three years ago and missed Europe and, mostly, Vienna. Before coming to Barcelona, he spent a few days there. He sat until dark chatting with Valldaura about common friends and new people. There had been many changes.

"Do you remember the wife of the English *agrégé*? I'd been in love with her, you know. A couple of years ago she was widowed, and, when everyone thought she'd return to London, she took off with Don Manuel's son, who is eight years her junior. They hushed it up as best they could." In Bogotá he was dying of sadness. "How can I marry? The hardest thing is to find a girl who doesn't wear a ribbon in her hair or play piano. It's obvious you've never been there. Besides, you know my trouble . . ."

Yes, Valldaura knew it: whenever he began courting a woman everything was smooth as silk, but he soon would be told to get lost. Quim spoke about his troubles as if he couldn't care less, but he was obviously depressed by the situation.

"If you knew how much I feel like saying to hell with it all and how I ache to settle back here, like you have done!"

"Don't do it," Valldaura blurted and after a moment, in a somewhat forced tone, added, "You don't have the temperament to be marooned in Barcelona."

Before Quim could answer, the door opened, and Gertrudis, slender and rosy, brought in the liquor tray. When she'd left, Quim said: "You see? If a girl like that one would take me, I'd marry her right away."

"You don't have bad taste," Valldaura said with a smile, "but she's already engaged."

Quim stood up and, with a glass in his hand, went to the window. "You see? They either leave me or I come too late."

Without moving, he looked outside. Facing the window, a little distance away, there was a large round bed with flowers of all colors.

"Boy, what flowers," he exclaimed in a low voice.

Valldaura came near him. "They're jonquils." He had spoken in such a cheerless tone that Quim, startled, turned his head around to look at him. Valldaura stood next to his friend, facing the garden. Yes, he looked changed, but it was hard to tell in what way. Perhaps his cheekbones were a little more marked under his tanned skin and his nostrils more flared. Perhaps. Quim could see that Valldaura was very sad. "He might still remember her, poor Barbara. I better be careful; but perhaps he'd like me to talk about it." Valldaura had gotten closer to the window and rested his forehead on the glass. Quim took his arm. "I should say something to him, but what in heaven can I tell him?" He realized that Valldaura had raised his head; his words were barely audible: "It's all right, Quim, it's all right; you don't need to say anything."

It was getting darker, and they could just see the trees in the background against the garden wall. All of a sudden they heard a strident scream.

"What an idea to have these animals!" He had turned his back to the window, and now, against the light, Quim saw his friend as a young man again.

"What animals?"

"The peacocks; my wife would not leave me alone until I bought a half-dozen."

Quim breathed easier; he had almost opened the door to bad memories, much as he would dislike doing so. But who could have imagined? The whole adventure had lasted but two weeks. The peacocks kept screaming.

"What's the matter with them? Are you sure they're not hungry?"

"No, they do this every day. It must be the hour when they realize they are in love."

Quim burst out laughing. "Imagine, if I had courted the English woman with screams like that!"

Valldaura patted him very hard on the back. "We would have received a diplomatic complaint, at the very least."

They laughed for a while. When they tired of it, they sat quietly.

"You have a splendid house and are living in the style you deserve. Your wife is sensational, but I think she doesn't like me one bit."

Valldaura reassured him, "Don't be silly; when she learned you were coming, she was very happy."

"If you say so."

At that moment Teresa opened the door. "What are you two doing in the dark?"

That evening, while she was dressing for dinner, Valldaura went into her room and told her that, as he had to go to Vilafranca next week, he'd take Quim along.

"I find him joyless, and I'll bet something is happening with him."

Teresa, who was putting on her diamond brooch, thought that Quim was a fool. "Good. That way he won't bother me here. But, believe me, don't worry. When he came to our daughter's christening, he was in love with the wife of the Japanese consul, don't you remember?"

They spent three days in Vilafranca. Quim had fallen in love with the estate there.

"What vineyards! And those porches! You never spend any time there, and I would never leave."

They had finished dessert but had remained in the dining room. Valldaura felt very satisfied.

"All my properties are good, but I prefer La Quintana because of the pines."

Quim was listening to him cross-legged, distracted. "And what do you do with the pines?"

"I sell them, what do you think?"

Sofia had come in without their noticing and, very quietly, came to her father to wish him good night.

Quim took one of her hands. "Come. Do you know that you have Japanese eyes?"

Teresa, from the door, called Sofia, who went running to her. "This gentleman said to me again that I have Japanese eyes."

Before they closed the door, Valldaura heard his wife say with an annoyed tone, "Let him rant."

The next day they went to the Liceu; Rafael and Eulàlia had invited them to their box to see *La Traviata* because they knew how much the Valldauras liked it. Teresa put on her white satin dress and the diamond necklace with seven rubies like seven red tears that Valldaura had given her to celebrate Sofia's birth. They had to wait for almost a half-hour, sitting in the vestibule, for Quim to come downstairs.

"He'll make us late." Teresa was fuming, and Valldaura, from time to time, looked at the stairs. Quim came down slowly, whistling an air from the third act; he looked like a model. When they got to the box's foyer, the opera had been going on for quite a while. From the stage they could hear, half-smothered, the tenor's voice: "Libiam ne' lieti calici."

Rafael must have heard them because he opened the curtain and came to them. "My wife was already convinced you weren't coming; don't make any noise."

Teresa, who had left her cloak on a stool, went into the box and sat next to Eulàlia. They weren't seeing each other as often as they used to because their friendship had cooled. Eulàlia whispered, "What happened to you?"

"Nothing; your relative here is taking his sweet time."

During intermission the three men went out to smoke.

"You look wonderful," Teresa said to Eulàlia, who was wearing an electric-blue silk dress with black chantilly lace.

"You too."

They remained sitting in the box, looking at the house emptying little by little.

"I would be surprised if I really did; my nerves are on edge. Quim, I can tell you, is driving me crazy."

"He drove me crazy a long time ago. If you'd seen the letters he writes to us . . . He is one of those people who spends his life making a fool of himself and then complaining about it."

Teresa straightened her necklace and was about to answer, but she thought Eulàlia was looking at her as if she wanted to tell her something but didn't quite dare.

"What's the matter?"

"Nothing; I shouldn't mention this to you. We've learned that he was responsible for that Vienna story."

Teresa looked at her. "What do you mean? What story?"

"It seems he insisted and insisted until he introduced them. She was a poor nobody who earned her living playing violin. It seems it was awful; he couldn't get rid of her."

Teresa thought, "How you must envy me, my dear girl." She wanted to change the topic, but Eulàlia, all excited, continued: "The bad thing is she killed herself. And, if there was a scandal, it was because Quim spread the news everywhere. You can't trust him."

Teresa felt upset, but she smiled. "All this is an old story, and it's better not to speak about it." She hadn't known that the girl had killed herself. She deserves more pity than he does, she thought, or than I do. Automatically, she took her purse from the balustrade, opened it, and closed it again without taking anything from it.

"Isn't it time to start yet?"

"Wait – it can't be long now."

Eulàlia looked toward the box's foyer. "Before the men are back, I'll tell you something else, and this one might amuse you. It seems that Marina Riera, the attorney's sister, has seen your husband a few times at the concert hall, all alone, and she found it surprising; she asked me where he left you. I told her you didn't care for music; what could I say?"

Teresa was very surprised. She was beginning to feel uncomfortable, but she managed to say in a calm voice: "It isn't that I don't like music, as you well know; sometimes when he asks me to go with him, I don't feel like going out. I don't imagine I should spend my life sewn onto his jacket."

People were returning to their places. Teresa saw Eulàlia wave to a gentleman who'd just come into the box in front of theirs: he was tall, tanned, with a tuft of hair falling on his forehead; a very pretty girl accompanied him. "Who is he?" she asked.

"Don't you know him?"

Before the three men entered the box, Eulàlia had time to tell her it was attorney Riera. "All of Barcelona knows him; the woman is his sister Marina, the one who told me about the concerts."

The day before Quim left, he told Valldaura during dinner: "Do you know what I've been thinking? You could sell me your Vilafranca estate; you never go there, and I would spend my life there. I am beginning to be tired of it all."

Teresa said nothing but looked at him askance. After dinner Valldaura and Quim went to his study and spent a long time there. When Valldaura came into the bedroom, he was agitated. "Quim is crazy. Do you know how much he's offered me for the estate? It's fabulous. I don't know what to do. I told him, of course, that I'd think about it. I want to discuss it with Riera, get his advice."

Teresa could not sleep. She hadn't dared remind Valldaura that they'd spent their honeymoon at the estate, that it was too good a property to end up in the hands of that ass, who thought that their daughter had Japanese eyes and who in a couple of days would be fed up with the place and would be chased away by the tenant farmers throwing rocks at him. Suddenly she felt she was still holding that apple blossom in her palm.

At dawn Valldaura got up to go to the bathroom. When he came back, Teresa was sitting up in bed. "Do you know what I think? That if Quim wants to live away from the city, in peace and without ladies to seduce, the best he could do is lock himself up in a convent. And leave us alone!"

Valldaura said, "Can't you sleep?"

7. THE BOY JESÚS MASDÉU

At midmorning on Saint Teresa's feast day there was a knock on the gate of the Valldaura villa. It was curious because at that hour only the delivery boys called, and they all knew that the side gate was never locked. Gertrudis went to open the gate. They must be bringing a present for the Senyora, she thought as she straightened her apron. There was a boy some ten years old, tidy and with his hair combed neatly, holding a bouquet of flowers in his hand.

"What do you want?"

The boy said he was Senyora Valldaura's godson and had come to wish her a happy saint's day. As they walked side by side under the chestnut trees, Gertrudis realized she'd never known the Senyora had a godson. She was about to ask him his name, but she noticed he had raised his head and was looking at her. "That thing you pull to ring the bell comes out of the mouth of a lion, doesn't it?"

Gertrudis said yes. "And sometimes it'll bite you."

He laughed. Before entering the house, he wiped his shoes very calmly on the mat. "Wait a minute; I'll go tell them you're here." Gertrudis left him in the vestibule and went to tell the Senyora. The boy had remained very still, but after a moment he went to look at the water that fell out of the brim of the stone bowl, and, when he got to the side of the pool, he crouched. The water in the pool was full of red fish, very big, with black spots, swimming under a bunch of leaves that seemed made of wax. He'd only seen flowers like those in the public park, once when his father had taken him. Some were white, some pink. He looked around and, timidly, ran a finger over the one nearest him. He was checking so intently whether the flower had left some dust on his finger that he didn't realize there was someone next to him until he felt he was being pushed. Frightened, he turned his head: it was a very well-dressed girl, with long wavy hair, who looked like a doll and didn't take her eyes off him.

"These flowers are not to be touched," she yelled in a fury. "If you touch them again I'll go tell."

She stood by him and asked him what his name was.

"My name is Jesús."

She looked at him stiffly, "My name is Sofia, and I am the girl of this house." Saying nothing else, she ran upstairs, and before reaching the second floor she leaned on the banister and stuck out her tongue at him. Jesús Masdéu felt a bit dejected but after a minute, looking up the stairs where the girl had gone, went back to the pool and touched the flower again.

Gertrudis showed him into the parlor. "Sit down, and don't break anything."

Jesús Masdéu barely heard her and remained standing next to the door. He didn't have enough eyes to look: the ceiling, very high, with pieces of wood in shapes like drawings; the gray velvet curtains on each side of the windows; the large painting over the sofa, of a hanging garlic wreath and a pumpkin on the ground next to two dead rabbits and a bunch of eggplants. By the door there was a tall vase with some feathers sticking out of it that had something like an eye at their tips. Jesús blew on them a few times from a distance and walked almost on tiptoe to the center of the room, where there was a table with claw legs and a red and golden chair on one side. He touched the chair's back and withdrew his hand right away: the fabric had little hairs and had given him a shiver. Behind the table, against the wall, he saw a shiny black armoire: on each of its doors there was a strange soldier, made with pieces of shell and with a gold saber in his hand.

Before Teresa opened the door wide, she looked in the room. A few days ago she had visited her aunt Adela, who almost never left home these days, to tell her she would like to get to know the boy. They decided they would write, the two of them, a letter to Miquel Masdéu asking him to send the boy to the villa on Saint Teresa's feast.

Aunt Adela was unenthusiastic. "Don't you think it would be better to leave things as they are?"

Teresa was not convinced and now, before her, stood that thin boy, wearing a school smock and carrying a bouquet of flowers in his hand. Jesús felt that someone was looking at him and stood dead quiet facing the armoire.

"Do you like these soldiers?"

He turned around slowly and saw a very beautiful lady, dressed in white. "Yes, Senyora."

"Why don't you sit down?" The lady sat in the chair and was pointing at a stool in front of him. Teresa didn't know what to say; she searched his face for something she couldn't quite find. Softening at last, she asked, "How old are you?"

"I will soon be eleven and a half."

Eleven years! A spurt of life. Of those downtown nights, embracing Miquel Masdéu, of all those bits of love, of so much innocence, all that was left was this frightened little creature. Teresa looked at her son: olive skin, thin lips, his hair as dark as a basket of blackberries, and his nose . . .

"You have a broken nose, don't you?"

Jesús brought his hand to it and laughed. "I fell from a tree and broke the bone."

"It must have hurt a lot." Without giving him time to answer, she asked, "Did you come alone?"

"No, Senyora, my father came with me, and he's waiting for me on the street."

Teresa turned her head and clasped her hands. "Wouldn't you like to eat some sweets?"

"No, Senyora, thank you; I just had my breakfast."

"Aren't you thirsty?"

"No, Senyora, thank you."

They sat in silence for a while. Jesús was thinking about the soldiers on the armoire but didn't dare look at them. All of a sudden Teresa pointed at the wall. "Do you want to pull that cord?" Jesús went to it and pulled on it shyly, as if he were afraid of breaking it.

"Pull harder, a few times; otherwise, nobody will hear you."

Felícia came in and looked at the boy: Gertrudis had already told her he was the Senyora's godson.

"Prepare a package with some sweets and lots of chocolates." As she spoke, Teresa realized that the boy was still holding the bouquet of flowers: a half-dozen yellow carnations and a few stems with small blooms that looked like a cloud. It must be for her, and he must be afraid of offering it.

"Whom did you bring these flowers for?"

Jesús Masdéu offered the bouquet, and Teresa took it without knowing what to do with it. "They are for you; to wish you a happy saint's day."

Teresa rose, and, with her back to him, before leaving the flowers on the table, she looked at her hands, so different now from when she was poor, red in winter, with split nails, like her mother's. Her mother would always examine Teresa's hands when she put on her over-sleeves to go to the market and tied the navy apron over her rumpled skirt. "They're very pretty, Jesús." She'd been wishing to ask him something for quite a while. "Does your mother love you?"

Jesús had been taught never to lie. "I don't know; she says I have to study hard so that later I may become a gentleman. And father also says I have to be a gentleman."

When, not even a half-hour ago, Gertrudis had told her that there was a boy to see her, Teresa had had to sit down because everything turned blurry. But that boy who, at the moment, seemed shy and spoke as if reciting by rote . . . No, there was nothing in that child. What had she expected? He sat in front of her, strange, far removed from her life as a rich woman, rather like a reproach. Felícia came back with a package wrapped in fine paper and tied with a gold thread.

"Put these flowers in a vase and bring them back to me."

Jesús, with the package on his knees, watched the chambermaid take away the flowers. Teresa told him, "Wait for me a moment now." She took quite a while. When she came back, she saw that Jesús was standing by the armoire touching the face of one of the soldiers. He must like to touch things, like me, she thought. Coming near him, she gave him an envelope. "Here, and don't lose it: I am happy you came to see me. But it's late, and you must go now." She felt a wave of emotion and, caressing his nose, added: "And don't climb any more trees."

Gertrudis was waiting in the vestibule. Before leaving, Jesús glanced at the stairs; the girl was looking at him from above, and he turned his head quickly so as to give her no time to stick her tongue out at him. He stopped suddenly by the stone fountain; before him, to both sides of the door, it looked as if a fire was raging. Four large oval windows, an escutcheon in the middle of each one of them, let in surges of light through their colored glass. Gertrudis turned around. "Come on. On your way now!" As they walked under the chestnut trees, Jesús felt a bittersweet taste in his mouth. He would feel it all his life, every time he'd go to that house. When he saw his father, who was waiting for him at a fair distance from the fence, he felt happy. He ran to him and gave him the envelope. Before sticking it in his pocket, his father opened it and saw it contained a few small gold coins.

From that day on, Jesús Masdéu paid his godmother visits from time to time. When he turned fourteen, he informed her that he had begun work as a painter's apprentice.

"And what do you paint?" Teresa had asked.

"Nothing. For the moment I just help Senyor Avel·lí, but I'll soon be painting walls like him." And he added that, twice a week, after work, he took drawing lessons. "You know? I would like to be a great painter of figures."

8. BEES AND WISTERIA

They were seated near the well, in the shade of the wisteria. Teresa said to Eulàlia, "Wouldn't you be more comfortable with your hat off?"

"No. It would be too much trouble to put it back on later. Do you like it?" On its brim there was a blue bird with jet eyes, partially covered in gauze.

"These women with delicate skin peak early," Teresa thought. Eulàlia's cheeks showed some very fine wrinkles: one could not really see them under artificial light, but the sun was unforgiving. Felícia came with the cart and started to place the tea service on the table.

"You've had her for quite a while, haven't you?" Eulàlia said, when the servant had left them. "I don't know how you manage. I can't keep a maid for more than three years."

Teresa smiled a little crookedly. "She's the only one left of the old team: Gertrudis married; Mundeta, you may not remember her, had to go to take care of her parents." She offered her the dish with the lemon slices.

"No," Eulàlia said, declining. "I just have tea with milk because milk hides its taste. You know I'm not crazy about tea."

Sofia came out of the house, white as a dove, holding a sheathed racquet in her hand, and went to say hello to Eulàlia. "How are you, godmother?" she said, offering her cheek to be kissed.

"You're prettier every day, child; you'll have a fiancé soon."

Sofia told her she didn't like young men. "I like gentlemen of a certain age, with white hair on their temples." And she left laughing.

Eulàlia blurted out, "And in a few years . . ." She didn't quite know what she wanted to say and stopped, but Teresa realized that Eulàlia had been about to say something untoward.

"Speak no evil of gentlemen with white hair; my husband's is begin-

41

ning to turn, and he looks better than when I first met him. It so happens that your goddaughter is in love with her father, that's the problem." She had picked up the teapot and was filling the cups. "She gets angry if we speak about it; young Lluís Roca has been taking her to play tennis for some time now. She enjoys the attention of boys, but you'll see how she chooses a mature man. And she'll be right."

Eulàlia left her cup on the table abruptly and with her hand fanned off some bees that were circling the pastry tray. Teresa could not help but laugh. "Don't be frightened: we've trained them . . . And if necessary my husband will come to your defense."

Valldaura, dressed to go out, was approaching them.

"We were talking about you," Eulàlia said to him. Valldaura kissed her hand and asked about Rafael.

"We barely see each other. He spends all his time in the factory and has many headaches about his workers."

"And what do you hear from Quim? I've been told he might go to Madrid, to the Ministry."

"We've also heard that, but last week we received a letter from him, and he said nothing about a move. He's about to publish a book and is thinking of nothing else."

"A book?"

"Yes, a book about his grandfather, the jurist; we are all excited about it."

They chatted for a little while longer, and finally Valldaura said he was on his way to the Ateneu.

"Are you also writing a book?" Eulàlia asked him, laughing.

"No. I just go there for fencing lessons."

They remained quiet for a bit, watching Valldaura leave.

"Should I get you a fresh cup? A flower fell in it."

Eulàlia picked up the flower with the tip of her spoon and left it on the saucer. "Not necessary, thank you." She took a couple of sips and covered her cup with her napkin. "It's nice to be in the sun, but both and Rafael and I are apartment people."

"That's why your face is so white. This little bit of sun will do wonders for you; tomorrow you'll look better." They could hear birds singing inside the laurel, and more flowers fell.

Eulàlia shook them off herself. "Did you know that Marina Riera has married an heir of the Quatrecases ironworks family? He could bury her in gold three or four times." She took a pastry and nibbled on it. "She got lucky; she's no spring chicken. At the wedding I sat next to her brother the attorney; you know him, don't you?"

"Isn't it too windy for you?" Teresa said, pouring herself more tea.

"No. You know. That's one who could make me do something crazy. He is one of those men who, whenever they look at you, seem to undress you. This business of his preparing wills all the time must kindle him. Of course, his wife's nothing to write home about." She spoke without pauses, raising her head from time to time to look at the bees flying among the hanging wisteria blossoms. "Can you figure it out? A man who could have had any woman, and he marries the ugliest thing."

"There are many men like that," Teresa mumbled, feeling suddenly on her guard.

Eulàlia went on. "But the poor lady has no grace whatsoever, and they say she is a little slow. He must take advantage of it. Very polite, to be sure, very serious – but I am sure he's got a lover, someone really good." She went quiet for a second and then added, "Of course, she's got nothing to complain about; on her ears she wears a pair of diamonds as big as hazelnuts."

Teresa had grabbed the bell and rang it.

"You scared me."

"If I didn't ring it loud, they'd pretend not to hear." Felícia came at once, and Teresa asked for hot water. "No, don't wipe the table; these flowers look nice on it." And, turning to face Eulàlia, she asked her if she wanted more pastries. "No more? You may take them away, Felícia; with the smell of the sweets the bees are driving us crazy."

Before Felícia had time to take away the platter, Eulàlia picked up a candied cherry. "The last one – I think I've eaten too many, but they're so good." And in the same tone of voice she added: "If I were a man, I wouldn't have liked to marry a woman named Constància."

"Constància?"

"Yes. On top of it all, her name is Constància. But enough about that – you'll think I'm a gossip. You, on the other hand, I don't know how you manage; you never speak ill of anyone."

Teresa picked up a blossom. "I," she said, "only like pretty things." She popped the blossom in her mouth and ate it.

"You're crazy. Are you sure you're not ill? And, now that I think of it, did you know Begú died? Eight days in bed and off to the graveyard."

"The jeweler?" Teresa had the feeling that time had just taken a leap back: the lamp with the green shade, the pearl on his tie, that obsequiousness of his, and all those anguished hours.

"But the business will continue; his son has already installed himself in the office and has begun selling jewelry."

"Why is she telling this to me?" Teresa wondered. "It couldn't be that . . ." Two or three bees approached them, and Eulàlia rose in fright.

"I'm leaving. It's late, and I am afraid I'll get stung by a bee." She brushed off the pastry crumbs that had fallen on her skirt.

Teresa thought: "You're scared? You've seen nothing yet." And she added out loud, "Before you leave I'll pick a few roses for you." She led her friend toward the washhouse; its walls were covered with blooming rosebushes. "Wait here. There must be something to snip them with inside." Teresa went into the washhouse and came back out with the pruning shears. "These rosebushes are cuttings that Fontanills gave us when we bought the villa; they come from Premià." She was picking roses very calmly, choosing those that weren't fully open. Eulàlia let out a scream.

"Hurry up, Teresa, can't you see this is all full of bees?"

Teresa turned around. "Cover your face with your hands; these are particularly vicious."

Eulàlia walked away quickly toward the house. Once she had gathered a good bunch of roses, Teresa approached her slowly. Through the kitchen door she saw Armanda next to the stove. "Will you tell Felícia to tie up these flowers?"

Eulàlia, who had been itching to leave for quite some time, asked Teresa to let her go to the bathroom to freshen up. "I've been in the sun for so long – I don't know what I must look like."

9. SPRING-CLEANING

Armanda looked around the kitchen and, since everything was in order, thought she better go upstairs for a rest. On the way she would check on the other girls. Even though the balconies were open, you could smell a strong odor of lavender: it came from two wardrobes with their doors ajar. In those armoires, the biggest in the house, were kept the old dresses, in the two smaller ones flanking the door, the house linens. Piles of winter garments lay on the chairs, and their dust cases were scattered on the floor; Cristina was picking them up and throwing them into a hamper to bring to the laundry.

"Come here, Armanda, and help us shoo away the moths," Simona said from inside one of the armoires, where she was dusting the wood, "and don't lock me in. I wouldn't want to die of suffocation."

On the ironing board, to one side, there was a huge cardboard box. Lluïsa was softly singing a song and folding a petticoat; she set it on the wicker tray and picked up a nightgown with lace on its collar and cuffs. Then she rubbed the iron with the wax bag and looked to one side.

"Do you like antiques?"

Armanda came to the ironing board and lifted the lid of the box. In the box, wrapped in tissue paper, was a purple piece of silk.

"Don't be afraid to look. It's a weird sort of robe. It's beyond me why they should hang onto something so old. I'd think it a bother."

Armanda, who had not opened her mouth, exclaimed, "What a pretty color!" She pulled the papers apart and carefully picked up the silk and spread it out. "It's a domino." In her house there had been a calendar showing a carnival ball with many ladies dressed in robes such as that one.

"Senyor Valldaura," Lluïsa said, "when he laid eyes on the Senyora dressed in this . . ." She had left the iron on one side and tapped her heart with a flat hand: "Pat, pat, pat."

Simona came out of the armoire and without a word picked up the domino and put it on. She was tall, willowy. Homely. Teresa always said that, of all the maids they had, Simona had the prettiest body and the ugliest face. As she strode about with the domino gathered around her body, she said: "Senyoreta Sofia will inherit this, with all the other rags. If Senyor Eladi sees her in this shroud, he'll say, 'Good-bye, my pretty.'"

Armanda helped her take off the domino, and, after folding it and staring at it, she put it back in its box over a dress with white lace. She'd been getting annoyed. "Can't you leave Senyor Eladi alone? You are all in love with him, all of you!"

"Don't get mad, it's not worth it. Any day I'll go to his shop and tell him: I am the chambermaid of the Senyora Valldaura, do you want to taste me?"

"As if he didn't know you," Armanda said, "and don't make fun of the shop. Besides having that shop, they own a corduroy and velvet factory; they are filthy rich."

Simona hung the dress she had just brushed and picked up another one. "And Senyoreta Sofia, so full of herself that she barely looks at us, will she end up tending the store behind a counter?"

Lluïsa said, "I like the young man who goes with her to tennis."

Simona, holding the dress in her fingers, came closer. "She's been going there by herself for more than a year now."

"By herself? Maybe he doesn't come to pick her up, but I'd bet an eye that they see each other as much as they want."

Simona turned to face Armanda. "And you, which one would you choose?"

Armanda left them. "Go on." She went to her room; she wanted to lie down for a bit and see if she could take a nap. From the balcony, far to her left, she saw the trees and thought they were just as they'd been the day she'd come to the house: they had not grown a bit. The laurel leaves were shaking beneath the balcony. Aunt Anselma had told her how lightning had split the bush a few days before her First Communion. A few years later Aunt Anselma asked Armanda's mother if she could have her daughter for help in the villa's kitchen. Anselma brought this up with Senyora Teresa, who agreed to it. "She can peel onions and tomatoes, I'll teach her to prepare the sauces, and she will polish the silver: the other servant girls have enough to do." Armanda closed the balcony door and lay in bed, straightening her skirt so it would not crease. And, come to think of it, she would soon have to start cleaning the bigger pieces: coffee and tea services, champagne glasses with their gilded insides, soup tureens. Her fingers knew those shapes by rote. They kept the silverware in a room next to the kitchen in a high cupboard with drawers lined in red wool.

Her aunt had told her many times, "You can't call a piece of silver clean until after you rub it hard with a cloth and it doesn't leave a shadow."

One day, as Armanda was cleaning the wrought-silver fruit bowls in the shape of two fully opened magnolia blossoms, the Senyora sat in front of her to chat. During her first weeks in the house Armanda, as soon as she heard the outside gate's bell, would run to open it, to the annoyance of Gertrudis, who claimed that it was her job. But she couldn't help it. Until one day Senyora Teresa warned her, "Armanda, when you hear the bell don't go to open it."

One day Armanda asked her aunt: "How come Senyora Teresa addresses all the maids so formally and addresses me so informally? Is it because I am so young?"

"Why else should it be?"

From the moment she had been admonished she'd never gone back to open the gate. But whenever she heard the bell, she had to make a great effort to stay put: she was itching to take off running like a hare under the chestnut trees. The kitchen, in winter, was like heaven: it was the warmest spot in the whole house. But in summertime . . .

"You can't have everything," her aunt would say, fiddling with the pots and pans, droplets of perspiration running down her neck. Armanda was beginning to feel sleepy. Lying on the bed, she thought of things. She recalled the first time Senyor Eladi came for dinner; he was elegant, reeking of quinine aftershave, dressed in dark gray and with a red carnation on his lapel.

"Today," her aunt had told her, "you will cook the pigeons; you can do a good job."

They always served pigeon with stuffed cabbage whenever they had company. That night the lady came to congratulate her. She was in a good mood.

"What do you say, Anselma? That young man with a carnation on his lapel and I with a rose on my bosom. We were a match!"

Whenever Teresa was to wear a rose on her bosom, she would pick it herself. She liked only those flesh-colored roses from the bushes that covered the washhouse walls. They were big as a fist, and their scent was dizzying. After that Senyor Eladi had come often. One day when she was washing the panes of the kitchen window, during a moment when Senyoreta Sofia had left him alone, he had come to her and said, "Is that beauty mark real?"

She had turned very red, and that night, before going to bed, she had examined her freckle in the mirror: right under her eye, small, very dark.

"Armanda, you're still awake, right?" Someone had knocked on her door and she had barely noticed. It was Simona, in a good mood. "Come see what we've found."

Armanda jumped off her bed and followed Simona mechanically. After having her eyes closed for so long, the light now hurt them.

"I see I won't get my sleep," she said, as Simona opened the door to the ironing room. Lluïsa, standing next to the board, was wearing a black mask with sequins.

"You have to hold it with one hand because the elastic is broken," Simona said, choking with laughter. They had never seen that mask. Some time before, during one of those ironing Saturdays, they had discovered the purple robe and the lace dress, but they had not seen the black mask, which lay beneath the paper, or the small fan, with mother-of-pearl ribs and a painted apple.

"One of these days," Simona said fanning herself, "I'll serve dinner wearing this old coat and this black thing on my face."

"For this you've called me?" Armanda asked. She was furious because they had interrupted her nap, but she heard steps from the corridor and said nothing else. Cristina, seated in a corner paralyzed with laughter, jumped up, threw the covers to the floor and started picking them up to pretend she was working. Simona left the fan on the ironing table. The doorknob was turning: it was the Senyora.

"Lord, what a smell of lavender!" She cast a glance around her and, addressing Lluïsa, said: "Don't forget to iron my cream-colored dress and the brown silk overcoat; I'll need them tomorrow evening." She seemed to be in a trance, staring at the fan. "Eulàlia's fan," she mused. "I had forgotten it existed." She opened and closed it a few times. Its tassel was faded. She turned slowly to face Simona. "Put things back as you found them in their cases."

Simona reassured her, "Senyora, it's not the first time we've tended to them."

Teresa took a moment to examine the ironed clothes in their basket and left.

"She might have rung, instead of coming over," an indignant Lluïsa said.

Simona replied: "She wanted to see what we were doing; she's becoming nosy. What I don't get is why she's taken the fan."

Armanda ran her hand over the purple satin. "If she'd catch you poking fun . . ." She went to the door and, before leaving, said, "And do not wake me up again." But she was not feeling sleepy anymore.

On the fourth floor there were two or three rooms with no furniture. Hers was quite large, like her aunt's. The girls had theirs on the other side, by the ironing room, one next to the other, small, with barely any room for a cot. Hers, on the other hand, was roomy, with a bed and a mirrored wardrobe made of lemon tree wood, the bedspread and curtain of a blue-gray cotton. She approached the beveled mirror and examined herself: she was short, on the heavy side. Her mother used to say: "You can't call Armanda pretty, but her skin is like silk. You might not think so, but this counts for a lot." She opened the wardrobe and picked up a half-empty tin box; she'd need to replenish it with cookies. But she still had several bars of chocolate. On evenings when she finally went upstairs, fatigued, she could not sleep, and in the wee hours she felt hungry. She would have been unable to explain how happy she felt leaning out from the balcony of that house, eating cookies and one piece of chocolate after another as the sky lightened and the birds began to chirp from inside the laurel. She still had time for a snooze. But she'd have to draw the curtains and get undressed. She took off her clothes and began to hang them up: her deep-blue apron, her percale dress with gray and white stripes, her petticoat with three layers of lace, one on top of the other, at the hem. Before taking off her shoes, she opened the balcony window wide so that the fresh air would relax her, and she drew the curtain slowly. She fell asleep seeing it swing.

10. ELADI FARRIOLS

His problem was boredom. He tried to cross his legs. Hard to do. He could not tell at what point he had begun to put on weight. He used to be so slim, trimmer than his father. Poor dad. Perhaps because his own parents had been unable to send him to college, he had always wanted to see Eladi become a great lawyer. To make his father happy Eladi had finished his degree, but he did not go on: other people's problems depressed him. His father was understanding, and one evening when they were both about to go out, on their separate ways, at the foot of the stairs, he took the young man by the arm and told him, a slight hint of melancholy in his voice: "Don't worry, Eladi. Everything will be all right." The following morning he paid a visit to his brother Terenci, who owned one of Barcelona's most renowned clothing stores, a business he had created by the sweat of his brow. They came to an agreement: he would invest money in that business on the condition that Terenci and Eladi become partners. Terenci was happy about the arrangement.

"I need someone to help me. The factory is running smoothly, but the store needs a good person."

Eladi's father had no trade. His fortune came from an uncle. He had squandered a good portion of it financing small investors. The death of his wife, a good Catholic, had wrecked him. The man who had poked fun at Eladi's mother's fixation with the church and the priests now took to attending the eight a.m. mass at La Mercè every day and to praying the rosary every evening. With great devotion he now asked the Protector of the destitute to help him live and bring up his son. He was thin, hunched, and looked much older than his brother. He had suffered from kidney stones and shuddered whenever he recalled how painful passing them had been. Getting into the carriage, the three of them, after signing the deed for the new company in the office of Amadeu Riera, Eladi burst out laughing. His father asked him, "What's so funny?"

"This attorney, who looks like a poet and keeps a rose on his desk."

Work, for Eladi, was light: he would show up at the store at eleven in the morning, perfumed, his hair parted, his mustache shining, a perfect dandy. Before the season began, he and his uncle would examine the books of samples and put in their orders. Once a year they traveled to Paris, both to get an update on fashion and to maintain a certain prestige. On afternoons when he was not busy at the factory his uncle relaxed at home or went out for a stroll; he was a great reader of French novels. Eladi, who had a more obsequious demeanor and a welcoming smile, tended to the customers. He would greet them as soon as they came in and then summon their preferred salesman; if the salesman was busy, he chatted with the customers for as long as needed. On their way out, whether they had purchased something or not, he escorted them to the door most amiably. He could have taken advantage of his situation: there were many dissatisfied women in the world. At times he told himself with a smile that he could use his store to build a harem.

But work was work and bills had been invented to be collected. Besides, his weakness wasn't ladies; it was cabaret artists. Ladies intimidated him, but, for a girl with a sequined dress or naked under a spread of feathers and veils, he would have sold his soul to the devil. When he was twenty he had had political aspirations but had always resisted joining a party: he just could not decide which one. Once, when his father had asked him to read a biography of Talleyrand, he was filled with enthusiasm and for quite a while, strolling through the university grounds, dreamed of becoming a great diplomat. But his fervor abated, and, one good day, just like that, he joined Esquerra Catalana. The right-wing Lliga suited his temperament better, but, after years of hearing his father and uncle talk about it, he resented the fact that the Lliga's Francesc Cambó had gone to Madrid to welcome the king. Twice a week he got together with a group of friends in the Colombòfila, where they discussed everything. Everything except politics.

He was definitely getting fatter. He had become aware of this a few days ago, at the Colombòfila precisely, one evening when he sat in his armchair, by himself, and crossed his legs. It was the first time this had required an effort. Now, knotting his tie, he felt his trousers strangling his belly. He was dressing to go to the store. To the store . . . A couple of years ago, one October afternoon, when it was getting dark, a sensational woman came in; she was about forty-five years old and wore a bouquet of diamonds on her chest. He tended to her himself. Her face was fresh, with eyes that looked deep and a sweet smile. When it came to the measuring and cutting of the material, Eladi called up the most handsome of his salesmen. That lady had a great presence, something unfathomable, moving. Even though she did not look at all like her, he thought of his mother, who, when he was little, kissed him a lot and smelled of rosewater. The next day he mentioned the lady to his uncle.

"It's Senyora Valldaura, one of our best customers. I am sure you've heard about her."

She visited the store often, always by herself, in part to pass the time and in part to see nice things. One Sunday Eladi, who had found her address in the business ledger, went to see where she lived, out of sheer curiosity. As soon as he found himself in front of the villa, everything came back to his memory. When he was little and his mother was still alive, his father would take him for walks in the residential parts of the city and let him ring the bells of houses with a front garden so that, by the time anyone would arrive to open the door, they could be quite far away, with no need to run. He had rung that bell dozens of times, pulling on the chain that came out of a lion's mouth and watching the lonely house at the end of the walkway with the chestnut trees. "Next time Senyora Valldaura comes to the shop," he thought, "I will be unable to keep a straight face." But when she next came he was taken aback because she did not come alone.

"I believe, Eladi, that you have not yet met my daughter; her name is Sofia."

Eladi would have never imagined that Senyora Valldaura could have a daughter who was so skinny, unfriendly, and with such airs of superiority. The next day he mentioned it to his uncle.

"It's true; what can one do about it? Sometimes from a spectacular mother you get a colorless daughter. But beware of calm waters."

Eladi though often of Sofia; there was something in her that attracted him, even though he had found her disagreeable. He liked graceful, cheery, innocent girls, with big, dark eyes. Sofia had small eyes, as if she could not quite open them wide; she parted her hair in the middle and bunched it in the back. He had seen young ladies with hair like hers in an illustrated edition of Balzac's novels that his uncle kept as a prized treasure. From that day on Senyora Valldaura would always go to the store with her daughter, who was hard to please. Nothing was good enough for her; she drove the salesmen up the wall – no sooner did they see her come in than they started quaking. Why did she have to be so difficult if she dressed so plainly? Her tastes ran to the informal, and she always chose neutral colors: grays or tans. Before she could settle on the exact hue, the salesman's feet would have grown roots. She avoided loud jewelry, unlike her mother: a simple gold bangle and a green stone on the little finger of her left hand. One day, while Senyora Valldaura was looking at crepe for lingerie, Eladi said to Sofia, "What a beautiful ring you are wearing!"

She took it off by turning it around; it fit very tightly and left a red mark. When he gave it back to her, Eladi caressed her fingers furtively.

"It's an emerald with no specks, a deep one." After a pause he added, with meaning, "Beautiful." Later, under a spread of silk, they held hands. Sofia seemed unstirred. Eladi was astonished: "We've quite the girl here!"

To see if he could lose some weight he joined a tennis club recommended by a friend.

"The most distinguished people in Barcelona go there."

The first person he met there was Sofia Valldaura. She was dressed in a satin skirt, opened onto one side and showing a splendid piece of leg, and a white blouse with a raised collar and a tie. She was a splash of milk, seated in the shade of some acacias, her racquet on her lap. It had been about three months since he had last seen her in his store, and they greeted each other coolly. "She might imagine that I've joined the club just to be able to see her." She was almost always in the company of Lluís Roca, a guy who looked English and drove a Hispano automobile. Sofia and Eladi gradually became better acquainted. Eladi was disconcerted by that young woman. One day after they'd gone together to watch a match, Senyora Valldaura asked him to dinner.

"We'd love to have you. Wouldn't we, Sofia? Would a Sunday suit you?"

He went there two weeks later. "Who could have told me," he thought as he pulled the chain from the lion's mouth, "maybe it is now when I should run and hide." The maid ushered him to a room with the walls covered with books. Teresa Valldaura came immediately to greet him.

"Please come to the dining room; it's sunny there, and we shouldn't stand on ceremony."

As soon as Senyor Valldaura saw him he stopped reading the paper, left his seat by the big window, and greeted him very politely. He was a tall man, good posture, with a grand blond beard and an air of goodness about him. He dressed impeccably. "When I get to know him better, I'll have to ask him who his tailor is; he'll like that." It had been a long time since Eladi had met a person that so impressed him; he barely knew what to say. "He's quite a gentleman," he thought in awe. He had heard some time ago about an adventure Valldaura had in Vienna, when he served in the embassy, but couldn't quite recall it. Hadn't a young woman killed herself? When he became aware of Sofia's presence, she was standing before him; distracted with his thoughts about her father, he had not seen her come in and now felt bad about it. She wore a knit silk dress that clung to her body and a short pearl necklace. The dinner would have been much more pleasant if Sofia had shown any cordiality. She appeared distracted and barely said a word. Teresa spoke most of the time with Eladi. Valldaura looked at him from time to time with some curiosity. He was a man who felt great respect for people, but that young man, polite, pleasant, university educated, a man who should have been able to split the sun in half with his teeth but who was letting his youth die away inside the walls of a store, did not quite satisfy him. "Fundamentally," he told himself, "he must be a mediocrity."

Valldaura took him to the library for coffee.

"The women need a rest," he said with a little laugh. "They've earned it." The men sat down, and then Simona served the coffee. Eladi did not have enough eyes to look at her.

"This villa," Valldaura began, after offering Eladi a cigar and as he calmly removed the band of his own, "used to belong to the Marquis of Castelljussà family; it was their summer residence. I bought it for a song when I decided to retire from my post. The last marquis was a disaster. He wanted to change his coat of arms because he didn't like the old one, which I've never seen, and he did not rest until he fashioned a new one: three cypresses on a field of azure, just as in the coat of the Guerets. But with a difference: on the Guerets's, in front of the cypresses, there is a deer, and in this new one there's an ax. My financial advisor used to say, 'It's little wonder they have so few trees left.'" Valldaura realized that Eladi was barely paying attention and changed the topic. He asked Eladi if he was satisfied with his work in the store.

"Yes and no. But business is good. My uncle . . ."

Valldaura did not want to pass the time chatting about Uncle Terenci and broke in. "Don't you think this coffee is too bitter?"

"Bitter? It seems fine to me," Eladi replied. "Life in Vienna must have spoiled you." He took a sip and put the cup back on the table very carefully.

Valldaura looked at him in silence. He could not find a topic of conversation; he was ready for Teresa or Sofia to come back in and say something. "By the way," he said, all of a sudden, "I can remember a store just like yours near my hotel in Vienna. The owner had the reputation of being the most beautiful woman in Vienna."

"Not an easy accomplishment," Eladi laughed, and he thought, "I smell regret."

Valldaura asked: "Have you ever been there?"

"Where?"

"Vienna."

"No. Once or twice I've almost gone, on factory business. My uncle seems to think that we could find customers there; I am not convinced."

"If you have a chance to go, don't miss it. A friend of mine, a diplomat, from Lleida, who had been posted there, used to say it was a city with a unique charm. This is a commonplace, I know, but it is exactly true. For me cities . . . What I like are details, small things. Do you know why I like Vienna? Because there violets are a deep lilac in color, I think. And because music sounds different there. Although this last thing is not exactly a detail."

When Eladi left, they all walked him to the front steps and Sofia all the way to the gate. Before shaking hands with him, Sofia told him she was going away to London to improve her English at a boarding school.

As soon as she returned from London, they invited Eladi over. He found her changed: more mature, less inhuman, her little eyes shinier and penetrating to an unbearable point. He was asked to dinner several Sundays. After a year and a half, having thought long about it, he proposed. Soon thereafter he and his father, dressed to the nines, went to ask for Sofia's hand. Uncle Terenci was elated and celebrated the engagement by drinking a bottle of sherry. That winter Salvador Valldaura died of an attack of apoplexy. Eladi felt it deeply. Sofia was saddened to the point of falling ill. She wanted to observe full mourning: they would wait two years before the wedding. Early during that period Eladi Farriols fell in love with a cabaret singer from the Paral·lel.

11. FATHER AND DAUGHTER

When she was little, her father wanted her to come down and greet him each morning once she was dressed, everything in place, her curls shiny. One morning when she was ill he came to see her unannounced. He sat her on his lap, and after a few moments, pressing his cheek against her hair, he told her, "My child, some people can fill their whole life with just one memory."

She asked, "What does one memory mean?"

"You will know soon enough; perhaps this moment will be one for you, many years later."

In church, the day of the funeral, Sofia felt as if something were collapsing inside her, and she saw herself as small, seated on her father's lap that morning. "What does one memory mean?" She was seized by a torrent of tears and had to be taken to the church office. Armanda, who had also gone to the church, was dumbfounded. "And she seemed so hard and unfriendly." By nighttime Sofia had calmed down but could think of nothing else than moments with her father. On days when Mother went out, he used to take her to look at the pheasants. They walked under the trees; she was so small that she had to raise her whole arm to hold his big hand. Grass rubbed against her legs, and, up above, the leaves playfully eluded her touch. Some afternoons they sat in the iron chairs in front of the birdcage and watched in silence. Sofia was terrified of the pheasants because of their color. But then she'd climb off her chair, go to the cage's door, and, on her tiptoes, grab the knob. "If I went in, they'd be scared, right?" Just after saying that, she'd run back to her father, turning her head to make sure the pheasants had not escaped to pursue her. He would then pick her up, laughing, and hug her. It was as if he were hugging a cloud. The first time he took her to look at the birds he explained what birds they were.

"Those with reddish feathers and a shiny blue and green neck are the pheasants; the guinea hens are the black ones with splotches of white. The peacocks and the peahens . . ."

Sofia interrupted: "Which are the ones that shriek?"

"The ones with blue circles at the tip of their tails."

Suddenly her father, as he'd done often, fell silent, and she thought he couldn't see her. She tapped his thigh with a fist.

"Let's go," he said, coming to.

One afternoon he unlocked the little back gate that opened to the fields.

"Step outside and look."

She was amazed – she thought the sky had been emptied of leaves and the sun was lord of all. The day of the violets was a very windy one. Her father was seated in front of the birdcage; she noticed a line of caterpillars and followed it, crouching, to see where it would lead. She found herself before a tree with a huge trunk and with moss at its foot. On the mossy part there were clumps of wild violets, some with purple, some with blue, flowers. She started to pick them. They were small, loaded with perfume, wet with dew. She heard her father calling her name but did not answer. Maybe she shouldn't be picking those violets and her dad would scold her. When she had gathered a bouquet, she brought it to her chest and looked around, motionless, until she saw her father's shadow.

"I'm here."

As she saw him emerge over the tall grass, she raised an arm and showed him the violets. He stopped, staring at the flowers, and lifted her to his shoulder. Branches were groaning. With her arms around her father's neck she tossed off the violets one by one, strewing the path with them.

She had never loved her mother much. Seeing her with her shawls embroidered with rhinestones and her herringbone stockings, the girl wished her mother would go away and never to return. Once, when her mother scolded her and dragged her off a flowerbed near the chestnut trees, she thought she would have to kill her. Because she frequented the kitchen, she had seen how those animals cowered whenever Armanda was about to kill a rabbit or a chicken. Much later, perhaps because Felícia had spread the news, she learned that her mother had been married once before and that she had her husband wrapped around her little finger. "I will never be like my parents because my heart is dry," she thought. She was convinced of this since the day Armanda informed her that her parents had been looking for a gymnastics teacher to wean her off the habit of raising one shoulder higher than the other: she spent three days without speaking to anyone. What possessed them to think that one of her shoulders was higher than the other? She had seen people doing gymnastic exercises. Her father took fencing lessons at the Ateneu: his coach was a Valencian named Bea, who, the lesson over, made him lift weights. He had taken her with him once. She was distracted watching all those novel things, when suddenly she thought her father was dying: he was very slowly raising and lowering a bar with a big ball on each end and the veins of his neck and forehead were swollen like snakes. When the bar was near the ground, he dropped it quickly and jumped out of the way.

"See how heavy it is. Go ahead."

Sofia couldn't even make it roll. Bea told Senyor Valldaura that, from the time the Ateneu had opened, only two people had been able to lift those weights. "You, Senyor Valldaura, and I, when I was younger."

Sofia had almost forgotten that Armanda had told her about it, when one morning the shock came. They were having breakfast, and her mother was pouring more milk into her cup.

"We have a gymnastics instructor for you, Sofia. You begin the day after tomorrow."

She turned white as paper.

"What's the matter?" her father asked her. She stared at him silently for a moment, her eyes filled with rage; then she threw her cup and saucer to the floor and burst into sobs. When he rose to come to her, she receded a few steps.

"Leave her alone," her mother said; "if she wants to be a hunchback, she can be a hunchback."

She did not take any lessons, and her anger lasted a long time.

Two years later Sofia had her First Communion, and her father fell ill; he had never been sick and was scared.

Doctor Falguera tried to raise his spirits. "You, Senyor Valldaura, are strong as an ox; a little illness now and then helps with your overall health."

The first day he was able to leave the bed, he took Sofia for a stroll. Walking under the trees, he mentioned his pearl tiepin, which he used to let her touch when she was little.

"It's a gray pearl, and when I die I want you to pin it on me; I'm telling you now because I am sure you will remember." He stopped and put his arm on her shoulder. "I'll leave you a fortune. All I have will be yours. But you are not to tell anybody, agreed? It's a secret."

She was happy to share a secret with her dad. A secret consisted of a few words said in a low voice to be heard not even by the birds. That night she dreamed that she was already rich: she wore a shawl embroidered with stones and black herringbone stockings. Perhaps for this reason, when years later she went with her mother to the attorney's office to be read the will, she was shocked to learn that the villa would be her mother's. She bit her lip so hard she needed to stanch the blood with her handkerchief. As they walked under the chestnut trees, the two women in rigorous mourning, their veils flying behind them, she realized her mother now entered the villa in a different way: she looked with satisfaction at the trees, the flowers, the pink marble columns holding the balcony, the coat of arms, the alabaster in the foyer. "Teresa Goday, the widow Valldaura," Sofia thought, "now enters her house." She, who was now one of the richest young women in Barcelona, cried tears of rage and shame until the wee hours because her father had deceived her.

That slightly dank smell of her parlor made him queasy. His liver might be giving him trouble: he ate too much, drank too much, and chain-smoked. When the maid, taking his hat and cane, informed him that her mistress was taking a bath, he felt peeved. Pilar knew that he always came on time; why didn't she take her bath before, or after? Whenever he thought of her and he was in a good mood, he enjoyed calling her Lady. *My la-dy.* Lady Godiva was her stage name, and calling her Lady made him feel soft inside. With her satiny skin and her exotic green eyes, she reminded him of an orchid. On rainy days she looked melancholy, and when she was melancholy she was divine. "*Dis moi, ton coeur parfois s'envole-t-il, Agathe?*" Early one morning he had pestered her so much repeating that line in that wide bed, under a coral pink bedspread and with pillowcases heavy with Valenciennes lacework, that she struck him in the head with her fist. She hurt him, but he laughed and kept moving his lips as he repeated, "*S'envole-t-il, s'envole-t-il, s'envole-t-il . . .*"

He walked toward the balcony and looked out through the sheer curtains. He pulled them aside: the glass pane on the lower right had a bubble. He had no idea how glass was made; with sand, he thought. He did know how they made bottles: by blowing. The evening was upon them, a bit gray, a bit windy. Then, right beneath the balcony, the music began. A tiny man, dressed in black, with a red kerchief on his neck, turned the handle of an organ that had faded flower garlands painted on its sides. The music irked him, but he began mechanically to tap the beat with his foot. "Some welcome," he said out loud. Finally he couldn't take it any longer; even though he wasn't happy about being seen from the houses across the street, he went out to the balcony and tossed down a couple of pesetas. The organ grinder looked up, and, when he saw Eladi gesturing for him to go away, he picked up the coins, looked up again, pleased, took off his cap, and pushed the organ cart down the street. Eladi left the balcony open for a while to freshen the air inside; he felt the bubble in the pane with one finger, drew the shade back, and sat down on his armchair. He was surrounded by disagreeable colors: burgundy walls, linden green rug and curtains. That afternoon the colors appeared more repulsive to him because of his liver, and to make things worse all those trinkets, those macassars, all those side tables. "Only the mistress is missing," he thought. In the middle of the mantelpiece there was a bust made of blue paste, with a big tulle wrap over its bare shoulders, an erect head and exquisite features. He was sure the large bouquet of hydrangeas on the piano was artificial because he'd never seen them faded, and the small picture next to the door must have been a new acquisition: on a background of white silk, painted in sweet colors, a young shepherd kneeling before a milepost cross. He got closer to it. "It's not a painting, damn it; it's an embroidery." He heard steps and sat down in a hurry. No one came in. He pulled his watch from his waistcoat pocket and checked the time. His uncle had given him that gold watch when he started working in the store. "To know the exact time is the most important thing in life. A man is made of seconds, of minutes."

About a year before, one evening when he felt bored, he went to the Edèn-Concert cabaret. The first three girls who went onstage to sing weren't worth much. But, when he saw Pilar singing onstage, naked, atop a guy disguised as a horse, he was delighted. One could barely see her face, with her long tresses down to her kidneys, but her legs and her thighs, her belly, that freckle on her breast, and her nacre skin . . . After her performance he sent in his card, and Pilar received him right away: she donned a pink robe pulled all the way up to her neck, with wide sleeves, held at the waist by a golden cord. She pulled up her tresses, and the sleeves fell to her shoulders. Eladi went breathless. He had never had a lover. Whenever he wanted a girl, he went to Madame Lucrècia's and chose the one he fancied best; the next morning he'd have forgotten her. He fell in love right away with Pilar Segura, madly in love. She was sweet; she had something in her at once vulgar and refined that made her endearing to him. "So different from Sofia. If Sofia could look more like her mother in some things, even if just a little!" But Sofia was a sour, secretive woman, full of admirable qualities that took a bit too long to uncover.

The relationship between Eladi and Pilar Segura had been very intense from the start. Almost daily he took her from the Edèn to her home, and Uncle Terenci did not take long to get a whiff of the affair. "It really doesn't matter," he told his nephew the day they discussed the matter, "it's nothing the clock will not fix, I mean time. Enjoy it while you can, but remember that your fiancée is a very rich girl and comes from a very good family."

A noise close by distracted him from his thoughts. As the door opened, so that he would appear to be doing something, he picked up from the table next to him a letter opener with a horn handle and a silver blade. Pilar came in scandalously perfumed, naked under her orange muslin robe tied with a sequined belt, barefoot.

"Did I make you wait long?"

Eladi got up and kissed her behind her ear. Then he sat her on his lap. The miracle was unfolding. The mere presence of Pilar made him feel outside of this world. Powerful. With the tip of the opener he pulled the front of her robe open to look at the freckle on her breast. She wore a necklace he had given her, a cross made of platinum and diamonds hanging from a thin, almost invisible chain. Pilar looked at him raptly. "*Moesta et errabunda,*" Eladi thought as he averted his gaze to dodge those beguiling eyes.

"Shall I get you a drink?" She went to the door and pulled the cord. "My new maid is half-deaf, and whenever she is at the other end of the apartment she hears nothing—but," she added with a laugh, "if I need her, I ring the bell, and, as she does not show up, I go to get her. Do you mind?" The charm had been broken. He felt surrounded by the silence and realized it had gotten dark. The blue paste nymph was staring at him from the fireplace. Eladi threw her a smirk and closed his eyes. Suddenly he could see the water lilies in the foyer of the Valldauras. "They are also nymphs—or better nympheas," he mused, "but for the rich."

Pilar had come in silently with a liquor tray, which she left on the table to turn on the lights. Behind the glass panes of the balcony it was night. Eladi had been feeling strange for some time now. It was a kind of restiveness quite different from the unease he had felt when he first came in. Perhaps Pilar was going through a rough time and he, somehow, felt it. Generally, as soon as she'd see him, she'd talk to him about her day; she'd tell him everything people had said to her and show him the cards that she'd gotten with the flowers. "Here. You can tear them to pieces!" She might have run out of money and didn't dare ask him for more. She might have had a fight with another girl, "*quelque chose que je ne peux pas saisir . . .*" Not that: she came to him smiling with a cordial glass in her hand and sat in his lap. What was that infernal perfume she had on? It suffocated him. She must have doused herself directly from the bottle. He felt his good humor return. No, his liver was fine. He would tease her.

"Do you remember, Pilar?" He softened his voice to a murmur: "*S'envole-t-il, s'envole-t-il, s'envole-t-il?*"

She brought her mouth to his and spoke very softly a few words he didn't catch.

"What did you say?"

She repeated her mumble. Despite his fear of appearing ridiculous, Eladi could not stop himself from asking once again what she had said.

"Didn't you guess?" And she mumbled again. He looked at her quietly. "I'm pregnant. Can you hear now?" She caressed his cheek with a finger and kissed him on the forehead. "You are pleased, aren't you?"

13. MASDÉU THE PAINTER

With the palette in one hand and a brush in the other, he took a step away from the easel and thought he should darken the longest fold in Moses's tunic. It was hard to paint on velvet because velvet soaked up the color too fast and made it difficult for the brush to glide, even though this canvas was cotton and had a low nap. The outline was drawn: water in front, parted; clouds on the horizon; all the personages. Without his having meant to do it that way, Moses looked like Senyor Valldaura. He still had to put the finishing touches on the frieze of dark-green leaves with little red berries half-hidden among them that framed the biblical scene. Jesús Masdéu painted tapestries for the Eudalt chain of stores: they commissioned one every two months. He now realized that *The Crossing of the Red Sea* was plagued with difficulties. It was his own fault; when Senyor Rodés had requested *Adam and Eve*, Masdéu had proposed *The Crossing of the Red Sea*. "You'll love the tapestry!" He picked up the brush and applied it to the velvet, thinking: "I'd like to see the kids who exhibit in galleries wrestle with this; all they paint is four pears and an empty bottle, and the critics are open mouthed." He was born unlucky. His father used to tell him: "Go pay a visit to Senyora Valldaura from time to time; she's rich, and you are her godson." She had paid for his studies; whenever he went to see her, she gave him money. He went through the gate full of inhibitions, but, as he waited to be admitted to their living room, he looked at the oval windows, rich with color, and he felt his chest fill with the wind of greatness.

One day he went to see his godmother with a tapestry rolled up under his arm: *The Rock of the Sirens*. He thought it was prettier than the still life with a pumpkin and a rabbit that hung in their living room, but she barely glanced at it. Another day he dared suggest that he'd like to do a painting of their foyer: the fire of the coat of arms, the water stained by color. Senyora Valldaura, fanning herself with that fan with a painted apple, stared at him piercingly, "You still have a long way to go, Jesús; as my husband says, anybody can make a daub."

He left disheartened. He stepped on the gravel as if it were gold and as if Senyor Valldaura, who always greeted him looking surprised and worried, would scold him for taking along some of that precious dust on the soles of his shoes. He now applied a few strokes with half-closed eyes. The hours he would have to stand before that piece of velvet that might never find a buyer! Suddenly he felt a flare of inspiration: he would have the woman to Moses's left wear a Prussian-blue tunic and the child she had in her arms a lemon-yellow one. With a hard squint and a frown, he took a step back and examined the pleat's shadow.

Jesús Masdéu was neither tall nor short; his eyes were black and kind. At work he wore a beret. Tacked on his desk his commercial poster was drying: "Your nose, Senyor, is a nest of microbes. *Antimic* will kill them all." He was sure it would cause an impression. He had drawn the profile of a Greek nose surrounded by bugs. He had been working for two years for a pharmaceutical firm and five years for the Eudalt galleries. The poster would earn him handsome money; the tapestry would cost him some. Senyor Rodés would never reimburse him for the hours he had spent on the *Red Sea*. His *Adulteress*, yes, that had been good business. He worked his hands to the bone; whenever he needed a break, he stepped outside and looked at the expanse of roofs all the way to the sea. He was happy to have his atelier in such a tall building. He was happy with a feeling grafted with melancholy that he must have been dragging since his days as a child: his mother did not love him much; his father left home every evening to go to work lighting gas lamps on the streets.

When he was little his father took him along his route, and Jesús had never quite caught how his father, with his long pole, managed to open the little glass door and ignite the lamp. They owned their own house.

As soon as he started to paint with oils, his mother took to complaining about the smell of linseed and turpentine and of the mess he made cleaning his brushes. "I'll never have a clean sink." To get out of her way he had rented that room, an attic with a side alcove that served as his kitchen, and he moved in. Every other week, in the evening, he paid his parents a visit; they chatted for a while and had dinner. Other evenings, after cleaning his brushes, he threw some water on his face, changed his shirt, tied his soft bowtie, and went to see Senyora Valldaura, not because he expected anything but out of affection for her.

So as not to waste time, the following morning, before climbing up to his studio, he did all his shopping: vegetables and fruit from Senyora Matilde's shop. She was grouchy, walked like a duck, and her store was a shambles. Milk from Senyor Seré, who always topped up his can and sold him delicious curdled milk. The butcher's name was Laieta: she watched her scales with an eagle eye but sold meat fine as butter. After finishing a tapestry, he'd show it to them: they admired his work and held him in great esteem: "What are you working on now, Jesús?" He never complained about his life because, at certain moments, three steps away from his easel, he felt a warmth in his heart and a kind of madness in his brain that nothing outside of his work could have given him. From his pigeon coop, looking at the spread of roofs and terraces with laundry swaying in the sea breeze, he would not have exchanged his life for anyone's.

14. SOFIA'S WEDDING

As the waiters served the appetizers, Eulàlia went with Sofia to the washroom.

"You couldn't look prettier," she told Sofia, hugging her once they were alone. And, moving to one side, she added, "You can tell a mile away that Eladi is madly in love."

Sofia faced the mirror and smiled. "And I am not?"

"Oh, you . . . have you ever been in love?"

Sofia did not answer. Leaving the church, she had spotted Lluís Roca's car on the other side of the square. She kept hidden away a few letters that Lluís had written her after she'd become engaged. They were not love letters, but she could read between the lines. "My friend Sofia . . ." "My dear friend . . ." "My friend . . ." She should not think about that anymore! She adjusted the orange blossoms next to her face and began to put lipstick on.

"May I tell you something?" Eulàlia had also gotten the lipstick from her purse and was applying some. "It's taken you two years to get married, and more than once I've been afraid that Eladi would get tired of waiting. It's been more chancy than you think."

Sofia, with her back to her godmother, was pulling up her stockings.

"Does it bother you to show me your legs, which I saw when you were born?"

Sofia turned around and winked. "They belong to my husband."

She did not want Eulàlia to comment on her stockings that were too bright. For a couple of months Eladi, as if to annoy her, had given her from time to time a small parcel tied with a golden cord. It inevitably contained a pair of pink stockings. She would walk him to the front gate and pinch him on the neck. "You wicked boy." The women left the washroom and walked past three young men in animated conversation. One of them said out loud: "I wish I were the groom. Not now. Tonight."

Eulàlia squeezed her arm. "Men."

Sofia felt nervous all through the dinner. Her mother, seated between the attorney Amadeu Riera and Jesús Madéu, chatted and laughed constantly. Why did she invite Masdéu without consulting her? She did not have him on her list. He wore black and a tie, but he needed a haircut and looked out of place. Constància Riera, in a light-blue dress, loaded with diamonds worth a fortune, sitting very straight next to Josep Fontanills, turned often to look at her husband: you could tell she was uneasy. For a moment Sofia was afraid; Masdéu was conversing with the woman next to him, while her mother and Riera were exchanging blissful gazes. When the champagne was served, the tables were bursting with liveliness, and Uncle Terenci had to beg for silence as he glanced at the gardenia on his lapel that he must have fondled because it showed a couple of smeared petals. After his speech he raised his glass and toasted the happiness of the newlyweds.

"I don't know what we are doing here," Eladi said as the waiter served him a cup of coffee. Sofia kicked him under the table.

In the middle of the dance Sofia and Eladi decided to leave without telling anyone. They almost ran into Rafael Bergadà, who was preening himself in front of a mirror, and they took off running and waving to him. Eladi's father, from a distance, saw them get in the car. "A day like today," Teodor Farriols thought bitterly, "a man should have his wife alive with him. If at the very least they had seated me by my brother . . ." He scanned the room for his brother, and when he saw him he calmed down. "Terenci knows how to live, and I don't – I never have." With sadness he traced his way amid the dancing couples across the hall filled with music. He lifted his tails and, as he sat down, looked at Teresa Valldaura, who, with bright eyes and sparkling teeth, was laughing with one hand on her chest. Who would have thought that Riera . . .

Sofia would have preferred for them to have their own place, at least for a few years. She had not brought this up to Eladi, but she was taken aback by the enthusiasm Eladi showed when her mother told them she'd be afraid to live by herself in such a big villa. "Where could you be better? You'll keep me company, and I won't get in your way." Sofia accepted reluctantly. What she did not like at all was her mother's insistence that, before the honeymoon, they spend a couple of days in the villa: "This way the memory of the first night will stay within these walls." So as not to intrude, Teresa would spend those days at the Fontanills, her dear friends. "Poor Mama, how sweet!"

The maids, in their Sunday uniforms, were waiting for them by the front steps. Eladi tried to bring Sofia into the house in his arms, and she thought that grotesque. Those girls would have a good laugh. Sofia was only happy to be seen by Armanda, since she had caught the girl once or twice looking at Eladi with droopy eyes. Her dress felt tight in the back, and before she finished climbing the steps, just for a second, she was afraid she'd fall. She found herself standing in the middle of her room, facing the large bed. She was now married. Just as Eulàlia had done, but with bad intentions, one of her tennis friends, Ernestina, older than her and jealous, had told her one day: "Are you sure you will get married? Eladi is more sought after than you think." She set her bouquet on the dresser and started removing the pins of her veil. She was very pale. She let her hair down to the middle of her back; she shunned fashion and had kept her hair long. It was brown, a little lighter than her mother's. Eladi had come next to her and without saying a word was caressing it. "Eulàlia, Ernestina . . . What had possessed them?" Why should they doubt that she could ever find a husband? Did they think her so insignificant? So pathetic next to Eladi, who always appeared as if just unpacked, polished, perfect? She felt him behind her, breathing through his narrow teeth, his chest heaving. "What's the matter with me?" she thought. "What's wrong with me?" Her father had been dead for two years, and she had never felt so alone. Once he had told her: "You are everything to me: daughter and son." The only person who had loved her. The other one, Eladi, had emerged from behind the counter of a clothing and lace store, smiling, full of himself, with the phony kindness of one contemplating a move. She was sure he had been dying to marry her. And there he had her, his forever. "Yes, Godmother, I have managed to marry a boy, a bit petulant, who looks good, of course, and who thinks I should be grateful for life. That's right: for life." Eladi turned her around and began to kiss her. "There's no stopping you, clearly. This fear of looking ridiculous . . ." She pushed him away, put her foot on the dresser's stool, and pulled up her skirt: a cloudburst of tulle and gauze. Her flesh-colored stocking, taut, shone in the light.

"Kiss me, but on the foot. Do you hear? The one you fancy best. You may choose."

Eladi, taken aback, was about to embrace her, when she pushed him off.

"You heard me, didn't you? On the foot."

She pulled her skirt a little higher; her legs were pretty, shapely, with a round, smooth knee and an exquisite ankle. Eladi ran a finger under his shirt collar and muttered, "Sofia."

She pointed at her foot. "I am not asking for anything extraordinary; if my stocking is in the way, why don't you take it off?" Automatically, he removed her garter and pulled her stocking down. Her foot was small, young. "Before you set out you might want to get comfortable. Do it as if you were at home."

Eladi threw her a fierce glance, threw his jacket on the bed, and undid his tie. She was looking at him amusedly.

"Do you mind if I don't let you get sentimental, as if I were a chambermaid?" Eladi had bent down and was rubbing his cheek on the curve of her foot. "This is the way, Senyor Eladi, like a good dog. And now, go wash yourself." She put her foot on his forehead and pushed. Eladi went to the bathroom and ran a wet towel on his cheeks and lips. Then he spit. When he returned to the bedroom, Sofia was brushing her hair. Leaning against the bed, with his hands grabbing the wood of the footboard, Eladi spoke with his voice muffled by repressed anger: "I thought I'd wait to tell you one thing. I might never have told you, but the sooner we get this over with, the better."

She stopped for a second and thought she had not heard him right, but she soon realized that what Eladi had to say to her was important, and she felt alarmed. "It will be better if I pretend I didn't hear him." She got up and, with a smile, pulled at a little blossom from her brassiere.

"You see: something blue." Then she removed her other garter and, throwing it at his face, said: "See? Something new." Finally, she threw him a little handkerchief she kept in her bosom: "See? Something old. The English say that these, all together, bring good luck."

Eladi, who had not left the foot of the bed, looked at her as if she were far away. "What do you think? Do they bring good luck or bad luck? Make up your mind. And do me the favor of answering when I ask you a question."

He held her look for a moment and then, in the most brutal way, mumbled, "I have a daughter." He saw Sofia open her mouth wide as if she hadn't understood him. "Didn't you hear? I told you I have a daughter."

Sofia sat down at her dressing table, threw her flowers to the floor with the back of her hand, changed the position of a perfume bottle, and picked up her brush. Her hands were shaking. She asked softly, "And who's the mother, if I may ask?" She turned around slowly. "If what you have told me is true, you have chosen a fine moment, don't you think? But if what you wanted was to botch something . . . with what you've told me . . ." She got up, finished undressing, almost tearing off her clothes, and, naked, went to him, hugged him hard, and stuck her knee between his thighs, pushing all the way up.

She stepped outside and crossed the opening under the stars that soon would fade. Eladi, after they'd made love, had fallen asleep. She took a few deep breaths, hesitated for a moment, and entered the mass of black trees. She walked as if afraid, pulling aside the low branches. The acacias flowered in the spring, and the lilacs, in a bunch, barely blossomed. The profusion of savage greenery covered the paths she knew by heart. The pheasant cage was empty. The birds had died gradually: the guinea hens, the pheasants; the peacocks had taken longer. The servant girls said they had died of old age, but her mother said they were not old. In her husband's lifetime, if a bird died, he rushed to replace it with a new one. What happened, and her mother must have been right, is that the servants did not change the water often enough, and the birds were poisoned. Near the cage stood the tree with violets around its trunk. It was her tree. The day of her betrothal to Eladi she had etched S.E. on the trunk with the tip of a knife. She now looked for the initials and could not find them. She remained motionless for a while. That daughter of Eladi's . . . a young child . . . She recalled a sentence from an English writer: "I honour you, Eliza, for keeping secret some things." She started walking but had to stop because she felt sick. She would react the same way that her grandmother she had never gotten to know reacted. She would want that daughter of Eladi in her house even if she could never come to love her. She was a baby and was called Maria. If Eladi figured that one day she'd be his . . . There would be time to decide what to tell their friends. When Sofia got to the wisteria, she looked up. She was thinking about what room to choose for the baby.

In the dark she walked into the library. When she was little she liked to climb the ladder used to reach for books on the higher shelves. It had wheels, and her father had her step on it and pushed her from one side of the wall to the other. "I am teaching you to travel," he told her with a laugh. She went through the foyer; halfway up the stairs she paused, and, grabbing the banister, she looked at the coats of arms aglow in the murky light. She did not want to go in but finally opened the door; the cigar smoke made her reel. Eladi sat in bed holding a drink, which he quickly set on the bedside table. Sofia opened the balcony wide. She knew Eladi was staring at her, and she contemplated for a while the moonlit garden in its misty light as if each grain of sand were breathing. She slowly took off her robe and, after turning off the lamp, sat on the side of the bed. Without a word Eladi took her arm and made her lie next to him.

"You smell like the trees," he said in a sad voice.

Sofia jumped on top of him and started to bite him furiously, laughing.

15. BIRTHS

When Sebastià Sànchez, the impresario, learned about Pilar Segura's condition, he immediately offered his country estate for her labor. He was a middle-aged man, the son of Andalusian parents, charismatic, with an easy laugh, but who at the slightest provocation turned sour and started yelling. "You better not say anything to him until he's calmed down," those who knew him used to say, ignoring his rantings. He had a good eye for cabaret artists and treated them better than he did his own daughters; his fifth had just been born. Ursula, his housekeeper, who was from L'Hospitalet and uglier than sin, but faithful and efficient, once asked him if he could find a position for her son. He asked what the boy could do.

"Well, he's never had a job. He's not good for much, but he's a good kid."

Senyor Sànchez put a hand on her shoulder and told her, "Don't worry, I'll find something." He knew a girl, Pilar Segura, pretty and shapely, whom he got in touch with from time to time. Her voice wasn't great, but she could carry a tune. Still, she was not quite a success. One afternoon, in his office, chatting with the Tullido brothers, the acrobats, he had an idea: he summoned his housekeeper's son, Felip Armengol, a guy who looked like a gypsy, and Pilar Segura. He had them sit down, was silent for a bit as if deep in thought, and finally proposed to them his idea for the horse and Lady Godiva number. When he finished, he stared at Pilar as if to see what she was thinking and told her softly, so as not to alarm her, "You will have to sing stark naked – no body stocking." Then, happy, seeing that Pilar accepted, he added, "You won't mind singing from such a high position, will you?"

Pilar laughed and said no. Senyor Sànchez asked a musician for a tune, "something like a march." He ordered the horse outfit, commissioned a few rehearsals for Pilar and Felip, and, on opening night, the Lady Godiva number was a hit. Pilar became the dream of many a married man and of almost all the students in Barcelona.

Felip Armengol went to the country house with Pilar. He would not leave her alone, and he practically saw the child being born: a lovely girl, chubby, who opened her curious eyes right away. The midwife told Pilar, "I have never seen a girl so eager for life or one who just at birth opened such clear and pretty eyes."

Pilar felt sad. Eladi had told her he would not recognize the child. "It is difficult to explain. I am sorry, as you can imagine, but it's out of the question. I'll find a solution."

Pilar sought the confidence of Senyor Sànchez and confessed to him, "I have no option but to take life as it is given to me."

Senyor Sànchez, who took pity on Pilar, knowing that she found herself in this predicament because she had fallen in love, consoled her as best he could. "An artist, before all, must live for her art."

In the country house, while Pilar was having her breakfast, Felip went to the cradle, pulled the netting aside, and looked at the girl sleeping like an angel, wearing nothing but a belly button bandage and diapers because Pilar felt that babies shouldn't be hindered by clothing. Felip wrapped the girl in a towel, picked her up, and, as he rocked her in his arms, asked Pilar, "Can I have her?"

Pilar, sitting near the fireplace, did not answer.

"I see I can't. What name will you give her?"

Pilar, white as a sheet, the skin of her hands looking transparent, said: "Maria, like the mother of God. Maria . . . Segura." And she burst into tears. The young man felt bad; he brought the girl to her mother and caressed her hair.

"I am nobody. You know my last name is Armengol, right? What would you say if your daughter took the name Maria Armengol?"

A few days later Sebastià Sànchez came to see Pilar armed with a bouquet of flowers and a huge box of chocolates. She had just gotten up, and they went for a stroll along a path in the wheat field. Pilar wore a woolen shawl on her shoulders and walked slowly. He stopped suddenly and took her arm. "I came to give you good news. A lawyer showed up in my office yesterday; Forcadell by name, I think, but it does not matter. He told me that a very rich couple, childless, would be willing to take the girl. On the condition that you never see her again. You would have to sign a waiver. What do you think?"

Pilar, amid the greening wheat shoots, looked at her impresario as if she were drowning in the middle of the sea. She kept quiet for a long time.

"I don't know what to say. The thought had never crossed my mind."

She waited two bitter months; she could not make up her mind. At last, exhausted, she agreed. More dead than alive, she surrendered her baby to her impresario. She also gave him a light-blue box. In it there was a silver bracelet, with little bells.

"It had been mine. Tell the couple who are taking the girl to give it to her when she is older."

Sofia Valldaura got pregnant a month after her wedding. She had a bad pregnancy, vomiting constantly and with paralyzing pain in her kidneys.

She couldn't stand the sight of Eladi and didn't even let him touch her. One night Armanda, who had marinated some meat with vinegar and herbs for herself and the other girls, found herself unable to ask anyone what they wanted for dinner the next day: the young lady was ill, and the Senyora was out to supper at the Fontanills. Only Senyor Eladi was at home. With some amusement she thought, "Let's see what face he makes when I go ask him what he wants to eat."

She rapped on the library door with her knuckles. There was a line of light under the door, but no one answered. "Perhaps he's gone upstairs and has left the lights on." She opened the door and saw him seated in his armchair, smoking.

"I am sorry to bother you, but what would you like for dinner tomorrow?"

Eladi looked at her absently. She repeated her question.

"Come closer, I can't hear you." When she was very near him, he stuck his hand under her skirt and grasped her garter, pulled on it, and quickly let go. Armanda said, "Ouch!" Thus began the affair between Eladi Farriols and Armanda the cook.

Exactly nine months into the pregnancy, when Sofia was about to get out of bed, she felt a piercing pain in her kidneys. The midwife had been staying over in the villa for a few nights already, and Eladi went to call her. Senyora Sílvia took Sofia's pulse, felt her belly, and said: "Your water has broken. Do me a favor: each time the pain subsides, get up and try to walk about a little. Let's try to make this go fast."

The next morning, back from the kitchen, where she'd gone to request hot water, she ran into Senyora Valldaura, who was going upstairs to see Sofia.

"I am concerned about your daughter because she's very narrow. I am afraid we will have an endless labor."

A worried Teresa asked her, "What do you think, Senyora Sílvia, should I call Doctor Falguera?"

Sofia spent two days screaming and moaning. Doctor Falguera told Teresa that he might have to cut the baby out but that he would not do anything unless it was absolutely necessary. Sofia gave birth to a boy, and Doctor Falguera did not have to intervene. The boy was born with a head in the shape of a melon.

"It'll get better," the midwife told them, "I had to squeeze it so that he'd come out without too much tearing."

The day of the christening Eladi wanted all the lights in the house turned on and gave money to the midwife and servants, who had been working overtime. Eladi's joy hurt Armanda. The child was named Ramon; Sofia would have preferred Salvador, like her father, but Eladi dissuaded her. "I've always disliked naming a baby after a dead person. It's too sad. Of course, all names are names of dead people . . . But you know what I mean."

Three or four months after the birth of Ramon, the daughter of Marina Riera, the attorney's sister, had a girl. She was named Marina, like her mother and her grandmother. Teresa saw the announcement in the newspaper. She remembered Marina Riera vaguely; she had seen her once, years before, one evening when she went to the Liceu for a performance of *Traviata* with her husband and the Bergadàs. That was the first time she had seen Amadeu Riera. When older, that newborn girl would fall in love with Ramon Farriols i Valldaura.

Ramon turned three, and Sofia became pregnant again. She did not mind at all. "Maybe I'll have a girl." She was sure that, if she could give Eladi a daughter, she would separate him from Maria, who was very pretty and who, as everyone realized, loved her father more than Ramon did. All those who went to see Sofia took to telling her that she'd have a girl, and so did Senyora Sílvia.

"Your belly is round, and it is well known that round bellies hide a girl inside." She recommended that she eat very little and walk as much as possible. "If the girl comes out reedy, don't worry: we'll fatten her."

Teresa asked if the labor would be smoother.

"Quite. I am sure this time it'll go without a hitch; we've paved the road."

The second child of Sofia and Eladi was born prematurely, at seven months. They had to fill his cradle with hot water bottles, and for a long spell the whole family lived on tenterhooks because if he cried for too long or caught a fever he'd have a seizure: his tongue would curl up against his palate, and his eyes turned white as if he'd died. Armanda, aware as everybody else of how much Sofia had looked forward to a girl, felt a sort of vicious joy.

"It serves her right. And, besides, the child is like an overripe fig!"

It took the family a while to christen him, and finally they named him Jaume. Teresa, upset by seeing that boy so small and sickly, could not make it to the ceremony. The day of the christening, as she prepared to go down the front steps, she dropped to the ground like a dead weight. Eladi and Uncle Terenci had to lift her and carry her to the parlor. Doctor Falguera came at once.

"What ails you?"

Teresa, pointing to her legs with her fan, told him: "It's as if I had no ankles: these don't hold me anymore. My right foot has been twisting for a while now. But I didn't pay much attention."

Doctor Falguera, worried, prescribed a potion for the nerves and massages.

"Don't trouble yourself about finding a masseuse. I know a nurse who's very good." And he urged Teresa not to let herself go. "If you are afraid of walking, have someone put a bandage on your ankles and buy a cane."

Teresa fixed her eyes on him and hit her knee with the fan; she was enraged.

"Before seeing my legs in bandages, I'd rather not move at all!"

Doctor Falguera shook his head as if he were about to say something.

"Don't. Don't say a thing! You and I have known each other for so long that we do not need to speak to understand each other." She raised her arm for him to kiss her hand. "And don't you laugh; I am not doing this to seek sympathy. It's sheer egoism. There is so much death inside of me now that a kiss on the hand will be soothing." Looking at the branches swaying outside the window, she added: "Come see me as often as you can. Please do."

16. THE SERVANTS IN SUMMER

Before starting to clean the two chickens she had just placed beside the sink, Armanda went out of the kitchen and, looking at the terrace with half-closed eyes, thought that the heat would be the end of her. Behind her the ivy, punished by the sun, seemed asleep; it was not like the ivy growing and creeping next to the pond or the vines that choked the trees, clinging to their rough bark. They stayed green all year. The ivy on the kitchen wall, like that on other walls of the house, turned the color of blood in the fall and climbed the smooth walls because it had little hands. She pulled a long shoot to look at the leaves; it looked like a lizard. Sometimes children made themselves wreaths with shoots like that one. "Now, back to work," Armanda muttered to herself, wiping the perspiration off her neck with a sparkling clean handkerchief. She took the shears from the kitchen drawer, and, as she cut open the breast of a chicken, she remembered the garbage. For about two years now, on the street they were opening nearby, two apartment buildings with shops had been built; the grocer who had rented the largest of the shops had developed the habit of tossing his debris by the little door that opened from the villa's yard to the open fields. She took notice of that and mentioned it to Senyor Eladi. The grocer was fat, bald, and sported a tiny mustache that looked as if it would fall off. Senyor Fontanills went to complain; the grocer, all kindness, told him not to worry. After two or three weeks of good behavior the garbage again. Senyor Eladi, who was not a man to pick a fight, told the gardeners to burn it. The empty cans got buried. But one day, perhaps because he'd started out on the wrong foot, he said he was fed up with the garbage and again sent Fontanills to have a word with the grocer. But that grocer, whose name was Àngel and who, according to Armanda, was a nobody, just laughed at them. The more Senyor Fontanills went to complain, the more garbage he left by the door.

The whole house was resting. Senyora Teresa must have been taking her afternoon nap. The young senyors had gone to Mallorca. "We never leave the house, and our children travel all the time." That morning she had received a postcard from Sofia; her daughter informed Teresa that Eladi's liver had been acting up again and that he was feeling so weak that they would delay their return for another eight or ten days. Miquel, the chauffeur, as the young senyors were away, had gone to his village to visit his parents. When they fired poor Climent and sold the carriage and the horses to buy the automobile, Armanda cried. Whenever she heard the purr of the motor, her heart filled with rage. But the other servant girls loved it. Mostly Olívia, who, at every free moment, would pester Miquel, even though he paid her no attention whatsoever. "And speaking of the devil," Armanda thought. Olívia had just come in with her uniform unbuttoned, dropped herself onto a chair, and spread her legs.

"This kitchen is hotter than hell, Armanda!"

Armanda turned around, holding a chicken gizzard in one hand and a knife in the other.

"If you dislike this so much, why don't you go out and check if they dumped their garbage again last night? We'll soon be eaten alive by flies."

Olívia, a disagreeable woman, shrugged. "It's not my job."

Marieta and Esperança came in from outside carrying a hamper with dried laundry.

"If I don't die this summer," Marieta said, "I never will."

Esperança went to the sink, pushed Armanda to one side by grabbing her at her waist, and rinsed her face and the back of her arms.

"You've got it easy, in the laundry. If you had to spend the days like me, ironing . . ."

Armanda had plucked and singed the chickens and now rinsed them, set them in a colander, and covered them with cheesecloth to keep the flies away.

"We will soon have horseflies in here, and there won't be enough aprons around to shoo them."

She did not know why, but she was happy.

"Go get Miquela, and then we'll all be here, and I'll make us a pitcher of fresh orange juice."

Olívia got up and, returning with Miquela, said: "I've had an idea. Since there is no one in the house, we could all go outside for a splash."

Olívia was tall, shapely, with a good head on her shoulders, and she walked slowly, like a queen. She and Miquela went to the laundry shed to fetch a tub and the hose. When Armanda saw Marieta and Esperança taking off their clothes, she warned them not to take off their panties in case the children, who might be anywhere, showed up.

"They are very small, and it won't matter; if they saw us only half-dressed, they might get spooked," Marieta said.

She had taken her corset off and pulled at her skirt. She was from Gràcia. Senyoreta Sofia had hired her on sight because she was young and very pretty and had astute eyes that gave her a desultory look.

"She always chooses pretty ones," Armanda reflected. "She amuses herself that way, driving Senyor Eladi crazy. If they are stupid, they fall for it, and she gets a kick from the fact that they have to do it on the sly and in a hurry. If they are smart, they tease him, and then, for the Senyora, the game is priceless."

She had been the first to fall and for two years had thought herself the mistress of the house. When Senyor Eladi got tired of her, she stayed in the house, desperately anxious; Sofia, who saw everything, got her revenge for the bad moments she'd had. She had been jealous of Armanda; she had felt so humiliated by what happened right under her nose that only her pride prevented her from firing Armanda on the spot. But that would have been tantamount to confessing that she'd known all along. And Armanda, more than once, had felt like quitting, although she always ended up staying. Then Eladi began to set his eyes on a chambermaid named Paulina, stroking his mustache with a finger. After a few bitter months Armanda got over it. Felícia, who had retired some time ago because of her age, had told her, "I think the young lady's husband likes to play the field." A grandmother of Armanda's, a country woman, explained that soon after she married, coming home from getting the eggs from the chicken coop, she caught her husband with a servant girl on his lap. She said she'd been unsettled but that she ended up relenting: she made her servants work like beasts. "If they think that a few nudges in a dark corner will let them get away with anything . . ." Armanda had inherited a sort of resignation from that grandmother. Going to bed with a full belly and a sleepy feeling, she reflected that she had a job in a good household and that she could take almost all her earnings to the savings bank. "All the rest is nonsense!"

They had taken off their clothes. "The oldest of these girls," Armanda thought, "must be twenty-five, if that old." They hooked the hose to the outside faucet and filled the tub. Marieta was the first to get in. Her boyfriend was a soldier from far away, from Cadaqués, and in uniform, in Barcelona, sorely missed his sea. On Sundays they went to the park and, sometimes, to Arrabassada. Marieta used to say, "He has kissed me only once, quite timidly – I told him not to do it again." Then, turning sad, she'd add, "If he were from Gràcia and not from Cadaqués, things would go faster because the folks from Gràcia get straight down to business."

Green and pinkish bubbles burst on Marieta's downy skin. She observed them, uttering halting sighs.

"You have breasts like lemons," Olívia told her. "Two sun-bleached little lemons."

Marieta was rubbing her sides with soapy hands. "Talk less and spray more!"

Olívia began to hose her, and they all burst out laughing. Then Miquela got in the tub, covering her breasts with her hands.

"You're quite loaded, for a young one," Esperança told her. Miquela turned beet red.

"Turn around; your front is already clean."

Miquela, her back to the sun, shrieked: Olívia had splashed her without warning, and the water was now quite cold.

"Don't make so much noise!"

Armanda was alarmed. Senyora Teresa might wake up and ring the bell and ask her if the coal delivery men were there, because whenever there was a commotion she asked if the coal men were there. Poor lady, how she had deteriorated, with her swollen dead legs. The worst was that Doctor Falguera had said she'd never recover. Not even Senyor Amadeu Riera came to see her now, and he'd come so often. While Senyor Valldaura was alive, Riera had been asked for dinner many times; he came with his wife, who looked like a little bird. Later he came alone, for visits. And then he stopped coming, as if he'd died. Senyora Valldaura never mentioned this, and her eyes had turned sad.

"It's the sadness of wine," Olívia said. "Couldn't they make her quit?"

"What do you want," Miquela replied, "she spends her days sitting in her chair; she doesn't do any needlework, any knitting; she's got to do something."

Armanda felt sorry for her. Her aunt Anselma, who was no longer working, would ask her every time she went to see her, "How is poor Senyora Teresa?" Aunt Anselma lived by herself in a small apartment in Barceloneta, eating only garlic bread and ham and drinking mugs of coffee with milk. "It makes perfect sense," she told her niece, who was appalled at seeing that diet, "I've spent half my life with my nose in the pots, and I've had it." Armanda knew that Senyora Teresa was a good woman. You just had to see how she looked at Jaume, her youngest grandchild, who had legs like matchsticks. Armanda also loved him a lot because he was so puny. She heard it said that rich people's children grew poorly because their fathers slept around a lot and their blood thinned. The worst was that the children were made to pick up the pieces.

It was Olívia's turn, and, as she soaped herself, she looked so pretty that they all stopped laughing and gazed at her without moving. Olívia was from the same region as Marieta's fiancé and was used to bathing in the sea. She explained to them that, at times, by night, she went to the beach with her sisters.

"There is nothing in the world like stepping into the sea on moonlit nights – not the sea as it is in Barcelona but a clean-water sea."

The others kidded her and told her that she didn't go skinny-dipping with her sisters but with her fiancé. Olívia never had a fiancé. Olívia had money in the bank, and they gossiped that it came from an old man who'd fallen in love with her. If they mentioned it, she changed the topic; if they insisted, she denied it – no one knew who had started the rumor. Olívia had long thighs, a thin, hard waist, a small mouth, red as a cherry; she moved her head with such absolute composure that she stopped their gossiping without saying a word. Armanda had noticed that Senyor Eladi had begun to ogle her in his peculiar way. Miquela was hosing her now, and after a while, since they all itched to get in the water, Armanda, who had kept her clothes on because she did not want the others to see her prematurely sagging breasts, volunteered to spray them. Since the hose was very long, Armanda started to chase the girls around the terrace, and for a long time they did not stop running and screaming.

There came a bit of a breeze, and the ivy leaves were swaying to and fro. The sun was still strong, and it was very hot. The children came out of the park's shadows and stopped at the edge of the trees, taken aback. Then they ran over. Ramon, the eldest, was the first to arrive, and Maria after him, and they stepped into the jet of water with their clothes on. The small one, Jaume, simply sat on the ground, took off his shoes and his sweater, and approached them slowly, his skin excited under the splash, his eyes closed, and his arms in front of his face, squealing like some little beast. Ramon slapped him on the back. "Shut up, stupid!"

Children and servants scampered about, chasing each other, red with sun, crazed by the heat. "It's a good thing Senyoreta Rosa went out," Armanda thought. Senyoreta Rosa took care of the children, she was very strict, and, if she'd seen what they were all doing, she'd have a stroke.

"That's enough!" Armanda yelled at the top of her lungs to be heard. "If the little one gets sick, I'll be the one they'll blame."

She dropped the hose to the ground, turned off the faucet, and dried her hands in her apron. Maria, dripping wet, stood next to her. She was eight. When they took her in, Senyoreta Sofia explained that she was the daughter of some distant relatives of Uncle Terenci who had been killed in an accident. But once one of the servants told her, although after some time Armanda couldn't remember which one, "You can be sure, Armanda, that behind this girl there is a mystery." She had not replied. She did not mind the servants gossiping behind the senyors' backs but did not encourage them. "A family's secrets," she reflected, "are sacred."

When she must have been three, one afternoon Maria came into the kitchen at snack time, and Armanda, leaning over, asked her: "What would you like, sweetie? A roll with chocolate or with butter and jam?"

Maria thought it over for a bit, putting a finger to the side of her nose. Armanda was dumbfounded: Maria had just made the gesture that Senyor Eladi made at dinnertime whenever he could not decide what to choose for dessert. And the girl could not have seen him make that gesture because she never ate dinner with her parents. Armanda, appalled, thought: "She's his daughter."

17. THE CHILDREN

They were crouching behind the curtain. Jaume felt Maria's hair on his cheek and the weight of Ramon's hand on his neck. Ramon, from time to time, said: "Be quiet. They're coming." No one was coming; they all knew it – but, each time Ramon said "Be quiet. They're coming," Jaume was seized by panic. Hidden behind the curtain, they waited for Senyoreta Rosa to go upstairs to her room to powder her belly button with talcum and for their parents to go out. Papa would come down first, erect, dressed to the nines, the tips of his mustache raised. Once Ramon had reported that Papa slept with some gadget over his mustache, but Jaume did not quite understand it. Mama would walk by after that. The world behind the curtain was small and safe, a world for the three of them only. That piece of velvet, lined with crimson satin, with its heavy folds, separated them from the green and mysterious world of the garden. They could hear each other breathe, caught in a kind of complicity that existed nowhere else. The dragon from the book, with red scales and fire coming out of its nostrils, the one Ramon and Maria beat up, would never find him, so small he was.

"Senyor Jaume," Grandma Teresa would say, "drink, drink – wine will make you grow."

Miquela, seated near the window, keeping his grandmother company, was knitting a scarf, while the boy held up the pink glass with a green stem. Under that wing of velvet Ramon and Maria were different: they did not push him around, even if he was in the way, nor did they pinch him to pester him so he'd leave them alone. Outside, the deserted and windy garden, seen through the glass panes, did not seem the same as when they went out to play. The stone benches, the gazebo with the wisteria, even though dry now for the great winter sleep, the great sandy spread of the terrace, everything, everything, seemed whiter. The laurel tree, with branches groaning in the wind, was darker; full of arms, full of voices, a shudder of light on each leaf. Its trunk, if he scratched it with a sharp stone, oozed a sap. He said softly, "The laurel leaves are looking at us."

Ramon pinched him on the neck. "Don't start saying weird things."

Maria turned her head, moving the curtain to look at the branch swaying behind the glass. Jaume realized that Maria's hair no longer rubbed against his cheek and felt suddenly alone. Someone was leisurely coming down the stairs: it was Papa. He was putting on his gloves, fitting each finger. After he had them on, he'd come down faster and would hit the last steps with the cane that hitherto hung from his arm.

"What does Papa put on his mustache?"

"What do you think, you silly? A mustache protector."

Jaume was about to ask what a protector was, but Maria went, "Shhh," and stepped on his foot. They heard their father's voice asking, "Where are the children?"

"They are playing," answered Senyoreta Rosa, who, whenever Papa went down the stairs, tried to come up. "On windy and rainy days, as soon as you leave the dining table, they spread all over the house."

Papa looked up for a moment, turning his head, and left. Ramon knew what he would do. Closing his eyes, he saw him walk under the chestnut trees to the little door by the main gate, grab the knob, turn it. The wind would make his pants cling to his legs, and he would hold the brim of his hat with one hand, leaning forward. As soon as he would close the door, and everyone knew this, he would pull on the chain coming out of the lion's mouth and would wait a while, listening to the bell ring far away.

"Mama will come down soon," Maria thought. "Mama, with her porcelain face and her moist lips, leaving a trail of perfume." Whenever she was alone, Maria imitated her: she went to the mirror of her dressing table, stuck out her tongue, wet a finger with saliva, and rubbed her eyebrows. She then pinched her cheeks and her earlobes to make them blush.

Ramon said softly, "Tonight we'll climb on the roof to kill the witches that the wind has put there."

"What are they like?" Jaume asked, his voice barely audible.

Ramon pinched his neck again. "Green and purple. They ride a broom the color of flies."

Ramon saw only colors: Mama was the color of roses, Papa the color of coffee with milk, Maria white, Armanda the color of earth, Grandma red. Jaume came out from behind the curtain and did two somersaults; he always did that when he was happy.

"Quick, hide, Mama is coming down," Ramon whispered, grabbing him by the arm; it was an arm thin as a reed, and Ramon thought of the branch he had discovered in the wildest part of the garden; it was shaped like a fork, with two twisted ends. Ramon had hidden it because he felt it might come in handy someday. The pond was deep, the banks steep. That corner was shady and desolate, and the water, surrounded by dead shrubs covered with ivy from the ground, appeared green. In the water you could see the elongated reflections of the trees and the black splotches of the leaves among sprinkles of sunlight. Ramon would stare at the water with his hands in his pockets; he would spit to make circles and, if alone, urinated in it. The water would shiver, and the circles would die at the edge. The ivy made bunches: black, dense bunches of berries with a bitter taste. In summer, when the water level was low, the mud of the sides teemed with worms and dead leaves. Somewhere, in the high branches, the turtledoves nested. Some days the wind came laden with clouds pushing back the sky, but the stubborn sky always came back: blue, blotted with leaves, scratched with branches – a sky lost beyond the walls crowned with pieces of broken glass. The sky that Jaume saw many afternoons, his eyes misty, through his grandmother's room window.

"Drink, Senyor Jaume. Wine makes blood." Teresa let Jaume come into her room and Maria too. But Maria seldom went because she found her grandmother's hands icky. Teresa would have nothing to do with Ramon because every time he came he would start hitting the feathers in her vase. "Every time he comes for a visit, he has to upset me."

One afternoon, some time before, they found an old, worn robe in the garbage and tore it to shreds. Ramon and Maria took Jaume and tied a strip of robe around his head and another around his middle. They picked lily leaves and stuck one on each side of his head under the strip. "They are an ass's ears."

Then they stuck two on his belt and one behind. "You've got a tail now."

They forced him to run up and down with a sheaf of twigs on his back. "Giddyap, giddyap! Yah!"

He told them he was tired, and they made him run even faster; he was a skinny boy, and the doctor had prescribed injections for the rashes on his neck and armpits. He had a sunken chest, a protruding belly, the bones on his back stuck out like fins. They made him run, and he was out of breath. Ramon and Maria tied him to a tree and told him that no one would come looking for him. "And the dragon will come and eat your hands."

They left him and turned around from time to time to thumb their noses at him. He was terrified of ants. What if the ants saw that he could not move and they attacked him in crazed mobs? When he was not tied, he would pick them up one by one as they left their burrow and would stick them in a big box until they dried up and formed a black cake. He saw the sun setting and made an effort to free himself – but he failed. He was afraid of everything: of the birds flying through the trees, of the groans coming from God knows where, of the swishing in the grass. The cold licked at his cheeks; the shadows began to climb up the tree trunks. He heard turtledoves but couldn't see them, and he burst out crying. "They are a witch's birds that will gouge out your eyes and eat them." At last Senyoreta Rosa, tired of looking for him everywhere, found him and took him by the hand, almost dragging him. "Be quiet, be quiet, be quiet; you're too old for this," she kept telling him.

The first time Ramon and Maria climbed up the trunk of the plane tree to jump from the garden wall to the open fields, they found two cans in the pile of garbage. They spent the afternoon kicking them about, and Jaume, unable to climb out, was fuming. When the two got tired of playing out in the fields, they tossed the cans over the wall. Right away Jaume picked up one that had a loose label with a very good picture of green peas, and he hid it under a bush. The next day he hid the other one. They were his. He caught a centipede and kept it in the pea can. In the other, a smaller can that had two tomatoes painted on its label, he stuck an orange and black ladybug that was clinging to his fingers, unwilling to fall in. "My pretty, my pretty," he kept telling it. He covered the can openings with stones. When he went back to look at them, he found that the caterpillar had escaped. The ladybug was shrunken, her wings folded. Ramon and Maria did not take long to discover his cans and went right away to the garbage pile to look for others. They caged crickets and lizards together; they mingled dragonflies with worms and beetles. Ramon covered the cans with a piece of paper full of holes fastened with a piece of string. The beetles' backs shone in different colors as they moved. Finally, they took the cans to their bedrooms. They each had two. Jaume, snug in bed in the dark, could hear the bugs stir under his bed, and he'd fall asleep happy. Ramon would get up at dawn, take all the cans in a basket he'd found in the laundry hut, hide them behind the stone benches, and run back to bed, before Senyoreta Rosa came to wake them up. On occasion he'd open the cans and make changes, keeping the prettier bugs for himself. The big dragonfly was Jaume's; one morning he realized it was gone. He kicked Ramon, who then beat him up. Maria, to make matters worse, pulled the paper from all the cans and tossed out the bugs. That night, with no noises under him, Jaume could not sleep. He would tell his grandmother what they had done to him, and she, as usual, would tell him, "Senyor Jaume, we'll have to teach this wicked Ramon a lesson."

And his grandmother would signal to Miquela to approach. "Look at this child's ears. Don't you think they are growing too big?"

Miquela, with the scarf she was knitting and the skein of yarn in her hand, would reply, "They are very thin."

He did not like that at all – but there were two things in his grand-mother's room that fascinated him: the huge vase, on the floor, at the foot of the window, with all those golden feathers with blue eyes in their ends. Grandmother knew he liked them and might tell him, "Senyor Jaume, if you want to touch the feathers, you may do so." He approached the vase slowly, placed one hand on each side, and moved them all the way up to the blue eyes. Then he turned to look at his grandmother; she would strike the arm of her chair with her fan and say, "Very well, Senyor Jaume – you may leave now." The other object of his fascination was the elephant. One day Grandma Teresa explained that its name was Bernat. It had a trunk curled upward and a translucent red stone on its forehead. It was quite large. What he liked best of all were its ears, which looked like two fans. At times, being very still before the elephant, when he thought that Grandma and Miquela could not see him, he felt his own ears to see if they were as big as Bernat's.

One day he found a longish slat of wood under a tree and placed it on the water. Crouching, he blew on it and saw it move away. He made it come back by poking it with a twig. Then he ran to the laundry hut, picked up a hammer and a box of nails, and went to the kitchen.

"Armanda, can you make a nail hole?"

Armanda was busy cleaning shrimp; she showed him one that was moving.

"You see? If I leave him in the sink, he'll get mad. Come back later."

He sat on the floor. After a while Armanda asked him what he wanted.

"Make me a hole in the wood to put a stick in it."

Armanda made the hole, careful not to go through the slat, sharpened the tip of a piece of kindling, stuck it in the hole, and tied a piece of fabric on top of it.

"There you are, and with a flag too."

Jaume went back to the pond, put in the slat, which tilted a bit, blew on it, and saw it glide. That afternoon Senyoreta Rosa was drawing pictures of the children for them to give to their father on his birthday. Jaume stood in front of his siblings, holding his ship as if as an offering.

The day after he found the forked branch, Ramon showed it to Maria; he paraded for a moment, holding it high. Soon Jaume, who had followed them, joined in. Maria went to the kitchen to get a knife, and Ramon, seated against a tree, started to sharpen the tips of the branch. Jaume was busy with his boat. Then he got bored and went to see what his siblings were doing. Maria pushed him toward the water and said, "Play by yourself, and don't bug us."

Standing, pouting, on the verge of tears, he watched Ramon peel the branch. His eyes were fixed on the knife blade, on the chips of gray bark falling to the ground, on the fresh and white wood. Maria yelled again, "Go away!"

But he was transfixed and barely heard her. His boat, unattended, was calmly turning on a sparkling dark surface. Suddenly Ramon got up, put the branch to Jaume's neck, and slowly made him step back.

"Throw him in the water!" Maria said. Ramon kept pushing him back, and Jaume was frightened; his fists were closed tight; his neck stiffened between the two prongs of the branch. At the edge of the pond Ramon removed the branch from Jaume's neck and went back to sharpening it. Jaume wiped his wet skin and, keeping his hand on his neck, turned around: his ship was stuck in the mud.

The doctor had said that Jaume should be outdoors as much as possible; his schooling could wait. Whenever Senyoreta Rosa instructed the older siblings, Jaume went to the gardens. He liked being there by himself. He always found new things: a flower he had never seen, a dead bee, the shiny path left by a snail's drool up a tree trunk. One day he went past the rusty aviary. Its door was hanging from a single hinge; some time ago Ramon and Maria had pulled the other hinges out in an attempt to lay the door flat on the ground. There was not a breath of wind. Farther out he saw a tree surrounded by little butterflies, part green and part white. He stood there, his arms hanging to his sides and his head pulled back. The butterflies chased each other; they moved in and out of the branches as if they were flowers that would not stay still. He went closer and lay on the ground; holding his breath, he observed the comings and goings of the butterflies, all identical, all equally big, crowding around those leaves they had been munching on when they were larvae. One would fly toward the sky, come down again to join the others, so mixed in with the rest that you could not tell which one it was that had escaped. The next day everything was different. There were a few left, but the huge cloud had fled. He had seen few things like that, but, when the weather was good, the gardens were full of surprises. On rainy days, if the grown-ups annoyed him, bored and with nothing to do, he would go to see his grandmother. He knocked on the door with the palm of his hand, and Miquela came to open it. His grandmother would look at him, and, seeing that he didn't dare enter, she'd say, "Come in, come in, Senyor Jaume – do not stand on ceremony."

Then Miquela brought a stool to the Senyora's chair, and he climbed on it. His feet did not touch the floor and felt heavy. He wore gaiters, fairly high ones, for ankle support. Ramon had told Jaume that he had to wear that kind of shoe because his bones were weak; without them his legs would bend. Senyoreta Rosa had taught him how to button them. It took him a while to learn to guide the buttons through the holes using that gadget with a hook on its tip; often the buttons slipped out, but Senyoreta Rosa insisted: "You are old enough. You must dress and put on your shoes all by yourself."

Bent over, his nose to the gaiter, the buttoning hook in his hand, his eyes filled with tears, he struggled to fit button after button to their corresponding holes, while Ramon and Maria came out of their bedrooms leaping and ran to breakfast, where they got dibs on the best pieces of toast. As he sat on the stool, his grandmother, without a word, looked at his ears. His growth was not good; he was runty, had a big head. He waited for his grandmother to tell him something, to ask Miquela for the wine glass.

"Will you please give the glass to Senyor Jaume?"

Miquela pulled it from the armoire with the soldiers holding gold sabers. One day his grandmother told him: "Senyor Jaume, your grandfather Salvador, who was my husband, was a great traveler, and he bought a set of wine glasses in Vienna. This is the last one; all the others have been broken."

Jaume was puzzled: he knew what a grandmother was but had never heard of a grandfather before. From that day on he held his wine glass without daring to tighten his fingers on it too hard, for fear of breaking it. Miquela filled his glass to the middle, and Grandma, to make him laugh, drank from the bottle.

"Senyor Jaume," she told him, "you must never drink this way; you come from a good family."

He took a sip and did not move. Without swallowing, his mouth full of the burning wine, he stared at the buttons of his grandmother's dress. If he could not control his urge to laugh, he would swallow the rough and fragrant wine; he rested for a moment and took another sip. His grandmother advised him, "Take small sips, Senyor Jaume, small sips."

One day, when he felt very sad, he climbed down from his stool, went to his grandmother, and snuggled by her skirt. His grandmother realized he was very sad and caressed his hair a few times; then she left her open hand on his head, without weight, leaned forward, and told him, "Your grandma loves you to pieces."

He felt a desire to insert his whole being inside his grandmother and to become a grandmother, a big fat one, and to be able to tell a small child like himself waiting at the door, "Come in, come in, Senyor Jaume."

Sometimes Miquela, without lifting her eyes from her knitting, would ask him, "Have you seen anything interesting out there these days?"

At first he was baffled but then would gather up his courage and answer, "I have seen many leaves and a crazy ladybug."

And he spoke of the dragon in the book. Whenever Ramon and Maria turned a page and that beast appeared, they struck it with their hands because it was evil and because, if they did not stun it from time to time, it would get out of the book whistling, its nostrils spewing fire, ready to whip their legs with its tail. If Jaume had finished his wine and no one said anything, he'd walk to the window, prop himself up with the cushion, and stick his nose on the glass to look at the rain. That room (his grandmother had told him) had three things that were his own: the wine glass, the stool, and the cushion by the window. If the glass was fogged up, since he was forbidden to wipe it with his hand, he'd go back to the stool. One day his grandmother had him drink two glasses of wine very fast, and he told her something he shouldn't have: that there was a tree that made white butterflies that flew ceaselessly, came in and out, paired off, danced for a while, and chased each other, laughing. He realized at once they didn't believe him.

Grandmother beckoned Miquela: "You see? The wine turns them red."

Miquela touched one of his ears. "And warm."

"Pour him another glass."

When he had drunk it, he held it up in the air for a while because he loved looking at it, but Miquela snapped it away without a word. He let his legs dangle, and, at one point when his grandmother turned around, he touched her skirt with the tips of his fingers: it felt soft.

"Why are you touching me, Senyor Jaume?"

He did not answer as he did not know what to say; he saw his grandmother like a great mountain crowned by her head that spoke through a red hole and said things that made him laugh as if they tickled him with the golden feathers from the vase. The day he explained that Ramon had stolen his dragonfly, his grandmother asked, "And what did the dragonfly say, Senyor Jaume?"

He was seized by such an urge to laugh that he covered his mouth with his hand, pressing hard, so they wouldn't notice. The first time the servant girls had bathed out in the open, after Armanda gave him dry clothes, he went to see his grandmother and told her all they had done and that Ramon and Maria had also asked Armanda to spray them. Grandmother was reading and looked at him over her glasses.

"And they showed their intimate parts?"

He thought about it for a while and then nodded. His grandmother, her hand loaded with rings, pulled him toward her skirt, and he felt that pleasant smell of grandmother and wine spreading out of the chair. "Don't you tell this to anybody, Senyor Jaume. Mum's the word!"

When he was by the door, on his way out, he heard his grandmother tell Miquela, "I think this child is seeing visions."

In autumn, when the leaves turned the color of fire, the children played at burying themselves. They lay down on the ground under the trees, threw handfuls of leaves on themselves, and waited for more to fall. Whenever they saw a leaf falling, they'd cry, "Come!" Maria said the leaf always fell on the one who called it best. They delighted in breathing that musky smell and picked the fungi off the trunks. Maria already knew that their world of shadows and branches would not last forever. Papa and Mama used to say: "When Maria is all grown up . . . When Maria marries . . ." She would have preferred for things not to change: the dollhouse, the music box, the ivy and the flowers . . . and Ramon. She had a vague sensation that she only wanted and would only want that – as if the stagnant water drowned all other desires. Jaume, if leaves did not fall fast enough, would fall asleep. Then the older two climbed onto the sycamore, and from the sycamore onto the wall, and from the wall they jumped out to the fields: happy, full of light. They came back clinging to the hanging ivy, sticking the tips of their feet in cavities of broken bricks. Under the trees everything was darker. The moss and the ferns with tiny snails behind their fanning leaves were a deep green. They went to the fields to kill lizards. Ramon made Jaume believe that he had to kill them because they were spies for dragons. One day Jaume saw them kill a little one at the foot of the aviary and did not stop whining until bedtime. Ramon threw pebbles at them and almost always made a hit. Once he had them stunned, he cut off their tails with a bit of wire. If Jaume awoke and found himself alone, he felt uneasy. He knew what they were doing to the lizards. He went to look at the water; his little boat, abandoned, on its side, was rotting.

Some days, rather than going to the gardens or to see his grandmother, he went to Maria's room: it reeked of stale cologne water and of the old cardboard of her dollhouse that was now quite broken down. On the sides of the dollhouse front door two rosebushes were painted climbing the walls. The façade opened out if you undid the small latch hidden under the roof; inside you saw the dining room. Its sideboard was full of shelves with lined-up cups, small as thimbles. On the table was a brass pitcher; Maria had put in it a few painted feathers from the Easter cake decorations because, when Papa bought the house, there was nothing in the pitcher. The bedroom had two beds with a boy in one and a girl in the other under sheets with an embroidered cover, gray with dust. Once Maria took the boy out of the bed and put him back in right away because he had no feet. By the staircase leading to the second floor stood the parents; it seemed they were returning from the theater and were going upstairs to see if the children were asleep; they stood with their backs to the front door, and their clothes were moth eaten. Jaume's grandmother, when he explained that the doll parents had holes in their clothes, exclaimed: "It's the moths' fault. A moth that harms a doll must be very wicked. I am surprised, Senyor Jaume, that the moths haven't eaten up the whole thing." Jaume would kneel with his hands together in front of the dollhouse. He'd been forbidden to touch anything, and, leaning forward, he sniffed. One day he could not control himself and turned the parents around to see their faces. The man had a mustache but was lacking an eye. The woman had a necklace down to her knees and, stuck on her hair, a diamond star. He thought he heard a noise, closed the house, and left. That night Senyoreta Rosa asked him: "Why did you turn the parents around?" He said he had not touched them. No one had seen him. He would never again open the dollhouse.

If Ramon and Maria sat on one of the benches under the wisteria, he'd join them at once. In the spring the wisteria opened its blossoms, and he listened to the humming of the bees around the flowers. As soon as they saw him, Ramon said to Maria: "The bore's here." Jaume watched them from a distance so as not to be shoved aside by them. Then the two looked upward as if they'd seen something, and he looked up too; he could not help himself, even though he knew Ramon would make a strange sound with his tongue and the two would laugh. Sparrows flew into the laurel and zoomed back out.

The kitchen girls were singing. Facing the bench where his siblings sat, Jaume was holding his ear in his hand. Ramon had tugged it very hard when he found out that Jaume had told Grandmother that he'd heard them on the roof, and Grandmother had told Miquela, and Miquela had told Senyoreta Rosa, who'd rushed to tell their parents. "The roof?" And Papa had said he'd teach them a lesson: "No dessert and to bed with the chickens." Jaume cowered in a corner more frightened than the other two. Then Papa paced for a while and added, "If you do it again, I'll tie you every night to the railing of your balcony." Jaume's ear was burning and hurt a lot. Petals were falling from the wisteria blossoms. Suddenly, while he was distracted looking at a bee sucking pollen, Maria came up behind him on tiptoe and poked him. Ramon and Maria, content, left him alone. He sat on the bench. It felt good under those quiet flowers falling next to him. The sun hit the terrace; even though it wasn't very hot, the girls had been showering out there for two days already.

He crouched behind the curtain. Mama was coming down the stairs buttoning her gloves. She always wore long gloves and, after buttoning and pulling them up tight, adjusted them back down in a couple of studied folds. Just as Papa did, once she had adjusted her gloves, she came down faster. Whenever there was someone down in the foyer, she took her time. The three of them were surprised because, instead of leaving right away, she went into the dining room. They pulled the curtain aside to see what she was doing: she was staring at herself in one of the ornate mirrors flanking the mantle. The mirrors, framed in gold, blurred her features – as if the reflected person were grimacing. Facing the mirror, Sofia realized her children were peeking at her. She left walking slowly, pretending she had not seen them. Jaume liked the buttons on his mother's dresses: the ones on her blouses, made from mother-of-pearl; the glass ones, round as balls – Mama complained they were useless because they slipped from the hole; the ones on her overcoats, some of which were gold and some silver, with such filigree that they seemed made of stiff lace; the bone ones that looked like the horn in the living room that was a vase for flowers. Buttons, lace, feathers . . . a soft and fragrant world. Maria wanted to be like Mama and wear dresses embroidered with stones. The very dresses that, as soon as Mama left, she ran to put on, while Papa, who was a late riser, sang in the bathroom.

Mama opened the front door. In the living room, seated in the red chair, Grandmother, fat and with sad eyes, drank wine. Nobody suspected they knew anything, but they knew everything. Miquela, like a frightened dove, always with her eyes wide open, always with her feet about to take off running, always pulling up her stockings. Miquela, with her gaze like lightning, her ear attentive to all that was said in Grandmother's room, with her hurriedness, her neat uniform and well-starched apron, and her headband held with hairpins. Maria had found a headband on the floor; she wore it pinned behind the tie of her tartan uniform. From time to time she ran a finger under her tie and felt for the pin to make sure she had not lost it. Miquela kept Grandmother company, that lady who had been so beautiful that all the gentlemen knelt at her feet. She never scolded them. She was not like Senyoreta Rosa, who got mad whenever they forgot their lesson.

Senyoreta Rosa, after dinner, would go upstairs and lock her door with a latch because the key had disappeared. Ramon had thrown the key into the well in order to spy on her as she applied talcum powder to her belly button, which developed rashes because it was very deep. Also in the well lay a silver bracelet with bells, from the time Maria was little. Jaume had thrown it in there, on the sly, one day when Maria had told him he was a revolting lizard.

As soon as Mama left, Jaume ran out from behind the curtain and did three more somersaults. They were alone and free to play. It was windy outside, and on windy days they played the thieves' game. Maria was a wealthy lady leaving church. Jaume pretended to be a beggar, and, when the lady stopped to give alms, he'd steal her purse with a jerk. Ramon was the policeman.

But that day Jaume did not feel like playing the thieves' game. "I'd rather go to the garden."

Ramon pushed him against the window. "Can't you see how windy it is?"

You could hear the whistling of the wind, the laurel branches rubbing against the wall. From time to time a leaf would go flying by like a bird. Jaume looked at Maria; she was very pretty. Everybody said so. One day she had a temperature, and her hands were boiling; the doctor looked at her as he took her pulse. Before leaving, he caressed her nose. "This girl is very pretty." Mama stood erect and looked at him the way she could look when speaking with a gentleman. "Really?" Ramon remembered the day the two of them had fallen in the water, holding hands, because they were playing at walking backward, and, as they fell, Ramon had tightened his hold on Maria so that she would fall too. The water felt cold; her dress had lifted, and the hem of her petticoat had stuck to her thigh: lattice and waves and flowers. The water surrounded them, thick, murky, without sky and without leaves, and they felt lost in the middle of that sea of jumping fish and slow-swimming whales with their backs above the bottomless sea, whales that spray with their two-nose blowholes, because there are whales that have many noses and swim with a harpoon stuck in the wall of fat that surrounds all they have inside, their guts and their liver and their heart, all that people have inside them but much bigger because the whale is the king of the sea, stronger than a frigate with all it carries of broken masts and torn sails and rotten wood; with all the whale has working inside, the juice of so many things that come and go, and the blood that is not quite blood and makes the heart beat and that, if you run too fast, bangs against the inside of your ribs, the red water bathing your liver and a pouch like the pouch for the clothespins that the servant girls fasten to their belts when they hang to dry the bedsheets they have washed with suds and soap. The water around Maria's thighs and the lace with lattice and flowers, all very delicate, and the two of them dirty with mud and Ramon still gripping her hand, don't be afraid, and a sticky spider fallen from a branch brushed their foreheads, and they hollered and slowly came out among the trees and went into the kitchen, and then one heard Armanda shrieking: what is all this mud? And he lifted her skirt and again the flowers, the waves, her skin blazing, terse and dirty.

While Ramon was looking at the light with his nose stuck to the window, Maria came down the stairs pretending to be putting on her gloves. Armanda came into the dining room. "Acting silly again?"

And Jaume said, "If Mama finds out we are playing in the dining room, she will punish us."

How would Mama learn about this if he didn't snitch? After Armanda left, Jaume insisted that he wanted to go outside to play with pieces of wood, and to shut him up Ramon hit him in the head with a fist and to scare him told him he would ask the gatekeeper to lock him up with the rats.

"There are no rats."

Marta, one of the maids who served in the house, had told them that her fiancé had been thrown in jail and had explained how he was surrounded by rats trying to bite him. But Senyoreta Rosa, always mingling in other people's affairs, said there were no rats in jail. Maria went to Ramon and passed him a needle: "Prick him in the neck!" Jaume, like his father, was revolted by blood. Ramon and Maria played at bleeding; they pricked each other's fingers on purpose, and blood appeared on their skin, red, round, shiny. Without a word he went to the door and looked at them slyly and then burst into tears yelling that they were trying to hurt him.

Senyoreta Rosa, materializing from nowhere, said: "Shame on you! Poor Jaume!"

Clinging to her skirts, he said that one afternoon they'd slipped live ants down his back, and Maria pulled his hair, and Senyoreta Rosa said shame again, that she'd have a word with their papa, and Maria replied that she couldn't care less because Papa would believe only what she told him. Then Jaume, his eyes popping out of his head, yelled: "Adopted! Adopted!"

Senyoreta Rosa got upset and ordered him never again to use that word. "Where did you learn that?"

She took Jaume in her arms, and he told her that Maria was not theirs, that she came from another family. At that moment their mother, who had forgotten some samples, came back in, and Maria ran to her. "Mama! Mama!"

Sofia asked what was causing such a stir.

"They are nervous, Senyora – must be the wind."

Jaume kept quiet: his mother the princess was there. He was no longer afraid.

He heard them laughing on the roof. The balcony was open, and the moon was out. The heat had awakened him. That afternoon they had played well: they had taken shoes out of Mama's closet and tried them on. The ones he had tried changed color: they could be gold, and they could be purple. Maria had worn the ones with diamonds. Ramon's were boots that reached to his knees and had patent leather toes and heels. The three of them strutted around the room for a while. Suddenly Jaume realized he was alone. He went into the playroom to look at his top. You wound it with a key stuck on its side, and, as the top spun madly, the key unwound slowly. There were red, yellow, and blue bands on the top; as soon as the winding mechanism stopped, the toy would waver until it fell on one side, dead: it smelled like a faucet. When the top came to a stop under the couch, he went to see his grandmother, but Senyoreta Rosa, coming out of the room, told him she was asleep. She tried to explain to him that they had given Grandmother a shot. As he didn't know what to do, he went to bed without saying goodnight to anybody. He felt uncomfortable there. A mosquito had snuck inside the netting, and, listening to its buzzing, he heard laughter on the roof. Trying to climb down from bed, he got entangled in the sheets. The mosquito was silent; it must have been getting ready to sting him. The moonlight had vanished. A bolt of lightning crossed the sky from top to bottom like a whiplash. Finally, he lifted the netting with his feet and jumped to the floor. When he arrived in the corridor, a thunderclap made him shrug his head between his shoulders.

Groping his way in the dark, he went upstairs. He was glad for the lightning; he stopped and covered his ears with his hands in case more thunder came, and he thought: "They are up there, and they're laughing." He kept climbing the spiral staircase; the steps were wide on one side and ended in a point on the other. He was holding the banister tight. Through the wall openings came a dead clarity and the smell of night; the door to the roof was wide open, and he peered down. He didn't dare climb down the iron ladder. The moon, round as an orange, stood amid a sea of black clouds. He saw the two shadows and the rope tied from one chimney to another. They lay on their backs with their feet against a lace-like iron cornice. He felt a great desire to join them, but the ladder made him uneasy: it was straight and with a simple iron bar as a guard. He shouted, "What are you doing?" and they did not answer. He turned back, worried that he'd find the mosquito still flying inside his netting. He went to the balcony, and another stroke of lightning forced him to close his eyes. A fat drop fell on his forehead, and he went inside. He soon heard the sound of rain on the laurel leaves.

The next day they told him they had spent the night on the roof to see daybreak. "And now, go and tell!" He walked to the trees and heard their steps behind him. A fine rain was falling; water dripped from the leaves, and the cooing of the turtledoves soothed him. He was thinking: "They have seen daybreak from the roof, but I saw butterflies, and they didn't." When he woke up, he ran to tell his grandmother, who was having her breakfast.

Grandmother had replied: "You astound me, Senyor Jaume. Roofs are made for people to be under them. You better never go up there!"

He shook his head, and then Grandmother said to Miquela, "Show Senyor Jaume the cardinal."

Miquela opened a small cabinet and took out a tree branch with a red bird on it.

"I am keeping it for you, for when you grow up. This bird had been alive and now is dead. Touch it, touch it, Senyor Jaume."

He didn't dare; looking was one thing, touching another. He asked his grandmother if Ramon and Maria had seen it.

"They have not seen it, and they'll never see it!"

He looked at her with slanted eyes and laughed.

Now, when he got to the place with the turtledoves, he raised his head, but, as usual, he only heard their cooing. Ramon and Maria must have been following him on tiptoe. He was dying of fear but did not want to turn around. He walked slowly, his hands pressing against his thigh, barely daring to breathe. He'd forgotten to tell his grandmother that they had played at wearing Mother's shoes. He would go and tell her before Senyoreta Rosa sent him to bed. He would also tell her he'd been followed under the trees, to be hurt.

Ramon got next to Jaume and, without looking at him, asked: "Did you go and tell that we were on the roof last night, you snitch? You didn't waste any time, did you?"

And he struck him in the middle of the chest with a fist like a rock. Jaume took off running toward the water, but Ramon had longer legs and caught up at once. He had picked up the forked branch from the ground and pressed it to Jaume's neck.

"Don't move!"

Jaume bumped against a tree trunk. "Stop, you're hurting me!"

Maria caressed his cheek, like his mama did, and said, "Poor little wimp." Her hand felt sweet, and her eyes shone like the tiny stars falling from the leaves.

Ramon yelled, "Now!"

Maria held the needle with her fingers. Feeling the prick on his neck, he looked at her like one who did not understand and started sobbing with his mouth open. His hands felt tense; he looked at them. He tried to move the fork away from his neck, but Ramon pushed him. He fell to the ground; none of them moved for a little while.

"Adopted . . ."

Suddenly the woods lit up. A small and round orange sun ricocheted among the trees and the leaves that had turned red. He had time to recall looking at his hands against the light and seeing the outline of his bones surrounded by pink flesh. The fork had taken him to the water's edge. He was in the water, lying on his back, as the leaves on the branches became smaller and everything seemed very far away. He made an effort to move but simply turned around half-prone and felt a great pain in the back of his head and felt very, very cold.

18. A TURTLEDOVE AT THE WINDOW

The first thing Teresa Valldaura saw when she opened her eyes was a turtledove on her windowsill. Smaller than a pigeon, with coffee-and-cream colored plumage and a black collar in the middle of its neck. How cheeky. A sudden anguish tightened her chest. The day Valldaura died a turtledove had been cooing on her window. She knew it was a turtledove because Sofia had said: "Look, Mama, a turtledove. And they're so wild." Teresa had not thought of that again. The turtledove, before flying off, let out a laugh. Teresa rubbed her eyes, covered her mouth with one hand to drown a yawn, and, last of all, touched her knees: wooden. As she neared her great voyage, she felt like setting fire to everything: all she had loved, furniture, trees, house. All to die in flames. Purified. No more memories! And, in the center of it all, she, blended with the eggplant and the rabbit of the still life. She thought the colors had become darker. Or was she losing her sight?

The door flew open, and Sofia, still holding the knob, asked if she'd seen Jaume. Teresa had to think about it.

"This morning, I think. He muttered something about butterflies and some worms with a lantern. Can you tell me where Miquela could be?"

Sofia closed the door without answering.

Behind the glass, in the same spot where the turtledove had laughed right before taking off in flight, she saw Maria's face, white and sad like an apparition. Those deep eyes, with their still pupils in the center of the dark water of their lakes. She leaned forward to call her, but Maria disappeared slowly, walking backward. Uneasiness seized her again: for having to sit, for being unable to move about, for having to muffle her heart wound up with emotion. She felt thirsty but was too far from the table and could not reach the bell. She jolted along, and her chair advanced a little; she heard a groan from one of the legs and was afraid it would crack. Her malaise increased. Why did she refuse to be put in a wheelchair? She would be free to go wherever she wanted: to the table, to the window, to the door to shove it open. Armanda had gone out to buy sweets. Miquela, what was she doing? She heard voices in the foyer but did not dare to call and thought she heard the turtledove laughing in the branches, brownish, with the dark line on her neck, elegant, tender.

She felt like taking flight, like running toward any danger and looking it in the face. As if Maria's face behind the glass had been the face of a dead Maria who'd come to make her follow to the land of shadows. She was suffocating. She opened her mouth a couple of times with her head back. Better not to think of anything. Not to think had been her salvation – or just to think idiocies. She made an effort. What a pearl-colored sky for an end of the day! She recalled the pearl on the silk of her lover's tie that had been the pearl on her husband's tiepin, and she recalled the white cherry blossoms by the balcony in the villa where she and Amadeu used to meet to make mad love as if the world were to end in glorious evenings with red sunsets and black clouds. Why did they have to love each other so much, and why did they have to lose each other, and why did the years have to drag on so, and why had everything taken the color of a fulsome life that was not quite hers? There were more white blossoms in her youth. A vase with white lilacs. Where? Lord, tell me where the vase of white lilacs was! Were there indeed white lilacs? Or are they flowers her memory has invented to torment her? She would ask Armanda as soon as she'd come in. "Is there such a flower as a white lilac, or have I dreamed it?" Armanda would stop in her tracks to look at her and would answer yes, or no, there were no white lilacs. And if they existed she would say: "For God's sake, Senyora Teresa, don't you know there is a bush of them at the foot of the fence next to the purple ones?" Thinking of Armanda's reply, she remembered, yes, there were white lilacs, and, when they were in full bloom, she, with one of the servants, went to pick them and filled a basket with branches and perfume. To die for.

She found herself, not having heard her come in, next to Senyoreta Rosa, her eyes deep within a pair of dramatic eyeglasses.

"If you please, Senyora Valldaura, do you know Doctor Falguera's address? The children must have hidden the phonebook away, and no one can remember where he lives."

Armanda and Miquela sat Senyora Valldaura on the wheelchair and pushed her to the library, where Jaume, amid the flames of candles, seemed asleep. Next to her dead grandchild she did not know what to do, as if none of that were real and a gesture, the slightest, would bring to life something that was better not to know. She asked to be taken closer and placed a hand on the child's bulging and cold forehead. She would never again see him come into her room with those huge boots of his and his frightened face. "Drink, drink, Senyor Jaume." She drowned a sob. On her fingertips she held the ice of death. Her hand slid off, and Armanda picked it up and put it on her lap.

"Can't I touch him again? He's my grandchild."

Miquela started to pray. Senyora Valldaura asked Armanda to bring a feather from her vase: "The tallest one." Armanda handed it to her, and she, before returning it, observed it for a while: iridescent, with a strong, mysterious blue eye on its tip.

"Here, Senyor Jaume. Show it to the angels."

Armanda placed the feather in the coffin, near the body of the dead child. She crossed his forehead.

"Water has killed him. But, Senyora Teresa, may God forgive my evil thoughts. Maybe I shouldn't say anything. Poor little one: he was a creature with no defenses."

She pulled down the white silk handkerchief on Jaume's neck, and Teresa could see a dark mark cutting his skin – a purple collar like the black collar on the turtledove.

"When the doctor looked at him, this mark wasn't showing." Armanda ran a finger over the dark line. "Water doesn't do this, Senyora Teresa."

Part Two

Leave, O leave me to my sorrows!
William Blake

At the foot of the gate, before opening his umbrella, he ran a finger over the pearl on his tie: it had been a while since he last wore it, but that day he had to put it on. The marble of the threshold was soiled with mud; somehow, if you saw footprints on it, the whole house looked poorer. He took a few deep breaths, pulling in his belly as he inhaled and letting it out slowly as he expelled the air. Oxygen. He stepped onto the street with an open umbrella. The night before had seen a lot of rain, but since midday today there was but a sprinkle, and a bit of a breeze pricked his cheeks and his sad double chin. As he walked, he tried not to lift his feet too much so as not to splash the bottoms of his new trousers. From time to time a drop would fall from a balcony – plop – onto his umbrella. Its handle ended in a perfect curve and was capped by a golden acorn that often popped off. Not knowing anyone who could fix it, and embarrassed to make inquiries, each time he hung the umbrella from his forearm he'd feel to make sure the acorn was in place. Oxygen renews the blood; it is odorless, tasteless. With age it is difficult to renew one's cells. In life everything, little by little, crumbles away. Plop! The raindrop again. He remembered that Constància, his dead wife, when they were young and went out at night, would say that lights, on rainy days, shone on the ground with more color than in the street lamps. Poor dear. He was sure that she never even suspected that he and Teresa . . . The cherry branches are still in bloom, Teresa Goday de Valldaura. The day he met her he thought a fresh wave had just entered his life. She had stopped for a second at the door of his office, pulling at her skirt, a blonde and white-skinned woman, with an exuberant bust, a wide brim hat atop the castle of her mane. Perfumed. Exquisite beyond all explanation.

"I'm Teresa Valldaura. You might remember me – we met when my husband purchased the villa."

Attorney Riera shook his head, not taking his eyes off her, fascinated.

"You meet so many people, of course. But I do remember you and would have recognized you out of a thousand. Once, with my husband and some friends, we went to see *La Traviata*, and during the inter-mission my friend said: "Look: Attorney Riera." From then on . . . You were with a stunning lady; Eulàlia told me her name was Marina. From then on . . . You had . . . No, of course not. I did not meet you when we closed on the villa, but that night at the Liceu . . . after so long . . ."

She stopped talking and looked distractedly at the piles of papers on his desk and the pitcher with a budding red rose. Constància had been nursing a cold for a couple of days, and the scent of elder blossoms pervaded the whole apartment. Aware of the smell, Attorney Riera felt embarrassed that, of all afternoons . . .

"Long after the night at the Liceu, coming out of an exhibition, my husband introduced us." Teresa raised a finger. "Your wife accompanied you, yes, yes; she wore a blue-gray dress and earrings with diamonds and aquamarines. You surely remember that. You don't? I remember it as if it had happened just now because you had, oh, excuse me, you have such a romantic head. Not many people would say that. Oh! I do not mean to say that an attorney could not have nice hair. Well, you know what I mean. And, if you do not remember me, still you must know who I am."

Attorney Riera asked her to please sit down, and he also sat down because, even though he used to receive his clients sitting down to impress them, pretending to be reading, no sooner had he seen Teresa than he had rushed to his feet and moved to greet her.

Teresa had taken a small handkerchief out of her purse after digging for a bit, and she stood with her handkerchief in her hand as if she did not know where it had come from or what she was supposed to do with it as she looked at the important attorney, with his round eyes and half-open mouth, expecting him, the important attorney, to guess why she'd come to see him.

At last she muttered, "I'm so embarrassed!" She started talking about a country estate her husband was reluctantly thinking of selling to a pestering friend. "I came here to entreat you because I am sure my husband will seek your advice on the price to charge for the possession." She knew that, besides being her husband's attorney, Riera was his trusted advisor. "I mean, if he comes to consult you, please advise him not to sell it. It would be very foolish to let go of the country house. My husband can be rather weak." She lowered her eyes and brought the handkerchief to her lips. Then she raised her head vivaciously. "The gentleman who is interested in the estate is a close friend. As a matter of fact, he is the brother-in-law of my friend at the Liceu who told me: 'Look: Attorney Riera.' You might know him: Joaquim Bergadà."

Attorney Riera flashed a benevolent smile. "I do know him."

Teresa sighed and, leaning forward a bit, ran a finger along the edge of the desk. She moved her hand away and then touched the desk again.

"I am no good at giving orders or asking for favors – I always give in and end up doing whatever my husband tells me to do. But, even if I dared tell him 'Do not sell the house,' he would pay me no heed. And I would feel so bad." She looked Attorney Riera in the eye. "I need a powerful ally, and I thought this ally could be you." Then she inquired, as if with a great effort, "Would it be very hard for you to help me?"

The office filled with silence. Teresa Valldaura kept her handkerchief in her brocade purse, the one with a silver handle, and remained silent, expectant. She heard a door slam at the other end of the apartment. Attorney Riera slicked his hair back a couple of times, and before he got up, putting away some papers, said, "I can promise you nothing."

He showed her to the door. On the landing Teresa gathered her skirt and, before descending the first step, turned around and smiled her angelic smile. Going down the stairs, she thought: "He did not kiss my hand, either when I arrived or when I left. What a fool!"

Thus, Salvador Valldaura did not sell the Vilafranca house to Quim because Attorney Riera, a man with a head on his shoulders and very trustworthy, advised him to think twice about it because the country house would only grow in value and it better be him and not another who should benefit from that. And the important and famous attorney and the milk-and-silk lady . . . well . . . someone figured out that for years they met and pretended they loved each other, or really did love each other, because these are things that God only knows.

He crossed the street and went to the streetcar stop. He had refused to take the car. This visit would be his secret. They were old. The years had taken away that ephemeral force that makes a man and a woman fall for some nonexistent grace. He could not say there'd been a falling-out. They would always be friends, even if years went by before they saw each other again. The proof. Teresa had written him asking him to please come: she had to talk to him. And he came. And he wore the pearl. There was a thin, continuous rain. With indifferent eyes he observed the sign on a café, the ad for a pharmacy. Shiny cobblestones, gleaming automobiles. Raindrops dangling everywhere, playing at falling or not falling. Everything shone in a tender gray – a kind of sadness attenuated by the clean smell of the air and by an expanding clearing in the clouds. The sparrows motionless on the trees. He used to leave bread crumbs for them on the railing of the terrace. Age made him pay attention to little things, and on boring days he thought of himself as one of those English ladies, happy with the company of a cat or with a cup of tea nearby, writing a letter to the editor to announce that the first lily in the garden had bloomed or that the first bird had sung on their eaves.

He had dreamed of a different life, very different from the one he had lived, very different from that of his father, a life designed by his will rather than by circumstances, always thinking that he would be have time to rectify it but ultimately with not much desire to rectify anything. He had seen so many vile people, so much misery, so much, that he now delighted in casting crumbs to the sparrows, which soiled his railing and flew away when they saw him move. A man is a mysterious thing – a machine put together in a way you never quite understand. Doctors and men of science say it's this or it's that, and they always fall short – the very humors, the very twisty paths inside one – but each man, with his soul, just as . . . However hard he tried to explain this to himself, he felt he understood nothing. The principle of solitude, he reflected, is this great originality of each person to work his own machine. Yes, all men are the same in unfathomably different ways. He had made love to Teresa for years: an infinite repetition of the same gestures and the same words. Just like the coal dealer or the grocer or the prime minister. The same gesture but each with an accent distinct from the others. Had Teresa been a font of life for him? Perhaps she had been but a pretext to persevere in that world that was slowly corroding him, the world discharging those droplets of rain on the silk of this old attorney's umbrella. He hadn't tired of Teresa. The proof was that he was now going to see her with a fast-beating heart and that nothing in the world would have kept him from going.

He was tired of himself, of each one of his automatic reactions. As if he had been seized and forced to sit in his chair behind his desk and forced to strike the wood with the palm of his hand, one, two, three, four times, a hundred times, two hundred times . . . "Enough," he would yell, even though the pleasure of hitting the wood with his flat hand may be the most intense in the whole world. And all of a sudden, as the streetcar stopped in front of him, something burst inside and filled his mouth with the useless sweetness of old kisses and tender lips. He folded his umbrella and climbed in. His eyes, tired of preparing wills and deeds, saw the houses go by, the shop windows, the street lamps, all diffused by the streaming droplets. A bit empty, a bit dreamy, he was led, amid indifferent folk, sickened by the stench of varnish, he who had had a romantic head and a youth full of fire.

Before handing the umbrella to the maid, he picked off the gold acorn and slipped it in his pocket. He cast a glance at the foyer, which he'd seen so many times, at the colored windows, thin and tall, at the large stone bowl overflowing with alabaster fruit. Time had not damaged the august mansion surrounded by ancient trees, crowned with chimneys, with tiled roofs and towers, as welcoming as Teresa. Teresa, there, sat against the light, with a halo of gray radiance, motionless, as if listening to the rain. They were facing each other, with no regrets, with a kind of throttled joy. My God, so much suffering: why? Life was there, creased with wrinkles, her hands shaking slightly, still loaded with diamonds, her eyes full of smartness and patience. "Sit down." They were alien and acquainted; their words of love from old times were nicks of shrapnel on a tired rampart. "Sit down." Teresa's voice had not changed. Attorney Riera took her hand in his.

"No. So much water, so much, under the bridge. I asked you to come because I want to prepare my will."

Someone made a noise behind the half-open door. Riera raised his head. "It's nothing. My attendant is given to spying. You know how it is."

Teresa rang the bell and had wine and pastries served. They ate and drank.

"More?"

"Won't it disagree with you?"

Teresa was no longer hiding the bottle under her shawl, as she'd done when little Jaume was alive.

"Disagree? Can't you see this is but sugar and the warmth of the sun?"

She had the wine decanted into a small crystal and silver carafe. Crystal and silver, just like the vase with the red rose that Attorney Riera unfailingly had on his desk. They met in all the churches for early mass, all except Santa Maria del Mar. "You don't think I pray? Well, I do," he had said offering her holy water. One morning Teresa had been late, and he hid behind a confessional because he thought an old woman was staring at him. Teresa burst in. All in gray. He saw her go to the holy water basin, and, instead of wetting her fingers, she caressed its edge over and over. What must she have been thinking?

"I asked you to come because I want to prepare my will. I want this house to go to the little girl, to Maria. If I do not take care of her, no one will. Maria," Teresa went on, "does not love me. But I love her. Just see how she looks at my hands with such a load of revulsion. I don't care."

Attorney Riera reminded Teresa that she had a son – that, like Eladi, she had had a youthful slip.

"You could leave him the money from Rovira's houses."

"Money has always slipped from my hands."

"Think that your son has your blood."

And Teresa, like the girl she used to be, replied, "What do I care of my blood or of anybody's blood?"

They laughed. About themselves, about what people knew of them, and about what they did not know, which, instead of pulling them apart, united them.

"Thursday next you may come to sign it."

Teresa picked up her fan, and, as she gazed at the green apple leaves, she told him she would not be able to go that Thursday or any other day because she had no legs. He did not quite understand it, and she had to explain that her legs were dead, that she'd been unable to leave her house for years now, that he should bring the will ready for her to sign and for the witnesses to sign. It would be best for him to come Friday rather than Thursday because Thursday was Senyoreta Rosa's free day, and she would like her to be around. Before he left, Attorney Riera asked what had happened to her legs. Teresa took a while to answer. She had had a friend, she said at last, and, when he began to neglect her, her sorrow had been so violent that the nerves in her legs had died.

"It's terminal."

They looked at each other as shipwrecks would; he took her hand to kiss it, and she hit him with her fan.

"Don't bother."

He walked out, inebriated with the old times. It was the time of the shrieking peacocks, the time for love with Teresa. The time for infinite gratitude. Attorney Riera looked at the sky. The clouds, receding, had become a field of fire toward the west. With his umbrella hanging from his forearm, he crossed the street and stopped by the opposite wall to look at the house. He could smell the moist earth, the drenched leaves, the rain that had just ended. An ivy branch rubbed the side of his forehead. He caressed those leaves with an unconscious gesture and found a bunch of berries in his hand. He knew that at the end of the park, by the water, there was more ivy like that ivy, and he knew it was just as shiny. From the white of cherry blossoms to the black of ivy. From the whiteness of the skin to the blackness of the eyes. Big, intelligent eyes, their pupils fixed and expectant at the time of love, dilated after love. Everything took on a new meaning, provoked new sensations, different intensities. Teresa's fingernails, pink and tender, were all made of fury in moments of passion. Teresa's teeth, snowy as they were, left dark marks on his back. A mysterious transformation that drove him crazy and each time filled him with new sensations, with a fuller life. Why did he tire of feeling the way he did at the time of loving Teresa? Had he been, with Teresa, the man he would have liked to become but whom he had never dared to be, or had he just been the famous and respectable attorney? The face of love had become a tired face – each wrinkle, how much effort, how much time, to place it in its corresponding spot. How much blood turning round and round, how many burning rivers under the skin that was growing loose. An old desire burst in the center of his heart, gave him strength, made him feel powerful like the red glow of sunset, like pensive ivy atop a wall. But it was all a sham, all under the earth of the past. Teresa's lips, Teresa's mouth, her enigmatic smile and her happy smile. The most shattering smile in the world. Teresa's lips, open and giving at the time of the kiss of love, and her lips, slightly ironic, slightly maternal at the time of the friendly kiss. Teresa's voice, a murmuring of quiet water, and Teresa's love grunts, a waterfall of emotions. Teresa's hands, with an always unexpected caress. Their bodies together, her hand open against his cheek, her eyes on his eyes, and her inviting mouth. Teresa's tongue, warm, wise; her saliva like honeycombs. Teresa's breasts, naive, magnificent, loosened, like all the magnolias. A gust of wind shook water drops off the ivy. Slowly, the first stars came with a misted slice of moon over the waves. Why should he be dreaming dreams? As he stood under the ivy, the glorious years of his love came back to him. He could not get himself to leave. The cherry tree is still in bloom, Teresa Goday de Valldaura. All the joy we've lost becomes present at the end of a rainy day, just like that. The heaven and hell of consciousness wage war against each other. Invisible, the angel and the devil (which one is more beautiful?) are attempting to annihilate each other. They are both victorious – now the one, now the other. Triumphant or defeated, they take each other's measure and retreat, perhaps for an instant, perhaps for years, until they stand up again and, hitting with their wings, wage a battle they cannot decide whether of love or of hatred, and they paralyze an old attorney under some ivy branches.

A car stopped in front of the gate. Attorney Riera had not heard it come. Even though he was hidden in the dark, he pressed himself harder against the wall. The chauffeur stepped out of the car, went around it, went into the garden, and opened the two halves of the iron gate. He climbed back in the car. You could see two shadows inside. Eladi and Sofia? Slowly, the car took the chestnut tree alley and disappeared quietly into the darkness. After a while he saw the gate close slowly. He heard distant voices. Two of the balconies in the house had become lit. And he was still there, submerged in a nonexistent world. The Valldaura villa, with Teresa in it, Teresa who was not Teresa but who had been for a good while his center of gravity.

3. THE PIANO TEACHER

He would have to speak to Senyora Valldaura. He was not one to put up with the antics of Ramon and Maria, not one more day. Granados had been one of his schoolmates. He was a friend of Granados. If it hadn't been for the accident that left him with a deformed foot and a shorter leg, he would have been a great concert artist. With his physique he would captivate the most demanding audiences, particularly the young ladies. He was tall, broad shouldered; his hair was jet-black, his eyes myopic. And he had that which money cannot buy: the gift. And the personality. Before leaving home he had slipped the most affectionate letter from Granados into the inside pocket of his coat along with two newspaper clippings. One spoke of Granados's tragic death when he was returning to Spain aboard the HMS *Sussex*, which a German submarine had torpedoed. "Senyora Valldaura," he would say, "Granados was my friend, and, to save his wife, he threw himself overboard, and the two of them drowned." Then he would show her the letter, so she could see he was no ordinary piano hacker and that the jokes of those children should be nipped in the bud. Whenever he felt depressed, he thought of the afternoons spent near that brilliant man. Perhaps Ramon and Maria would have respected him. "He was a man, Senyora Valldaura, who would wonder at each little thing, as if at every moment he were discovering the world." He was not too fond of Granados's music. He adored Marcello, Corelli, Bach. And Mozart, because of his grace and melancholy. No. There were some things that just should not be done to him.

He was sure that if he brought this up with Senyora Valldaura, such an understanding lady, she would listen. She would insist with Senyora Sofia, and Senyora Sofia would talk to her children, who were disobedient and growing up with the devil inside them. He had many students – rich and not so rich – and they respected him. Talented, studious children. Whenever he took on a disciple who was too young, whose hand could not reach an octave, he felt soft and took his tutoring even more seriously. A man as kind as he, a man such as he, as patient as Job, a man who walked the way he walked, who was unable to run. The other newspaper clipping, the one he would show Senyora Valldaura first, he had gotten from his sister. It was the portrait of an artist, Lady Godiva, who was the spitting image of Maria. That artist, like so many others, had died in a poorhouse after having been the queen of the theater district for years. "Don't you lose it," Angeleta had told him. "I love it, because the face of this artist is the exact face of the Madonna." A true saint, his sister, quiet and sweet; no man ever went after her because she was a chosen soul, nearer heaven than earth. Like himself. If he had ever been in love, it had been a platonic love: a smile, an affectionate gaze, an expressive handshake, that was all he had needed to fill his heart with joy.

He led a simple life and ate frugally: a soft-boiled egg for supper and a glass of warm milk with a bit of lemon rind in it. He managed to make his suits last for years, but he was always clean and tidy. He allowed himself only one luxury: his bedsheets. He needed to sleep between sheets that were changed frequently and smelled of apples. Neither too new nor too old, soft, caressing. They had to have embroidered hems adorned with ample lace. He once mentioned his indulgence to Senyora Valldaura, and on his saint's day she offered him two sets of linen sheets. He was most thankful for the gift, but his sister remarked that the family probably got them cheap at Senyor Farriols's store, which purchased them wholesale. From that day on he eagerly awaited his saint's day – his name was Joan – because his sister made his bed with those sheets, fresh as a mountain stream. He felt a great affection for Senyora Valldaura, who, like Granados, emanated a kind of warm grace that filled his soul with waves of peace, with the naive and melancholy joy of Mozart's music. Often, whenever Ramon and Maria took their time to come down or were out prancing in the park, which they did intentionally because they hated piano, the maid asked him to wait in Senyora Valldaura's room. He had come close, several times, to speaking to her about his dreams as an artist, but he'd never dared. Some inexplicable shyness kept his confidences in check. But no more of that. He would show her the newspaper clipping and the letter. He was sure she would empathize and that she'd tell him with her velvet voice, looking at him with those eyes of hers filled with the water of dreams, those eyes that in her youth must have done great damage, "It was a great loss." He remembered Senyor Valldaura with veneration, and Senyora Valldaura knew it. He'd met him at the Vilalta's. He always spoke about music – and he had no way to imagine, even remotely, that one day he'd be his grandchildren's teacher – about Vienna, about that Beethoven concerto that Senyor Valldaura confessed he could not hear without feeling a lump in his throat.

On Fridays Senyora Valldaura had her pedicure, a visit that coincided with one of his lessons. Even with the podiatrist present, if the children were late, she asked him in, and, as the maid took off her shoes, he went to the window and looked out to the garden. Poor Senyora. He had an impaired foot, but he was better off than one who had to spend the whole day sitting, unable to earn a living. At night, taking off his shoes, he hid the one with the monstrously thick sole under the bed.

"For quite some time" – they sat before each other, she facing the window, he with his back to it – "your grandchildren have been giving me as much trouble as they can. Please understand. Maria is a talented girl, a fine ear, nimble fingers. But she does not practice. The same goes for Ramon. If you knew how hard it is for me to bring this up to you. Many times, during my lesson with Maria, I've been startled by a blare right in my ear – and it is Ramon tooting his toy trumpet. The first time really shook me. Horrible. And neither of them laugh. They do it in cold blood."

Teresa Valldaura brought her fan to her mouth and then unfolded it and folded it back a couple of times.

"I am truly sorry. We will have to do something about it. But you, Senyor Rodés, you must discipline them. Put some fear in them with a bit of yelling."

"Senyora Valldaura, for the love of God, how can a cripple like me," and he unconsciously stretched his short leg ending in his deformed foot, "earn the respect of those two children, who look like archangels?" He had gotten the most difficult part out already and went on, "I'd like to show you something special." He pulled out the newspaper clipping of Lady Godiva and gave it to Senyora Valldaura. "Look at this face, if you please."

She took the picture and examined it for a while.

"Look at those eyes, the nostrils, the line of those lips. Those lips are Maria's lips; she is the creature with the most charming mouth in the whole world. As I am a bit myopic, I thought at first it was a picture of Maria; she might have been at a costume ball. But a girl from a good family would have never climbed on a man dressed as a horse."

He was about to take back the clipping, but Senyora Teresa stopped his hand with a quick gesture.

"Senyor Rodés, you must realize that pictures can lie."

"Sure. But that girl is Maria's double. Look at the hand on the thigh. Look at those long, thin fingers with square nails."

Teresa Valldaura put the picture face down on her lap and covered it with her hand. "There is some likeness but quite slight."

Senyor Rodés was becoming impatient, so he pressed on: "Changing the topic, had I ever told you that as a young man I'd been a friend of Granados? That if it hadn't been for the streetcar accident I would have been a remarkable concert artist? Granados and I were very close friends; he confided his dreams in me, and whenever he had famous people in his home he introduced me as a great promise. He exaggerated, of course. When I met your husband, may he rest in peace . . ."

And he mentioned the Beethoven concerto and a performance at the Konzerthaus and explained that Senyor Valldaura carried a program from the Konzerthaus, old and yellowing, in his briefcase.

"Many times, to hear the concerto with his eyes closed, Senyor Valldaura went all alone to the Palau." He thought Senyora Valldaura was not listening. "Beside the trumpet episodes . . . I don't want to pester you, but it's a bit much. One day two of the keys weren't working. Do you know why? They had tied up the hammers."

The chambermaid came in and announced that Senyoret Ramon and Senyoreta Maria awaited Senyor Rodés in the music room. He'd run out of time to show the *Sussex* wreck or Granados's letter beginning "My esteemed friend." He left the room with the maid and forever carried a grudge against Senyora Valldaura for having kept the newspaper clipping with the picture of Lady Godiva. From the corner of his eye, he saw her sneaking it into the album she always kept on her table.

4. ELADI WITH A CHAMBERMAID

At the moment of lowering the door knocker, he realized there was a couple next to him. He smiled at them. They did not seem to be much in the mood for love. Senyora Filo opened the door as if she'd been right behind it. She looked at Eladi, and she looked at the gentleman and the lady. She took Eladi by the arm, somewhat nervously. "You are at home. You know the way. Do not stand on ceremony."

Eladi knew the room where he was to go: the settee facing the window, the mahogany bed with its voluminous comforter, the night table with a piece of newspaper neatly folded under one of its legs to prevent wobbling. As he was taking off his raincoat, he heard steps.

Looking in from the door, Senyora Filo said: "The couple who came in with you are prospective buyers and need to see the house. Would you mind greatly stepping out into the garden? If you knew how terrible I feel about this . . ."

Senyora Filo had been a widow for some years now; she had a small pension, and to make ends meet she rented out rooms. There were five of them in her house that the good woman tried to decorate nicely with damask curtains, shiny bedspreads, a few flowers in vases, postcards tacked to the walls, strategically placed mirrors, and as much cleanliness as her income and tired old body could afford. It hadn't been a month since she had informed Senyor Eladi, whom she considered her best customer because whenever he came he rented out the whole house, that she had put the villa on the market. She was worn-out. With her equity she'd get an annuity; she'd move to an apartment and wouldn't have to work so hard.

The garden was long and narrow. At dusk now, the gray light from the sky, the trees and greenery, it all seemed shipwrecked. Standing by the loquat tree, he saw a shiver of water before his eyes; the shadow of a blue mermaid, splotched with algae, spied on him through a growth of mint. He rubbed his eyes. Toward the end of the abandoned and thirsty garden two hazelnut trees were laden with tender hazelnuts, poorly hidden by the leaves the way the mermaid was hidden by the mint and protected by their coarse husks with frilly endings. He heard a flutter of wings from the top of a tree, raised his eyes, but saw no bird, just a shaking branch. The mermaid was not to be found. Had he lost her down the path, or had she been frightened away by the flight of that invisible bird, she who was meant to play with silvery fish only? A shipwrecked garden. Raising an arm, he picked a hazelnut.

Senyora Filo, stealthy despite her obesity, beamed at him: "They're gone. They've come from Lleida, and it seems they like the villa a lot. It's for a son who's getting married."

The air felt nice with the scent of dry earth. Eladi slipped the hazelnut into his pocket, and, as he walked, he pulled up a sprig of mint. A delicious mix of scents: garden, evening, and mint. Where had the mermaid gone? He was tempted to ask Senyora Filo, who could be startled by the slightest thing, if she kept a mermaid around on a leash. Watch out, she's gotten loose. They heard a knock, and Senyora Filo took off running toward the house saying, "This time it must be for you."

Eladi went into his room; he was sorry that soon he wouldn't be allowed to use it. He was not fond of luxury houses. He had visited so many and so often that he knew them all by heart. He was tired of running into acquaintances there; they would either wink at him or pretend not to know him. He could not quite explain – what could he explain? – why Senyora Filo, with hairpieces that did not match her natural color, obsequious, carelessly dressed, and old, by her mere presence created an atmosphere that was at once exciting and relaxing? She'd been a find, and her sheets were clean. That good woman put him in touch with things and got him away from stuffiness and calculation. The more time went on, the more he felt like being unnoticed. He walked to the mirror, which returned his face with his disillusioned eyes, wide forehead, flabby cheeks. He combed his thinning hair and realized one of his fingernails had split. He hated that. Sitting with his legs crossed, he began to file it, deliberately. When the door opened and he had before him that girl who'd come for him to dispose with at will, he felt on his forehead the friction of the wing of imbecility. Without interrupting his nail filing, he asked, "Aren't you coming in?"

"Yes, Senyor."

"Don't call me 'Senyor.'" He decided to file every one of his nails to unnerve her.

"Then, what shall I call you?"

He sensed that she felt embarrassed, uncertain; it was her first time: a novice. The girl crossed the threshold, adjusted the door behind her, and at last closed it. If all that were to end, if he could no longer look forward to afternoons like this one, he would hit his head against the walls. He filed his thumbnail.

"Elisa . . ."

"Yes, Senyor." He had trimmed the nails of one hand and began to file those of the other. He worked slowly, deliberately, pretending to be absorbed, sensing that Elisa was getting more nervous. As if impelled by an inner demon, he amused himself with making her itch. When he had filed every nail, he got a handkerchief from his pocket and started to polish them. He blew on a nail from time to time and then, moving his hand away, checked their brilliance. A little more. I must make this last, as if I were all alone, he told himself. At last, with a deep sigh, he got up.

"Ah, you're here? I was getting ready for you."

He went toward Elisa and took her by the shoulders, smiling. She was not too pretty or too ugly; she had what she had to have for him to find in her the spice he needed. Girls who were too sumptuous burdened his desire. Hugging Elisa, he breathed in the scent of her youthfulness and the fatiguing smell of her rosewater.

"I am sorry I was a bit late, but Senyoreta Rosa detained me. A piece of work, that Senyoreta Rosa – if you only knew . . ."

He covered her mouth with one hand. He had never stood so close to her, and until then he had not realized how freckled she was. Small, blondish freckles on her cheeks. Her eyes were small but lively, set quite apart, she had fleshy lips and thick eyebrows. She wore a black suit, with a very tight skirt, that had been Sofia's. Her snakeskin handbag also. He took off her jacket, gave the back of her neck a long kiss that provoked a little screech from her, and threw the jacket to the floor. He picked her high up in his arms and let her body slide down slowly, rubbing his. He threw her onto the bed. He was looking at her without blinking, bent over her. Elisa covered her face with an arm.

"Does it bother you that I am staring?"

She shook her head and with a thin voice said, "I am not used to it."

He took off her shoes. Careful not to frighten her, he lifted her skirt. Her legs and thighs showed her taut stockings tied to her girdle with four fasteners. He undid them. On his knees, he put his cheek to one of her feet: a toy. Suddenly he passed the tip of his tongue under her toes. She squealed. Every girl he had known who had calloused hands had her hidden skin smoother than silk. His heart began to pound; he could almost hear it in the absolute silence of the room. He got up and made her get up. He forced her to put a foot on the armchair. Crouching, he kissed the arch of her foot.

Turning her head away, she said, "Oh, please, Senyor, don't . . ." She spoke softly but was angry.

"Easy, easy," muttered Eladi, "easy!"

His brow showed drops of sweat; his lips were dry – he put them to the foot again but could not manage a kiss. He felt a fist in his stomach, his tie was choking him. He almost tore it off, along with his collar button.

"Give me your foot!"

Standing, she looked at him uncomprehendingly.

"No! If you think you've asked me here to kiss my feet and for me to see you sweat, you are wrong!"

Eladi took one of her arms and dragged her brutally toward him. And she had seemed so sweet . . . Elisa wore a thin, translucent blouse, a pink slip under it.

"Let go, you're hurting me!"

She had pulled back to a corner and pointed a finger at him.

"Senyoreta Rosa warned me: all he does is play." Her eyes had narrowed to dark points – they were shooting sparks; her lips trembled. "I knew about you, but I didn't want to believe it. I didn't think you'd do this to me. And the thing with your nails. It's clear you can't get past the feet."

Eladi went to her with bulging eyes, and she put out an arm to fend him off.

"I don't like to be made fun of, even if I'm only a servant girl. Nor to be taken by what I am not. Enough!"

Eladi stood looking at her, frozen; he was panting. He wiped his forehead a couple of times. After a moment, his mind made up, he gave her a few bills, which she took.

"Here. You may leave now."

He sat facing the garden now completely in the dark, his mind empty. He felt that bit of fresh air that was taking away the dank smell and the scent of rosewater. He left the house. In the middle of the street he put his hand in his pocket: he felt the hazelnut. He shucked it under a street lamp. The shell, between his teeth, felt soft; under it there was a thick and bitter layer and under that a bit of juice. Altogether nothing.

5. ARMANDA'S EARRINGS

She was very happy. She had gotten what she hadn't even dared dream of. To never again work as a cook and remain in the house. She read the doctor's certificate again. It was true that the heat from the iron stove made her gut bulge. If she didn't have to be on her feet for so many hours and stopped doing kitchen work, her belly would get well. She had given warning to Senyoreta Sofia to find another cook; she told her that, whenever they found themselves in a pickle, either because the new cook was ill or because she left before they could find a replacement, she would go back to the kitchen for as long as they'd need it. Senyoreta Sofia had said to her: "I appreciate it; but you're not leaving, you're staying. This house has jobs for everybody."

From that day on her job would be to supervise the servants, pay their wages, give the cook the money for the shopping, and go over the receipts. And mostly to keep Senyora Teresa company because the other girls got tired of it. Armanda had become the person of trust in the house. She had earned it because she had put up with a lot. She put away the doctor's certificate in her closet's upper drawer and got out the box with the earrings. She pressed the golden button, and the lid opened. She opened it wide. She had always felt too embarrassed to wear those earrings. And because of the posts. She loved the two little diamonds, stuck in the middle of a gold star. They were very fine. She was never one for jewels. If, instead of having been born a servant, she'd been born a lady, she would not have worn jewels, or very few. Just like Senyoreta Sofia. She would not have been like Senyora Teresa, who was a woman to wear them and who could look like a display case. Many of the servants laughed when they saw her, before her legs gave out on her, ready to go out loaded with rings on every finger and the diamond brooch, the one with the flowers, big as a tray. Senyor Eladi, giving her those earrings, showed very good taste: he had given her a piece of jewelry that she immediately loved. But she'd never been able to wear them. She would have enjoyed hearing Senyoreta Sofia tell her, "Those earrings you're wearing are very nice, Armanda." And she would have been laughing madly on the inside, as she knew that it was her husband who'd given them to her. And she would have answered: "Diamonds are very expensive. They've put quite a dent in my savings."

As far as she knew, Senyor Eladi had never given jewels to any other servant of the house. Once she asked Olivia, as if joking, "Has the Senyor ever given you jewels?"

Olivia looked at her over her shoulder. "What a thing to say!"

But she couldn't trust her, and at the first chance she got she went and searched her suitcases and her whole bedroom, taking her time. She did not find what she was looking for. She breathed easy. Senyor Eladi, she was convinced, considered her different from the others, and that's why he had shown himself to be so generous with her shortly before they broke up because he'd become infatuated with a chambermaid named Paulina, a pretty girl but very dull. How they shone, in the sun, her little diamonds; you'd think they were two little demons. She pulled one earring from the box and looked at its post – the little gold bar had too sharp a point; it hurt whenever she stuck it into her earlobe. Since she had never worn earrings, the holes in her ears were tiny, almost closed, the post didn't go in easily, and, halfway through, got stuck. Once or twice, standing on the balcony facing the garden, she pushed the thing in furiously and drew a drop of blood because she had pierced her ear. If the post had had a rounded tip it might have followed the hole through instead of getting off track and drilling a new hole. One of these days, now that she wouldn't have so much work, she would take them to a jeweler to have them fixed. She wouldn't want to die without having worn them. It was almost her duty to wear them because they were a token of love and to make sure the other girls could see she was someone and that she had diamonds. But what would happen if the jeweler, as she'd heard some jewelers did, swapped the gems for an inferior pair? She smiled at her own misgivings. She'd wear them, mostly, to needle Senyoreta Rosa.

6. EULÀLIA AND QUIM BERGADÀ

She felt horribly depressed. Truly old. She honestly felt old inside. Teresa was not well and was sleeping. Sofia, right after lunch, excused herself: she had appointments with her hairdresser and dressmaker, and since they'd been invited out to supper that night . . .

"Why didn't you tell us sooner that you were coming? You will forgive us, won't you, Godmother dear?"

Eladi left after coffee. Ramon and Maria had spent the whole time observing her inquisitively. She had no defenses. When she was young, she felt proud to be looked at. She knew why they were staring at her. But now . . . She thought Maria was very pretty – more than pretty, stunning. A face of pure beauty and, at once, slightly diabolical. A girl capable of anything. Of anything, really? She could not explain it. Capable of taking and capable of letting go. An unusual face, with an original expression. Eulàlia had her intuitions. If that girl were her daughter, she would be a little afraid of her. She thought Ramon was a boy like so many others. Magnificent eyes, but not necessarily expressive, and sensuous lips like his father, who was infinitely more attractive. Ramon had nothing of Sofia. If you searched deep, perhaps you'd find he had something of Teresa, not much. A kindness in his gaze, perhaps. His expression changed quickly, in a flash, as if all of a sudden he had forgotten how to control himself. With a sigh Eulàlia thought she had discovered a deep, meaningful, disturbing gaze. She thought she was reading things into that look of the boy's and that behind her impressions there was nothing more than the impossibility of understanding extreme youth. Seated on a chair in the library, she missed Quim, who had stayed in

Paris. She missed her home. She missed the fine rain and dull sunlight of Paris. She had come to Barcelona on a sort of sentimental journey, and she had the impression she would come out of it destroyed if she didn't manage to react in time. The Passeig de Gràcia was no longer her Passeig de Gràcia. Her friends were disappearing one by one. Everything had changed without quite having changed. On days like this she held to her memories as if her life depended on it – what was left of her life.

The Luxembourg, that day, was gray; the orange trees looked puny in their huge wooden planters, painted green; all the statues of the queens of France on their pedestals had an empty gaze, and their hands had missing fingers. She and Quim, sitting by the railing, looked at the pond and the little boats with white sails floating upon it. Quim had gone to pick her up and took her to the hotel. That day (she was so tired!) he'd let her rest; the following day he would figure out how to attend to her. She was still mourning Rafael and felt like crying. Not because Joaquim reminded her of Rafael, they were nothing like each other, but because he had received her with a joyful attentiveness that had touched her. The next day they dined together. She wore a gabardine suit and a white straw hat with a black veil that fell to her back. On her lapel she had pinned the brooch her husband had given her when they were first married – it was the first time she'd worn it after the tragedy: a diamond and topaz horseshoe that Teresa detested because, she said, horseshoes brought no luck, not even to horses. Eulàlia loved Teresa, but she resented her marriage to Salvador Valldaura, a marriage that she had somewhat brought about since she hadn't quite imagined that an immensely rich and pedigreed man such as Valldaura would fall for the spectacular but unrefined beauty of Teresa. She had, rather, on certain moments, felt he was attracted to her and had received his affection as an homage. Despite that scrap of jealousy, she loved Teresa, and she loved Valldaura and deep down regretted that Teresa had smeared her life with a love affair that would bring about no good. For a time she hated her as you hate someone who has erred and over whom you'd like to have some influence to get back on the right path. Salvador, and she had talked this over with Rafael, did not deserve the lot he had. They ate their duck, and then Quim took her for a walk. Later they were to see *Tartuffe*. But they never made it, and the tickets ended up as mementos in Joaquim's billfold. Quim. For Quim was tired of his life as an aging bachelor, of disappointments, of postponements, of now yes now no; tired of his apartment empty of affection, of the disquieting sensation of a life that's going nowhere. He needed to love and to be loved, and Eulàlia, with her halo of loneliness and sorrow, had come at that sweet point when changing a man's fate is the easiest thing in the world. Quim took her by the arm each time they had to cross a street, and she appreciated the gesture deeply. Finally, he took her arm exactly as Rafael had taken it when they were courting. He didn't link arms with her but, rather, clasped her arm with his hand, and she could feel the slightest pressure of his fingers: confident, attentive to the least sign of danger. And since they walked in silence, either because he didn't know what to say or because he respected her own silence, a sight came to her memory in a brutal way: the splotch of blood in front of the entrance to her apartment building, on Carrer Consell de Cent, where Rafael had been assassinated one morning as he was leaving home with his factory's foreman to discuss a settlement with some workers who had been fired. She trod on that stain of blood every day, willy-nilly, because she couldn't get around it, and she felt like dying. She wrote Quim, who had come to the funeral and had been very nice to her to the point of offering her anything she would need – she, who needed only her husband, but who would love to go to Paris, if even for a few days, because Barcelona weighed on her and because not even her country house or the woods there could take away that obsession: seeing that dark stain that everybody trampled on the stones of the sidewalk right by her door. She couldn't take it any longer.

As she crossed the Luxembourg, she shook the hand holding her arm and grabbed Joaquim's arm with both her hands and broke out in tears, the tears she had held in for so long when her friends began to desert her because no one likes to be the friend of a woman whose husband has been assassinated. Eulàlia thought her brother-in-law was a refuge, and now that she had him there ("I am very sorry, Quim, do forgive me") she was pestering him with her teary outburst, tears like a river. She was crying because she was crying. "I cry because I cry." At last she calmed down, and Quim did something he'd never done with a woman: he put his arm on her shoulder as if she were his buddy and took her to a seat by the railing, while some children pushed their sailboats on the pond. Before they left he showed her a few French queens, in marble, all very beautiful, all with maimed hands. And, as he looked at Eulàlia looking at the queens, Eulàlia felt that Quim was discovering her, admiring the tender pink of the skin on her face, her flaxen hair, her greenish eyes, her well-traced eyebrows. One of those faces – Rafael had told her more than once – that improve a hundred percent when you have them close.

"I will never let you go back to Barcelona!"

And now, an old woman, sitting in the Valldaura's library, she felt a longing for Quim – she, who just a few weeks ago had felt a great longing for Barcelona. Quim, who had carried her like a flower and who still kept the two tickets he had bought for *Tartuffe*. And, despite the shroud of sadness choking her heart, she laughed to think that, when they were young, she had disliked him with a passion. Had his love been so good because he loved in her what she retained of his brother, who had died by violence, and because she loved in him what he had from birth of that husband of hers who had been the first love of her life?

The chambermaid came in to tell her that the Senyora had awakened and wanted to see her. She went into Teresa's room and felt sincere compassion for her. She felt she had to forgive that old difference that was better forgotten because, within their conscience, everyone is completely alone.

7. SOFIA

Sílvia had drawn open the shutters and with a moist cottonball began to remove the dried mask stuck to her face. Sofia, with a towel around her neck, felt as if she had new skin. Once her face was clean she sat up, rearranged her pillows, and picked up her mirror with the frame of roses. Her cheeks were smooth, her lips still soft, the arch of her eyebrows neat, and not a wrinkle on her forehead; her eyes, having rested for a while in the darkness, shone as she opened them. "Japanese eyes," Joaquim always told her, poor old Joaquim, who ended up seducing her godmother, a woman so spiritual and winged. No, not Japanese. Strange, yes. She could not open them quite as wide as other people. Her doctor told her once, "With a twist of the scalpel on each corner they'd be perfect."

She never agreed to that. She'd rather keep the eyes she could not quite open; they were her pride. Opened full, would they shine as bright? Would they be as bewitching in their uniqueness as her deep voice was? She jumped out of the bed, slender and nimble. Sílvia had drawn her bath. She tested the water with a foot. She loved and was proud of her body, of her face, of her estates, with the grapes to be picked, the wheat to be harvested, the poplars and the pines to be timbered. And her cork oaks. She was the full mistress of all that was hers. Full owner. Because of her ownership and because of the satisfaction with which she owned it all. Sílvia helped her with the navy-blue dress. She had taken her time to put on her makeup. She slipped on her emerald ring. She applied some Mitsouko, which was the perfume Eladi could not stand. She took her purse and, at the door, turned around and smiled kindly at Sílvia. She knew that every time she went out Sílvia tried on her dresses and her jewels. She knew that Sílvia, prettier than her, infinitely younger, hung on to every one of her movements, every one of her outings. That's why she was so kind to Sílvia – because she knew she was making her uneasy. She went into Eladi's bedroom. Even though it had been aired, it still reeked of tobacco. She found the smell of Dutch tobacco mixed with the smell of English tobacco from cigarettes unbearable. The daylight, gray, sweetened everything: the pipe stand, the baroque clock they had bought at an antique shop in Munich, the backs of the books. Eladi read Proust. He kept the volumes in a small bookcase, to the left of his bed, at hand. He read them bit by bit, never a whole volume at one time. Eladi's liking for Proust made Sofia smile disdainfully. She did not like Proust one bit because he had been sick in his body and in his soul. Besides liking the work, she needed to admire the author. Or perhaps she disliked Proust because Eladi liked him. Many of the things he liked displeased her, and that feeling was surely mutual. They had been sleeping apart for how long? You couldn't tell. She had never told him not to seek her. It was he who had given up, tired of so much distance and so much emptiness.

As usual, she came down the stairs buttoning up her gloves. A distinct memory made her stop halfway down: the first time she took Maria in her arms. Maria was seven months old, and she was returning from her honeymoon. In some black corner of her soul she knew that in accepting the child would lie her strength. That child Eladi had so tenaciously wanted would be his shame. At times, seeing him absorbed in his reading, she felt like knocking the book out of his hands and telling him he was a pitiful man who had fathered a child with a nobody. Maria lived in the house because Sofia needed her; the girl stimulated her spiteful sense of dominion. She had given Eladi two children: two males. While Eladi became weaker and weaker with his obsessions, she had slapped him with two sons. But her pride lost strength when she realized Eladi loved Maria and Maria was becoming a beautiful creature. She would have been unable to define what was taking shape in Maria: her grace, her restraint, her elegance. Lady Godiva's daughter had come into the world branded by some remote ancestor of Farriols. Now that Jaume was dead, she could pour her maternal instincts on Ramon alone. Part of his ordinariness must have come from that woman, who had been a fishmonger. Vexed, every time she saw his caddishness, she thought that Ramon must have the fishwife in him. Not quite, in truth. It was less true than she imagined, but to her it was the truth of truths. Some nights that truth kept her awake. It was the fault of Maria, who forced her to establish comparisons. At times, faced by a spontaneous and affectionate gesture from Maria when she was little, she felt won over. Maria, she reflected, loves me as if I truly were her mother. At moments like that Maria's black and deep eyes seemed to her the honey lode of the world. But that was a passing gratitude. Maria kept on growing, and, as she grew, she grew apart from her. Sofia brought her hand to her nose, smelled its perfume and saw herself years back, speaking to Senyoreta Rosa in the foyer as she scolded Ramon. Maria, no sooner did she see her, threw herself on her and hugged her: "Mama, Mama." And Sofia felt a great inner joy. Maria was hers. She finished descending the staircase. Senyoreta Rosa was coming out of the dining room.

"Senyoreta Rosa, tonight I need to speak to you."

That night she'd inform her that she was no longer needed.

8. SENYORETA ROSA

Sitting in her chair near the balcony, she was crying tears of rage. She had just two more weeks to remain in the house. She had been given three months. When Senyoreta Sofia informed her, she felt a great disappointment; then she thought that three months would last forever. She got up, unaware of why she was getting up. Ah, yes: the valise. She got one out of the armoire and placed it on the bed. She found a rag and started to dust it. The locks were shiny, just as when she had bought the case. From time to time she had to wipe her tears so she could see. She left the valise alone; she was not up to that. She had plenty of time to pack her things. The bulkier stuff would go in the trunk that was in the basement and which must have grown musty. She stepped out onto the balcony and looked longingly at the chauffeur's hut. The sun was pure fire, and she could not feel it. How would things go with Marcel once she was no longer in the house? He had assured her he'd find a way for the two of them to still see each other. So many nights she had crossed the garden to go to his hut! She'd leave through the kitchen door, always fearful of being found out. Marcel was a nice, charming guy. He had never mentioned marriage, but she was convinced that, if she were to continue in the house, habit, more than will, would have brought a victory. Now she saw it was all lost. She thought of her new employers; they seemed to be nice people. The lady had told her she would have to care for a five-year-old girl. She hadn't seen her because, precisely at the time, the girl was away at her grandparents'. But the lady explained to her that the girl was very docile, very affectionate, a bit sickly, poor little one, thin as a reed because she was growing too fast. She was five, and, from her height, you'd say she was seven. She would no longer live in a villa like this one. She had put up with a lot of discomfort so she could stay. Suddenly she felt a wave of outrage in her throat as she thought about the talcum powder. Ramon and Maria had amused themselves by hiding that rose-colored jar that she needed so often, particularly during the summer, because her belly button was very deep set and chapped easily. She had been patient but could not forgive them that they went on with the prank when they were more grown-up. She had attended to them when they were ill, had taught them French, had taught them all she knew, and they had always paid back her cares and concern with practical jokes that were unseemly in the children of a wealthy family. She sat down again and was seized by another burst of tears. She wiped her eyes and her mouth and looked sadly at her valise; she had bought it years ago in a fit of rebellion, bent on leaving the house. It was pigskin and had cost her a fortune. She wanted to be seen departing like a lady. After all, of all the servants she was the most important. She had always tried very hard to be kind to everybody, to appear unassuming, not to put on airs. She dressed modestly so as not to provoke Senyoreta Sofia's jealousy. She had been forced to live without luster. Her mother was a laundress who had slaved to pay for her studies. She had made a young lady out of her. Rosa spoke fluent French, without an accent. Before she went to work for the Farriols she had worked at the home of a couple from Perpinyà who were always telling her that her French was impeccable. For the last few years she no longer gave Ramon and Maria lessons; her job now was to accompany Maria and help her keep her clothes in order, a job any chambermaid could have easily done. But the goodness of the Senyora had saved her. She had put up with enough whims from Maria. Helping her get dressed to go out, she'd say she did not want to go out, that she had a headache. And she had to hang the dress again, put the shoes away. Not once, in those many years, had she been able to awaken the slightest feeling of tenderness in that girl. Maria thought her a woman one could humiliate. Ramon even more so. They called her chaperone. And she heard that damning word repeated over and over in her brain, as an obsession. She had kept quiet over many things; she had tried to understand. Superior to that boy and that girl who laughed at others so as to be able to admire themselves: Ramon did the impossible to awaken Maria's admiration and Maria to awaken Ramon's.

She rose like a snake and returned to the balcony, facing the garden, facing the chestnut trees that she had seen grow taller and taller, with their white flowers in the spring, each bunch of flowers like a flame of snow. Before leaving she'd talk! She went to the bathroom, brushed her teeth. She combed her hair. She had never been pretty, but her hands could be the envy of anyone. Her fingers were long and delicate, their skin white, smooth, aristocratic. She looked at them for a long time and again burst out in tears. She looked at her bedroom, wide, with light – colored furniture and flowery curtains. She went out onto the balcony, grabbed the railing, and shook it with fury. It would all remain the same: the servant girls, Armanda, the children; Marcel would continue to drive the car. And she would end up in a tiny room, right under the roof, with a washbasin barely big enough for her to wash her hands in. She had been deeply in love with Senyor Eladi, who never cast a glance in her direction, who spoke to her only not to appear rude. But one day, shortly after Maria's First Communion, she thought he was looking at her the way he looked at the other girls in the house. And she conceived hopes. She was worth nothing, she'd be the first to admit it, but she was better than Armanda. She opened her valise. In it, neatly folded, there was a negligee of light blue muslin. For a long time she had waited, her heart beating fast, to hear steps in the corridor. One moonlit night she would have sworn that her doorknob was turning. But she never saw anyone, and that was when she began to tire of that house and the children's pranks with her talcum powder. Since Senyoreta Sofia had told her she no longer needed her services, she felt uneasy, she avoided people, she felt they were all happy that she was leaving. That day she didn't feel like leaving her bedroom – but she had to face the music, and she went down to eat and swallowed her food, without having an appetite, so they wouldn't laugh at her. That night she went to see if there was light under the library door. There was a clear line; all the lights inside must have been on. She walked down a few times to look, before she went to meet Marcel. Not to go in but to get accustomed to thinking she would go in. To gain confidence. A week before her departure she made up her mind. She took a bath, put on the muslin negligee, for which she never had any use and which she had bought in case Senyor Eladi . . . If she had donned it for Marcel, such an austere man, he might have thought it in bad taste. She came down the stairs with a hand on her heart. The line of light under the door was tenuous now. She rapped timidly, and nobody answered. Perhaps . . . Once or twice the Senyor, unmindfully, had gone to bed leaving the lights on. She rapped harder. She heard Eladi's voice saying come in. She opened the door and stood there. Eladi looked at her in surprise and told her to come in, and, since she didn't say a word or move, he asked her what she wanted, his eyes laden with boredom, and then with an effort she answered that she had to talk to him. She slowly came closer to him, thinking more of the time when she had expected to hear steps along her corridor than of what she was about to do. Eladi fixed his eyes on her, and she had a hard time resisting that electrifying gaze. With lowered eyes she sat down. She kept her knees pressed together. She put a hand to her face and let it fall to her neck, moist with perspiration. As if mysterious forces dictated what she had to say, but saying it in a more direct way than she ever thought possible, she spoke about the children. It was the first time Maria had gone anywhere without her, alone with Ramon. It would have been better not to let them go spend the summer at the Balsarenys, those playful friends of Senyoreta Sofia. Perhaps he had never realized that between Ramon and Maria there was something more than sibling love. Because she knew everything. No, she was lying. She had overheard Senyora Valldaura and Senyor Riera, the attorney, talk about it, but she had kept mum. She was no gossip. The last thing she wanted was to create a problem, but she had kept an eye on them. Eladi looked at her with an expression that was hard to describe:

a mixture of curiosity and indignation. Senyoreta Rosa kept unraveling her skein of black yarn until, finally, before the impassivity of Senyor Eladi, she played her best trump. That the children loved each other too much and that one night, in the park, near the lilacs . . . She got up. Eladi did not say a word. His face was like fire. And Senyoreta Rosa, standing, further said that he should wonder why Ramon had such bad grades. "He will never graduate." She spoke as if casting a curse. She left the library, went upstairs on her shaky legs, and, once there, threw herself on the bed, exhausted from the effort and the violence she had had to commit. But it was worth it. In that house they would never again live in peace.

9. ELADI GOES TO GET HIS CHILDREN

He told Marcel to stop at the first café they saw because he was dying of thirst. He had already taken off his jacket and his tie. And he'd done a thing he hadn't done since he was fourteen or fifteen: as he waited for the traffic jam that had them stuck at Premià for a half-hour to clear, he began to bite his nails, without realizing he was doing it, because he did not feel like smoking. He had bit one nail too hard, and there was a bit of blood. The sight of blood horrified him. Before he died, his uncle Terenci had vomited blood twice, and he had to leave the room in order not to faint. He recalled a violent summer night when Armanda went to see him with a bandaged finger, the gauze lightly stained with blood. He felt like shoving her away immediately. After that, whenever she was near him, he could see that blood-stained bandage. That might have been the reason he broke it off with Armanda. He was sorry about that because Armanda was good in bed. Marcel parked the car, and they went to a bar near Llavaneres for a couple of beers. They went to his head. Probably because he'd spent a sleepless night thinking what he would do and say. Besides, he had skipped breakfast. The sea looked like a pool of oil. The heat made his skin sag. As the car devoured the road, he kept losing track of all that had tormented him through the night. Couldn't Senyoreta Rosa have been imagining things? A sudden stop of the car threw his head against the glass. Marcel let out a curse, and then he looked back and with a little laugh said sorry. A convertible coming in the other direction, trying to pass a truck, had come at them. He closed his eyes and felt even sicker. He lowered the other window. He hoped that those beers that his sweating struggled to eliminate would finally leave him alone.

"Your beer didn't make you sick, Marcel?"

Marcel shook his head and then said no sir. The sea was becoming a more resplendent blue. Without meaning to, Eladi started humming: *Celeste Aïda* . . . He stopped himself, lest Marcel might think he'd suddenly gone gaga. He would have liked to know what Marcel thought of Senyoreta Rosa's departure. He was sure the man was happy to see her disappear from his horizon; he couldn't look more satisfied. He felt deeply that, had he been able to sing at the top of his lungs, the way he did in the shower, most of his bothersome thoughts would fade away. And the beer might stop weighing on his gut. Having gnawed on that nail to the flesh capped his sickened feeling. He had five nails left to bite, those of his right hand. A couple of very white sails, far away, perfectly placed between sea and haze, sweetened his heart for a moment. When Maria was little and sat on his lap and said, "Papa, I love you to heaven," his heart sweetened the same way. She was his beloved, more than his sons, more than Ramon. He never quite loved the little one, Jaume, who made him uneasy with those reedy legs of his and that pale skin. He felt his premature death rather like a relief. Who knows what would have become of Jaume once he'd grow up, such a sickly person, a child that seemed rather like a punishment? He had pretended Jaume was his favorite so that Sofia wouldn't feel too jealous of his love for Maria. Suddenly he had the car stop. He stepped out and approached the sea. He needed to breathe free air, to stretch. But there was not a breath of air, and the sand was burning. He had to separate Ramon and Maria. Even if Senyoreta Rosa had been exaggerating. He would have to explain to Ramon that he and Maria were brother and sister. The truth.

He had not quite appreciated that both Sofia and the children accepted the Balsarenys's invitation. They had all insisted on going. It would be a season of pure bliss. They could go swimming. Neither he nor Sofia liked leaving town. Traveling abroad, yes. But the beach . . . Old Valldaura didn't like the country either. They were city people. And, if they needed greenery and trees, their villa had them aplenty. He would have to separate them. A wave of shame made him close his eyes; he covered them with one hand. When he removed it, he realized that the waves that almost licked his feet were small and silent. Wouldn't he have been happier if he had married a pennyless girl, that sweet Pilar, mother of Maria, who had never bugged him, who had been so in love with him? Maria was all Farriols. If he had another chance . . . No. If he had another chance, he would do exactly the same. He couldn't know what he had lost, but he knew he had gained a set of privileges that, had he married a poor girl, he wouldn't have dared dream of. His life might be a bit sad, but aren't all lives sad, however you live them? Socially, he was a man related to an important family. His silks and velvets? How are you? Come in, come in; how may I help you? He had sold his store long ago. And the factory. He had a small personal fortune, to be sure. All that had been his father's and his uncle's. He felt a little better now. In the car, and again on the road, he stared at Marcel's neck: thick, reddened skin, with three well-marked horizontal furrows. Marcel was a husky guy. Why must he keep his hair so long? Attorney Riera likewise. Mentally, he compared his hair to Marcel's. Senyoreta Rosa must like it long. She was a good egg who had always behaved very correctly and had worked well when Ramon and Maria were little. Little by little, the scene staged by Senyoreta Rosa, which had thrown him into a hell all night long, was losing consistency by the strength of sky, of sea, of light. He had to confess that he was no good for drama. He preferred to get the most out of the hour he was living. He thought of Valldaura. Shortly before he died, he had spoken to him about Vienna, about scentless violets, about violins. He confessed that he would have never imagined that his romantic adventure could have been found so amusing by so many people. Perhaps he might also become like a child and end up explaining to everybody that he had been mad about a girl who sang onstage. Or perhaps he'd tell the story maliciously, just to see the expression on the face of the idiot who might be listening to him. No, it was no laughing matter. He realized his queasiness had faded and that he was feeling hungry. Whenever he was depressed, he felt a distaste for tobacco and felt hungry, had a ravenous appetite. He could wait no longer. A good dinner was what he needed most urgently.

"Say, Marcel, aren't you hungry?"

He felt an impulse to eat a fine repast: fish from that sea so blue. A sea perch maybe, surrounded by mussels the color of oranges and by some rosy prawns.

"Marcel, say, don't you know of a place where one can have a good meal?"

And so Eladi Farriols did not go to get his children. He decided to write to them, asking them to return at once; he wanted them at home because he was ill. He'd send his excuses to the Balsarenys.

10. RAMON AND MARIA

At a distance from the house, surrounded by pines that obscured it, stood the church. From inside, through two round windows like portholes, you could see the sea. There were always artless bunches of flowers in many colors on the little altar. And burning candles dripping with wax. And a small Madonna, with the face of a child, the protector of sailors in peril, dressed in blue, and the bottom of the tunic and the hem of the mantle adorned with a blackish gold embroidery. At her feet two crossed oars. Over her hair and veil a crown of white roses. Ramon and Maria stepped in to look at the Virgin. Sunlight streamed in through the windowpanes and fell on the floor tiles next to the last row of pews. Their friends waited for them on the beach. They walked a bit, climbed down the rocks among Scotch broom. The sea was like a sheet: deep blue, sprinkled with lanterns of sunlight. The shade under the pines felt hot. Their feet were sinking in the sand. Maria looked at Ramon. The sea was theirs, the sea with its inlets of sleeping water, the pebbles on the bottom polished and polished again by the patience of the water. They were to spend the summer together: without Senyoreta Rosa – what bliss – without Armanda, without their parents. Maria wore a terry robe over her bathing suit. The group of young people greeted them with shrieks of joy, and Màrius, who'd been staring at them as they climbed down the rocks, went to meet them laughing, shading his eyes with his hand. They got in the water slowly, their legs splashing. Then they dove into the sea girding them. Maria in her red bathing suit, tanned, her hair falling on her bronzed shoulders. Maria in the water, all gold and fire, her feet like seashells. Maria a bud, a virgin like the altar's Madonna. Maria of trees and of ivy and of the park and of the moonlight on the roof. Maria alone, like a slab of stone under the fallen leaves of autumn waiting for the branches to rain more leaves on her. Maria in her blue bed of sea; farther out, a sail. Maria surrounded by the foam of waves only you and I all the way to the end of the world alone with the rain alone with the storms each lightning bolt to honor your name Maria my sister. Maria,

Ramon, Màrius. Maria between the two boys. Màrius skinny, tanned black as coal, his face with shrunken cheeks cut by the whitest laugh on earth. Màrius with Ramon in college. Màrius Balsareny. Friends, fellow students, so different one from the other. Màrius fleeing, pursued by a mounted policeman. Màrius arrested. Màrius in jail. Màrius rebellious. Màrius the revolutionary. Maria and Màrius had come out of the water and sat next to each other, happy upon the hot sand, and Màrius drew a large M on the sand, and next to it he drew another one. Màrius drew two M's, while the others swam and yelled and laughed. Ramon watched them, jealous to see them so close Maria false sister of mine. False false sister of mine. Maria amused herself making the legs of the M's longer and longer, the M's Màrius had traced beyond the reach of the waves so the water would not erase them. From time to time Màrius lifted his gaze and sought Maria's eyes, which were fascinated by the M's. Reedy Màrius, without cheeks, his nostrils aflutter, with veins and nerves under his burned skin, somewhat like a hare or like a bird. Ramon looked at them. He felt a sharp splinter stuck into some remote inner organ whose existence he hadn't known. He shut his eyes so as not to see the beach turning and turning with the red splotch that was Maria in its center like the eye of a whirlpool. Maria far out under the storms under the shifting light of the branches, turtledoves and butterflies her accomplices, the two of them virgin of mine. And the straight legs of the M's meant Màrius and Maria together. A bitter taste filled his mouth just like that night when he heard his parents. He'd peeked through the keyhole. He wanted to know. He had also peeked into Senyoreta Rosa's room. Their bedside lamp was lit; they were in bed. It was as if he'd been riveted to the floor; he was not breathing. He heard them. He climbed to the roof by himself. He felt choked by nausea. The world of the grown-ups was an ugly world. He walked on the roof with his arms extended, from tower to tower. The laurel's leaves were full of wind, and their rustling began to calm him down. Under his feet, under the tiles, under the beams, Maria slept. Over his head the night was going on, with small clouds drifting by, lined by the moon. Some lost voice pushed by the wind muttered, "Jaume." Suddenly tied to his dead brother by a voice wafting in the wind. He and Maria would jump out to the fields without telling Jaume, toward freedom, toward the garbage with its empty tins, their treasures. Grandmother and her wine. He'd go see her and smirk at her. She didn't want Miquela to let him in because this Ramon I am not sure whom he takes after. He kept splashing the salty water with arms and legs; the water at the end of the park was green and bred mosquitoes that flew and laid eggs. More mosquitoes were born, and they installed netting. Jaume like a fetus in the green water with mosquito eggs and him in the water salty like a giant's fetus a water with no belly. The sun would rise from it the sun would come out not between the legs of a woman spit out to life full of blood. To die in the water a death without a bothersome corpse, out, out, where the water is not the color of salt in the lungs. He took his head out of the water and spit. The white light made him close his eyes the forked branch after he peeled it was still more white and Jaume was receding and he looked at them and showed his puffed lips he had pimples in his armpits and on his neck big pimples that never dried and exuded pus and purple blood he was looking at them on the verge of tears without crying the creep. Jaume-Màrius like a tumor full of pus between him and Maria. He started to swim vigorously as if behind him all who had died by water were to pull on his feet and as if his salvation were that red splotch sister mine and he came out of the water panting and instead of joining Màrius and Maria he ran toward the pines in the blue shade with all his badness inside him gnawing on him and it would gnaw on him whenever he sat down to study, to walk, to remember a virgin sitting on the beach one summer morning because deceptively she'd been made a girl but she was a virgin between the thighs of blood and gold there was night and dreams. Maria was coming to him. She came from the light. Màrius was out swimming far. Maria ran a palm over his forehead: do you have a temperature? And all the peace in the world burst out between Maria's palm and the skin of his forehead all the peace you and me forever under the trees where the turtledoves say unintelligible things because they are utterances with all the innocence of the morning of life. Maria. What can the others know if they never saw her as a little girl a bird lost on the roof shut the door don't let the dolls escape the scent of laurel a quietness brought by sleep Maria the center of everything? What could they know of those tender eyes, of those cheeks where the rain slid down the skin lost in the bottom of the park holding hands in the bright light born of the green vomited by shadow to the sunlight? What could the others know, the folks on the street, those who ogle a girl a city to be conquered? And he took off running and Maria after him, and they jumped in the water together splashes of sun and of blue the two of them clean and shiny like olives without meanness without poison inside only you sister mine. When they came out of the water the beach was deserted. The sand burned their feet. Maria, distracted, walked over the letters and smudged them. Ramon rubbed his feet over the rest. She turned around smiling, but, when she saw that Ramon was erasing the letters, she went to him and gave him a shove. When they got to Barcelona . . . Their father had written the Balsarenys. He informed them that he was ailing and wanted his children near him. Maria got the dollhouse from her room and took it to the nursery. She did not want to see it anymore. She was a woman.

11. RAMON LEAVES HOME

He felt sorry for his father, and he felt sorry for himself, and he felt sorry for everything. He wanted to disappear, to erase his life that summer. His father was staring at him, not knowing how to tell him that he and Maria were brother and sister. That Maria was not the daughter of some cousins of his who had died in an accident, as he'd heard the servants tell when he was a child. The same blood. His father, before the truth had a chance to leave his mouth, walked to the window, then sat down, got up again, and with his back to him told him what he should have known from the start. He felt like running away, but his father's voice nailed him to the floor, his legs glued together, his head lowered. As soon as his father stopped speaking, he left the library, walking backward, not quite knowing what he was doing, his brain foggy as in a nightmare: he was small, playing with Maria and Jaume behind the velvet curtain of the dining room; his grandmother did not love him because he once messed up a feather from the large vase that stood at the entrance to the parlor. He climbed upstairs like a madman; he wanted to see Maria – but her door was locked. His sister was a prisoner because she loved him and because he loved her and they could not love each other. He banged the door with his shoulder, and the door did not open. "Maria," he called softly, and no one answered. Then he kissed the door panel to say good-bye to that Maria, to his own Maria, whom he would never see again. He needed to breathe, to free his lungs from all that squalor they'd been stuffed with. The staircase to the roof, which he used to climb without really seeing it, seemed to him too narrow, its steps too steep, its corners too violent. The night was limpid, loaded with fire. A waft of melancholy came up from his heart for all the hours spent on that roof. Lying side by side, brother and sister, covered with the whirl of the stars. A whole life had just died. He wanted to walk on the roof, to the next dormer, to the center, to that spot where Maria's hair had rubbed his cheek when they lay there in the wind. He couldn't make himself do it. He climbed back downstairs, stopped before Maria's door; his childhood was in there. He went to the playroom. He looked at the small tables where he and she had learned to write. Maria hadn't been locked in. Maria had refused to see him, had refused to open her door to him. He knew that; they had also told her. He kicked the cardboard horse, and it started to rock. He opened the toy cupboard. He looked at each one of the toys. On the lower shelf lay the wooden top with color stripes. Its string was torn. He got hold of the cupboard and dragged it under the lamp, tilted it, and all the toys spread out on the floor. He calmly started to step on them: he stepped on the top, hurt his foot, picked up the cardboard horse, and threw it at the window. A piece of glass slashed his hand: the same blood. Red, shiny, thick. Lifting his hand so as not to drip blood on the floor, he went to the balcony. The garden appeared black, sprinkled with moonlight. When they were little, his and Maria's garden appeared to have no end. He had an urge to shout his sister's name: so it would go out through the broken panes and spread through the night like a dog's howl. He went to the dollhouse. He picked up the man and tore its head off. He went downstairs with a hazy brain as if still in his nightmare. He crossed the foyer without stopping and walked like a shadow under the chestnut trees. He sat at the foot of the fence and looked out to the street, to the ivy branches on the wall across the way. He realized he was holding something in his hand and didn't know what. It took him a while to realize it was the headless man from the dollhouse. He stuffed it in his pocket just in time to cover his ears. Behind him everything was sinking; the stones of the house crumbled and fell near him, breaking branches, missing him but hurting him nonetheless. He couldn't tell how long he stood there as if he were dead. He went back in. He followed the alley of chestnut trees, climbed onto the bench by the wisteria; he stared for a bit at Maria's balcony and saw no light inside. He had lost the sense of time; he was walking down the streets as a lost soul haunted by his father's voice, by memories that kept pushing him into a dead-end street. At eight in the morning, feverish, he rang the bell of Marina, Attorney Riera's sister. He was classmates with Marina, her oldest daughter. A small girl he did not recognize opened the door.

"I am the goddaughter of Senyora Marina, and my name is Marina."

12. MARIA LISTENS BEHIND THE DOOR

She heard Ramon go by and opened her door to call him, but he was running downstairs so fast that she gave up. She sensed that something bad was imminent. Her father was not ill, as he had said in his letter to the Balsarenys. She stood for a moment on the landing not knowing what to do. At last she went downstairs, stopping from time to time, as if she wanted to guess what was going on without having to go all the way down. The library door was not quite closed. Her father, upset, was speaking, and she could make out that he was talking about her and Ramon. She crossed the hallway and went to the door. She had never known that the water in the fountain could be so noisy. She recalled an afternoon when Senyoreta Rosa, halfway through French dictation, had straightened her white collar, adjusted her cuffs, and, raising her head, said, softly, looking her in the eye, that she, in that house, was nobody. "You're nobody. Nobody. I'm telling you to punish you for all your smirks when you were little. You're less than nothing." She felt like spitting in her face. She responded angrily that she was making things up, lies, because she was ugly and envious. Senyoreta Rosa, her cheeks lit red and her lips pursed, said in an authoritative voice, "Dictation." And she corrected hers, crammed with errors, and for each mistake she underlined she clicked her tongue against her palate. When she declared the class over, she muttered: "I shall have to speak to your mother. I'll tell her you are a poor student because you have other things in your head. Ungodly things." Maria ran to see her grandmother, stood at her side, and burst out crying. When she could, she explained that Senyoreta Rosa had told her she was nobody. Her grandmother caressed her hair over and over. "Now, now. Don't you cry. You are my dear one, my love; you've always been my darling." She instructed her to open the middle drawer in the Japanese armoire and take out the purple box. Then Grandmother opened the box and picked up the bouquet of diamonds. She held it in the palm of her hand. "The day I die this will be yours." Maria felt like crying even more as she put the box back. Her grandmother came very close to her, stretched an arm, and, pointing at what was around them, told her it would all be hers: the house, with the trees and the birds.

She heard a great quiet in the library and fled upstairs, running with an uneasy heart. After a bit Ramon was knocking on her door. Covering her mouth with her hands to keep from answering, she stared at that door behind which stood her brother, who was the son of her father, as she was the daughter of his father. She did not open the door because she was no adopted waif; she and Ramon were brother and sister. Once they had kissed by the water, where, years ago, Jaume . . . She'd been looking at the water with her arms crossed behind her back; she was fascinated by the bugs swimming in the water, which made her shiver. Ramon stood next to her. "I know more things than you do. Do you know what grown-ups do when they are in love? They play with each other's tongues." He held her and made her turn to face him. "Did you know that your eyes and mine are made of water? It would be nice if the water of your eyes and the water of mine could mix." Maria saw leaves inside Ramon's eyes: a shiny and dark paradise that was sucking up her will. "If the water of your eyes and the water of mine mixed, I would be you, and you would be me. Would you like that?" She said yes with a weak voice. Then he kissed her lips with a tender and brief kiss. "This is how I'll kiss you from now on. Always this way." Maria had pushed out her lips and with moist eyes said, "More." They heard the sound of branches cracking and hid quickly behind a growth of honeysuckle. Ramon, after holding his breath for a moment, told her very softly that someone had followed them and was spying on them. "I know who it is." They went back to the house saddened, and by separate ways. That was three or four years ago. She now raised her head and listened. Ramon was on the roof. Then she heard him in the playroom. The whole house was a big silence broken by that storm in the playroom. Suddenly the storm stopped. Ramon was running downstairs, skipping steps.

"Maria . . . Maria . . . Maria . . ."

Someone was calling her name so far away that she could not guess who it was. She opened her balcony door and looked at the sky, the trees. Despite the darkness, she could make out the white splotch of Ramon's face; he was standing on the bench by the wisteria. She rushed back in. Crouched at the foot of her bed, she couldn't even think. Fear strangled her heart. She got up, went to the window.

"Maria . . . Maria . . . Maria . . ."

Where was that voice coming from, that voice that was nowhere and that repeated her name so she'd know she was not alone? Ramon crossed the garden and disappeared in the shadow of the chestnut trees.

13. ELADI FARRIOLS AND ATTORNEY RIERA

He got out of the car, crossed the sidewalk, and stopped before the house of the attorney. The entrance was imposing but dark, the elevator obsolete. He would walk up; that would give him courage. He climbed slowly; every two or three steps he stopped to rest. He slid a hand to the inside pocket of his jacket to check that the letter was there. He felt an irrepressible desire to forget about it all, to get rid of that noose of responsibility choking him. If any other person could possibly take care of what he was carrying out . . . Standing before the apartment door he read, one letter at a time, the name of Attorney Riera on the brass shingle. A lean young woman, with very large eyes (or perhaps they seemed large because her face was so small), opened the door for him. She stood aside to let him in.

"Does Senyor Riera know that you are coming to see him?"

"No." He gave her his card. A couple sat in the waiting room: a fat man and a blonde girl, with black eyebrows, who seemed to be his daughter. Eladi went to the balcony and pulled the sheer curtain a sliver. Dusk was setting in, the evening a little gray, a little windy. He was distracted from his thoughts by the red lights behind the cars hurrying down the street. Suddenly he was overtaken by a kind of uneasiness. One of the windowpanes, the one on the right, the lower one, had a defect: a bubble that reflected the tiny red lights. That defect brought him a memory as gray as the evening, a memory coming from who knows what depths, from who knows what dark paths, perhaps from when he was little. He took his eyes away from the bubble. The attorney's assistant, holding his card in his hand, came into the room. He sat down. The Isabeline-style chairs, upholstered in strawberry-colored velvet, were kept from touching the wall by a wood strip nailed to the floor. The assistant came to him to let him know that Senyor Riera would receive him soon and asked the couple in.

Attorney Riera looked at his rose. He had brought it freshly cut from his villa in Cadaqués. He himself had set it in that little vase made of silver and crystal he'd gotten from a maternal grandmother. It was a red rose, open, but still with a few petals in the center making a bud. He picked up the card: Eladi Farriols. That name did not sound familiar. He asked his assistant, "Has this gentleman come to see me before?"

"No, sir."

"Ask him in." He picked up a contract and pretended to read. Then he raised his head and told Eladi to sit down. He had forgotten the face behind the name on the card, but seeing him now he recognized him at once. He looked much worse. Eladi was taking off his gloves; when it was hot, he needed them more than ever because he hated his hands feeling sweaty. A glove fell to the floor. He picked it up and looked at the attorney. He'd come about a matter that had nothing to do with the law.

"It's about my son Ramon, whom you might remember. When he was little you saw him often."

Attorney Riera felt like looking at the rose. He said to Eladi: "Of course, yes, sure . . . I recall perfectly Senyora Valldaura's eldest grandson. He must be a man now."

The office felt stuffy, and the stuffy smell, deep down in Eladi's mind, blended violently with the uneasiness brought about by the bubble.

"Ramon, you understand . . ." And Eladi told him how his son, in a fit, had left home. "And Marina, your sister, has written to me explaining that he is staying with her. It seems that Ramon and Marina's oldest daughter, Marina, were students together."

Attorney Riera picked up the letter that Eladi handed him. He recognized his sister's handwriting at once. He interrogated Eladi with his eyes, "What does this all mean?"

"Your sister tells me that my son is in her house; well, after I . . . After a conversation I had with him."

Attorney Riera listened to that mumbling with little interest. Teresa had told him so much about that son-in-law of hers whom she held as a man of little substance. She was sure he had married Sofia for her money. After all, if Eladi Farriols was having a hard time with his son, it was his doing. Eladi spoke about Maria, of what there might have been between brother and sister. From time to time he wiped his brow and his neck. The stuffiness and the bubble and Attorney Riera, who seemed not to be there. Attorney Riera knew the story, not the recent one but the old one, the one about the cabaret singer. The story of Lady Godiva. He'd seen her more than once; not alone, with friends. She sang naked on top of a man with a horse's head, covered by abundant black hair. She had a nice belly, firm and exquisite. It was worth wasting a couple of hours to admire that belly. But why in hell did Eladi bring the artist's daughter to his home with his wife and legitimate children? There must have been a thousand more intelligent ways to resolve that problem. Very touching, to be sure, the natural child at home – but now he was paying the consequences. One always pays for one's foolishness, he sentenced mentally. All that family needed was a case of incest! Eladi was telling him that he'd come to see him in order to help his son.

"I'll write you a check so that, without letting my son know, you can send it to your sister. That's why I came to intrude on your time."

Attorney Riera, picking up the check and folding it without looking at it, said: "Why don't you try to go to my sister's to see your son? At times the most complicated situations can be resolved with a couple of words."

He quickly realized that he had to accept what Eladi was asking of him if he was to help him: no sermons or advice. Eladi was not a man to face anything requiring an effort. Deep down, despite everything, he felt sorry for Eladi. He assured him that he himself, in person, would hand the check to his sister; he would do everything possible to ensure that Ramon didn't know his father was helping him. Eladi started to put on his gloves, lowering his head to hide the emotion that was choking him. As soon as Eladi left his office, Attorney Riera took a deep breath, picked up the vase, brought the rose to his nose, and smelled it voluptuously. Poor Teresa . . .

14. MARIA

She had never felt autumns to be sad, only that one. The villa was surrounded by fences, by clouds that did not let her breathe. Why didn't everything just die? Her mother looked at her as if she couldn't see her. Her grandmother was always asleep. Her father was feeling down, and he sulked about with his eyes so full of sorrow that she couldn't bear looking at him. Her only company was the roof and the sky. Every night she climbed up there, and, facing the wisteria, standing, all white in her diaphanous nightgown ("like a bride's," Armanda had said long ago), she softly uttered again and again her brother's name; it was as if she'd just seen him atop the bench where in summer the bees and the purple flowers that fell and flew were sweeter than honey. She called him feebly because, if he were far away, wherever he'd gone, he could hear her with his soul and come back, even though they were brother and sister. The same way his soul had called her under the light of the stars. One night she tried to get all the way to the eave, the place where they had sat holding a rope, which they had tied from chimney to chimney. She then walked back, and, when she got to the iron stairs, she grabbed the railing hard and closed her eyes because her heart was beating fast. At that moment she made her decision.

At the bottom of the park all the golden and red leaves awaited her. She shook a maple, and a rain of helixes fell upon her. She filled her hands with closed eyes. She went to the water and leaned forward; in it her face was the face of a child. She threw a handful of dirt on the water, and her face disappeared. She began to drag her feet, making grooves in the soft earth. From time to time she kicked a root. "Like a snake," Ramon used to say; they'd pull on the root, thinking it was from a nearby tree, and it took them to a tree far away. A dead snake, made into a root by time and by storms. And then she saw the forked branch at her feet: dirty and white, with clumps of moss on the tip of its handle, half-buried. She took some steps back and could see everything again. "Don't move!" a voice inside her said. "Don't move!" In the trees the birds seemed to be listening. She bent down and picked up the fork. She struck it against the ground to rid it of the moss. She then hit the water hard. She hit it again, and the water splashed her left cheek. She wiped it with the back of her hand and licked it. It had no taste: just saliva and tongue and sky. She hit the water again, and the water splashed her left eye. She wiped her eye with her fingertips and ran a wet finger on her eyelid. The water on her eyelid and the water of a tear were the same, except that one was sweet and the other salty. Her face in the water was the face of a being with eyes of water, with saliva of water: a being of water and fire. A flame rose inside her soul: a high flame. A flame of love without knowing what love was. She broke as best she could the forked branch and threw it in the water, which again erased her face and the lips that no love of a man had ever kissed, that were never to be kissed by the love of a man. Her breasts tender as the spring, her knees sweeter than the calyx of a honeysuckle. A wasteland. At the foot of the oldest tree the violets stared at her. One by one she crushed them under her foot. With a stone she rubbed the trunk of the tree, deep, to erase those letters the sap had warped and which she had never quite understood. Then she went into the birdcage. She sat on the ground and stood for a while looking at the splotches of light and shade on her hands. In that place there had been large birds, colorful birds: peacocks with their tails unfolded in an iridescent fan stained with blue. Pheasants the color of autumn, all with a small head. Her grandmother had explained to her that she loved them but that the servants hated them as they were an added burden and had let them die of thirst. She would have also loved them, but Ramon would have gouged out their eyes. She had heard it said that blind birds sang better. She would have liked to hold one on her lap: a blind pheasant, with an open beak and a scratchy tongue. The shadows shook on her hands; her heart, well protected by bones and skin, also quaked. She wished she could grab it and throw it to a tiger. Here, tiger. And the tiger, with his claw, would turn it to see what lay beneath. Then he would have taken it with his teeth, careful to keep it whole, and would have taken it to his young, who awaited him hungrily. A yellow tiger lined in black and with live coals in his eyes. With a single leap atop a tree. She got up, hesitated, sat down again. She took off her shoes to find the earth. Nearby there was a violet, partly crushed. She picked it up delicately; if her eyes were a magnifying glass, they would be able to see such a crisscrossing of nerves, such a madness of lines. She brought the violet to her lips, plucked it with her tongue, and swallowed it. Bits of moss from the fork had clung to her hands. It was getting dark. The light had fled, and night descended. She liked the night. Maria . . . Maria . . . Maria . . . She got up. She touched the dangling gate and, bending her head, went out. Shoeless, she thrust her feet into the rotting leaves, the dry leaves, and she felt like a dry leaf, like a rotten leaf. Maria . . . Maria . . . Maria . . . She stopped and yelled with her hands around her mouth as if she had to climb down from a branch or from a star: Jaume! Jaume! Jaume! No one answered, and she no longer heard her own name being called.

She left the door ajar and opened the balcony wide. The wind pulled her nightgown to one side: a white wing reflected in the mirror. Her small breasts and her superb thighs showed through. Suffused with self-love, she looked gravely at her own reflection. Suddenly she was naked. An invisible hand from the other side of the mirror had removed her nightgown as if the wind had swept it away. Her breasts were the shape of a bowl, her nipples a light tan, her belly button knotted. The invisible hand put the sea at her feet. She was being born naked out of dead waves, with an engagement ring on her head, like a crown, studded with shrapnel of diamonds and rubies. Wedding colors. The red of rent virginity and the white of lost virginity. The ring fell off. She opened her arms, spread her legs, raised her head. She was making a star. Whenever she and Ramon tired of running and screaming, they came to a sudden halt and made five-pointed stars. They would remain motionless, to see who could hold the position longer. Jaume came and pushed them. "Move! Move!" Engagement ring, sea, and stars, all disappeared from the mirror, which now misted over. And she. Halfway up the stairs she needed to grab the railing for a moment. She stopped by Grandmother Teresa's room and listened. She turned the knob and opened the door. Grandmother's breathing was heavy. The breathing of someone who was very tired. What could she be tired of, her grandmother? The room was completely dark, but the faint light from the foyer windows let her see the table and the gold and red armchair. On the table there was the photo album Grandmother Teresa was fond of looking at. She picked it up. Before she closed the door, she felt like kissing Grandmother Teresa's hand, but she was unable to.

Carrying the album, she lit the small table lamp in the library and sat on the floor. She was looking for something specific. She turned the pages quickly. Was it all about Grandmother? Young Grandmother, with a rose on her chest. Grandmother in a décolletage, loaded with jewels. Grandmother in a suit, her brooch of diamond flowers pinned to its lapel. Papa and Mama. Mama like a pigeon, with a racquet in her hand. She in diapers held by a wet nurse. She with a bunch of mock orange in her hand. Finally! She and Ramon next to each other, Jaume in front of them with his small head, his thin legs, his bulky knees. As if carrying a tray, his hands held a slab of wood with a piece of white material tied to a stick that pretended to be a flag. Jaume's little boat. When she took the photograph to kiss it, a newspaper clipping fell to the floor. She saw a young woman with her tresses loose, mounted on a man disguised as a horse. She stared at the eyes of that woman, which looked like hers. Why should Grandmother have kept that clipping? She gave Jaume a long kiss and left everything the way she'd found it. She closed the album. Placing her hand on it, she thought for a while about the sad eyes of that young woman. She went out, walked to the wisteria bench. She leaned into the dry well. A moonbeam penetrated it to the very bottom. Down there she saw something shiny. Something Jaume must have thrown in. Whatever he didn't like he threw in the well.

With one hand she grabbed the iron railing, with the other she held her hair, which the wind was throwing onto her face, and she came down to the roof. A taut sky, veiled on one side by stardust, pierced on the other by large stars, gave her courage. With her arms spread to keep her balance, her hair over her eyes, she approached the eave with the lace-like grill; she again looked at the stone bench she could now barely make out, at the trees reaching to the sky. She licked her lips a few times. If you curl your tongue for a good while against the roof of your mouth, you will feel the taste of nectar. The laurel, leafing under her, swaying in the wind, seemed like a sea of black water. A roof tile got loose, and one of her feet slipped. At the moment of throwing herself over, a moan came out of her open mouth.

15. THE LAUREL

In the kitchen everything was shiny: the brass, the glass, the pots hanging in rows against the wall. Armanda came in to inspect: everything was behind schedule. Jacinta had not returned from grocery shopping yet; Júlia went along to help carry the bags. Before taking the streetcar, they went into a café for a leisurely cup of coffee. And the two of them, sometimes with the help of a waiter, added up what they had spent, increased the totals a bit, and, back home, gave the list to Armanda. Armanda recognized that Jacinta kept the kitchen spick and span. She went into the scullery. She opened a drawer in the hutch that was built to measure years ago to keep the silver. The amount of silver kept in that house was mind-boggling: the table settings from both marriages of Senyora Teresa, those of Sofia, those of Senyor Eladi's father and uncle. She closed the drawers and pulled open the bottom one, where the cleansing liquid and the rags were kept. She picked up a piece of cloth and rubbed a spoon with it, hard. Not even a trace of a black smear. That's what one called cleaning the silver right. She opened the closet with the trays, the tureens, the tea and coffee sets, everything solid. And on top of all that, in the basement, they kept the fancy silver from Senyora Teresa's first husband, whose name she could never remember. She went to the table; she had heard voices in the garden. Jacinta and Júlia were chatting with the man who delivered the cases of mineral water bottles.

Armanda saw him into the kitchen and turned the basement lights on. The girls had begun emptying their baskets: seafood, for Senyora Sofia; shrimp that were still stirring; meat, bacon, cold cuts, two chickens, a rabbit for the servants' rice. Júlia went to the dining room to get the platters for the fruit. She still remembered Senyora Teresa's dismay when she learned they had sent the old fruit platters away for storage, those in the shape of magnolias. Júlia returned the fruit platters to the dining room and then put the extra fruit in the refrigerator, which was as tall as the ceiling, a hotel model. From the basement the mineral water guy yelled that there were three return bottles missing, and Júlia, leaning down, told him they had gotten broken.

Jacinta put the baskets away, slipped on her apron, and told Armanda, "I'll prepare a rice dish that will make you lick your fingers."

Lighting the woodstove, Armanda offered to help chop onions and peel tomatoes; she was not busy, and chopping would help her pass the time. It was not simple to cook dinner in that household: everyone ate differently. Senyora Teresa was going through her french fries and grilled meat period; whenever she decided on a menu, she kept having the same thing until she could no longer stomach it. Senyor Eladi would die for lambs' brains fried in batter, and Senyora Sofia was a shrimp – and lobster – eating machine. Jacinta's arm hurt from making mayonnaise. When Ramon was still at home, one would say the young ones were old folk: they kept asking for broth; Jacinta boiled hen after hen, and with the meat she made croquettes for herself and Anna because the family wouldn't touch anything that might seem like leftovers. That day Armanda, Júlia, Anna, Jacinta, and Virgínia would eat rabbit rice. Sílvia had the day off. The bay leaf jar was empty; Júlia washed it.

"I'm going to get more leaves."

Armanda recalled the night of the storm: Aunt Anselma had explained that the wind was blowing the roof off and that little Sofia was crying nonstop. A lightning strike split the main branch of the laurel tree, but that mutilation made the plant even bushier. Once the lightning rod was installed they all breathed easier. It had been foolhardy to live in that house with all those towers without a lightning rod. Júlia went outside. She was dead tired; they had spent over two hours in the market, standing, going from one place to the next, because Jacinta, before deciding to make a purchase, took her sweet time looking at every stall. And she, Júlia, did not have much stamina. Had she been at home she would have gone to lie down, as she used to do with her mother every time they came back from the market. She stood outside the kitchen door looking at the park. She would not have dared go there at night. She'd been in the house for two years and was still afraid of trees; she felt they were all growing at once and said things to one another. Once Senyor Eladi told her that at the very end of the park there were three Lebanon cedars, and she replied she'd never seen one. "One day, if you would like, I'll take you to see them." She said thanks. The laurel by the house got sun only in the morning. It had low shoots and branches that the senyors did not want trimmed so that the cooks could pick the leaves without a ladder. She looked at the tree somewhat uneasily. There was something different about it. The main trunk was stained with ooze the color of red ochre. The ground, under it, seemed wet and was stained red. The ooze was shiny. She touched it with the tip of a finger, smelled it: it didn't smell like anything. She looked up. Among the thick leaves she saw something white, as if a sheet had fallen from the balcony and had gotten snagged in the laurel. She ran her finger again on the seepage and then took off running, frantically screaming that there was blood flowing down the laurel trunk. Armanda, who was seated and peeling tomatoes, and Jacinta, cleaning shrimp under the faucet, turned their heads. Armanda said, "Lets go upstairs to see what's going on."

She cast an ugly look at Júlia for being so shaken. They climbed up to the second story, went to the balcony, and looked down. Armanda covered her face with her hands and bent over as if she'd been hit by a fist in her stomach. The other two crossed themselves and closed their eyes.

It had rained hard that morning, and early in the afternoon the sky had cleared up a bit, but there were still clouds. The rain had done nothing to abate the heat, and the wind was hot, as from the desert. The bouquets and wreaths filled two vans entirely; the men who were moving the flowers from the house tilted against the wind that was spreading the smell of death. Eladi, ashen, was shaking the hands of all those people who were shaking his out of obligation. After all, they reflected, Maria was not the daughter of the Farriols, rather of some cousins, who knows. Sofia, pale, but with glistening eyes, accepted the condolences as if she really were the mother of the girl that was to be buried. In a corner of the kitchen, sitting on a low chair, Armanda was sobbing. From time to time she wiped her eyes with a corner of her apron. She had washed her face. That dribble of dried blood to one side of her mouth had stuck like a scab. And the belly, Lord . . . She had helped get her dressed. The men who had taken down the dead girl had almost fainted; she had to pour them a glass of brandy. She had combed her hair – that black and curly hair that she had bleached so many times against Senyoreta Rosa's orders. Sitting there, blinded by her tears, she listened to the wind. Maria liked the wind, and the wind had come to keep Maria company, to mingle with the black celebration. Maria had never loved her. Who had Maria ever loved? Who could she possibly have loved? One evening she'd come in the kitchen, years ago, looking for a knife.

"What do you want?"

Maria had answered dryly: "A knife."

"What for?" Armanda had asked guilelessly.

"I need it."

"You have no business with a kitchen knife."

"The others aren't sharp enough."

Maria was right, and Armanda showed her a small one. "Will this one do, Maria?"

To Armanda's astonishment Maria said, "From now on please do not address me familiarly; I am no longer a child."

Maria took a knife from the drawer after searching for one.

"A meat knife? You and Ramon are always taking knives from the kitchen. I can't see what you need them for."

"To kill Mama," she answered blithely.

"Be quiet! You want it for making trouble – I know you."

"I want it to open the pages of a book."

"If you need it to open the pages of a book, get a letter opener. You're not fooling me." She tried to take the knife from her, and in the struggle she cut herself. "You see? Do you like blood? You're wicked. Look at the blood."

And Maria, facing her, and standing just as Sofia would have, told her: "Having gone to bed with my father for a time doesn't give you the right to treat me as if I were a servant."

Armanda felt the blow. "Look at the blood, look."

Then Maria took the knife that Armanda had left on the table, put it back in the drawer, and left slowly, crying. The following day, when she was going out shopping, Sofia stopped before a chestnut tree. On the trunk she saw a huge hole, still fresh, that almost went through the tree and on the ground three kitchen knives with broken blades. She went back in, called her children, and asked them who had dug a hole in the chestnut tree. They said they didn't know.

"You are a bit old to be such idiots!"

Why, Armanda thought as she wiped her eyes, did she have to recall that ugly episode on the day Maria was taken from the house forever? She got up, staggered outside, and went to the laurel with a heavy heart; she looked at it from top to bottom, put her hand to the trunk a few times. Good-bye, Maria. And she burst into disconsolate tears.

When all the visitors had left and Eladi hadn't yet returned from the cemetery, Sofia went to see her mother and found her asleep with her head on her chest. She cleared her throat loudly to see if she could wake her up, but Teresa did not move. Sofia left the room, closed the door, and started to climb the stairs, her heart pulsating with a strange joy. Her bedroom's balcony door was wide open, and rainwater had come in. Along the driveway you could see flowers that must have fallen off the wreaths. She breathed in the warm wind mixed with sunlight and clouds. All passes. She went to her desk and sat down, as motionless as an object. The drawers had round knobs. She pulled on the knob of one of the drawers and slid her hand under a batch of bills: the small key was there. It was tiny and flat. She ran her index finger over it as if to polish it. The only drawer in her desk that had a key was the middle one. It was raining again in between sputterings of sun. The rustle of the rain on the leaves filled her with pleasure. She put her hand in the drawer and took out a bundle of letters tied with a discolored ribbon. She pulled on the ribbon, and it knotted; it took a while to untie it. She arranged the letters in a row in front of her; each one in its envelope, yellowed by time. She pulled one out, and, her eyes filled with tenderness, she read: "Dear Sofia . . ." She took all the letters out of the envelopes, tore them up, and threw them in the wastepaper basket. She had unfolded the letters on her desk; each letter was like a wave of youth that brought a taste of mint to her mouth, a precise memory of white outfits, balls and racquets, of acacias in bloom and walls with trellised roses. The gate was wide, painted green, and with a sign over it extending from side to side: TENNIS CLUB. "My dear Sofia . . ." They were from Lluís Roca. He had wooed her, but then she'd fallen for Eladi. She took a letter and tore it with a feeling of melancholy, and then she tore all the others. Before tossing them into the wastebasket, she paused. If one of the servants . . . Bah, why bother? Her forehead burned as if she'd been drinking champagne; she was always feverish after drinking champagne. She itched to have a cool drink, outdoors, next to a young man in white pants. The balcony in Maria's room was also open. The bed, the headboard, the skirt of the dressing table, all of white organza. Everything in Maria's room was incandescent. She thought: Why did I have to tear the letters? Why, after keeping them for so many years? She would go get the shreds, would piece them together with tape underneath, she would keep them again. But, why? Gone, gone. Those letters had softened her, and she hated feeling soft. A branch of the laurel was next to her. It didn't smell, even though the rain and the wind, she thought, should have brought out its fragrance. She pulled off a leaf and crushed it in her fingers. She stuck the crumpled leaf into her décolletage and smelled her hand. What a fine scent. She would have liked to find her mother awake to whisper in her ear, "You could have saved yourself the trouble of writing that will." Over the edge of the balcony emerged the branch rent by the lightning that ended in a sharp point. Sofia smiled as she raised her head and smelled her perfumed fingers. Whenever she was alone, she pulled her head up as much as possible to avoid having a wrinkled neck. Good-bye, Maria.

17. THE STONE SLAB

Eladi had to make an effort to go on living. His craving for girls had abated. Some cog inside him was not running smoothly. He developed a sickly passion for books; he picked them up as if they were jewels, moved them around, reordered them incessantly. He seldom went out, just to go to bookstores to seek and order rare books. He drowned in essays on Proust. Since at times he was fascinated and at others bored, he itched to find the key to that mystery. He tried his hand at translating fragments, which he later tore up. The maids were forbidden to clean the library. It felt stuffy and dusty in a bad way. There were piles of books on the floor, rare, deluxe editions, half-filled-out catalog cards, drawers to be filled. He polished the spines of books. He climbed on the ladder where Valldaura used to perch little Sofia to make her travel about; he moved the books he was less interested in to the higher shelves, making sure that no spine stuck out one millimeter past the others. But he didn't read a line. He got up in the middle of the night to work, chain-smoking. Sofia at times looked at the light from the library windows projected onto the gravel outside and thought that Eladi's nights, locked in there, were a madman's nights. One day all the pictures of Ramon disappeared from the house. Then those of Maria. He burned them and cried. Early one morning he found, behind the row of volumes of the *Comédie Humaine*, one of Valldaura's notebooks. He opened it at random. There was a detailed description of his estates. On the last page he read: "I sit at my desk when the peacocks cry, and I think of my world. Small: a golden ball no bigger than an orange. I supply the views; I give it life." Eladi felt a shiver down his spine and decided to light a fire. He made a pile of kindling, crumpled newspaper under it, covered it all with big logs, and lit a match. As the flames rose, he pushed a chair toward the fireplace and picked up the notebook. He started again: "I sit at my desk when the peacocks cry, and I think of my world. Small: a golden ball no bigger than an orange. I supply the views; I give it life. A river, a canal, and mountains with lilacs in bloom in spring. My dream is not dead; the more time has passed, the more violent the memory. I have loved Teresa, but I am not the man she needed – because an important corner of my soul has always been closed to her. At times, when I wanted to make love to Teresa (how inadequate 'to make love'; they call melting, giving oneself away until the loss of consciousness, 'to make love'), I felt in the palm of my hand the sweetness of Barbara's bosom burning me. That fire in this bit of skin barred the doors of pleasure for me. For this reason I have understood Teresa's sentimental deviation, although I have not always respected it." Eladi closed the notebook and became absorbed, contemplating the flames. The trees burning now had stored heat from the sun and light from the moon, millions of raindrops; what was burning before his eyes was the beauty of the universe reduced to a bunch of bluish and red flames, the sky and the sunlight now fleeing upward to rejoin what they had been. "I do not think I've ever loved Sofia the way parents love their children. I have been wanting in paternal spirit. Snuggling with her when she was little was a need for me. With Sofia on my lap, with Sofia to look at the peacocks, with Sofia to pick violets, it was as if I were finding refuge in a being with whom I could open the gates to my nostalgia without arousing curiosity or uneasiness. I've spent hours at the bottom of the park listening to the cooing of turtledoves. And the pond water surrounded by ivy has made me sad for Ophelia. Each reflection of light made her surface on her shiny bed, wasted, her hair adorned with violets oozing black water. Ophelia poisoned by the moon, floating in her night of death. The sweetness of Barbara's memory cannot be compared to any other sweetness."

Halfway through winter Eladi fell ill. Recovery took a long time. He was clearly diminished. By spring he felt a little better. He made an effort and came down the stairs with the same airs as before, buttoning his gloves, his cane hanging from his forearm. If he ran into an acquaintance, he'd greet him, but he never paused to chat with anyone. One morning in April he left the house early. He was going to take care of something he'd promised himself he'd do. He stopped for a moment to see Teresa, whom Maria's death had affected deeply. He found her old, and seeing her son-in-law she thought, "What a ruin." In town he walked with a straight back, a raised head, a tucked-in gut. He stopped in front of Senyor Jeremies's workshop. Two young men were carving a large figure with a wreath of flowers. Senyor Jeremies was running about the courtyard, amid the blocks of marble, and one of the young men went to get him.

He greeted Eladi with great deference. "What can I do for you?"

"Something very simple: a stone slab to put at the foot of a tree where my adopted daughter died. It should have big letters, carved deep, saying only *Maria*. Make it as soon as you can."

Senyor Jeremies thought for a moment: "I made the tombstone for your younger child – I remember his name was Jaume. And for Senyor Valldaura. And for the girl, Maria. Of course I'll do it, but I am swamped with work – do not ask for anything in a hurry."

"But a slab with one name, is it so difficult to make?"

They talked about measurements for a while and agreed that the slab would be ninety by sixty centimeters and the letters filled with fine gold.

"Perhaps they'll become dull with time, but you can always have them repainted. Besides, you know, if they are a bit dull, they look even better."

Eladi found a letter from Attorney Riera on the console table. He informed him that Ramon was no longer living in his sister's house and that he had found a job. But he didn't say where he was employed. A week after the visit to the carver, the slab sat at the foot of the laurel. Sofia thought it in horrible taste, but she made no comment. From that day on Eladi spent hours sitting on the wisteria bench, in front of the laurel, delighted with the stele. Before going to bed, facing the bathroom mirror that reflected back his demolished face, he thought that in his black eyes, gleaming still, were the same melancholy lakes as in Proust's eyes. What had happened with Ramon was a sorrow for life. Maria's death was a wholly different thing. His daughter's death had killed his own youth: the cabarets, the artists, the songs. Those nights when he left the house with an excited heart, full of anticipation. And the memory of Pilar, innocent and sweet, was the great memory of Eladi, the man who he had been and who he could never be again.

18. A NEW SET OF SERVANTS

Armanda, as usual after the midday meal, went upstairs to stretch out in bed. The heat was killing her. Sofia had gone to the hairdresser and the massage parlor. Virgínia had cleaned Senyora Teresa's room in depth. Whenever they cleaned it, two servants under Armanda's supervision sat the Senyora in her wheelchair and took her to the dining room. When they returned her to her room, Armanda made sure everything had been properly cleaned and that they had not overlooked any corners, because today's servants weren't as trustworthy as they used to be. She straightened the peacock feathers that the draft always mussed, and she stayed to keep the lady company until she fell asleep. The Senyor, she thought, will leave soon. After a moment she heard *riiiing, riiiing*. It was a wonder that, after so many sorrows and so much sitting by the slab, he was still in the mood for that old joke. Only for a short period he'd forgotten to press the lion's tongue bell, after the drama with Ramon and for a few months after Maria's death. It must have been a compulsion with him because, as soon as he felt a little better, he went back to the same prank. Or maybe it was just habit. One could never know. Where must Ramon be? He hadn't shown any signs of life since. As if he were dead. He was an ornery child but not a mean one. What both he and Maria needed was to be loved. She never thought them capable of anything evil, as that loose tongue, Senyoreta Rosa, had insinuated. Perhaps with time things would have gotten dangerous. She turned her back to the balcony; the light creeping in through the open curtain hurt her eyes. It had posed a danger, a big one. The stone with Maria's name at the foot of the laurel said it clearly. Then she heard the screams of the girls outside the kitchen: they must have turned the hose on. They couldn't be any jollier. They laughed at everything. When a new one came to the house, she soon acquired the habit of the old ones. Because the water felt so good on your skin in the sun. As soon as the senyors left, they rushed to undress and hooked the hose to the faucet outside the kitchen door. Under the spray they laughed like crazy and kidded around because their bodies were young, with thighs that seemed made of rock. She was dozing off. Senyora Teresa no longer asked if the coal delivery guys were there because by now poor Senyora Teresa could hear very little.

With great shrieks Jacinta said she could not get in the basin. She was afraid her belly would hurt like it had the last time. Very low, deep inside. Sílvia gave her a shove.

"Don't worry. You'll see. When it's so hot, it's just fine. Take off your clothes!"

The bell had rung a while ago, and Anna knew that it was Senyor Eladi, who was making passes at her; at his age he should be ashamed, a girl as young as she was, seventeen years old with milk and honey on her lips. He left through the gate. One day he'd told her that she had milk and honey on her lips; she'd been dusting a painting featuring three ladies with veiled faces. He left through the gate, went around the fields, and came back in through the back door. Stealthily, like a wolf, he snuck into the washhouse. One day, some time ago, she could not remember what she had been looking for, she noticed a round spot, no bigger than the mouth of a cordial glass, on the lower edge of one of the panes of the window facing the kitchen. Those panes never got washed, and that immaculately clean spot made her suspicious. Right at the foot of the window, a place that had been piled with stuff all winter, was now clear. From that spot Senyor Eladi spied on them. They could not see him because the sun blinded them. She could almost see him right there, crouching, his black eyes and thick eyebrows with some white hairs, tall and meager, his mouth watering, lost and lost again before so much bosom and so much thigh. She didn't tell the others; that afternoon they were overexcited. All of them. Perhaps because they had eaten too much grilled rabbit with too much allioli. Once they were all naked in the sun, she called them together and warned them, above all, not to look toward the washhouse because Senyor Eladi, whenever they showered, watched them through a peephole. He pretended to leave, rang the bell to fool them, and, hiding among the trees and the grass, snuck into the washhouse and peeped and peeped. He missed no detail. She thought the girls would rush back into the kitchen in embarrassment, but Sílvia – Armanda called her the Queen of the Pinks because on Sundays she pinned a carnation on her dress – who hated Senyora Sofia, brazen as can be (whenever she laughed, she showed the tip of her tongue between her teeth), took off running and stood facing the window. All the others burst out in mad laughter. Then she turned her back to the window and then turned again to be seen by Senyor Eladi, with his gloves and cane. She then walked back toward the girls, slowly, and they giggled even harder, and, as they avoided the jet of water, they ran and danced in front of the window. Armanda woke up and went to see what all that fuss was about. It was too much. She thought they had gone mad. They ran and skipped on the terrace, shimmering with droplets, their skin taut from so much watering, not the water of the spray but from the fire of their young blood underneath. She let them scream at will and went back upstairs. She was dead tired and lay down again on that bed where the Senyor had met her more than once when returning home in the wee hours. Senyoreta Sofia, stupid enough to miss the fun, had been asleep for hours already; she said that going to bed early kept you young and the following morning made your eyes shine.

19. ELADI FARRIOLS'S WAKE

At midnight Armanda, in her black silk dress, lace apron, and star-shaped diamond earrings, walked into the library with a bouquet of artificial roses. Masdéu, his back to the door, stood as soon as he heard steps.

"Oh, don't get up. It's only me."

The curtains were drawn. The table and armchairs had been pushed into a corner to make room for the low platform where the casket sat, with mammoth candles at its head and feet. From time to time Masdéu trimmed their wicks. Candlelight shone on the gold lettering on the backs of books. Armanda placed the bouquet of red roses over the belly of the dead man and thought: a man who looked like a god, and, see, stiff as can be and with one eye half-open. She crossed herself and began to pull with one finger on the stubborn eyelid. The cornea, under the light of one of the candles, seemed alive. Armanda kept her finger on the eyelid.

Masdéu said, "Look, his belly is already bloated."

Armanda lifted the roses and took a look. "It's really happening fast; it'll soon be higher than his chest." She replaced the roses carefully, making sure the starchy ribbon hanging from the bunch showed the gilded letters that read, "To Eladi Farriols, Armanda Valls."

At the foot of the platform covered in black velvet with a white fringe, the wreaths and bouquets of flowers that had begun arriving that evening were piling up. Tender roses and purple lilies with a burst of yellow in the middle of each petal. The library was filling with the bland smell of dead flowers withering in their empty sacrifice. They had dressed Eladi in a black suit and a bow tie that had proved more convenient. The man who dressed him could not tie a four-in-hand; the bow was held by two celluloid strips. Armanda explained to Masdéu that she had not heard that the Senyor was dead until the late morning and was sure he had died early in the afternoon the day before. But nobody knew anything for sure; the nurse intimidated the servants and told them nothing. She couldn't stand her; the woman wanted to be served like a lady and looked at the servants superciliously, as if they were not human, and forbade them to enter the sick man's bedroom. Júlia explained that Senyora Sofia had asked her to telephone Doctor Falguera, and, when he arrived, Sofia, all dressed up and her head erect, walked him to her husband's bedroom. An uneasy pall hung over the house all afternoon. No one knew exactly what was going on until the Senyora informed them the Senyor was dead. He had died without spiritual comforts, and they all thought that very strange.

Júlia said: "I've felt death roaming about all afternoon; one can feel death coming. The dogs are proof of this. It's a shadow nobody sees, but it paces about."

They did not know whether the Senyor had died peacefully or in pain – the matter remained unclear. Someone, whom the Senyora must have advised at once, had sent a wreath of yellow roses with a purple ribbon a foot wide before they knew anything or had time to prepare the library. None of his friends had come for the wake, only that gentleman who was a painter, Senyora Valldaura's godson, the one Senyora Valldaura said was a bad artist.

Masdéu raised his elbow and brought his thumb to his lips in a gesture and asked Armanda, "Do you think Senyor Eladi . . . ?"

Armanda, having succeeded at closing the fractious eyelid, answered, as she kept checking the eye. "Do you mean like Senyora Teresa, for years? No. But surely other things."

Masdéu asked how long ago Maria had thrown herself from the roof because he had no sense of time.

"You are thinking that the girl's death brought him down? Maybe."

Armanda folded her hands on her lap and pouted her lips. "The only child I saw him really love was Jaume, the one who died in the water. I still remember when he was born. What a christening, Holy Mother of God! Senyora Sofia was in a bad mood, perhaps for having borne another child so soon, and the Senyor slapped her with a grand christening feast. Better than Ramon's. The christening outfit was made of Malines lace."

Masdéu could not recall it because he'd never been invited to the christening. Looking at the books on the shelves, he thought of Senyora Teresa, whom he now seldom visited. He was afraid he'd bother her.

"And Senyora Teresa, what does she have to say about this death?"

"She probably doesn't know about it yet; I think she'll feel bad about it."

No, Masdéu did not often come to the house anymore, but, as soon as Armanda had sent notice that Senyor Eladi was dead, he rushed to offer his help for whatever they might need him. He helped set up the platform and cover it with the black velvet.

"At times," Armanda said, "when I think of the time when the children were small . . . Maria loved Ramon right away; she would say: I have a baby all mine, and she was very little. But, when poor little Jaume came, she at once became jealous. Ramon did too. They abused him a lot."

Masdéu interrupted to tell her that Eladi's death must have been a blow for Sofia. And Armanda, staring at that eye that seemed about to open again, said she knew very little of the things of the world.

"I am waiting to see what Senyora Teresa will say when she learns. But at this moment I would like to know one thing: what the Senyor died of, because a few weeks ago he appeared very changed, so much that he already seemed dead."

Masdéu said, "If you, who are practically family, don't know . . ."

When she heard those words, Armanda pulled a handkerchief from her apron's pocket and said, wiping a tear, "It is true I am like family."

"Me too," Masdéu said. "My father always told me to go see Senyora Teresa, who was very kind, and that I was her godson. Perhaps she'll take care of you. I don't care whether she remembers me or not – I've never come to this house with any interested motive."

Armanda, with a mysterious air, after putting her handkerchief back in her pocket, pulled out a small flask and said, "Look." It was a medicine vial, without a label to spell out what the medication was. It had been in the medicine cabinet in the bathroom for years. As soon as it was empty, it appeared, again, full, and none of the servants had gone to the drugstore for a refill. That vial seemed to go to the drugstore and return all by itself.

"I think Senyor Eladi took it out for walks. Smell."

Masdéu said it had a particular smell, and Armanda asked him if he knew anyone who could tell them what it was or take it to the pharmacy for an analysis of the few drops still left in it. Masdéu blushed and said he was no good for certain jobs. Armanda didn't dare either, but an idea had stuck in her head: to learn what the Senyor had died of. She explained that some time ago they had a chambermaid, Paulina, with a sculptural bosom, who'd stayed just one year in the house. One Sunday when she was off, Armanda got into her room and in the bedside table drawer found a bottle just like that one – it could be the same one – and she had smelled it, and it was the same particular smell. That girl left without notice, very mysterious; as soon as she'd left, that little bottle appeared in the Senyor's medicine cabinet.

Suddenly Armanda brought her hands to her chest, leaned over, and whispered to Masdéu's ear: "Are you sure he hasn't stirred? Look at his fingers."

Masdéu told her they'd been stretched out the whole time. Armanda observed the dead man for a while; the wick of one of the candles began to twitch, and Masdéu got up to snuff it out with his fingernails, which got blackened, and he said his fingers got scorched.

"A dead person is imposing," Armanda said, "and who knows up to what point we are dead when we die?" She caressed the dead man's forehead and muttered: "Like frost. Maria too, when I dressed her, was like frost. Can you remember her when she was eight or nine?"

Masdéu said quite and that he had wanted to draw her head but had never dared request a session for fear of rejection, and, since he was very sensitive, he never made the request so as not to have to face being denied.

"Her eyes were black, indeed."

Armanda asked him if he wanted a cup of coffee, and Masdéu said sure, if she could also bring some toast with butter or a few cookies because he hadn't had anything to eat since eight and was famished. "A night by a corpse is so long it never ends."

Armanda left him alone. Her shadow shivered on the wall and followed her to the door. The dead man's profile had rows of books as a background. The flames underscored all that time had wrought on the smooth face of youth – his sunken eyes, his bitter grimace, a kind of flabbiness of the flesh that the spiritedness of life had mitigated and that death would take away forever. Masdéu studied the dead man's profile: his well-drawn lips, his translucent nostrils. The flowers in the wake room were drooping, and, behind the petals, the stamens, and the bended stems, you could see the wreaths' supports made of wire mesh and ferns. The dead man's lips were white, their skin etched with tiny wrinkles; some ooze between his eyelids could not have come from the sorrow of the heart because this had stopped hours ago. Behind his right ear a dark stain spread and began to invade his cheek. The corpse's hands rested near the bunch of paper roses. And the feet, so delicate that the man could not walk for even a few hours without developing blisters, pressed against the coffin's wood. Masdéu looked at those feet. The library smelled of burned wicks, of sad flowers, of decomposing flesh. He took his paper pad from his pocket and picked up a pencil. Eladi's profile with the books as backdrop had a grave air that made it more than interesting.

"You here all alone, Masdéu?"

Startled, he turned around. Standing by the door, Sofia was looking at him. All in black, serene, tall, slender. Her hair combed straight back, gathered high, untouchable, as it had always been. She never allowed a single strand to be cut.

"I am awfully sorry you've been left alone. I was so exhausted."

Masdéu got up; Sofia begged him to sit down. And he, who was not a man to notice many things, realized that she was a woman on her way back from many a path.

Sofia went to the body. "I see his eyes are closed. One of them was always open. I told the nurse to let it be, that it would close of its own accord, that I cringed at the thought of her forcing it shut. Are you making a sketch?"

"Yes, the profile."

Sofia told him that the years had been unkind to him but that her husband had an extraordinary profile. Perhaps the only one to inherit his profile was . . . She cut herself short. She had grabbed one of the ribbons from Armanda's bouquet.

"I think he was one of the most elegant men in Barcelona. I don't mean by the way he dressed, oh no, even though he did dress terribly well. My mother said: my daughter has married a prince." Unmindful, she was pulling on the ribbon until she could read the gold lettering. She looked at the roses she had not seen before and burst out: "What is this? A charade?"

Masdéu lowered his head, not knowing what to say.

"What are these paper roses doing here?" Armanda came in carrying a tray. Sofia, as soon as she saw her, yelled at her with a harsh voice to take away those flowers right away – she didn't want them there. "The flowers, the flowers!"

Armanda threw a glance of loathing toward her, placed the tray on the table, picked up the flowers lovingly, and took them away. Sofia sat down to look at the dead man. She ate a bit and drank two cups of hot coffee. She munched slowly, chatting with Masdéu, her chest raised, her little finger drawn away from the cup, sipping as if she were onstage before an audience. A dead man? In that house he'd been dead from the first day, from the first night. Her marriage war? Indifference, rather. And now she sat there, and he was the stiff one, and he had died like everyone else. Curtain. She stood and shook bread crumbs off her skirt. She walked to the window. She drew open the drapes. The clarity of dawn was beginning to fall on the gravel, to climb up the windowpanes – a tenuous light that gradually would become a triumph. Soon they'd be able to read the death notices in the papers; soon it'd be time for the burial. She would have to think of the funeral and of her widow's outfit. And she would have to speak to her mother. As the light spread across the sky, she felt overtaken by a peacefulness that even she herself found excessive. Masdéu had gone back to sketching Eladi Farriols's profile on paper, a drawing that, once finished, no one would pay any attention to because Masdéu was a poor soul whom they allowed in the house out of sheer condescension and because mother was the way she was.

20. SOFIA

The very day after the funeral Armanda stood before her and showed her a little flask. "What do you want me to do with this?" It was a medicine bottle. Sofia picked it up mechanically, uncorked it, and smelled it. She felt Armanda's stare. She moved her head back with a grimace. "Where did you find this?"

And Armanda said: "In the Senyor's bathroom cabinet, may he rest in peace. It was always full, and the day before he died it appeared empty."

Sofia gave her back the flask. "Throw it away."

Armanda left, and Sofia could not quite figure out why she couldn't forget that little bottle that seemed perfectly ordinary. Why did Armanda attach importance to it? Armanda's few words, pronounced in a tone of voice . . . as if with her tone of voice she wanted to force her to think that behind those innocent words a shameful truth was hidden. Why had she smelled that flask? Why should she worry about it? But, despite herself, she kept thinking about the flask and Armanda's words.

Consol, the manicurist, looked at the garden from the balcony: the garage behind the chestnut trees, the washhouse with the old rosebushes covered with huge flesh-colored roses. She turned around quickly and walked away from the balcony because Marcel was looking at her from below and laughing. Sofia came in, adjusting her robe, and sat down. Consol, after leaving her toolbox on the side table, sat beside her. Sílvia came in with a basin full of sudsy water. Sofia didn't feel like chatting, but she felt obliged to ask how her mother, who had a bad heart, was doing.

"She lives in fear. Senyora Farriols, I must tell you something: Marcel makes eyes at me. Whenever I come, he stares at me and grins."

Sofia, just to say something, said, "We might hear wedding bells."

Consol blushed. She pulled one of her hands from the water and began to trim the skin around the nails. "I think he's nice, of course, but I think he likes all women, and, since I am very jealous, it would be death in life. I don't know why I am telling you this. After all, a few compliments do not mean much."

Sofia forced a smile. She was getting tired of smiling. During the funeral Attorney Riera had looked at her in a way she thought peculiar. And that had been months ago. She was apprehensive; she saw things that weren't there. She could not get rid of the uneasiness she felt about the episode with the little flask. Attorney Riera had looked at her . . . How exactly did he look at her? As if he meant to say: she's getting rid of her annoyances. Of course, she and the attorney had never liked each other. With her fingers spread wide, she waited for the nail polish to dry. Consol took one of her feet and set it on her lap. She started trimming her toenails with the clippers.

"Of all the ladies I do pedicures on, you are the one with the prettiest feet."

Sofia looked at her foot and realized there was a stain on it. "Consol, what is this stain?"

Consol rubbed it with the tip of the towel. "I had never noticed it, and it's a stain in the skin."

Sofia looked at the stain with worry. "Are you sure it's not a freckle? To grow freckles, at my age . . ."

When she was alone Sofia crossed her legs and observed the stain for a long while. It was very strange. When could it have appeared? It couldn't have been long ago because she would have noticed. She rubbed it with a fingertip. Some joke, if it began to spread. She went to the bathroom, took the bottle of peroxide and a bit of cotton. Perhaps with patience and time she could manage to erase it a bit. She put her foot on the stool. Her loose tresses fell down her back. She moistened the cotton ball and rubbed her stain hard and left the cotton on it. She leaned on the sink, her head to one side to keep her hair off her face. Pale, annoyed, she picked up the cotton ball; the stain seemed even darker. There, on the white enamel stool, was her foot, a bit removed at the end of her leg. Suddenly she pulled her head back and burst out laughing. After all those years, on the piece of skin that Eladi had rubbed with his cheek on their wedding night, she had developed a stain that she did not like one bit.

21. DREAMS

Teresa Valldaura, asleep, draped an arm off the edge of the bed and sighed. The pressure on her feet prevented her from moving beyond a circle traced she didn't know where. The waves of sand would end up burying her. The smell of gunpowder choked her before she heard the shots, and a violent fit of coughing shooed the clouds away, and everything became the color of blue porcelain but unreal. A blue with no vibrations. Sky and sand were getting mixed. She looked at her chest: all blue. Her feet: blue. She found herself facing a mirror of water with her face in it: all blue. She raised one hand: blue. She felt the dread of being blue inside. Heart, lungs, liver: all blue. She lifted her skirt. Her thigh? Blue. And her blood? A long needle pricked her finger. After a moment a drop developed from the prick, a drop of blue blood. What world had she ended up in? She was dreaming, and she dreamed that she had fallen asleep and that she could not wake up because the sky and the water do not sleep. Where were the sun and the moon and everything that is somewhere and which you cannot see? Was it daytime or nighttime? And the nearby waves, the waves . . . she heard more shots and felt surrounded by a circle of blue streetlights. She was nettled by so much blueness because she was reminded of something very much like anguish. A flower with five petals, blue, appeared on her lips; it smelled of mint, and a soldier with a sprig of mint between his teeth came to her. Badly burned, he dragged a rifle with a bayonet on its end. Masdéu threw away the gun and told her, in a gruff voice that sounded like Sofia's: my darling. They hugged and were no longer by the waves but on top of the church of Sant Pere Màrtir flogged by a stormy wind. They had to lie on the floor not to be swept away. The soldier undid her blouse: my sweetheart, my love. A violent rain of apple blossoms began to fall on them, no, they are not apple blossoms, the soldier said, yes, yes . . . they all are. The apple of the beginning shone in the middle of a sunset-red sky, green on one side, rosy on the other, just like the apple in her fan. Forever holding hands, oh yes, life of my life, mine, they went down toward the city, wet with an unending love until she became round with the apple inside her, hard, with seeds of iron. A doctor opened her belly; it's the world's largest apple. He left it on a table, and it became small, the size of a hazelnut, and again in her belly. With her hands she opened her belly and looked at what the apple was doing in there, until an old man threw the apple away and covered her with diamonds, diamonds that also got inside her as she slept, and the old man loved her upstream in her veins, each vein a river of diamonds, oh how painful. The door stopped in front of her, a door in the middle of a wall three kilometers long, as the sign said, beyond the narrow door the garden was blue: trunks, branches, and leaves – everything ranged from a tender blue to a dry blue. She was afraid to go in the garden because she knew she could never get out. A voice cried: Spit out the diamonds! She spit three times. Don't spit anymore, it's done. The hand from that voice was dragging her, and under the tree how many apples, the voice whispered you exalt my passion and you soothe my soul, you exalt my passion and you soothe my soul . . . you exalt and soothe, exalt and soothe, exalt and soothe . . .

She woke up unsure of where she was. Armanda stood in front of her.

"Where do you feel pain, Senyora Teresa?"

"It was a dream. Nothing – I was dreaming."

"You know it's time for your snack, don't you?" Armanda began to undo the string tying the parcel with the sweets. "Look at what I brought you. Fresh out of the oven – they smell so good."

"Don't you ever dream, Armanda?"

"What a thing to ask! Don't you remember that you're always asking me to tell you my dreams? What was your dream about?"

Senyora Teresa looked at her with her eyes filled with the desire to be believed. She recalled what Valldaura used to say about the mystery of time. She began: "Weird. It has been one of the strangest dreams I've had."

"Tell it to me. I'd like to hear it."

Senyora Teresa kept her waiting for a while as she reflected on what to say. "I'm not sure I can remember . . . wait . . . I think I can. I was in darkness on the verge of an abyss, all around me the wind was howling: time does not exist, time does not exist . . . And I had it in my hands; I could do whatever I wanted with it. I held it in my hands, and it began to flow out of my hands like water between today and tomorrow: it existed. The wind was quiet for a long spell, and then it began to summon time with a voice of thunder, and, since time was not coming, as it was measuring the weight of things remaining, the wind started to howl from one side to the other, here and there: it does not exist . . . it does not exist . . ."

Senyora Teresa took a bite from a sweet without taking her eyes off Armanda, who replied in a worried tone, "Quite the weird dream."

Senyora Teresa smiled. "It's now your turn to tell me your dream."

Armanda spoke with some sadness: "I always have the same dream – you know that. Last night too."

"The angel?"

"The angel," Armanda affirmed.

"You were flying upward, as usual?"

"No, Senyora. I was in my bed, and some smoke began to come out of my belly button in the form of me, and it was me, and it was not quite me."

"Your soul?" Senyora Teresa inquired, as she held a partly eaten little cake by her mouth.

"The soul. And, as it went through the roof, he came by."

Senyora Teresa knew and Armanda knew that Senyora Teresa knew that the angel of her dreams had the head of Eladi Farriols.

"I, as soul, had no breasts, they were so small. The angel, with the feathers of his wings a bit brown on the edges, had a mane of hair like a burst of night."

Senyora Teresa interrupted, "You never told me he had long hair."

"The last times he did. And he took me by the waist, with an arm like a belt, and, with the other arm extended and pointing with a finger, he took off toward the sky. I, with my feet hanging, half-fainting and half-deafened by the flapping of the wings, let him grab me. We flew beyond the sky and sat on the moon until the angel left, telling me he'd be back. He had set me down on a pile of moon dust, hard as a rock, and came back in love. And that is it, Senyora Teresa."

"But the other times the dream ended as you two sat down."

"Yes, Senyora, but a dream, if it is always the same, it seems to change. It is already a mystery for me to dream it again and again. Now every time I have the dream it is different, and as I go to bed I'm thinking: how will it be?"

"Look, Armanda, how many cakes are left; eat some before you go to bed so that their sweetness brings you your dream of love. Don't let it die, Armanda. Don't ever let it die."

Part Three

But time past is a time forgotten.
We expect the rise of a new constellation.
T. S. Eliot

She pulled open the drawer in her night table and took out the head of the gentleman from the dollhouse then brushed it with a tiny and very fine brush. After gazing at it for a while, she put it back in the drawer. At eleven she went down to see if the Senyora had awakened. She found her sitting up in bed, in the dark.

"Don't you see you could fall?"

She drew open the curtains, and the room filled with sunlight. Senyora Teresa, squinting in the light that hurt her eyes, smiled: "How is falling a bad thing? When I was young I used to fall a lot."

Armanda thought: "There she goes. And she used to be such a lady."

"Do you know what I would like? To be twenty and able to fool around."

Armanda went to the bathroom to gather what she needed to wash Senyora Teresa. She wiped her face, her chest, her arms.

"You must wash your hands all by yourself." She put on her robe, the woolen stockings. "We want to keep those feet warm."

When she was by the door, Senyora Teresa called: "Don't bring me coffee. I want chocolate, even if it's bad for me."

Armanda cast her a sad look and left.

Sitting in her red and gold chair, she looked out. Motionless, she was listening to something the garden was about to tell her any moment now, something it might have been about to tell her forever, from the first day. A secret guarded by the air, borne out of some split tree trunk, overcoming the flowers and leaves of the chestnut tree and which kept closing in on her misery. She raised her eyes; Armanda was at her side with the breakfast tray.

"While you were sleeping, Masdéu came wearing a red tie and a black armband. He came to tell us that his father died."

Senyora Teresa tore a bit of bread, spread butter on it, mumbled a few words that Armanda did not catch, and, before putting the morsel in her mouth, sighed. With her hands in her apron's pockets, Armanda watched her eat.

"He explained to me that they have declared the Republic. That he was wearing the red tie in celebration, even though he felt very sad."

Senyora Teresa brought another morsel of bread to her mouth, took a couple of sips of chocolate, and wiped her lips. She left the napkin on the tray and, with a deep look, said, "To be as I am, even though I never complain, is sadder than it looks." She stopped. Deliberately, she inserted the spoon in the cup and muttered, as if measuring each word: "You do know, don't you, that when I was young I sold fish? And that I fell for a man without knowing he was married? Youth sets one many kinds of snares." She rested for a moment then swirled the spoon in the cup a few times. Suddenly she told Armanda to take away the tray. The garden appeared brilliantly green. Each leaf was a warrior in the great army that the autumn rains would kill. She looked at her fingertips: swollen. She would be taken away from that house inside a box made of rare wood. In it she would rot like the leaves. She felt like crying. Because of that wave of spring that came in with the light and was completely useless? Armanda, the tray in her hands, seemed unable to leave. "Why do you look at me this way?" And with a thin voice, almost like a child's, she asked, "Tell me the truth, Armanda, you've known me for years: do you think I am a bad person?"

2. YOUTH

She couldn't sleep. She wasn't feeling sick but could not sleep. She began to see, with her inner eyes, the contours of some navy-blue flowers in the center of white tiles, on the risers of tall steps with eroded wooden edges. The staircase, at night, had to be climbed blindly, calculating every turn, a landing after the sixteenth step. Teresa Valldaura, stretched out in her bed, could visualize her mother's apartment. She thought she heard the finch in its cage, which at night was covered with a linen cloth with a lace border to give the finch a good night's rest. A finch with sparkly eyes, fluttering all the time, its face surrounded by feathers the color of blood. "From having pulled so many thorns from the crown of Jesus on the cross," Aunt Adela said, whenever she came for lunch. She arrived loaded with sweets: cake rolls and braided rolls. Teresa's mother had a colander chock-full of shrimp. The dining room was small, neatly wallpapered. The gas lamp was in the shape of a lyre. The round table, the Vienna chairs, the hardwood hutch with its glass case stuffed with china and glasses mixed with crystal of the kind that if you flick an edge with your nail it goes clink! Teresa's bedroom had black furniture, a flower-print bedspread, a shiny comforter the color of straw. There was a rocking chair at the foot of the bed. Everything was squeaky clean, tidy. On the balcony they had a flowerpot that had been without a plant for years. A lily had been in it, and the lily, because neither she nor her mother knew that a plant needs water, died. The pot stayed with a couple of dried leaves, crumbly, and the wind blowing in their alley made it totter a bit. Teresa Valldaura listened: in some part of the room there was something beating—she did not know what, perhaps the feathers in the vase. Or perhaps the flowers Armanda had brought along with her afternoon snack. Something she couldn't quite identify was trying to get her attention: one of those shadows that do not frighten you, a shadow that was she herself years and years ago. Why was that shadow here if she hadn't called for it? How many folds of memory did it need to go through before becoming a presence? What was that girl in a striped percale dress, a high collar, and long sleeves with cuffs up to her elbows doing in the darkened room? Her skirt ended in a ruffle, flouncy over her brown ankle boots, shiny as a mirror. Her mother, the widow of a train engineer killed in an accident, had sent that girl to learn embroidery from a cousin called Isabel; in the afternoons she engaged the help of Camilla in the fish stand and had to pay her, even though they'd been friends for years. Teresa left her house, clean, her hair combed, got lost in the crowd, advancing slowly, eager to taste the freedom of thought, keeping her thoughts from her overprotective mother. She soon learned to embroider, her hands beautiful in the summer but strained in winter, rough skin, red, the impossible hands of a moneyless girl, made to struggle with sea bass and bream, with slimy eels, as sneaky as water, shiny; hands made to gouge beady eyes out of all kinds of fish, those gelatinous sightless eyes that, out of the water, as the fish struggled for its life, were probably unable to see anything. Hands made for pulling off gills, for scooping guts from bellies she opened with huge shears. For playing, when she was little, with the suction cups of octopuses that stuck, taking the thinnest bit of skin, with the scales that spewed out brilliant and happy and that clung to her hair, that got on her clothes. Those fingers she would breathe on to keep warm soon produced wonders: twisty letters, sleeping flowers, bouquets and bouquets of roses and pansies. She returned home daydreaming, looking at the sky, the street lamps with the gas flame inside that accompanied her home, escorting her as if she were a queen. She would have loved to be one, with a scepter, wearing a blue mantel, sparkly with diamonds and colored gems. Perfumed with jasmine, no fish smell whatsoever, lost in a castle atop a rock made rosy by the sunset. Where had she ever seen a queen? Who had told her of queens? She couldn't tell, but she liked to think that queens sat tall so that everyone would fall in love with them.

"You are all laughter," Miquel Masdéu told her one day, "your mouth, your eyes, the blood rushing to your cheeks."

They had met at the end of one autumn when she was going to embroidery lessons. At the foot of a street lamp, on a solitary street of low houses, as she muffled herself with the black shawl her Aunt Adela had knitted for her, she saw a picture on the ground and bent down to pick it up: it showed a young man in a soldier's uniform holding a bayoneted gun over a footstool. She found it funny that the boy lacked any martial air, as if he had wanted to look imposing and failed. She was absorbed in the picture when she heard a voice behind her.

"Do you like it?"

She turned around slowly and found herself facing the soldier with the stool and rifle, now dressed as a lamplighter: a knee-length dark-blue gown with reinforced shoulders and pleated back, a cap, rope-soled shoes, eyes that she thought were like a wolf's, a sprig of mint behind his ear, holding the torch pole with more poise than he held the warring gun.

"I would have hated to lose it. But, since you found it, would you like to have it?"

Without a word she handed him back the picture, and he, without taking it, insisted, "If you keep it, you'll make me happy."

She gave it back to him then, but he pestered her until she took it. He would stop to light a lamp and then hurry to catch up with her. Suddenly he stood before her and delicately removed a thread from her sleeve.

"This thread will be our bond."

And he slipped it into his cap. That evening she did not go to embroider the bouquet of lilies she had begun on the fold of a sheet. That night, before taking off her clothes, she looked at the picture over and over. She liked, oh, how she liked that young man with shiny teeth, white as milk, with eyes hard and tender that took your breath away. A bit sad. She said softly, "Miquel."

Under the shaky light of the candle she placed her dress on the rocking chair and in her panties and corset went to the wardrobe, after slipping Miquel's picture under her pillow. She pressed her face against the mirror's coldness. "Miquel . . ." Saint Michael the archangel in his golden armor with his invincible sword fighting Satan with a whole legion of angels in full fury would not have impressed her any more.

They saw each other often, and the things he told her made her head spin.

"You are a doll in the shopwindow of the world."

The night he told her that, she could not sleep. She listened to the sounds in the house: the finch skipping on its zinc platform, a breeze flapping the laundry that hung from the balcony above hers. Her mother was breathing rhythmically.

The following day, at breakfast, her mother looked at her inquisitively. "You don't look well."

She laughed, trying to avoid the issue, but could not stop all the fire in her heart from going to her cheeks. She got up in a rush and went to get dressed. As she tied the ends of her shawl and put on her apron, the mirror told her she was pretty.

"My doll," she muttered, as if it were her lamplighter speaking. A doll in the shopwindow of the world. That evening, as they saw each other, he told her, "My damask rose." Then he started with, "Sweetheart." The first kiss had a taste of mint, of life. As she climbed the dark staircase, she licked her lips. And, falling asleep, she did the same. She'd get home late. "We had to finish a trousseau." "We're up to our eyeballs in work." She got home later every time. After a while her mother could not even hear her come in. She had to get up at daybreak, just as Teresa did, but Teresa did not mind losing sleep. Her mother, during the visit she paid each year to her first cousin on her saint's day, learned that Teresa had been absent from the embroidery shop many afternoons. Teresa gave excuses to Isabel, as she did to her mother: "Yesterday my mother was not feeling well." "My mother wanted me to go with her to buy a pair of woolen stockings because, as she stands in her stall, her feet feel frozen." "My mother needed me." "My mother does not want . . ." The following Sunday her mother locked her in. She spent the afternoon on the balcony staring at the bit of sky up above. She was calm because she and Miquel never saw each other on Sunday. For a couple of Sundays her mother locked her in. Every day she accompanied her to Isabel's. She never asked what was going on. She already knew. There was in the works an unrighteous suitor going after her daughter, who knows how badly . . . without showing his face to the mother. Teresa one day managed to escape her vigilance. She flew down the street.

Miquel Masdéu, enraged, as soon as he saw her took her by the arm and without asking what had happened, told her softly and with clenched teeth, "Today, as soon as I am done with my work . . ." Teresa felt scared. They went to the foot of the Tibidabo hill. They loved one another amid the brush and dry grasses. They loved and loved.

It was cold. A milky mist surrounded the calm flames of the streetlights. The trees in the gardens had lost their leaves. At times it was windy; at times it rained. They couldn't make love. Teresa was going mad. They could not go to his house. Or to her house. As a solution, Teresa thought of her Aunt Adela, who lived alone. She went to see her with trepidation. With passion and tears she explained her love for Masdéu. "Why don't you marry?" Aunt Adela asked her, as she placed the pitcher of chocolate on the table covered with a neat tablecloth. Teresa was stumped. Of course, why could they not marry? Why hadn't Masdéu ever told her they could get married? She sidestepped the issue, answering, "We're too young." "And what does your mother have to say about it?" "My mother," a dumbfounded Teresa answered, "knows nothing about this." Aunt Adela shook her head sadly, "You are asking of me something fraught with danger and with shame." But she gave in, overcome by the pleading eyes of Teresa, who hugged her vehemently and filled her face with kisses. Moved, Aunt Adela filled the two cups with chocolate. "Drink."

Then one night, when she got home, she found her mother waiting up for her, standing in the dining room and holding Miquel Masdéu's portrait; his face was half-erased from all the kisses Teresa had given it. It was three in the morning. "Why do you have to hide the fact that you have a boyfriend from me? I've been patient too long! Enough is enough!" Pacing around the dining room, desperately wringing her hands, she confessed. She was three months pregnant. The next day, following her mother's advice, with great difficulty, she had a serious talk with Miquel. He was stunned. At first she wasn't sure she understood him. Finally, he made himself clear: he already had a family. No, no children. He was married. But he loved her, if she could only know how he loved her. He made a gesture to kiss her, and she pushed him away. "I don't want to see you again." She spent the night crying. She wanted to die. Forever. She saw herself along the streets, hugging Miquel Masdéu, under a pink sky, under a blue sky, with stars, without stars, with wings on her feet, transported . . . Never again.

Her mother told her she would deliver in Camilla's house; she'd already spoken to her. Teresa suggested, "Why not at Aunt Adela's?"

"What would my sister say? I don't even want to think about it. She will find out soon enough."

Armanda came in with the breakfast tray and said: "While you were asleep, your godson came in to tell us that his father was dead. He was wearing a mourning band."

Her love went away slowly. During the last weeks Teresa went through hell. The fish stall repulsed her. Her mother, so that her belly would not show, pulled her corset tight to the point of suffocation. The neighbors were talking. Once, because whenever Miquel Masdéu was not dressed as a lamplighter he dressed any which way and did not comb his hair, she had called him "my ragged angel," her lips to his lips, not quite knowing what she was doing. He laughed, and he rarely laughed, and embraced her. Why did she, an old woman, have to recall that shred of her youth that had been buried in the deepest part of her soul, as if it hadn't been a fragment of her own life? Miquel Masdéu, with his death, had taken away, frozen inside him, all that Teresa had given him.

She had never told him where she lived, and she didn't know where he lived, but one Sunday afternoon, while she was in the dining room ironing clothes, she saw him on the corner across the street. He must have followed her, and, as she imagined the scene, she felt like screaming. What was he doing, glued to the wall, so still, without looking up, even though he must have known what floor she lived on? Concentrated and still, she thought that his whole body was shouting, "Don't forget me." Nervous, trying to ignore that presence, she went to the kitchen to get the hot iron to press her petticoat. She picked up the poker, revived the fire, and added coal; she placed the cold iron over the fire. "Don't forget me." She went back to the dining room with the red-hot iron. Throwing it on the rest, she looked outside. Masdéu was still there. She could take it no longer. She would tell him to go away, to please go away. She covered herself with a shawl and opened the apartment door. On the landing she felt a gulp of bile in her mouth. She got to the street at the moment when an old woman was passing by, and she accidentally pushed her and made her stagger. Embarrassed, she went back in. She stood in a corner, near the gate. She could feel the air from the street; she felt that across the street Masdéu was thinking of her, that he thought of her constantly. Her thoughts lost in his thoughts that were sucking her in, she was assailed by her tumultuous memories, filling her with desire. She went back to a far place, she fled toward the night in the brush, back to his embraces and kisses. Her head tilted back, her hands on her temples, leaning against the door, an offering to love, to nothingness, to the darkness of the staircase, she began to moan softly, open like a flower, her heart beating loud, her mouth dry. The sound of steps on the sidewalk snatched her from her dizziness. She ran upstairs, holding her skirt with one hand, the other hand on her splitting kidneys. She opened the apartment door, and the smoke and smell of burned cloth made her draw back. She rushed to the dining room. The iron had burned her petticoat, the old sheet, the blanket that lined the ironing board. She picked up the iron and placed it on the floor. She gathered all the burned material and dunked it in a basin filled with water; the smoke made her cough. She poured water on the ironing board. She opened the windows, the balcony, without looking down to the street. She hung the finch's cage outside to keep the bird from suffocating. She sat down to fan the smoke out. Was he still there? Still there?

Then every Sunday the same thing. On the corner, against the opposite wall, Miquel Masdéu seemed to be keeping guard. Teresa, one afternoon, went out in order not to have to see him, not to think of him. She walked fast, close to the buildings. He must have seen her leave. Near the harbor he approached her.

"Don't speak to me if you don't want to. But let me look at you. Even if it's for the last time."

She did not know what to say. She was shaking all over. Then Masdéu gave her a little package, and she took it mechanically. She was glued to the ground; her legs did not have the energy to make her walk. Next to her, below, larger than hers, was the shadow of Miquel Masdéu. She shut her eyes so as not to see it. When she opened them again, the shadow was gone. She walked and walked. Exhausted, she went back to the harbor and stared at the water shimmering with lights—the masts, the flags, so many ropes, so many prows, so many escapes, so many far-flung flights. The smells of pitch and mussels made her queasy, but the water soothed her, and then she returned home up the Rambla. She walked into her apartment. Her mother wasn't back yet. On Sundays she went to Isabel's, and the two of them made clothes for the baby. Teresa couldn't sew a stitch. No sooner had she picked up a needle when something inside her rebelled. When she had to grab the matchbox to light a lamp, she became aware she was still carrying the little package Masdéu had given her. With trembling hands, her heart aflutter, she tore the string off. Wrapped in three pieces of silk paper, there was a small box and in the box a soap in the shape of a heart. She stared at it, surprised, unaware of the passing of time. Finally, she brought the soap heart to her nose. It was purple and smelled of lilac. She took it from the box, and it almost slipped from her fingers. She rubbed it against her cheek, her neck . . . it was sweet . . . her forehead.

When her mother told her she should pack to go to Camilla's for the delivery, Teresa found, under a stack of shirts, the soap heart. She grabbed it angrily and rubbed it on her cheek: it was hard, cold; it had lost its fragrance. She felt like throwing it away. No, not the garbage. Not anywhere ugly. She took it wrapped in some clothing. Camilla's apartment was a lot like her mother's: on an alley, near the Boqueria market, by Petxina Street. Once she was alone, when Camilla had left to help her mother in the fish stall, she took a glass pitcher that was gathering dust on the top shelf in the kitchen, filled it with water, and tossed the soap heart in. She hid it in her bedside table. Later, once she had her child and returned to her ailing mother's, she looked at the pitcher. The soap heart had dissolved, and the water was murky. She poured it down the drain. She was fully conscious that she had just thrown away her youth.

She tried to turn over and couldn't. Her raw skin was burning, and she gave out a moan. When the doctor visited her, she told him, "You are a good-looking man, and your presence is a balm to me, but no doctor can do anything for what ails me."

He laughed and patted her cheek, and she hurt, oh how she hurt, for not having a young cheek. The doctor was the son of Doctor Falguera, who had been her doctor and who could tell what she had with just a look. His son was learned, truly learned, but he did not have quite the eye for diagnosis that had made his father famous. But, like his father, he mastered the art of making his patients believe that only the patient in front of him and only that ailment existed for him. She did not have the kind of disease that could be cured, however. She'd already told him that.

"Doctor Falguera, what I have is death inside me, and against such a fine personage nothing will work: not herbs, not minerals, not the scalpel. And not all your science."

She wanted to turn over because she was hurting, but she couldn't. Irritated, she tried again. She was nettled by the great areas of skin made raw by all those weeks in bed facing the ceiling, her lower back in agony, the liquid oozing from her legs all filled with boils, dead.

The oil lamp at her bedside was twinkling. Armanda had refilled it before going to bed, but no sooner had Teresa seen it than she knew it would burn poorly. She loved to look at the small flame. The round table held the pharmacy. She called all those flasks and vials "the pharmacy"; they were all bunched together, overflowing the table. She grabbed the ringer from under her pillow; it had such a long cord that she at times got tangled in it. She looked at the ringer and left it on the pillow fringe. What would be the point of waking up poor Armanda and asking her to help her turn if, no sooner she lay on one side, she would want to lie on the other? Sofia had suggested that Armanda should sleep in the room, on a cot that by day could be stored in the bathroom, but Teresa refused. She had a nurse for a couple of weeks but soon asked Sofia to get rid of her. The nurse always asked, "How are you?" with such coldness in her eyes that Teresa felt exasperated. The first day the nurse

178

said, "You will soon be able to get out for walks and take in the air." Was she born stupid not to see that she was a paralytic? Sofia then said she would install an electric bell on a cord and a ringer that would ring in Armanda's bedroom directly. She was not going to wake her up. If she were to die during the night, she wanted to die surrounded only by her disease. At daybreak Armanda had gathered some flowers from the garden; she prepared a mixed bouquet, with all different colors, the way she liked it. After a moment she asked her to take the flowers away because, locked in, having flowers near her made her sad.

"It smells of death. There'll be enough smell from the wreaths."

"Why are you saying things like this? You'll see how you'll get well, and we'll see you sitting in your chair again with all your rings."

When Armanda said "the chair" she did not see the chair, but, rather, next to it, sticking his little hand under her shawl to touch the wine bottle, she saw that poor child Jaume, the one who had the same eyes as Sofia, shaped like a buttonhole, and who died drowned in the pond at the bottom of the park, a pond good only for breeding mosquitoes and bugs that swam there with big heads and pointed tails. She could no longer wear rings; her fingers had become swollen. They had to be taken off by rubbing soap between the fingers and the rings. She was depressed about her inability to wear her rings. She needed to look at beautiful things, and diamonds were drops of dew. "Dewdrops on a flower," Attorney Riera had told her one evening when they had made love. Still lost in the world of caresses, she looked at the bouquets of cherry blossoms. She raised her hand mechanically and dropped it as if letting a stone fall. She slipped her hand under the sheet and felt her belly. Where did so much useless flesh come from? She, who had been so proud of her wasp waist, of her bumblebee waist, as she joked, and of her belly as flat as an ironing board. Where did all that was pretty go? She moved her hand, and at that very moment she was overwhelmed by that horrible thing, that suffocation that made her lift her body, she who was now unable to turn over. The smell of paint helped with the suffocation; all the balconies had been repainted recently. She opened her mouth and opened her mouth and felt that her eyes were leaving her head. Her heart was bursting, and that living death seemed to her to last an eternity.

With a cheek against her pillow and breathing as if the world had exhausted all its air, she thought that she would not last the night. The next day the doctor would find her cold, and she would not be able to tell him, as she did every morning, "Good day, Doctor." And, if she were still alive, she'd tell him, "Here's a patient whose cards have been dealt." And she would smile saying it, but with death in her soul, and the doctor would soon realize that her heart was crying, because he had his wits about him. "Senyora Valldaura, be serious. Do not court the foul weather." Whenever he took her arm, he appeared deep in concentration and finally said, "I can't find your pulse." And she said that it had not escaped, that it was hiding. And poor little Jaume, always, before leaving the room, touched the blue-eyed feathers and sipped his wine to be able to remain longer in the room with her and Quimeta. And she, who never left her room now, two years after poor Jaume's death, asked Armanda to take her near the pond, out there, to see where he had drowned, and it was sad, oh, how sad that there under the tall trees and in the green water and the green ivy so green and everything there so murky. She wanted to leave right away, but one of the chair's wheels got stuck in the mud, and Armanda had to get help, and, as they pushed her, Armanda moved a branch aside that looked like a fork and barred their way: barkless and white as a bone. And when Maria and the laurel branch . . . She rubbed her eyes, unsure whether the oil lamp had died or whether the darkness around her was caused by fog in her eyes. The night of the day when she was taken to the end of the garden she kept thinking about that weird branch that had barred her way. Butterflies. Poor Jaume had explained to her that he had seen many butterflies, clouds – and clouds of butterflies – and she hadn't believed him.

All food had been banned for three weeks. She felt a sudden calm and thought of a few nice things; she felt she ought to die thinking of nice things, flowers and flower buds and flames, neither blue nor red flames but the color of oranges, tongues of fire, those flames she had watched when she first came to live in the villa and the lilacs were little and the rosebushes had few blossoms. She had three regrets in her life: Masdéu's son, poor Jaume's death, and Maria's impaled death. And a big regret is like a drop of water that keeps carving a hole in you. She closed her eyes and saw the pearl tiepin. Iridescent and huge. She saw it pinned to a dark tie. Sofia was standing watch over her father, and at midnight she had left the library nervously. "Where is Papa's pearl? This morning, when they brought him down, he was wearing it. I saw it with my own eyes"

– and she pointed at them. "I had pinned it on him because it was his wish to be buried with the pearl, and now the pearl has disappeared."

Sofia suspected everyone on the staff, but it was she, Teresa Valldaura, the wife of Salvador Valldaura, who had taken the pearl from the dead man's tie. Too beautiful to end up in a graveyard. She had pinned it to her bodice before leaving the library, and no one would ever find it. Not ever again. Two men had worn that pearl. She had given it to the second to forget the first. A gray, pink, and blue pearl that seemed alive and that she would remove from Amadeu's tie with her teeth. She wanted to feel her belly now but could not move her arm. "Here we go again," she muttered, "just like my legs." She tried to move the other arm but did not have the strength to slip it under the covers. She would have liked to feel her own belly, which had grown big from her eating so many good things.

She had put mountains of cream and custard in her mouth. When Armanda brought her a cardboard tray full of sweets, she said, and that game lasted for years, "Leave me." Armanda knew that Senyora Teresa wanted to eat her sweets by herself, without witnesses, to stuff them whole into her mouth and feel herself filled with sweetness, her eyes fixed on the tray as she chose the next morsel. She adored candied fruits, the colors of the watermelon and the pear. And the bread with butter and honey and the pignoli cakes from the bakery – she could eat six at a time. And the liquor-soaked biscuits. She fell to pieces before tea cakes, those that looked like bows and those that were balls. Some balls were yellow, and some were white, and the white ones and the yellow ones both had coconut. Armanda said, "The yellow ones aren't coconut, Senyora Teresa; they are egg yolk." She ignored her because she couldn't care less what Armanda thought; they were coconut. And the big cookies. Despite the burning skin of her back, her mouth watered just to think of them. She cut them into pieces, and then she licked the knife. Sweets topped with butter and topped with chocolate crowned by a chocolate swirl done with a pastry funnel. She had grown old the lazy way. Her flesh had lost its tone: jowls, double chin, flabby upper arms. Sofia was also growing old but in a different way. Like a mummy, her skin clinging to her bones. She had lived, and she still lived, surrounded by lotions and perfume. Was it worthwhile? She sighed. Old Rovira had fallen in love with a simply dressed girl, a girl who helped her mother sell fish. He had fallen for her as he drank coffee on the Liceu's terrace as she walked by arm in arm with that friend, such a close friend she couldn't remember her name. Until the day she walked by on her own. He followed her and spoke to her; she had a love and a child. She allowed his love. Soon came jewels and adoration. She had known three men. The first one looked like a ragged angel, and the others, two great men. Nicolau Rovira had been the jumping board that catapulted her to the world of Salvador Valldaura. No. Not three. Four. Amadeu Riera had satiated her thirst for love. The others . . . The love she had felt for Salvador Valldaura had melted away, and she still could not explain why. Masdéu had been a spurt of madness spread over deserted streets at the time of the first stars and at the time of the last stars, when the dying sky and the newborn sky are the same color. She screamed. The burning pain returned, and the suffocation that made her open her mouth seeking a thread of air that barely reached her lungs. Her whole skin was on fire, and her insides were a hell. Then she prayed to God and asked forgiveness – all her sins . . . She had time to think that she'd been forgiven years ago; as a sign, God had sent death to her legs: "I keep you in mind." She needed her fan. She would have brought it to her face so that the walls wouldn't see her die. The fan lay on the chair. She could not reach it. Droplets of perspiration ran down her neck. A shiny warm tear hung from a corner of her eye.

4. CLOSED ROOMS

Sofia Valldaura de Farriols wanted to end her mourning. She had worn black for two years for her father, two years for Jaume, two years for Maria, two for Eladi, and, for a few months now, she'd been wearing black for her mother. Black, which had been so becoming, now made her look old. But it was for a deeper reason that she had liked mourning: because it closed her in, it protected her. She had not expected the good memories her mother left her. Sofia could see her mother's beautiful face, with that air of hers of feeling happy in life even if her life had not always been golden. After all, she reflected, I owe my power to Teresa Goday. Death made her realize that her mother had been an exceptional woman, and she, faced with that departed splendor, felt diminished. The respect she inspired she owed to that shadow, which nobody could forget. She had stopped being Sofia. She would have liked to be called Teresa. Suddenly, in her black outfits, her blood, her muscles, her nerves, were demanding something else, something more: to breathe the air and the sunlight and fill her lungs day and night, like the plants, like the earth, like the sea. She was becoming reconciled with her own house, the house that she had thought ugly and old – overstuffed with memories, with rooms she had stopped entering because they were filled with anguish. She would revive old relationships. She would travel to Paris to visit her godmother, Eulàlia, and her godfather, Quim, even though he could be caddish. She would start to wear her mother's jewels – especially that necklace of diamonds and rubies that so scandalously suited her. When she was little, one night when her mother had come up to tuck her in and kiss her before going out, she had pulled it off her with a jerk and had ruined its latch. "Why did you have to ruin my necklace? Why?" Her mother, holding the necklace, slammed the door, after putting out the light. Alone in bed she thought that her mother, dressed in such good silk that it rustled, had been forced to leave that blinding necklace of water and fire at home.

She felt like going into Maria's room. She found its door locked. And Ramon's. And her parents'. She called a chambermaid. "Please tell Armanda I want to see her." She went to the landing and waited there for a while, taking in the beauty of her house. Armanda did not come right away. Sofia went downstairs and stood before the door to her mother's room.

"Were you calling for me, Senyora?"

Armanda had gotten fat, gullible; she breathed goodness – it must have rubbed off from her mother from all the time she had served her. Sofia asked for the keys to the empty rooms, and Armanda stared at her as if she hadn't understood. Finally, she got a bunch of keys from under her apron and gave them to her. From each key hung a label: "Maria," "Senyors Valldaura," "Senyor Eladi."

The room was dark. She turned on the light. The vase with the peacock feathers, the Japanese armoire, the golden table, everything was clean, alive. Mechanically, she opened the Japanese armoire; on a shelf sat a pink glass with a green stem. She remembered there used to be many like that one and a matching pitcher. She did not know there was an undamaged one. In a vague way she felt there was something changed in the room but could not figure out what it was. Until she saw the armchair cover. The chair had never been covered during her mother's life. She left the room on tiptoe. The *M* in *Maria* on the key label had a little flower drawn at the foot of each vertical line. The balcony, once wide open, let the sun in. Each organza ruffle on the bedspread, on the canopy, on the dressing table, seemed freshly ironed. Armanda's love for the dead of that house was touching. Sofia was aware that every Friday Armanda lit a lamp before the picture of Sofia's parents she had on her dresser. And something strange happened. Outside, not one leave was moving, but on the right side of the dressing table a flounce swayed. Imperceptibly, but it moved. Sofia rubbed her eyes. It was not possible. She felt eyes piercing the middle of her back, a gaze sharp as a stiletto that made her turn around. Behind her there was no one, but she felt a presence. She would have that room cleared right away. She wanted no more memories of Eladi's daughter. Armanda was waiting on the landing, and she felt annoyed.

"Take the keys. But from now on I do not want any more locked rooms in my house."

That organza flounce with an indoor breeze had made her uneasy. She put a foot out of the bathtub, and at that moment Miquela, a distant relative of that Miquela they had many years ago, came in and told her in her voice like a spoiled cat's that Senyor Fontanills had just arrived and that she had asked him to wait in the library. That good man, who managed her affairs, had the virtue of dropping by for a visit on days she did not feel at all like chatting with him. He was the most inopportune person she'd ever met. She felt a pang in one tooth, exactly in the one next to her left eyetooth. She would have to go and see her dentist, which she hated. One day she told him that. And the dentist, a very pleasant man, answered that, rather than going for a visit when her teeth did not hurt, she should wait until a toothache did not let her sleep and then she would beg on her knees for an appointment. They laughed. She was taking her time getting dressed. Let Senyor Fontanills wait. She felt no desire to talk about properties at that moment, even less about tenants. Or about that roof on the Rambla property that leaked like a nightmare. She entered the library all dressed up and perfumed. Senyor Fontanills had left his famous black briefcase filled with papers next to the chair where he sat. He tried to get up, but Sofia stopped him with a gesture. She knew he suffered from arthritis in his knees. They shook hands. Fontanills's palms were sweaty both summer and winter. Their wetness was different from Eladi's: stickier. She sat in front of Senyor Fontanills without knowing what to do with the hand that had touched his. As usual, he started speaking about the weather, the heat that so oppressed him. He was a winter man.

"The first cold spate revives me. And at Christmas, when the air is thin and cuts your skin, you might not believe this, but I feel younger."

Sofia did not know where to look because she had heard that story more than once.

"Every afternoon, from my office, as soon as I have a free moment, and if I don't have it I take it, I look at the divine light above Sant Pere Màrtir, and all my worries disappear." Then inevitably would come his energetic: "Well! To business!" He pulled his briefcase open and spread out its papers. "The house on the Rambla is on its last legs. There is no point in fixing the leaks; it would be throwing money away. The roof must be redone. Houses die by the roof, you know." And almost without a pause for breath he went on: "The plumbing and all the downspouts in the house on Portaferrissa have to be replaced. The contractor said they can no longer be fixed; it'd be a waste of money. And the water tanks for the first-, third-, and fourth-floor apartments in the house on Carrer Viladomat . . . And you ought to give some thought to installing an elevator there because . . ." Senyor Fontanills had a soft spot for Senyora Munda, a very old lady who occupied the fourth floor. He had promised her to do the impossible, to convince the owner to install an elevator in the building. "The marble of the sinks has been eroding, and you could say that there's barely any left."

Sofia listened distractedly and told him to prepare budgets, and then Senyor Fontanills, triumphantly, got a bundle of papers held together with a clip from his briefcase. "Here they are." Sofia held Senyor Fontanills as a most trustworthy man. She took the papers, threw a glance at them, and, without noticing what they said, gave them back to him.

"Order the repairs immediately."

"If we're still in time," muttered Senyor Fontanills, as he put the budgets back in his case. Sofia looked at him as if he'd gone mad.

"What do you mean, if we're still in time?"

"Well, you see, a few generals have risen in Africa, and everyone says there'll be trouble."

Sofia smiled and told him that people were alarmists and that the rebels would end up celebrating their promotions to general with a banquet. "Besides," she added, "I am not in the habit of worrying until I see my head three steps away from myself."

5. COME BACK SOON, SENYORETA SOFIA

Miquela, seated at the kitchen table, was threading a needle. She put on a thimble and began to sew the seam of a small bag. She had made five of them – fifteen to go – for the most valuable jewels. The others would be left in the small coffer. Armanda was watching her sew, seated in front of her. No other servants remained in the house – just the two of them. The cook had been the first to leave. Then Marcel. He had quit without saying where he was going or what he intended to do. The other maids, headed by Rosalia, left as a group: to give blood for the hospitals. The little bag Miquela was sewing carefully, the tip of her tongue between her lips, was to hold the brooch with the diamond bouquet. Armanda passed the time looking at the boxes. She opened a big flat one. She had never seen such a splash of diamonds. It must have been worn by someone dead centuries ago, some conceited and proud Valldaura woman. Miquela, once she made all the bags, would have to sew them onto her girdle and onto Senyoreta Sofia's girdle. Distributed nicely. The day before Senyoreta Sofia had left very early and had returned very late, crazed with joy.

"God bless Marcel. It turns out he is now in charge of passports. He has arranged everything for me to be able to leave. He will come get us at midnight. In exchange for this favor he'll keep the car and will make it available to the committee."

Sofia had decided to go abroad. Things were getting complicated. Senyor Fontanills was beside himself with fear. Houses in town no longer had owners, and in the country the caretakers said the estates were theirs. Miquela, deeply worried, confided in Armanda: "They will all realize we are hiding jewels, and we'll be killed before we reach Andorra. They'll put a tree trunk across the highway; they'll get us out of the car, hands up, Marcel also, a blow on the head with the butt of the rifle to save ammunition, and fare-thee-well Miquela and Senyora Sofia. I'm shaking in my boots."

"And I am staying here," Armanda said, as she caressed the worn velvet lining of one of the boxes. "Do you think I am not at risk? The revolutionaries keep the villas they like; one today, another tomorrow . . . Senyor Fontanills said it very clearly."

"Relax. They won't take this villa. What use could it be to them?"

"What use? Bring other people to it. But I won't leave. If they are to kill me, let them kill me here. After all, once you realize you are about to die, it's as if you were already dead. I won't even take off my earrings. I don't care if they dislike me for wearing diamonds. God will help me. God, who made me small to be able to reach down to the kitchen fires. And fat, not because of all I have eaten but because of all the dishes I've had to taste. A little more blood, a little less, what?" Blood, for Armanda, had been her daily bread. Fish blood, the more spectacular chicken blood, the blood of pigeons and rabbits brought live from Vilafranca. And suddenly now it was men's blood, men who fell. Shiny blood.

A purple halo sat over the darkness of Barcelona, descending like slow lava, blood that was life, hidden blood. Dicing onions to make soup, Armanda could think of nothing but blood. She was a pitcher of blood, from head to toe. When the pitcher broke, blood oozed and slid down the laurel tree. The onions made her eyes tear; she could not see. Perhaps her eyes burned so much because she hadn't slept all night. Tired of being awake, she'd gone to the ironing room and looked into the closets. She got out the purple domino from its big box. Behind the mask edged with overlapping sequins, Senyora Teresa's eyes must have been like flares.

She heard Senyoreta Sofia's voice behind her.

"What are you thinking about? Can't you hear me? Come closer." Senyoreta Sofia had left a bunch of bills on the table. "Here are fifty thousand pesetas for you. I imagine that before you spend them all I will be back. They're yours. Hurry up, Miquela. Tonight, Armanda, after we leave, I want you to drink a bottle of champagne. Wish me luck."

Her hands on her chest and her mouth open, she walked under the chestnut trees and under the night. The heat was stifling. A good thing she had put the bottle of champagne out to chill. The garden felt like an oven. She would take the money to the bank, put it in her savings account. The house was practically hers. Senyora Teresa had written it quite clearly in her will: "Faithful Armanda will live in the villa until her death. And, until she dies, my heirs will pay her wages." When she'd take the fifty thousand pesetas to the bank, the bank director, who'd known her all her life, might think she'd stolen them. No! She would not take them to the bank. She would bury them! She would live frugally to save most of the money. An intense joy now filled her. She came close to yelling: windows and shutters all closed! To sleep! She went around the whole place. She turned on the lights and left them lit behind her. If she went by a mirror, she turned her head away so as not to see herself. "The devil lies in the mirror; don't you ever look at yourself in a mirror at night," her mother used to tell her. She stopped in front of Senyor Eladi's bedroom.

She went up to the ironing room to get the purple domino and put it on. At the front gate, when the car took off with Senyoreta Sofia dressed as a maid, Miquela next to her, the two of them loaded with jewels, Marcel sporting a red kerchief around his neck, she had shouted, "Come back soon, Senyoreta Sofia!"

The domino dragged on the floor. She opened her arms wide. "I must look like an old eagle." She bent over to pull up the robe so as not to trip. She grabbed Senyoreta Sofia's looking glass, the one with a frame of silver roses. She finished pointing with an outstretched arm all around the house, the mirror raised before her like a torch. She went from the second floor down to the foyer holding the mirror: she saw the reflection of bits of ceiling, bits of balustrade, designs and garlands of the rug that covered the steps, all alive and out of focus, and when she got to the last step she tripped and fell to the floor wrapped in violet-colored folds. The mirror had broken. Most pieces remained in the frame, but a few had fallen out. She picked them up and tried to put them back in the spaces she thought they would fit. Did the pieces of the mirror, having lost their level, reflect things as they were? Suddenly, in each piece of the mirror she saw years of her life spent in that house. Fascinated, crouching on the floor, she could not make sense of it. Everything passed, stopped, disappeared. Her world took shape in it, with all its colors, with all its strength. The house, the park, the rooms, the people: young ones, older ones, corpses, the flames of candles, children. The outfits, the décolletages with emerging heads, laughing or sad, starched collars, ties with perfect knots, freshly polished shoes walking on rugs or on the gravel in the garden. An orgy of time past, far, far away. How far away everything was . . . She got up disquieted, still holding the mirror. She heard shots. Just like every night. The hour for the champagne had arrived. She needed to drown a dull fear that came from inside her and surrounded her like an aura. She went into the kitchen and got the chilled bottle. She turned on the big chandelier in the dining room. Everything was gleaming. The house was hers. All of it. From top to bottom. She spread out the fancy tablecloth. She took a cut crystal glass with a long and thin stem: a flute. She should have uncorked the bottle in the kitchen. But so what if she sprinkled herself? She rolled up her sleeves as best she could. The champagne bottle felt cold. The night was made of fire. She grabbed it by the neck with one hand, and with the other she began to rip the gold foil that hooded it. She twisted the cork from one side to the other. When it popped, she felt a jolt, and she filled the glass with light and foam. She liked champagne better than wine because it tickled her and got to her head quickly. Zoom! To the very top. She had left the mirror on the table; it reflected bits of the ceiling, chandelier crystals deformed by the cracks. She raised her glass. "All the money, underground!" With raised glass she let out a few moans, something like those love cries that the peacocks used to let out. Those cries coming from her throat didn't seem like hers. The pheasants, how golden . . . Red like autumn. She turned her gaze to the mirror, giddy with that voice that filled the dining room. She rubbed her eyes with her free hand. Had her eyes turned blurry, or was she going mad? It's gone to my head, she thought. On a piece of the mirror, a long and narrow piece with an edge stuck into another piece like a knife, there appeared a skeleton hand. A bunch of bones, together, thin, pale. It wasn't a child's hand. It was the hand of an older person who had become tiny to fit in that little piece of mirror. She drank more champagne without letting her eyes off those bones that had come she could not fathom from where, whether from her head or from a grave. She rubbed her eyes with her fists, hard, hard . . . When she looked again, the hand was no longer there, but in front of her, each seated in its chair, three skeletons were laughing with convulsed jaws. She stared at them with her eyes hurting from watching so fixedly. Where did all those bones, so nicely held together, with no flesh or skin to cover them, come from? Letters were forming on the foreheads of the three skulls; she couldn't read what they said, but, as she stared at them, they became lit by a soft greenish light, as if each skull had a little lamp right behind the forehead bone. The first forehead to her right read "Eladi," the other "Teresa," and the third "Valldau" because there was no room for the *ra*. She had the three of them right there, right in front of her. At the head of the table, seated on a high chair, a girl was staring at her. A girl in a white dress, her arms made of rags and a black butterfly in the middle of her chest. Armanda, with a shaky hand, brought the glass to her lips; before taking a sip, she raised it. She was offering it to the dead in a toast of fear that was not quite fear. In the glass, swimming in the golden liquid, there was a speck: a boy, as small as a fly, holding a tiny boat in his hand, amid the bursting bubbles. She picked him up between index finger and thumb; she did not want him to drown, but, as she was about to set him on the table, there was nothing between her fingers. The girl was now standing on her chair; she looked up as if looking for the sky. Her belly was cut open. Armanda emptied the glass and refilled it without taking her eyes off that belly. Holding the glass with both hands, she went around the table to see the backs of the skulls. They weren't there. She touched the back of each seat. She came to hers, sat down, and again the skulls were before her. They were laughing. Their jaws – shuck, shuck, shuck. She filled her glass one last time and threw the bottle away. She drank calmly, reflectively. Then she leaned over as if stabbed and, in her purple cloak, fell to the floor in a heap. Before she lost consciousness a voice came from within, went through her dry lips, rose over her tired body and her sweaty armpits. She closed her eyes, all alone in her purple mourning, half-lost in the well of time.

6. THE VILLA

She would always remember it. During the day she had made changes. Her clothes and the pictures of the senior Valldauras that she had taken to Senyor Eladi's bedroom. She would sleep there. She would not get as tired going up and down the stairs. She checked her provisions. She had oil and coal at least for a year. Three cases of condensed milk and six liters of fresh milk. Beans, chickpeas, canned tomatoes, pasta, rice. Everything. She would never run out. She had filled crates with the silver (the grocer's wife had hidden her wedding ring inside the stovepipe) and had carried them one by one to the gardener's wheelbarrow, which she then pushed to the laundry shed. She would bury them later; for the moment she covered them with dirty laundry and some old mattresses. The jewelry left in the little coffer she buried right away at the foot of the birdcage; she stomped on the ground, placed a big rock on top, and covered everything with dry leaves. By late afternoon she felt satisfied and dead tired. Seated before the kitchen balcony, she looked at the terrace absentmindedly. "Is this a true beauty mark?" Senyor Eladi had asked her when she was still good-looking. She would sleep on the bed where he had slept; she would remember him until her death. A tranquil sun was setting, as if life were life as always. The trees shone as if nothing had happened. She felt like taking a stroll under those trees that were so much hers, so well known, and without worrying to think that someone might say: "What's Armanda doing over there?" She stopped to look at the colors of the trunks, pulled clumps of grass, picked leaves: there were no flowers left. Here and there, unexpectedly, you saw a red daylily. She opened the gate to the fields. Two or three mice ran to hide under the pile of garbage now shockingly tall. She locked the door and continued her walk. At every step the green was deeper. When she got to the pond, the bits of sky among the leaves appeared a humid gray. The water was breathing darkly, spotted with sky. The ivy was the mistress of the place: on the ground, clutching and caressing dead tree trunks. She pulled a few bunches, sat on the stoop of the birdcage, and began weaving a wreath. Some vaporous grasses had blue flowers. She stuck a few among the ivy leaves of the wreath and walked back to the house, to the bench under the wisteria, to the laurel tree. She placed the wreath on the stone slab. She straightened up with difficulty. As soon as she stood, an invisible cobweb rubbed her cheek. She brought her hand to it. As she withdrew her hand, the cobweb rubbed her again. She raised her head. The thickness of the laurel was above her, dark. Where were the birds? Had the shots heard every night scared them away?

She chewed slowly. Drank her coffee in small sips. Washed the cup and the saucer. She closed the kitchen door and went up to the third floor to get some things from her old room. She felt a strange desire to climb onto the roof. To see what the children had seen. The lightbulb went out. She tried the light in the room next door. The foyer's. The power was out. She felt her way back to the kitchen, pulled a candle from a drawer, and lit it. The flame went out as she left the kitchen. She retraced her steps patiently, lit the candle again, and again it went out as she left the kitchen. After lighting it for the third time, she put the matchbox in her pocket, and then the candle did not go out again. She sat on the first step of the stairs. Holding the banister with both hands, she looked ahead, up; she felt she was spinning from looking at everything so motionless. A voice lost in the night was calling a name, and she could not make out what name was being called by that weak lulling voice. Waves of breeze came to her, waves of moonlight, waves of star fire – each star the home of an angel. Beyond the sea, from each luminous house, came a red angel; a troop of angels was coming down to greet her; they came from all sides, from the east and from the west, troops and troops; the tips of their wings caressed her face sweeter than honey, fresher than a sprig of parsley. She laughed, she laughed, she laughed, caught in a mesh of infinite tenderness. The angels had no faces, had no feet, had no body. They were wings with a diaphanous soul, like a mist within so many feathers of love.

The screech of brakes woke her up. Day was breaking. A strip of red sky spread at the end of the sea crowned by mists the color of ash. She heard words, or was she still dreaming? The sound of a motorcar came to her. She went into Senyor Eladi's bedroom and opened the balcony. She backed off quickly. Just below there was a red and yellow van and three automobiles. She started thinking. She could hear people talking in the kitchen. She went there and found them seated at the table, drinking her milk. They had forced the balcony's lock.

Next to the table, on the floor, were some guns. A very ugly militia-man, an older type with caramel-colored eyes, faced her and asked her where she'd come from.

"I'm the housekeeper."

"And the owners, where are they?"

She told him they were all dead and that the young lady, the only one left, had fled to France. A curly haired boy sitting at the table burst out laughing and told her with a stare that the mistress was better off away because, otherwise, she'd be kindling. They had taken possession of the villa under orders from the committee, and the villa would never again have a master. Everything was everybody's. And they would make a public garden of the woods in the back for poor folks' children to play.

They spent the afternoon moving the furniture around, bringing in desks and file cabinets. Then, stuffing them in baskets, they took half the books to the basement. They did not want to burn them because they respected books, but they were in the way. They loaded some of the furniture in the yellow and red van. The next day they and the van returned. They unloaded more desks and more cabinets. She had locked herself upstairs and was crying her eyes out. Looking down, all she could see were men with red handkerchiefs around their necks going up and down the chestnut tree alley, laughing and yelling. Toward the end of the morning she saw a handsome man, dressed as a militiaman with a black beard and mustache to inspire fear and with a revolver hanging on each side of his belt. It took her a while to recognize him: it was Masdéu. He had the air of being in command more than the others. He was continuously giving orders right and left. After much hesitation she ran downstairs. Masdéu was turned away; she tapped him on the shoulder, and he turned around. She heard a happy cry.

"Armanda!" He gave her a big hug and lifted her, and, holding her up, he turned around a couple of times. "Armanda!"

They walked inside, and he asked right away what she was doing there. He had thought the villa was abandoned. With tears in her eyes she told him she was looking after the house. Masdéu burst out laughing like she had never heard him laugh.

"Whose house?" But seeing she was so disconsolate he told her, "If there's anything you need, just ask."

She asked, for the love of the dead, that they keep out of Senyora Teresa's room and the bedroom that had been Maria's. Masdéu, without a reply, called two men and told them: "The rooms my sister tells you not to touch must not be touched by anyone. Tonight I'll discuss it with the chairman."

Then he asked her if she wanted to remain in the villa or would like him to find her an apartment. She answered that she wanted an apartment. Masdéu kept his word. She spent the remaining wartime in an apartment very near the villa, an apartment that after the war would become hers. It was on a narrow street that at night filled with lovers making out; it was weird to see so many young people in the mood for love amid that great tragedy. As soon as the war ended, she went to see the villa. She found the gate ajar. After two or three months she moved back in, to those large rooms without furniture, her steps echoing as if a whole lot of people were pacing inside. One day she yelled, "Oooooh!" and her voice returned to her through all the doors. Startled, she turned around and ran upstairs; she locked herself in the room that had been the Valldauras's. She looked for a job. She spent time in her apartment and paid the rent, but she slept in the villa, as if duty-bound. She could not let go. Until she married. To have company rather than out of a wish to marry. She married the older militiaman with caramel-colored eyes who had asked her where she was coming from. They had run into each other on the street, and he had recognized her right away. Then she went to see Senyor Fontanills, who'd spent the war years in Monistrol at the house of a sister.

"Senyor Fontanills, here are the keys. The big one for the gate too."

She had found it by freak chance. The militiamen, or whoever came after, instead of locking the gate, had thrown the key to the ground behind a shutter.

7. THE VERY OLD ATTORNEY GOES FOR A WALK

He slept the whole afternoon, and when he woke up he dozed for a while. A sparrow was chirping as if he'd gone mad: the noise came from the mandarin orange tree. He went into the bathroom, washed his hands, and splashed his face; he changed his shirt. It took him a while to undo the buttons; he put on the fresh one, and it was still hard to button it up. About two weeks ago he'd told Sabina, more gaga the older she got, to tighten his buttonholes because his shirts came undone merely by his breathing. But Sabina had made them too small, and he wasted time in the buttoning and unbuttoning operation. He licked his lips; they were always dry and chapped easily. Standing in the hallway, he waited for a while, unsure of what he had to do. Finally, he got a raincoat from the hook and put it on. It was cool, or perhaps not; perhaps the bit of coldness he felt on his back came from the great sleep he'd had; it had been so good he'd drooled. He straightened the brim of his hat with one hand and then stuck it on his head. He thought for a while; he was sure he'd forgotten something he had to do before leaving. The nap had made him groggy. Suddenly he said, "Ah, yes." And he ran to his den. The desk, the bookcases, the armchair . . . so different from those in his office. He had had to give up his practice because of his age, and he still felt hit hard by that. Nobody needed him now. To feel useless ate at him, and he didn't know what to make of his days, all the same. He sat behind his desk and locked the bottom right drawer.

From the foot of the gate he stared at the front garden, small, with two cherry trees; his own, with blooming branches that could be seen from his bed, had died the same year he left the office apartment and moved to his villa. He looked up and down the street trying to think. Yes, he'd go. It had been years since he'd gone there. It would be a kind of pilgrimage, a tribute to memory. His desire to go see the Valldaura villa reminded him of a letter from Sofia he'd gotten that morning. He read it a couple of times because the first thing he saw in that letter was the signature: Sofia? From its contents he surmised it was from Sofia Farriols, Teresa's daughter. But her last name disoriented him because it was French. Sofia Desfargues? He and Fontanills had looked after her interests. Old Fontanills, who got help from the son of a cousin, was still in pretty good shape, even though his back was hunched. And his wife was still living! Maria Recasens, the daughter of Recasens the banker, who had been engaged for a couple of years to Attorney Esteve's son and nobody ever found out why they had broken up. Suddenly he stopped as if he'd been riveted to the ground and wondered if he'd done that thing he always had to do before leaving home. He slid two fingers into his waistcoat pocket and felt the key to his desk drawer. Yes, he'd locked it. Was he sure? It was not five minutes ago. He kept a medication there that he absolutely did not want Sabina to find because his ailment was growing worse and vexed him. He went back in a mood, went upstairs, opened the door, went into his office, and, yes, the drawer was locked. He would have to get a notebook and write down right away all that he did. He would save time that way. To reassure himself he set out the strip of paper. For some time now he'd had the feeling that someone, as soon as he went out, opened his drawers and searched them carefully. Since he did not dare lock them all in order not to offend Sabina or Roseta, he bought a pack of cigarette papers: he'd pull out a piece, cut a small strip, stick it in the narrow gap between the drawer and the tabletop. If the drawer were opened, the strip would fall to the floor. Thus, he'd know if someone had opened it. It would be well nigh impossible for the unknown spy to realize the strip of paper had flown. And it would be even harder, if he noticed, to put it back in the same exact spot where it had been placed: exactly above the keyhole. Reassured, he went out again and went up the street, yes, the Recasens boy, no, the Recasens girl, had married Fontanills the business manager, and the Recasens son, after a while, married Josefina Ballester, a girl as pretty as she was dull, and he had never liked dull women. And Attorney Esteve, whom he only knew by name, had prepared Salvador Valldaura's will, he heard through the grapevine, instead of him. Valldaura must have heard something. And all the money went to Sofia. Poor Teresa. And to think that he, the best of friends, had betrayed a friend. Once Teresa, and she never did this, spoke to him lightly of Salvador Valldaura, and he covered her mouth with his hand. Life is complicated. Indeed. Too complicated. Could he swear that, even for a fleeting moment, he had not felt the satisfaction of stealing a friend's wife? And could it be that, after Valldaura's death, his passion for Teresa had waned because there was no rivalry nor a need to have her choose him over her husband? But he had adored Teresa. He had never been a ladies' man. When young, he had always thought that married men who had a lover were ridiculous. He had disapproved of that. After making love, he'd look at Teresa slumbering next to him and thought that for her sake he had gambled his self-respect. Regrets. But, when in his arms Teresa raised her head and looked at him with those eyes of innocent black water, he felt smitten. He was living in another world. In heaven. His whole life was erased, dead. How many paths of love they had followed! Teresa's mouth, Teresa's voice, Teresa's hands. Those times when she slipped under the covers and bit him sweetly like a newborn goat. Oh, yes! Once in a while he had spoken with Maria Recasens about Esteve's boy, the one who'd dumped her to marry that pudden-head Josefina Ballester.

It was cooler and breezy. He had always worn his hair long; that's why as a young man he hated the wind, because it mussed his hair. Now he no longer cared whether the wind mussed his hair or not. He had so little left. He pulled his hat down because the wind was coming from some snowy mountain, and where he most felt the cold was on his head. He was happy to be able to breathe: that was what truly mattered. To be able to breathe. He wished for nothing more. A few years after Teresa's death he went for a walk up the street and in front of the villa. He needed it as a medication. He could not understand himself; after she called him to make her will in favor of that girl who'd fallen from the roof, he had been back with some frequency. Then he just stopped going. Not because he didn't want to but because he couldn't stand seeing her always seated and with that insistence of hers to have him drink a glass of wine in the middle of the afternoon. Then he saw her obituary in the newspaper. For days on end he felt muddy inside, so moved he'd been by the announcement. He stopped under a streetlight and touched his tie. He no longer wore the pearl, which had fallen off its pin just as his acorn had fallen off his umbrella handle. When Teresa died, he had already begun locking up his medication during the day. As soon as Sabina and Roseta were asleep, he went to his office to get it and kept the tube of ointment under his pillow in case he'd need it. The pain at times made him clench his teeth and brought drops of sweat to his forehead. Early one morning he found the tube squeezed in his hand and couldn't remember whether he'd used it or not. Two girls went past him. He moved aside to let them go: they looked like two goldfinches. He was from a time when people were people. He kept his thoughts vague to avoid thinking of all those weighty things inside him – as if life had accumulated in his very center and made him realize he was as useless as the bits of nail trimmed from his fingers. He trimmed his nails over a sheet of newsprint for tidiness's sake, then he crumpled it and threw it in the trash. Dead and dead again. He stopped. He was panting. Lost in thought, he had started to walk fast and could not keep up the pace. He had to do everything slowly, thinking about each step because of his bad memory. Of course, he was hearty, and many of today's young would like to get to be his age and be as strong as he. He'd never been to the doctor. He did not know what illness meant. When some time ago his only ailment began to bother him he went to the pharmacy, told the pharmacist what was the matter, and the man recommended the ointment. Later, as he wasn't getting any better, he thought he had a fistula, and he worried because he had heard they needed to be burned with silver nitrate, which hurt a lot. But, no, it wasn't a fistula, and he was glad.

He got to the villa's neighborhood. Everything seemed the same as before, like years ago – gardens everywhere. That neighborhood had seen little construction, and it still smelled of the trees. He stopped. Not like the lover he'd been but like a pilgrim. He stopped in front of the house and looked at the magnificent grilled gate with a bell that looked like a lion's head. A lion's head or a fist? Teresa's daughter in her letter told him to get in touch with Fontanills. The two of them had been collecting earnings for her, but he didn't know whether Fontanills had sent her money. He never asked him. Sofia explained to him, she sounded as natural as if they'd seen each other the day before, that she'd married a French industrialist, that she had become widowed recently and inherited a considerable amount from her husband. She told him she would be coming to Barcelona soon, for a short visit, and that she had already told Fontanills to sell the house on Carrer Unió and the two buildings on the Rambla, they were too old, and she wanted to tear down her mother's house and on the lot, which was bigger than a couple of hundred thousand spans, have apartment houses built in the most modern style. She was sure to have found a good architect, recommended by some friends of her godmother, Eulàlia. And she added . . . Phooey! It was Sofia's letter that had made him leave his house that afternoon because he wanted to see, perhaps for the last time, that magnificent villa, which he had helped Salvador Valldaura buy and which had made him dream so. Across the street, under a growth of ivy that had grown thick with the years, he stopped to contemplate the villa. He heard steps and got all flustered, as if he'd being doing something naughty.

A good thing the street was dark and the ivy sheltered him. A fat woman coming up slowly stopped by the gate, stood there for a while, and then raised an arm and threw something into the garden. Then she bent down, and he realized that what she'd wanted to toss inside had fallen back out. The woman raised her arm again, again remained motionless, and then left. Not forward but back, the way she'd come. She limped, followed by a dog. Once woman and dog were out of sight the moon came out. A round moon lit a whole side of the villa in that half-white, half-green light, and he, his eyes entranced, looked at the roof. The towers . . . Near the lightning rod he saw a dark spot, and it took him a while to figure out it was a small bush. He crossed the street and tried to look through a crack in the door but saw nothing. He put on his glasses, after wiping them with his handkerchief; he'd forgotten the chamois on his desk when he was not sure whether he'd locked the drawer. He looked again, and he thought the garden was filled with overgrown grass and bushes like the one he saw growing on the roof. He jerked his head back because something very light had rubbed his cheek; he brought his hand to it: it was nothing. Perhaps a cobweb. Young children . . . He lost track. He couldn't recall what he was thinking about young children. He couldn't remember who told him that Eladi Farriols, when his son ran away, fell apart. And what do you know? When Marina, his sister Marina's goddaughter, married, a young man who looked old came to him at the church's door. He was balding, his eyes nested in crow's-feet. He addressed him with great respect.

"How are you, Senyor Riera?"

He added that he hadn't been invited but that he wanted to see Marina's goddaughter's wedding, even from the last pew in the church, because when she was little she'd opened an apartment door when he didn't know where else to go. The young man took his leave, but he grabbed him by the arm and asked him who he was because he could not place him.

"I am Teresa Valldaura's grandson, Ramon. Sofia Farriols's oldest."

He was astounded. He had seen him as a child running in the garden like one possessed and dragging Maria by the hand, with tiny Jaume, who could not keep up, following them at a distance. He took a closer look. He had the air of one with a heavy conscience, as if he'd done something really bad. Now he looked again through the crack and saw a shadow, a kind of long, whitish wing, stopped among the chestnut trees. He took off his glasses; they must have fogged up. He thought he had behaved badly with Teresa. He thought about what he'd told her about her legs. His selfish unloving might have . . . Or it might have been a story she'd made up to move him. But, facing the silence in that moonlight that he would never again see on the abandoned garden, he had to acknowledge that she had always behaved nobly with him. Very nobly. She was a woman worth a dozen. He saw himself as an old guy applying the ointment before going to bed because hemorrhoids are a nasty thing. And he saw himself tall, young, making love to that woman who seemed a queen among queens. Fire and silk. He thought he should go on a diet: fish and vegetables, if he wanted the inflamed capillaries to grow smaller. He had read they could grow to the size of an orange, in which case neither the preparation nor all the saints in heaven would be able to cure him. Boiled carrots, boiled hake, refreshing tomato salads, the tomatoes peeled and seeded, because, to top it off, his intestines were misbehaving. He raised his head and saw, atop the wall, a rat as big as a rabbit. Where did this ugly rat come from? He waved his hand to shoo it away, but the rat didn't move. If there were a twig or a pebble on the ground . . . That street, before, was full of such things, but it had now been paved. He could tear off an ivy branch and whip it. Three kinds of beasts disgusted him: rats, slugs, and snakes. Snakes because they slithered on the ground, slugs because they were slimy, and rats because they were always gnawing, even if they weren't hungry. Before he made up his mind to look for the ivy branch, he looked up the wall, and the rat had vanished. He yelled, "Dirty rat!" Nothing. Then he felt the ringer with his fingertips: it was a lion's head.

8. THE MOVERS

The moving van stopped by the gate, and three men got out. Oleanders, old lilacs with their bunches of dried seed, and parched rosebushes hung over the wall. Next to the gate there was a small door. The bell was in the shape of a lion's head. The ample gate's grill had a reinforcing iron plate completely eaten out by rust. Anselm, the oldest of the movers, inserted the key in the lock but could not make it turn. Only after a long patient while, when he was afraid the key would break in two, could he open the door. But he could not open the gate wide. The years and the rains had piled up sand behind it. All the men teamed up to push, and finally Quim, the youngest, thin as a reed, managed to slip through the opening and get into the garden. He dug out the sand with his bare hands. Right behind the gate, on the ground, were a bunch of dried bouquets. One of the bouquets, marigolds, was still green. It took them more than an hour to open the gate entirely. The tall, three-story villa stood at the end of a chestnut tree alley. Two towers, with embrasures and several chimneys, gave it the air of a manor from another time. Supported by four pink marble columns, a porch protected the main door. Leaves were beginning to fall from the trees, and wild chestnuts lay strewn on the ground. One of the chestnut trees had a hole in its trunk; Quim stuck his fist in it. Before going into the house they went around it. In the back was a large terrace with tall grasses, at the end of which began the park thick with trees of all kinds. To one side, almost touching the villa, an arbor covered with wisteria that now dragged on the ground, a stone bench, and a dried well faced an enormous laurel tree. Its main branch, broken, was surrounded by other taller branches. Anselm stopped before a stone slab covered with moss; he could use that slab for his own yard. The entrance to his washing shed, every time it rained, flooded; his wife used a wooden plank to avoid getting her feet wet. Quim said: "I see some writing." He scraped the moss from the stone; a name appeared: *Maria.*

As soon as they got the main door open, the stench of dust and dankness made them reel. In the foyer there was nothing but a large billiard table and a grand piano with its keys pulled out. They went into a very large room. Through the French windows' dirty panes they could see the stone bench; the light coming in was bottle-green in color probably because of the laurel. They brought their ropes to that room and their lunchboxes. You could see three or four desks and a busted armoire with strange soldiers on its doors. In one of the corners, a gilded armchair had lost its legs. It was upholstered in red velvet, full of stains and tears. On a round table, with its marble top cracked, sat piles of papers. The few chairs left were sitting room chairs, with their upholstery as sorry as that of the gold armchair. Next to the door there was a heap of newspapers, pamphlets, magazines, mixed with shoes, perfume flasks, pots and pans, and bowls. They stopped to look. Quim bent down and picked up three pictures. He dusted them with his sleeve. "Look: kids." Two boys and a girl. The girl was very pretty. The youngest of the boys held, as if a tray, a piece of wood with a stick wedged in its middle; at its top a bit of fabric served as a flag. The other picture was of a lady of great beauty. Low-cut dress, naked arms, a bunch of violets in her décolletage. "Forget this junk. To work!" The third picture was of a bearded gentleman. He looked important and had one of his hands on his chest. "Before we begin," Anselm said, "help me dig up the slab by the laurel. I'll put it at the door of my washing shed with the letters facing the ground."

9. MARIA'S GHOST

Don't take this stone away . . . Don't take this stone away . . . Oh, brother of mine . . . I fell on the laurel, and the branch of wind and rain went through me and came out my back. Married to the laurel. She's bled to death, they said as they took me down, and Papa kept a vigil, and Armanda cried: she was still a girl. She brushed my hair, washed off the blood. She was still a girl. Do not take this stone away. This stone is me. Don't take away anything that was my life. Oh, brother of mine, when we played with autumn leaves we were little we hid in the ivy we climbed out to the fields on a spotted sycamore branch. You who are young like me hear me, don't you understand? I belong to this house, and everything belongs to me. You who are old and know a lot: do not take away this my stone. I used to play games shooing rats, entwining ivy branches so they didn't know which way to grow; I plucked rose petals and squeezed their buds so they would rot before opening. Until now I knew the light of summer nights. I came to dance on this stone, on the letters that are nothing, that are not me but that call me in their sequence. I slid down the lightning rod; I glued myself to the walls. I made castles with the fog, turned on the faucets, and once I took the bathtub stopper and put it on the garbage heap next to a can of peas. And Grandmother Teresa. This big sorrow making me feel like crying without eyes and without tears, where does it come from? He went to the gate, and then he came back and climbed the bench of the wisteria and looked at the balcony, and I was not a shadow, I could call his name, I waited for him. Do not touch this stone. Wait. Wait. I impaled myself on the laurel, and for many, many years I've roamed here and there loving the laurel that helped me to a quick death. Leave my bed alone. My room was white. I pricked the palm of my hand and sucked the blood the blood of my brother. Do not carry away the porcelain clock or the box filled with herbs we would fill cans with water and put green polliwogs in them. On the roof. Oh, brother of mine. Everything that is beautiful I will give to you, Maria. And Papa fell ill, and he called me my sweet daughter and the drops of blood were like the stones in Grandmother's necklace we loved one another with love forever, and when I undressed, by myself, the mirror and I, I saw myself white and would remain so to the hour of my death. Don't slip, you could fall and death could take you and would take you to that secret realm where shiny stones are born the red ones the yellow ones the white ones. Leave everything that had been mine; while things are the way they were, I won't be completely dead. What makes me go from one place to another? I startle the birds they have flown there is not a single one left. The turtledoves. A cooing atop the leaves and a feather in flight. You who come and go hear me. I hide so they return, and not one bird wants to come back. They can hear me. If I could make them understand that I won't hurt them. The water and the ivy have gone bad. The muddy water. Don't you understand that even if I am only half-dead I can feel all the pain? The blood returns to my belly the leaves cry can't you hear them? They cry for me they are fog. Those who kill themselves keep on living next to the things that had been theirs a very slow death. We would look at the book of butterflies together close together brother of mine. Together. Each butterfly pierced by a pin. I wanted to die like the butterflies, black and orange, belly covered with fuzz. If you cart away my things, the ugly ones will come, the ones that died of disease, the putrid, the truly dead. They will grab me, they will pull on me, they will suck me up with their lipless mouths. They will take me away with them under the ground, where there are no trees or wind or leaves or flowers. They've been waiting for me for years I can hear them. Me, who has no bones who is a sigh who is not even the feather I will blow to scare you away. Once they have taken me, everything will be erased. Without time. Without memory. The moon who sees me knows how I am and how I was. Go away. If you knew what you were doing to me, you would die of sorrow. Someone is crying for me, Maria. What have you done, Maria? I have no words, I cannot say what's happening to me, my words are nowhere. I shall caress your cheek, and you will think it's a spiderweb, but, if I caress your cheek over and over, you will be afraid. I will make you feel that someone is touching you, and you'll turn around and look and look and will see no one. I will scare you, and I want you to love me. I was left alone with what was mine: walls, pieces of wood, shaking leaves, small grasses and buds that strive to unfold. A piano key. Who made the hole in the tree trunk? Who strung the piano key? How scary the toy trumpet how scary and alone in the house we screeched our happiness and ran holding hands and roped ourselves to the chimney. Armanda! The children will fall in through the roof and the rain will come in you broke everything hobbyhorse and striped tops. I have in the well the lady of the dollhouse with a necklace to her knees and a star stuck in her hair she was coming back from the theater. Her neck was stained with blood. Oh, brother of mine. We played with the knives and made holes in the trees. Many nights I went out to the garden and standing before the gate I waited I wanted to be you to feel what you felt when left alone forever. I tired of calling you I tired of hearing myself call you. The laurel my husband to death stabbed on a thorn like a leaf.

She ran up the chestnut alley mad as hell. How dare they? She had rushed to ask one of the boys loading the desks who was in charge. The owner of the moving vans, they informed her, had told them to take everything out of the house and on to the furniture storage. Sofia said she was not going to pay rent for furniture that wasn't hers, much less pay for the moving. As soon as she went into the room that had been her mother's, she saw Anselm dragging a file cabinet.

"I am Sofia Valldaura. You can drop all the office furniture, and, instead of moving it, set it on fire."

Anselm looked at her with surprise. He did not quite dare tell the lady with the hoarse voice that he could find some use for all those pieces. A good thing he had already loaded the stone slab; otherwise . . . The two boys came in with a desk and asked Sofia where she wanted them to put it.

"Behind the house. In the middle of the terrace. So you can burn it."

She asked them what they'd been doing since eight in the morning. Anselm told her they had loaded two vans with furniture from different rooms in the house, that there were quite a few left, and that they would have to end up loading by candlelight. Sofia shrieked. A rat as big as a rabbit had run by her feet and had disappeared through a hole. Quim said the house was infested with rats. That near the basin with the birdfeeder he had destroyed a nest made of rags and wood shavings. An old rat had defied him, and, as he was about to hit him with a piece of wood, the rat reared on his hind legs and showed him his teeth. He had to laugh, such a brave beast.

"But the rat, that's nothing. A rat is a piece of cake. What's really frightening is the ghost."

The other boy said, "You know, when we went to load the furniture from a white bedroom, a box on the dresser moved."

He looked at Quim, and Quim nodded. The box had turned around. At first they thought their eyes were playing tricks with them – no way, it was true. And, if that weren't enough, after a while the balcony curtains waved all the way up to the ceiling, and outside not a leaf was shaking. And when, loaded with the bed, they started to go down the stairs, Quim, who was in the rear, felt a cobweb brushing his neck. There were plenty of cobwebs in the house but not in the middle of the stairs, which they had climbed and gone down quite a few times. They had told Anselm, and he said they were imagining things. "But the cobweb has brushed my neck many times." And Anselm had told him he must have a scared mother who must have told him horror stories when he was little. And later, while they had their lunch, the peacock feather passed right in front of Anselm's face. "No, not flying like a bird, don't you think? Hovering over the floor as if someone lying down were blowing on it." Sofia threw them a pitiful look and made no comment. She asked them if they had any more candles because she was waiting for a visitor.

Anselm lit three candles, dripped some wax on the table, and stuck them in it; while he was doing this, a poorly dressed balding man came in and stood there. Sofia, her back to him, could not see him. Ramon looked at his mother: old and slender, straight as a lightning rod. She turned around. On the lapel of her jacket she wore that diamond bouquet that had been Grandmother Teresa's and that in the wavering light of the candles seemed even more blinding. Sofia was asking Anselm if they had moved an armoire with double doors, with a Japanese soldier on each, the blades of their swords in fine gold. The things she is asking about, Ramon thought. An armoire that, when the room was dark and the moon shone on it, was a wonder. No one would ever again know that villa and that park under the ice of the moonlight. Anselm answered her that, yes, of course, they had moved the armoire, quite dilapidated. "It had only one door and none of the shelves." Then he left. The boys followed him. Ramon walked to his mother with lowered eyes and said to her, "Don't you recognize me?"

Sofia looked at him for a long time. She controlled a slight tremor of her lips, excused herself: "It's so gloomy here. You have changed a lot."

The boys came back in loaded with a crate so heavy that they had to bend as they lugged it. They dropped it on the floor and straightened themselves with their hands to their kidneys. They had found that box in the basement; there were two more covered with rat-gnawed books. Sofia asked them to open it; it was filled with something like iron pine cones. Anselm picked one up and said it was a hand grenade.

"If you don't pull the ring, they won't explode."

Sofia asked, "What should I do with these?"

Ramon said the best thing would be to call the police. Sofia took him by the arm and walked away a few steps.

"I always wanted to know where you were." She was quiet for a moment; she didn't know how to go on. "Do you need money?" Faced with her son's silence, she went on: "As soon as the war ended, I wrote Fontanills and Attorney Riera. I couldn't count on the attorney because he always answered me a year later and always off on a tangent. I asked them to search heaven and earth and find you. It was only years later that I learned you had returned to Barcelona after living in South America." She kept on talking, talking; she had always been his mother. They would make an effort to forget all that had happened. She talked, saying what she thought she ought to say. Truth be told, she had asked her son to come to the villa because she did not want to face him alone. She felt very apart from him, and the past scared her. But she had wanted to see him and help him out, to soothe her conscience.

"Excuse me a moment." She went to Anselm and gave him two large bills. Even though it's quitting time, please take all the office furniture to the back and burn it right away."

She went back to her son and asked him what he did, how he earned his living. He told her he had come back from America in poor health but that he'd rather not talk about it.

He'd gotten married, he later explained, to a girl who worked as a dressmaker. They had a boy and a girl. The boy's name was Ramon, the girl's Maria. The candles went out, all three at once. Anselm lit a match, and, as soon as he had relit all three candles, they went out again.

"See what we told you? Perhaps now you'll believe us."

Sofia smiled and explained to Ramon the story of the box and of the feather. A fat, short woman carrying a basket and a bouquet of flowers had come in followed by a dog. She stood by the door. Finally, Sofia noticed her, and, when the woman saw that Sofia was looking at her, she went to her with open arms: "Senyoreta Sofia! I thought you were all dead."

Sofia took a step back to avoid Armanda's embrace. Armanda looked at Ramon and asked him if he was Ramon. He had changed, to be sure, but she had recognized him right away. Just as when he was small, whenever he was sad or worried, he stood real straight and kept his feet together. And she burst out in happy cries. She had seen him at birth, had held him on her lap. Oh, that christening! Anselm, holding the matchbox, listened raptly.

"Just imagine! The firstborn son! Senyor Eladi was beside himself with joy – he could not believe it. The day of the christening the villa was lit from top to bottom until the wee hours. Burning."

Armanda told Sofia that she wanted to have a word with her in private. They left the room. She told her quietly that the coffer with the jewels was buried at the foot of the peacock cage. "You'll see a round stone, quite big, that sits on top of it." And the silver under the window of the laundry shed, the window that opens to the terrace. She had covered everything with those cans the children used to collect from the garbage heap, to fill with beetles and tadpoles, and empty sacks and mattresses. Had Senyor Fontanills never mentioned it to her? She had taken the red curtains from Senyora Teresa's room; if she wanted them back, she just had to say so. Of course, she'd had to shorten them because the ceiling in her apartment was much lower. She had also taken a couple of old silverware utensils and a spatula for serving sweets.

"You do not need to return anything. Keep it all for memory's sake."

One afternoon, after leaving some flowers on the laurel tree slab, she'd gone to the back gate and found it on the ground, half-buried in rubbish. Armanda was gushing out her words; her eyes shone.

"Yes. They're still dropping garbage there. And Senyor Eladi had been so annoyed by that ill treatment. Oh, Senyoreta Sofia, if you only knew . . ."

Her husband, who was not yet her husband when he came back from the war, found a job as a cook in a restaurant on the Rambla, and, once married, they had always had something to eat. They were able to save more than half his earnings after paying the rent and the few inevitable necessities. Masdéu had found her the apartment. She lived there all through the war without paying a cent because the owners had disappeared.

"You remember Masdéu, don't you? He always wore that soft bowtie."

He died at the front, in battle. The newspapers had all spoken about it and shown his picture on the front page. More than five thousand people attended his funeral. Flowers galore. Finally, she and her husband had decided to board the back gate and close the garden. They went there one Sunday, carrying a ladder. They closed the gate and secured it with tins across the opening nailed with a thousand nails. They gathered big stones and made a mountain behind it. Once the gate was secured, her husband climbed the wall, using the ladder. She too. She was still agile then. Then he pulled up the ladder and placed it on the other side so she could climb down. Three of its rungs cracked, and she was this close to breaking a leg. She managed to jump. Her feet hadn't developed this problem that made her limp now. He climbed down, holding onto the sycamore branch, and they took the ladder away. They went back into the room.

"Senyoreta Sofia! Senyoret Ramon! Isn't life full of surprises!"

Sofia explained that she had arranged for her son to meet her at the villa on such and such a date because she was not sure what hotel she'd stay at. She briefed them: she meant to tear down the house and use the lot to build luxury apartments. She broke off her explanation to again ask her son if he needed cash. Ramon turned beet red.

"We'll have a big party. I have investments abroad. I'll have to divide my time between Paris and Barcelona. A big reunion party. I'll meet your children, my daughter-in-law. But right now I can't do it."

Armanda asked Sofia to pardon her, but, if as she said, the villa had to be destroyed . . . She had come in because she walked by often; she did not live far. From time to time she threw flowers into the garden for the girl's soul. She'd seen the front gate open and the moving van and a taxi waiting. If the villa was to be torn down, she wanted a souvenir: a couple of shoots from one of the rosebushes. The one with the flesh-colored roses growing on the laundry shed wall. If she were allowed, she'd go get them now. Sofia said yes. She walked her to the kitchen, and Armanda explained more things from the time when she was in the house alone. Finally, Sofia left her. She fixed her hair. She told Ramon she had to go, that she could give him a ride in the taxi. Ramon said he would walk. By candlelight Sofia wrote a check and nearly forced him to take it.

"And Armanda?" Ramon asked. "I'd like to say good-bye to her."

"Leave her be. She is looking for flesh-colored roses in the dark."

11. RAMON

He started to walk with one hand in his pants' pocket, grabbing the check his mother had just given him. He took a side street and slipped into the first portal to take a look. No more meager dinners, no more late-due rent, darned bedsheets, shirts with only the front ironed because power is expensive and the meter never sleeps. His wife, a woman with a frightened look and a shrunken heart, could breathe easier. She was always hunting for the worst food because it was the least expensive. Overripe fruit. Using rejected clothes to sew outfits for the children. And she had to put up with the yakking of the downstairs neighbor, who loaned them her sewing machine. He was walking away from the villa in the company of the scent from the trees, that old air. For years he had to make an effort not to recall the place because its memory would mean perdition. He found it hard to forget. He'd suffered from insomnia, a murmur in the heart; he was convinced he had a bad heart. No one could fathom how mangled his nerves were. In summer he was ill. He was ill every summer. Mysterious ailments, without a name, made him stay in bed. His innocence had ended the moment his father had started yelling with his eyes full of reproach. His father, in one moment, had done away with his youth. His life as a man began one night on the streets and continued years later in the war, with all his mates telling family stories and reading letters and asking questions, and he had to tell them that he had no one, that he was all alone. And thinking of the Ebro and the Catalan highways leading to France, he felt a taste of bile in his mouth. A taste of bile, of tiredness, and abandonment. As if an endless desert could suddenly become a scratchy ball that got into his throat and choked him. In his hand he held the check, made out for a lot of money. Without realizing it, he smiled. Just imagine: an heir! Walking down the street, his suit reeking of age, each fiber of its fabric steeped in poverty, he thought of the wind in the park that had tousled his hair when he was little. He had thought so much about the park. But little by little he stopped remembering the trees because a man's heart can be defeated, or worse. He walked slowly so as to take longer in leaving his childhood behind, and his thoughts went to his wife and children. His mother: she was in great shape. As she glanced at the pictures of his children that he had hurriedly showed her under a streetlight a moment before she climbed in the cab, she told him they took after him. His thoughts ran off. What must have happened to Marina, the oldest daughter of Senyor Riera, who helped him when he was lost? She had fallen in love with him. A naive love. Impossible. At the time love, for him, more than a sin, was a curse. Marina, young, maternal, saturated with compassion and tenderness, her sweet eyes and her hands of an altar Virgin, had loved him when he wanted to die rather than live. He needed to marry a woman who'd know nothing of his life: an unknown marrying an unknown who had broken with his family and who never asked him what the rift had been about. His wife had a brother killed in the war. Perhaps his wife's sorrow for the death of her brother had made him marry her. His thoughts brought him the forked branch with Jaume's thin neck between its prongs. Every time he saw a river, every time he saw the sea, he had vertigo; he had to lie down because he could not bear seeing a body of water. The spreading water sucked him in. He recalled his mother under the streetlight looking at the picture of her grandson and her granddaughter, whom she did not have time to meet this time around because she was in Barcelona for just a couple of days. A boy and a girl who were growing fine. His wife was not like before. Neediness had undone her. But he saw her like she was before because she'd been the great tender spot in his life. And when he was roaming a country that wasn't his country, even though he did not want to, he thought of his father. One day, with his children, he'd go to the graveyard to visit Grandmother Teresa's tomb. Grandmother Teresa had loved Maria more than him. For a while Marina kept writing to him. She kept him up on who'd died. He should bring flowers to Maria as well as to Grandmother Teresa. But to take flowers to his sister he'd go to the graveyard by himself.

12. ARMANDA

She was so eager to tread those grounds that she did not know where to begin. Standing next to the kitchen door, her dog by her side, she could not get the words of that boy out of her head: that there was a ghost in the house. The candles had died, blown out by someone they could not see; just as years ago, and she had almost forgotten, the candle she had lit was blown out the night she climbed onto the roof before she began to feel afraid of living in the villa by herself. As she walked, she ran a hand on the wall; she found the faucet that the girls had used for their showers. She was tempted to turn it on but held off. How many years that faucet had been dry. Two shadows loaded with stuff crossed the terrace, arguing loudly. That high watermelon slice, the moon, made the sky only darker. Underneath, the great mass of trees rested quietly.

Walking as if on eggshells, she went toward the laurel amid shrubs and weeds. She bent one knee to look for the slab but only found dirt. She left her flowers on it. If it hadn't been for her habit of throwing flowers over the fence, she would never again have seen Senyoreta Sofia or Ramon. She'd been tossing flowers over for years. Before securing the back gate and giving the keys to Senyor Fontanills, she would go in and simply place her flowers on the stone. She never went in the house. It seemed to her that, the more time passed, whatever had happened in there became more horrendous: the whole thing was pitiful, scribbled walls and furniture destroyed for the pleasure of destruction. She sat on the wisteria bench. Senyoreta Sofia had asked her where she lived. "When I come back to Barcelona, I'll come visit you." And she had felt thankful for those words. Even if she did not mean them. The little dog came over to her skirt and started to whimper. Really . . . She brought a hand to her cheek; a spider must have jumped off a branch, just a spider. From the bench she could see one of the French windows of the dining room. She closed her eyes, and everything came back to her: the big bunch of gardenias, the air of celebration, all that work. It was the first time they had the attorney and his wife to dinner. It had been Senyora Teresa's idea, saying they should be nice to such a serviceable attorney. The day before she'd spent more than fourteen hours cleaning all the silver they would use and the magnolia fruit bowls. Senyora Teresa came down to see her progress and joked, and everyone laughed, that, if she did not shine the silver enough, she would have to ask the attorney's wife to do it – her name was Constància. That morning Senyora Teresa took your breath away, in her white gown, a bunch of lilacs pinned to her waist, the flowers made of such delicate ribbons that you could only find them in Paris. Before she left the kitchen she told them that at dinnertime she wanted all the servants entirely in white and their boots like mirrors. And most of all she did not want to see any bit of petticoat showing under the skirts because that was a sign of laziness. This happened to Filomena at times. Filomena blushed and said tearfully that it wasn't her fault if her petticoat was longer than her skirt. "Take it up!"

Her little dog came to her side, and she saw the darkened house and a moving shadow next to the lightning rod. Her eyes could not quite make it out, but it could only be a weed. You could not hear a single bird among the branches, and that laurel always used to be full of birds. Sofia, the day of the dinner with the attorney, had been up to her old tricks.

They had dressed her in the outfit made of lace they had ordered from Switzerland and with a large bow of white satin on the back. And they had done her hair in curls, which drove her mad because she was forced to wear the iron curlers all night long. At dinnertime she confronted Anselma: "If I am not allowed to eat at the table with the grown-ups, I will not eat." Armanda went to tell Senyora Teresa: that Sofia was giving Aunt Anselma a hard time. And Senyora Teresa picked up the train of her turtledove-gray dress, made of a stiff silk that rustled at every step, and you could see the heels of her satin pomegranate-red shoes. She said that, if Sofia didn't want to eat in the kitchen with the servants (she had thought she'd have a better time there), let her have her dinner in the playroom. Sofia, small as she was, replied that, if she could not eat with her parents and their company, she would not eat. She undid her sleeves' bows in a huff. Senyora Teresa could not control herself and gave her two clamorous slaps. The girl, rather than crying, stuck her tongue out to her mother, who turned away, pretending she hadn't seen.

In the middle of the table the centerpiece with the mermaids full of flesh-colored roses shone bright; to each side of it they had placed the salt dishes for great occasions: two gold and crystal swans with their golden spoons. Everything was wonderful: the Empire china and the silver with initials surrounded by a green enamel wreath and the champagne glasses in the shape of tulips and the tablecloth of the finest lace made by hand with a technique she could not remember the name of. To go into the dining room was like entering heaven. By two o'clock the sun began to come in, and everything sparkled. Filomena served the wine, in white gloves, slender as a lily and with the eyes of an odalisque, and she spent the whole dinner behind Senyor Valldaura's seat. The Senyor, with his thick beard and mustache, seemed like a biblical patriarch. They said that before his marriage he'd played the field, but as a married man he was a saint. They had an open-casket wake for him in the library, the room they used for that, and Senyor Eladi's dad and his Uncle Terenci had sent wreaths fit for a king. The one from Eladi's father had dark-red and light-red roses, and Uncle Terenci's was all made of tree of Jesse shoots and had a foot-wide purple ribbon. Sofia dismissed it: "Uncle Terenci has sent a wreath that would be proper for a lady." Aunt Eulàlia's wreath was made of roses and lilies and Senyor Bergadà's, that gentleman who lived abroad, of striped and coral camellias. Who knows where they could have gotten those flowers in the middle of winter? In what greenhouses had those flowers bloomed? It seemed a miracle. All the flowers of the world to accompany Senyor Valldaura in his final journey. How sad that death had been. He lost consciousness right away. His eyes were open, but he couldn't see. His death rant lasted three days. He had gotten more flowers than Senyora Teresa, Armanda recalled. She had kept wake for her when everybody got tired, and, on tiptoe, she'd gone out to pick one of those flesh-colored roses the Senyora loved madly, the ones that bloomed on the wall of the laundry hut. She hid a rose in her cleavage so that Senyoreta Sofia could not see it; she didn't want to repeat what happened with the bouquet of roses she'd placed on Senyor Eladi, which, with a reprimand, Sofia told her to remove. Mundeta and Antònia served the oysters. She had opened them and placed them on the platters over a bed of crushed ice. As soon as they began to eat them, as Senyor Valldaura brought the first one to his mouth, he exulted, "An oyster is the spit of a mermaid." The attorney's wife turned white as paper and was unable to taste a single one. She was not very pretty: she was flat chested and had weak ankles. On the other hand, everything was generous in Senyora Teresa, and the attorney, from time to time, could not avoid ogling her. You could tell a mile away he fancied her a lot. There was nothing left of the pigeon rolls, not one teaspoon of sauce. "How happy I am," Aunt Anselma had said, "I've not killed myself making them for nothing." While doing the dishes, Filomena told them that Senyora Valldaura must have worn one side of her shoe bare from playing footsie with the attorney. The two gentlemen had their coffee served in the library and the ladies at the little table by the dining room French doors. They probably had nothing to say to each other – they were so different – and after a while they went to see what their husbands were doing. Filomena came into the kitchen laughing. She said they were smoking hard and Senyor Valldaura had proposed going to the second-floor hall to play a few rounds of billiards. Senyor Riera declined. He was no good at games. Then they started to talk about Vienna. "The violets and the violin?" Aunt Anselma asked. Senyor Valldaura appeared to be showing off. The Danube was gray. One of the saddest rivers in the world, right by the city. But the woods . . . The songbird woods, the fisherman's lea . . . Some time after seven Mundeta helped Senyora Constància put on her caramel-colored fur stole lined in a silk print, and the Senyor and the Senyora accompanied them all the way to the gate. The next morning an errand boy brought a bouquet of gardenias that filled the living room with perfume. Senyora Teresa picked it up, buried her face in it, and said with her cheeks rosy from so much joy, "Even if they turn black." She put one in her décolletage and wore it all day. It must have been the one that even after many years she still kept in her snuffbox next to the card from Senyor Riera. Before turning in, she went to kiss Sofia good night. The girl was grounded because Mundeta had brought her a tray with her dinner, and when she went to pick it up the girl had not tasted a thing. Sitting on her bed, stark naked, she was about to eat the last of the chocolate bonbons from the box the attorney's wife had given her. Her Swiss lace dress was on the floor, all torn.

The fear I have felt in this house, Armanda was thinking. At night, locking herself up in her bedroom, she thought she heard noises downstairs, and when she was downstairs she thought she heard noises upstairs. Windy nights were worse because the howling wind didn't let her hear a thing. But the noises were there. She stood before the laurel and said the Lord's Prayer. She had taken a few pictures to her apartment so they wouldn't be lost along with the memories. Looking at Senyora Teresa in her gem-studded dress, her heart laughed. Sofia and Eladi as bride and groom. The children. She sighed. Maria wore a jasmine tiara on her First Communion day. She again felt a caress on her cheek. She stopped, with her dog running furiously around her. She had come out through the kitchen; she'd go back in through the kitchen. From time to time she stopped. The dog yelped short continuous squeals and lowered his tail. She wanted to follow the path that led to the back door, but it was too dark, and the silence frightened her. She froze. Once again she felt the caress to her cheek. More solid than the touch of a flying shred of spiderweb. As if an invisible hand were caressing her cheek sweetly, a love caress under her eye, down her cheek. She was not scared.

Standing before the trees, she muttered, "If it is a dead one from this household who now thinks of me, may God help him and give him the repose he needs."

She stood there as if her thoughts had stopped, alone in the middle of a desert, with no sky and no earth. She regained her composure little by little, and very near her, level with her eyes, the black trees as background, something drew her attention: a shard of mist, almost nothing, hesitant, a transparent wing that moved away and finally vanished as if the earth had sucked it up. She felt a cold fright inside, and, as soon as she could, she crossed herself.

The laundry shed walls were surrounded by rosebushes. She ran a finger over the windowpane through which Senyor Eladi used to peep on the girls' hose showers and cut two rose branches. Her heart quieted at once. In the foyer the movers sat on the floor, smoking and drinking among lit candles.

"The Senyora and her son have already left," Anselm told her. Of course: she'd been out there so long. She wished the movers good night. She gathered her thoughts. Something weird had attracted her attention, and she could not remember what it was. To gain time she went into the dining room, trying to figure out what it was that was bugging her. On the table a lit candle was stuck to the surface with wax. She looked at the rose cuttings and immediately realized they were dead. She had suspected as much as they made a dry sound when she cut them. She left them besides the candle. She was limping more than ever but felt sweet inside. She stopped on the porch, climbed down the steps. She walked between the rows of chestnut trees. She crossed the street and from the other side, under the ivy hanging over the wall, looked at the villa. The moon's sickle had gotten close to the lightning rod. She sighed without sadness. The dog followed her calmly. After some fifty steps, as if a light had turned on inside her, she understood that strange thing that had come to her thoughts from some recess of her soul: Ramon, now so different from the time he left home, was the spitting image of Jesús Masdéu.

13. THE RAT

Huddled amid wood shavings and gnawed-off rags, with red eyes and a hairless back, he listened. There was a thick silence. Something stirred inside him, and he started to crawl. He walked over scattered papers, through rooms with gilded ceilings, rooms with crystal chandeliers, with broken porcelain candlesticks woven with cobwebs. Rooms with buckling wallpaper, hanging loosely in the dampest corners, and furniture, vases, drawers, piled up on the floor. People used to live there. Of the vanity, the hatred, the shards of love, all that was left was dust and a sad spectacle of splendor and forgetfulness. He went right through the vestibule; beyond the fountain, over dead water plants, under the urn bursting with grapes and pears – all broken. He kept on. He knew where he was going. He was sure of himself, as if a well-organized mechanism had energized him and nothing could detain him. He went up the stairs, grabbed a flap of a curtain, climbed to the window, went out through a broken pane, ran along the sill, grasped the rainspout, and descended carefully. He got to the ground and proceeded amid tall grasses and over the gravel. From time to time the trunk of a puny isolated sapling detoured him. He walked in front of the bench under the wisteria, ran over roots that emerged from the ground as if they were the earth's nerves. Suddenly he stopped. He heard blows on the outer wall; they were dumping garbage. He lifted his head, attentive. Behind him, very tall, rose the lightning rod, the two crenellated towers, and the crest of the wrought-iron cornice. All against the blue of the night, flat as cardboard. The blows to the wall stopped, and he entered the great zone of shadow. There the trees grew wild, surrounded by brambles and sleepy ferns, while the fallen leaves, all dry, let their shiny shoots emerge. He only dared to go in there late in the evening, far from the three fateful cedars, into that thick mixture of wild rose and honeysuckle, where the acacias, with their crumpled bark, held onto their desperate need to bloom again in the spring. The mulberries, the oaks, the lindens, cloaked all sorts of bushes and lilacs that had forgotten how to make their plumes burst out. They mingled with the dense boxwood and clumps of American bamboo, with canes thick as the arm of a man. And everywhere the climbing ivy, choking, invasive. Ivy all around the water. Dark ivy, with unyielding leaves that did not quite hide the bunches of their small black berries. What had once been ordered and well managed, neglect and the passing of the seasons had turned into a disease. One day, years ago, the birds had all decamped from the old branches, from the new branches, from the branches torn by the wind and burned by lightning, from all the burrows under the leaves. The centuries-old trunk of the sycamore, with its two branches shading the garbage heap, was covered with a green fuzz that was not quite moss. And he climbed up, toward the yellowed leaves watched over by a star, among heaps of dry straw, under the tender humidity of the twilight, under that trembling diamond nailed to the sky. When he got to the top of the wall, he stopped and wiggled his snout. He looked for the ivy and climbed down almost to the foot of the heap of garbage. Calmly, he started to rummage through the debris, guided by the scent of cheese

rinds. Bits of paper packaging rustled under him, and, when he found what he was looking for, he clutched it in his front paws. From the other side of the clump of grass two other rats came, small rats. And from the side open to the field, running and stopping, like bits of living darkness, came another four.

When he was sated, he came out from under the wood shavings and began climbing through the leaves, followed by the two small rats. He went back the way he'd come but suddenly veered west, to where the front wall of the house had been covered with a different kind of ivy, with leaves of a luminous green that lit up in autumn. That ivy had been dead for years, but the hairs that the ivy stuck on the wall were still there holding up dry branches that grew thinner as you went higher. What had been a luxuriant sea of fresh ivy, waving in the sun under the breeze of the good days, had become a jumble of dead branches and hairs. He kept climbing up that jumble, followed by the small rats, the three of them filled with the rinds of the cheese that the grocer down the street sold by the ounce. They got to the roof, walked along the cornice, and finally went inside the house through a crack in the tower.

Awakened by a hard blow, he cowered in his corner. He saw three tall shadows going back and forth. He remained in place for the whole morning, and toward noon one of the shadows went to his corner and messed it all up. He froze, anxious with curiosity. Then he saw a plank of wood lifting, and with fear in his heart, eyes popping out of their sockets, with his broken tail, he rose upright, defiant. And then he took off running and hid under a pile of paper. It was getting dark, but there was light inside the house, a few trembling flames rising and falling amid shadows. Taking advantage of a moment when the lights were not visible, he stepped out slowly, and once he got to the terrace, his snout up in the air, he tried to listen. Next to the well he heard the groaning of some animal. Everything was the same; nothing had changed, but he felt uneasy. He was surrounded by danger and did not dare to move. That well-known shadow, a wing of mist slithering like a flame, came by so close and so low that it brushed his ears. He started and took off running for as long as he could. He stopped, with his heart bounding inside his chest. Then he saw the three shadows building a huge pile with all the things they had removed from the house. They set it on fire. He heard crackling sounds and saw the red flames rise up to the sky.

The branches and leaves of the nearest trees in the park appeared to be burning. The fire lasted the whole night. He did not know where he could go to sleep. He roamed the house. Nothing was safe. He couldn't find even a rag. Breathless, feeling ill, he got to the alley with the chestnut trees and climbed up a trunk. He found a hole and sneaked in.

A few days later other shadows came to cut down the trees and to raze the house. Soon they saw by the trunk of the chestnut tree a disgusting rat, with a head that had been gnawed on, surrounded by a bunch of greenish flies.

Rose Mellie Rose
By Marie Redonnet
Translated by Jordan Stump

The Man in the Pulpit
Questions for a Father
By Ruth Rehmann
Translated by Christoph Lohmann and Pamela Lohmann

Abelard's Love
By Luise Rinser
Translated by Jean M. Snook

A Broken Mirror
By Mercè Rodoreda
Translated and with an introduction by Josep Miquel Sobrer

Why Is There Salt in the Sea?
By Brigitte Schwaiger
Translated by Sieglinde Lug

The Same Sea As Every Summer
By Esther Tusquets
Translated and with an afterword by Margaret E. W. Jones

Never to Return
By Esther Tusquets
Translated and with an afterword by Barbara F. Ichiishi

The Life of High Countess Gritta von Ratsinourhouse
By Bettine von Arnim and Gisela von Arnim Grimm
Translated and with an introduction by Lisa Ohm